JOAN SLONCZEWSKI

"A strong and gentle voice...
A fine book by an up-and-coming talent."
Detroit News

"A thoughtful and unusual
after-the-holocaust novel...
Rewards the reader with
beautifully developed characters and a
hopeful view of humanity and its future."
Publishers Weekly

"Courageous and intelligent...
Seldom have I read an SF book
that so completely convinced me of
the actuality and solidity
of its created world.
This is a wonderful book."
Nancy Kress,
Nebula Award-winning author of *An Alien Light*

"Fits well with modern classics
by Yolen and Le Guin...
Sure to be an award contender...
A work not to be missed."
OtherRealms

the wall around eden

JOAN SLONCZEWSKI

AVON BOOKS ◆ NEW YORK

AVON BOOKS
A division of
The Hearst Corporation
105 Madison Avenue
New York, New York 10016

Copyright © 1989 by Joan Slonczewski
Cover art by Nicholas Jainschigg
Published by arrangement with William Morrow and Company, Inc.
Library of Congress Catalog Card Number: 89-34064
ISBN: 0-380-71177-X

First Avon Books Printing: December 1990

AVON TRADEMARK REG. U.S. PAT. OFF. AND IN OTHER COUNTRIES, MARCA REGISTRADA, HECHO EN U.S.A.

Printed in the U.S.A.

RA 10 9 8 7 6 5 4 3 2 1

For my son, Daniel,
who told me that God will appear as a
mouse creeping out from the wall

I

AT THE TOP of Gwynwood Hill the path dipped, the mat of pine needles fell away, and without care you might slip down the cliff in the darkness. But Isabel Garcia-Chase knew the path too well; she stopped herself at the edge, breathing hard from the hurried climb.

Tonight the angelbees would appear in the clearing below, as they did each month at the new moon. But what if they caught her and Daniel watching?

Isabel turned off her flashlight, her hands shaking with apprehension. She stared out upon the shrouded clearing. In the clearing beneath the stars rose the Pylon, a six-sided pyramid, white and pointed like a sun-bleached rib. The Pylon was where the angelbees would appear.

Angelbees had ruled what remained of the human race since the Death Year, in enclaves like Gwynwood. Each enclave was imprisoned by an invisible airwall like the Gwynwood Wall, an immense dome of pressure some ten miles across. Just outside the Wall lay another sort of wall, of piled bones and even complete skeletons, all sun-bleached whiter than the Pylon.

The angelbees would communicate only with their chosen Contact, here at the Pylon, which stood at the center of the enclosed land. But now the Contact, Daniel's grandmother Alice Scattergood, was confined to bed, dying of leukemia, like so many others in the twenty years since the Death Year. The moon was dark, but Alice could not come. What would the angelbees do without their Contact?

Isabel planned to find out. Whatever she learned, she would use, somehow, to resist those masters of Earth.

"Daniel?" she called softly to her companion, a fellow graduate of the Gwynwood "high school." Along with three classmates, theirs was the first high school class to graduate since the Death Year.

Crickets chortled steadily, and from a branch above her the cry of a barn owl wheezed and choked off. Daniel Jacoby had fallen behind as he picked his way up Gwynwood Hill at a more studied pace.

For a moment Isabel felt amiss, as if she had broken the silence of Quaker Worship. What if Daniel had fainted again, as he often did from his anemia?

Daniel's steps sounded at last, heavily, as he pushed back a branch and appeared at the cliff's edge. Like her, Daniel wore faded farmer's overalls. His face was pale in the starlight, his mouth small and serious as usual, though in a tranquil way that made her yearn to touch his cheek. Why had he agreed to come, Isabel wondered; why had he bothered with what she expected him to call a fool's errand?

"Daniel, are you all right?"

His eyes turned toward her. She could barely see in the dark, but she knew his eyes so well, the most beautiful eyes she knew. *Like lodestars,* she recalled from *Midsummer Night's Dream.*

Daniel said, "I am fine, thanks. And thee?"

"I'm okay. Just watching."

Daniel's anemia had troubled him since childhood, thanks to the radioactive poisons that seeped in from the deadland beyond the Wall. Isabel knew all about it; she kept the card file for her mother, Dr. Marguerite Chase, the Town's only doctor. Daniel's card said that he might not live out his twenties. A bone-marrow transplant would save him; but the only place to get it was Sydney, the one City left on Earth. If only the Walls would fall.

Isabel clenched her binoculars. "Wait till we catch those angelbees. We'll find a chink in their armor yet." Few chinks had appeared in twenty years. Tunneling the Wall, disobeying the Pylon, potshots at angelbees—the only result was the whole town got put to sleep for three days. After that happened, the Town Meeting forbade any more resistance.

Daniel said, "I don't see any angelbees. Perhaps they know that Alice is sick."

Isabel tossed her black hair back over her shoulder and searched the valley again. She was tall, and her profile jutted a bit harshly, like a "Spanish aristocrat," her mother used to say, referring to her Chilean-born father. In the daytime, she could have seen past the Pylon and the farms all the way to where the invisible Wall enclosed Gwynwood, and the ring of bones lay outside, marking the edge of the Pennsylvania deadland. But now the valley was dark, and you could not even see the Meetinghouse; that is, the Church, if you were Lutheran. The field below twinkled with fireflies, while above, the sky glittered with stars that came out of hiding when the moon was gone. To the west, a meteor streaked down, a straggler from the Perseid shower the week before.

And up there in Leo, tracking steadily, was a reddish satellite, believed to hold the Hive of the angelbees. But still no sign of angelbees at the Pylon.

"Oh, look—"

A dusky glow filled the Pylon, as if a candle had been lit within, delineating its six faces. Isabel's pulse raced. She stared, and the binoculars became slippery with sweat in her hands.

Wisps of cloud appeared around the Pylon, thickening until the Pylon was obscured. The fog grew until it filled out a hemisphere, about the height of an oak tree. The surface of the hemisphere, Isabel knew, was a miniature airwall which kept humans out of the Pylon's domain, just as the greater Wall around Gwynwood kept them in. But angelbees could pass through the Pylon's airwall, as did the Sydney mailbag, and once even a criminal transportee from Chile, who later became her father. How did things "arrive" there, in that little space around the Pylon? Something happened to time and space, something that defied what humans knew of physics, her favorite class at school.

"The Pylon won't talk," Daniel warned. "Alice is not there."

Alice Scattergood was the only human in Gwynwood whom the angelbees would "talk" to—once a month, when the moon was new and least interfered with their night vision. They did not really "talk," but made "visions" appear in the Pylon, as the Contact put it. "Visions" might warn of an impending storm, or advise the destruction of a radioactive corn crop, or herald the arrival of a transportee from another Wall-town, like Isabel's father.

There was no other way out. No human had ever breached a Wall.

Below, within the Pylon's airwall, the fog receded a bit

and an unfamiliar dark object appeared. Isabel pressed the binoculars to her eyes and winced in pain as the eyepiece jabbed her skull. The object looked like a long, jointed spiderleg with a cupped foot pressed into the ground. The spiderleg was visible barely long enough for Isabel to be sure she had seen it before it vanished again in the fog. "Daniel, what is it? A spacecraft of some sort?" It looked so fragile. Mentally she filed this datum for future use. *Spacecraft—fragile.* The Underground might want to know about this.

Above the hemisphere of fog emerged the first angelbee, a pale reflective globe, like a miniature moon. It floated upward, followed by another, and then another. Each globe had a dark eyespot that passed across its face as it rotated. The fourth angelbee had a secondary globe growing out of one side, a budding daughter cell.

The first people to see the creatures, when they had appeared after Doomsday, had called them "bees" because they arrived in a swarm, out of a spaceship of hexagonal cells, it was said, though none had ever seen the ship since. Others had called them "angels," for the beauty of their shimmering forms. So they were "angelbees," the diminutive limbless destroyers of Earth.

"Why did they come?" asked Daniel, as if to himself. "Whatever brought them to Earth, in the first instance?"

"Why indeed," said Isabel dryly. "*Veni, vidi, vici.* They've used Earth as they pleased, ever since Doomsday." June twenty-third that was, twenty-one years before. Isabel's arm itched, irritated by the sweat rolling down, and she tried not to scratch at the scaly patches that were not just dry skin. Epithelioma, said her card in the file.

"But why," Daniel wondered. "What do they want from us?"

Isabel frowned. "They want nothing particular from us. What did the British colonists want from the New World?"

"They took such trouble to preserve us."

"So we're an Indian reservation."

"They must have a conscience, then."

"Conscience!" Isabel laughed briefly. "'A very gentle beast, and of a good conscience.' Come, Daniel. Even Quakers can't make excuses for the creatures that started the Six-Minute War." On Doomsday the angelbees had jammed the radar of both sides with illusory missile trails. In six minutes the world was crippled by fire; it took another year to die of ice.

"Nahum says that's not how it happened," said Daniel. Nahum Scattergood, whose mother was the Contact, was Daniel's uncle. "Nahum does not believe the *Sydney Herald*."

"Nahum is such a literal old Quaker, he wouldn't believe a black sheep was black on the far side."

"Thee should not talk so, Isabel."

She smiled at his annoyance. Isabel's mother was a Quaker too, though not a strict "plain Friend" like the Scattergoods. But Isabel was getting tired of Quakers; they were as bad as the Lutherans about her attempts to join the Underground.

A mosquito buzzed in her ear. She slapped at it and lost the view in her binoculars for a moment. When she looked up, she blinked in surprise. "Those angelbees—so many of them."

All at once there seemed to be dozens of the moonlike globes, floating across the plain, toward the abandoned highway where they had made a bit of marshland to wallow in. Angelbees fed themselves in the marsh by soaking up methane, most of which was metabolized to hydrogen, which filled the buoyant spheres.

"Isabel." Daniel's voice was lower but not tense, which for him meant he was beginning to get worried. "Thee knows that we should not be here."

Yet he had come, after all, because she had asked. Perhaps he might yet join the Underground, even though he was a "plain Friend."

"The angelbees may see us here," Daniel warned. "They see . . . warmth, beyond red."

"Infrared." The angelbees could "see" out to wavelengths more than ten times longer than red light—the wavelength of body heat. Like rattlesnakes, angelbees could see you in the dark.

Against the stars, a touch of light caught her eye. Dropping her binoculars, she caught her breath and craned her neck toward the sky. A streak of pale orange grew into a jagged branch, limbs of it creeping into the black as if the sky itself were cracking and peeling.

Isabel gasped, her forehead turned cold, and she leaned against a birch trunk to steady herself. She tried to speak, but she could not, as the trail of orange bled into the night sky. It was two years since the last time this had happened, the sky going wild as the upper atmosphere boiled away, ensuring that the ozone would never return to screen the murderous ultraviolet from the sun's rays. This was how the angelbees kept the deadland dead.

She watched, transfixed by the spectre of the tortured sky, until she barely recalled where she was or how long she had been there. She became aware of Daniel's arm around her shoulders as he watched the sky with her, and his voice repeating lines from Isaiah. What good was that? Daniel would die, perhaps they all would, unless someone drove out the angelbees.

"Conscience, indeed," she whispered. "We're worse off than slaves." Isabel reflected on her own slave ancestors and wondered, not for the first time, what they would have done.

"God will send us freedom," Daniel said, "when we've earned it."

"When we fight for it." She thought about the Underground Resistance in Sydney, and about the radio she was building in secret to get in touch with them. If only she could convince Daniel to help her.

From across the valley came the sound of the hospital alarm, its distant ring competing with the crickets.

Daniel's fingers dug into her arm. "It must be Grandmother Alice—"

"Or Ruth's baby at last. It could be a dozen things. Come on." In any event, Isabel would be needed at the hospital.

They hiked swiftly down to the dirt road, where they picked up their bikes near Anna Tran's house and rode another mile through fields of wheat and soy. All the while, the sky above was cracking and peeling like orange cellophane.

The road turned onto the old highway, a stretch of cracked pavement overgrown by grass and Queen Anne's lace; it cut straight through Gwynwood, coming in from the deadland and leading out again. The light from their pedal-driven headlights pulsed across the old gas station, and the store-fronts which had been empty as long as Isabel could re-member, windows gaping empty like the eyes of a skull. The town, whose survivors numbered a hundred forty-one, had no need of stores.

At last they turned up Radnor Lane, and another block up was Isabel's house, a white colonial with a faded rose pattern in the slate roof. The hospital was on the second floor.

Isabel leaned her bike next to the garage, where her ma-chine shop was set up. Breathing hard, she noted the horses tied to the fence; the bay mare hitched to Liza Scattergood's carriage, and the piebald hitched to Ruth Weiss's. So it must be Ruth Weiss having her baby, and Nahum's wife, Liza, had come to help. Isabel sighed with relief and headed up the steps, not waiting for Daniel.

The interior was dark, with just a fifteen-watt bulb above the stairs. A smell of ammonia drifted down, from recent cleaning. Isabel went on upstairs.

Voices came from the far end of the hall, formerly the bed-room of her grandparents, where the birthing was done now. Inside, Ruth Weiss stood leaning over the back of a chair, her blouse dark with perspiration, her black hair matted over her face. Beside her sat her sister-in-law, Becca Weiss, the blind schoolteacher whom all the kids called Teacher Becca. Teacher Becca had kept them riveted with her reading of *Midsummer Night's Dream* the year before. Becca had been blinded on Doomsday; a twelve-year-old climbing an apple tree, she happened to be looking toward Philadelphia when the nuclear flash hit.

Gently Becca massaged Ruth's shoulders and brushed the hair from her face. Isabel's tongue thickened, recalling that Ruth's husband Aaron, Becca's brother, should have been here, only he had succumbed to melanoma two months be-fore. Aaron's last days in the hospital came back to her, but she forced herself back to the present.

"Breathe, breathe," murmured Becca.

Ruth's breathing was good and regular, about every five seconds. It sounded like a mid-phase contraction.

"Active labor, four centimeters." Isabel's mother, Dr. Mar-guerite Chase, spoke for the first time from behind the tray of instruments. "Looks like a hole in one." She meant, the head had plenty of room to descend. Marguerite had Isabel's dark complexion, her African features unusual in this town, with tight waves of black hair caught in a green surgical cap. Her busy hands were red and chafed from incessant hand-scrubbing; the doctor could not risk spreading infection when the nearest batch of ampicillin might be a continent away.

Isabel crossed the room to bathe her own hands in disinfectant. Ruth's breathing quieted as the contraction subsided, and she paced across the room to relax. Isabel nodded to the remaining two women seated in the corner: tall Liza Scattergood, and Grace Feltman, the orphaned "Special Child" whom the Scattergoods had taken in. Despite the heat, both Liza and Grace wore "plain dress," a long skirt of gray homespun with the hair pinned back in a white cap. Grace was the only survivor born during the Death Year. Two years older than Isabel, she had reached a mental age of five. As Daniel appeared in the doorway at last, Grace flashed a broad smile and clapped her hands. Daniel taught the children in Sunday School.

What had possessed Liza to bring her, Isabel wondered. Grace's presence would hardly be a comfort at a birth.

"Good evening, Friends," Liza spoke in a firm voice. "Grace was so anxious to come," she added, as if answering Isabel's unspoken question. "She loves the little babies."

"Good evening, Liza," said Isabel. Liza's remark troubled her. By age eighteen, they said, you had to start the babies since two out of four would not make it to adulthood. Even then, you would not live to see them grow up. That was the fate of those born since Doomsday.

But Isabel had other plans. Isabel wanted to go to the Sydney Uni, to get a real education, as her mother had. For now, she studied physics with Teacher Matthew, and even Latin when the elders insisted.

"Water," Ruth asked hoarsely. Marguerite nodded, and Liza got up to pass her an ice chip.

"Isabel, dear, please check the autoclave," Marguerite called to her daughter. The buzzer had blown a couple of years ago and had not been replaced.

Isabel dutifully went to check, passing Daniel, who followed her down the hall. "Ruth is okay," she assured him. "You can go home now," she added reluctantly.

"That's okay, I'll stay and help." His eyes were so wide and hopeful.

"But tomorrow's Sunday; you teach. You need your strength."

Daniel looked away, and the dim light from the birthing room cast jagged shadows over his face. "That is true. Good night, then." He touched her arm, then left. She looked after, wishing she had let him stay.

The autoclave had been installed in the bathroom several years before. Sparks of color played across its steel handle, reflected from the ghastly light show out the window. Isabel turned the handle; the cross bars pulled in and the steam hissed as it escaped. Gloves on, she reached inside for the contents, sterile linen and bottles of saline in case they needed an IV.

The red indicator light went dark. Isabel blinked. "Mother?" she called, looking down the hall, which was dark.

"The power's gone," Marguerite called back.

Isabel flicked on her penlight and raced downstairs, trying not to stumble. In the cellar, the circuit breakers were still on. It was just as she feared; the autoclave had overdrawn the solar storage. She switched on the diesel generator, thinking at this rate Gwynwood would have to go without electricity for a month to save for the winter. Physics by candlelight.

In the birthing room, now, Ruth lay on her back in the bed, taking rapid shallow breaths, with Becca on one side and Liza on the other. "Breathe, breathe, breathe," murmured Becca, much faster now. Ruth was in transition now, the baby's head entering the birth canal.

"Oh," Ruth sobbed, "I can't go on, I—"

"All right," said Marguerite, "you can push now."

Ruth's face went taut with strain as she pushed with each contraction. At the perineum a round patch of baby scalp appeared. As Ruth cried out, the head emerged.

Isabel swallowed hard, and her stomach knotted with fear despite herself. The Wall that kept people in did not keep radioactive poisons out, even after twenty years. What if the baby was deformed, limbless like her best friend in school, or, worse, like Grace? Liza should not have brought Grace, she thought again.

Then suddenly there was the wrinkled little creature hanging by its feet from Marguerite's fingers: the one hundred forty-second citizen of Gwynwood. It let out a squeaking cry, and a stream of urine projected out from its tiny organ.

"Well, at least that part's okay." Marguerite nodded to Isabel to take care of the umbilical cord. Isabel stripped the cord between her fingers back toward the baby, to save the extra blood, then she clamped it twice. Then Marguerite laid the little boy on Ruth's chest, where he quieted and opened his eyes, staring.

Isabel held up the pan for the afterbirth, a dark mass like a muddy fist within the pale torn sac of the amnion, the vessel that had enclosed its occupant for nine months. An amazing piece of engineering, insubstantial yet as sturdy as an airwall.

"Just as I thought," said Marguerite, "a hole in one." She grinned and hugged Isabel around the shoulders.

Everyone cheered, though they knew, of course, that faulty genes might not appear for years. The little bundle was passed from hand to hand, even Grace getting to hold him briefly above Liza's protecting arms. Then he settled to nurse for just a minute before falling asleep.

Liza opened a hamper of dinner for Ruth, lentil pie with corn on the cob, a thermos of goat's milk, and fresh-picked raspberries for all. Marguerite told Isabel, "You did great. You're getting to be a real baby-snatcher."

Isabel smiled, warm in her mother's praise. Still, though, to become a real doctor she would have to go to the Uni. Somehow, someday. Isabel took up the mop and started to clean the floor. She glanced at the clock; four A.M., her father would be getting up to milk the goats and sheep.

Teacher Becca caught her arm and gently tried to pull her close, as if to whisper in her ear. "Isabel. Do you see anything?"

"What?"

"Outside; out the window. What do you see?" Becca had only a trace of peripheral vision left, fleeting shadows around the grayness.

"The sky is burning again," Isabel told her. Liza and Marguerite, too, had turned to the window, where they murmured over the spectacle, their voices low.

Becca paused, then nodded. "Yes. Anything else?"

Isabel approached the windowsill, uneasy for some reason. She flicked on her penlight and aimed it out the window. To her surprise, a point of light reflected from something shiny hovering outside, the mirrorlike surface of an angelbee.

"It's an angelbee. There's another one, I think." Isabel remembered that angelbees liked to look in on a birthing.

Becca said, "I thought so. Isabel, you should come and see me again. My screen window needs fixing; the mesh is loose, and the bugs come in."

Watching her, Isabel smiled slowly. The last time she had gone to Becca's place to patch the leak in her roof, Becca had left an old electronics manual in the bottom of the basket of garden squash she sent in return. Radios were forbidden, everyone knew, but Isabel had been working at one on and off ever since. Becca was on her side, about the angelbees and the Wall. She had a good head for figuring, and she must have figured out something new.

"Of course, Teacher Becca. First thing Monday, we'll fix your window screen."

II

ISABEL AWOKE WITH her father nudging her shoulder, first gently, then more playfully as he saw she was awake. She blinked in the sunlight and stretched groggily on her cot in the garage, where she slept on nights that were too hot for upstairs.

Andrés Garcia was standing over her, his black hair slicked down, dressed in his much-mended best suit, which he had had the foresight to wear when he was transported to Gwynwood. He had appeared one day at the Pylon, sent there somehow by the angelbees, from Valdivia, the Wall-town in Chile. Transport was the ultimate punishment for criminals; the angelbees no longer tolerated human executions, although they had caused several billion on Doomsday. Andrés said he deserved his fate, but he never told what he had done. A model citizen in Gwynwood, he had married Marguerite and taught the town a lot about farming.

"Dad, what about the milking?"

"It was done long ago. You were busy pulling lambs, Belita."

"Right." She smiled as she dragged herself to stand, her nightdress damp with perspiration. Andrés was the one who really delivered the lambs, and trimmed the apple trees, and tended the corn.

"I've hitched Jezebel," he said. "We're all set for Meeting."

"I'm going to Mass."

Andrés laughed. "A Mass in *la ruca!*" he exclaimed, his scornful term for the Meetinghouse. "I'll join you, if you can find a real Mass. After so many years, I'll have plenty to confess." He gave her a quick, bone-crunching hug, then turned to go.

Isabel picked her way out of the garage, between the sewing machine of Anna Tran's that needed realignment somewhere, and the Scattergoods' attic fan, and the forbidden radio receiver in progress. It was not much, so far, just three tuned amplifiers in series with a diode detector, a circuit cop-

ied from Teacher Becca's electronics manual. But Isabel
would get it working—why not? The angelbees need never
know. Still, the Town Meeting would probably send a Committee of Concern to speak to her about it one of these days.
What a disgrace. Why didn't they send a Committee of Concern to the Pylon, about what those angelbees were doing to
the sky?

Outside the sun was beating down, and the blue sky hid
the deadly work of the angelbees. Isabel drew a bucket of
water up from the cistern, pulled off her nightdress, and
sluiced herself down. Immediately she felt much better. Perhaps it would not get as hot as yesterday. After Meeting for
Worship, she would have the afternoon to work on her receiver. The Underground had set up a powerful new transmitter somewhere, according to the *Sydney Herald*. The *Herald*
appeared at the Pylon each month with the medicines and
other goods from Sydney. Why newspapers were allowed, but
not radio, no one could say.

She reached for another bucket of water, then noticed that
the level in the cistern was low, a good ten centimeters lower
than she had seen before. She paused, then put down the
bucket. They would have to tighten the water rations. There
was something called ground water, many meters below;
maybe it should be tested again.

Despite her parents, Isabel refused to wear special clothes
for Sunday, although she did pull on a clean set of overalls;
her own version of "plain dress," she said. With that, she
jumped up to the driver's seat of the carriage, Andrés and
Marguerite seated behind, his arm around Marguerite's
shoulders, stroking her hair. They knew Isabel loved driving
the horse. Horses, sheep, even the field mice in the barn; animals always made more sense to her than people, somehow.
They used what brains they had and did not put on airs.

The reins drooped loosely in hand, she clucked to Jezebel,
who lifted her head and swished her tail at flies. The hooves
tossed up dust from the road.

"The baby had a heart murmur," Marguerite was telling
Andrés. "I warned Ruth, before she left, to watch for distress
signs. Also the head circumference was on the small side; I
didn't tell her that. Nothing she could do about it, anyhow."

It was understood by both husband and daughter that Dr. Chase needed someone to talk with in confidence. They were her only colleagues.

"At least it's a boy," said Andrés. "Another suitor for my Belita."

Isabel did not reply to this ridiculous remark.

Marguerite added, "Our water's critical. Another week and all use will be restricted to drinking."

"No." Andrés's voice changed. "Impossible. We'll lose the vegetables."

"But otherwise, we'll lose livestock."

And people, Isabel added silently. She turned her head back. "When did you last test the ground water?"

"Last month," said Marguerite. "The level is still far too high, by two orders of magnitude. The puzzling thing is, now it's not only strontium-ninety, but cesium-one-thirty-seven. A new leak must have opened in the ground somewhere, probably around Philadelphia."

"Beggars can't be choosers," said Andrés. "We drink radiation already."

"Not ten rads a week. In a year we'd all be dead."

The road passed the charred remains of a house that had burned down before Isabel was born. The woods at either side sang with cicadas, and a cardinal flitted across in a flash of scarlet. Isabel turned off onto a winding trail that skirted the marshland which the angelbees had generated to fuel themselves. The mud looked mostly dried up, but above the trees Isabel saw two angelbees, shimmering in rainbow colors, a patch of sun glinting off each one.

The angelbees would have to pick a new Contact, it occurred to her, though she felt guilty to think about Alice dying. Who would the angelbees choose? Why they had chosen Alice in the first place remained a mystery.

"Our population is shrinking, as it is," Marguerite continued. "Even in Sydney it's still in decline."

"But the rate of loss is slowing," said Andrés. "They say it will turn around."

"So they say. But there goes our ozone, or whatever's going on up there. The truth is, I'm bearish."

When Isabel had been small, Marguerite had used outdated phrases from before the Wall when she did not want the child to understand. She had never lost the habit, though Isabel knew well enough that "bearish" meant things were rather desperate. Her pulse quickened, and she gripped the reins hard; Jezebel snorted and had to be calmed down.

Maybe now the Town Meeting would face it at last, would do something. But how? What could they do?

The horse turned a bend, and there stood the Meetinghouse. It was just inside the Wall, although thankfully a stand of pines obscured the view.

The house of worship, which Quakers called a Meetinghouse and Lutherans called a Church, was a log cabin with a dirt floor, built shortly after the Wall cut off access to regular churches. Andrés called it la ruca because to him a church meant stained glass and a statue of the Virgin. To be sure, there was a small bell tower, donated by a Sydney Bible society. When Carl Dreher wanted to put up a cross, the Quakers had been scandalized. They had compromised by putting up a Star of David next to it. That satisfied all but Nahum Scattergood, who maintained to this day that he would never worship in a "steeplehouse." Whatever its name, the survivors of Doomsday agreed that there was room for but one place of worship behind the Wall.

To Isabel's surprise, another angelbee floated just past the window, close enough for her to see its black eyespot rotating slowly. A nosy little creature. Was it seeking a new Contact already?

She cast down her eyes and reined the horse in. As she stepped down, her father put his arm around her and kneaded her shoulders. "You are a woman of few words this morning."

"I'm thinking about the sky."

Andrés shook his head. "It does not pay to think too hard. You could age a thousand years in a day."

Inside, there were rows of benches built of crossed logs. Isabel slid into the place saved for her by her best friend, Peace Hope Scattergood. Peace Hope's blue eyes sparkled, and curls of blond hair strayed from beneath her Quaker cap. Beside Peace Hope sat her mother, Liza, without Nahum of course. Grandmother Alice, still critically ill, was absent too.

Farther down the bench sat Daniel, who had lived with the
Scattergoods since his parents died of typhoid, and next to
Daniel sat Grace Feltman, well behaved so far.

Worship opened with twenty minutes or so of Quaker silence. The silence began, silence unbroken but for the breathing of a hundred-odd souls, and the occasional click of Peace
Hope's metal gripper-hands. Isabel nudged her as usual, and
the clicking stopped.

Now was the time to center inward, to relax one's will and
catch the Spirit. Isabel herself had never felt particularly good
at "catching the Spirit." She found herself gazing over the
familiar heads and shoulders and wondering who would the
angelbees choose as Contact?

Certainly not Sal or Deliverance Brown, Isabel's classmates at school. Nor Jon Hubbard, who flashed Isabel a bright
smile which she returned with polite disinterest. Behind
them sat Anna Tran and her son and daughter, whose round
faces and high cheekbones marked their descent from refugees of the war Isabel's grandfather had fought in. Anna's
house stood within view of the Pylon, and she detested its
dominion. She was unlikely to be chosen by the angelbees.

Carl and Deborah Dreher, holding their well-worn Lutheran Bibles, sat with their three children. There was six-
year-old Miracle Dreher, so named because he took two days
to be born, and it seemed a miracle he had ever arrived. The
brain damage was minimal. The girls, Faith and Charity, had
done better, and with luck the fourth now growing in Debbie's
womb would turn out the same. Debbie would be a likely
choice for Contact, if they did not pick Alice's daughter-in-
law, Liza.

Somewhere a shoe scraped on the hard earth. The air rustled, and a breeze carried in a whiff of fresh-cut grass. In the
light from the windows, shadows of maple leaves made a
lively dance upon the backs of the benches. Her head nodded,
exhausted from the night before.

Then it happened. Isabel's heart beat faster, and she could
not escape the sense of being overcome, the sense that something, a presence of God, had entered the room, was pouring
itself slowly in. If only she could last until it filled the room,
there would be an answer—

But it never came. Was there really a God out there, she wondered. Perhaps there was nothing out there, nothing but the sunlight and the angelbees, and the Wall, the skeletons, the deadland. Nothing her soul could connect with.

The radio in her workshop was her best chance of connecting something, connecting to the Underground. That afternoon she would have to check the connections with her voltmeter; the last time she had closed the circuit, a resistor had burned and split in half, leaving a sooty trail. Between that and the Town Meeting threatening to send her a Committee of Concern, she would never get it done. What they ought to do was—

Send a Committee to the Pylon. A Witness, rather, a "Witness to Crimes Against Humanity," as Grandfather Chase had done, years ago at the missile plant outside Philadelphia. In those days, Quakers had really meant something.

There came a rustling of clothes and feet as the children slid themselves off the benches to file out with the teachers. Daniel was waiting at the door till his Specials were all through; Grace caught his arm to lean on because she had a slight twist in her leg.

Now the programmed service would begin, led by Carl or Debbie Dreher, or another Lutheran. Isabel shifted herself on the bench and hoped the sermon would be brief. She generally found the Bible stories lacking in taste, let alone morality. That woman Jael, for instance, who hammered a tent peg through Sisera's head and got nothing but praise for it. The New Testament was little better. Why had the city of Jerusalem put up with that trial, especially the false witnesses? There ought to have been a Committee of Concern somewhere. There ought to be one now, for the angelbees. She would tell them, she decided, as soon as Worship was done.

Instead of the Drehers, today, Matthew Crofts rose to lead the service. Matthew was a former chemist at Union Carbide who taught the science classes in high school. Isabel liked Teacher Matthew, even if he was a Lutheran.

Matthew ran a hand through his speckled gray hair. His receding chin gave him a diffident appearance. His build had a slight stoop, and he tended to roll his eyes upward as he spoke.

"Today is a special day," Matthew began, "for a new soul has been born into our community. Yet while we rejoice in this gift, our joy is overshadowed by the inexplicable events in the heavens." So Matthew would speak to what the angel-bees were doing. Isabel took a deep breath.

"It would be easy for us to feel bitterness, to question God's wisdom in permitting this suffering, in bringing about such a curse upon the day of this birth." Matthew paused to open his Bible. "In one way or another, the birthdays of men have been cursed since the time of Abel and Cain. The suffering Job actually spoke a curse upon the day of his birth:

"May that day turn to darkness; may God above not
   look for it;
nor light of dawn shine on it.
May blackness sully it, and murk and gloom,
cloud smother that day, swift darkness eclipse the sun.
Blind darkness swallow up that night;
count it not among the days of the year.

"Doesn't this verse hold special meaning for us?" Matthew asked. "Doomsday should have been a birthday to over two hundred thousand souls. Imagine it—a population greater than that of the whole Earth today, all born on a single day. Yet that birthday for thousands became the Death Year for billions."

Isabel shivered inwardly. What would that Death Year have felt like? She herself had not yet been born, nor conceived, thank heavens. She recalled the solar eclipse, just over a year ago, when darkness had swallowed the sun, and the stars came out. But for a whole year—a blind darkness, without stars...

The elders never spoke of the Death Year, not in detail. Matthew had lost his family outside. But then, even within the Wall, four fifths of the town had died off during Isabel's childhood. As her father said, the loss was slowing now.

"How shall we explain the events in the sky today?" Matthew asked. "More to the point, how shall we explain the events of Doomsday and the Death Year? Why did God allow these events, leaving us trapped as we are here today?

"To answer these questions, let us return to the mythic birthplace of all questions, the first Garden. There God's people first tasted the fruit of the Tree of Knowledge, knowing how to question, what is good and evil? This knowing of good and evil came at a price: mortality, eternal subjection to the laws of nature, the limits of the physical universe.

"But we forget that there was a second tree in the Garden: the Tree of Life, which meant Godlike mastery of the physical universe, the power of eternal life—or eternal death. God never gave us the chance to approach that Tree, the Tree of Life or Death. Instead He barred the way with a flaming sword.

"Why, then, have we mortals schemed ever since to get at that second Tree, to master life and death? Despite that flaming sword, we have calculated like Caiaphas that one man should die for the life of a people, ten for the life of a hundred, ten million for the life of a hundred million. We burned heretics at the stake; we exterminated the natives of our American shores. The advent of modern science only heightened our calculation: millions burned in one war, billions in the next."

Matthew paused as if for breath. "So as we mourn our imprisonment, and shake our heads at the evil disturbance of our skies, let us recall the road taken. If we ever should regain our mastery of Earth, let us return to the Tree of Knowledge and learn to master the evil within."

Isabel blinked at this sermon, perplexed. It was the angelbees who had destroyed Earth, as surely as if they had sent the missiles themselves. Why had Teacher Matthew turned the blame around? Any Quaker knew that killing humans was wrong, but as for angelbees—that was different.

What an odd turn Teacher Matthew had taken, like the neck of the Klein bottle he described in school. Absorbed in thought, she missed the closing hymn, "A Mighty Fortress Is Our God."

As the worship concluded, the room filled with shaking hands and people leaning across benches to greet their neighbors. Isabel clasped Peace Hope's shoulder, not her gripperhand.

It was time for announcements. Suddenly her heart was

pounding. Someone would have to speak up about the burning of the sky. Surely someone would want to do something about it.

Liza Scattergood, as Town Clerk, stood first, her hair pinned neatly beneath her cap, and her black skirt flowing down her straight profile. "Ruth's newborn boy welcomes visitors," she announced.

"A boy!" Peace Hope whispered.

"Yes," said Isabel. "She hasn't named it yet; isn't that odd?"

"Of course she won't, silly; not till the *bris.*"

Isabel frowned, annoyed when Peace Hope used a word she did not know.

Marguerite announced the water crisis, and she confirmed that the ground water still contained too much strontium-ninety.

Peace Hope nudged her again. "Why is strontium still a problem, does thee know? What is its half-life?"

"Thirty years—that means it's still here, Scatterbrain," Isabel whispered, triumphant this time.

Children burst in upon the room with exuberant squeals and hands signing to the deaf Pestlethwaite twins. They seemed to be continuing one of Daniels's "sunshine games," the object of which was to call out, "This is a hug!" then squeeze your nearest companion as hard as you could. "This is a hug!" called Grace, and she threw her arms clumsily around Daniel. The twin girls signed the same with their hands, crossing their arms before their chests; then they embraced him.

Daniel managed to extricate himself with good humor, but he looked paler than usual. It was probably about time for another dose of his medicine, or even a blood transfusion.

"Are there no more announcements?" Liza asked.

Surely now someone would speak up about the sky? People were standing to leave.

Isabel leaned tensely on the bench in front of her. She rose to her feet, and she nearly blacked out as the blood rushed from her head. Her loss of sleep was catching up with her. "I think we should do something." Her voice sounded thin and strained. "About the sky. About what the angelbees are doing."

People gasped as if taking a collective breath. The depth of their reaction took Isabel by surprise. "There must be something we could do," she hurried on, louder over the voices. "We could send a Committee of Concern to the Pylon."

From his seat up front, Carl Dreher stood and half turned toward her. "The Town Meeting will consider this, I'm sure."

The next Town Meeting was a month off. It was even worse than she had feared. They were not going to face it; even this time they would give in to the Pylon without protest. She tightened her grip on the bench in front of her, inwardly burning.

"Isabel is right." Her mother stood beside her, laying a hand on her shoulder. "We need to do something, about the angelbees and about the survival of this town. We were saying so, just last night, Liza."

Liza nodded. "We must consider these things. I invite everyone to a discussion, at our house this afternoon."

There was a rush of voices as people got up to leave, some remaining to talk in worried tones.

Marguerite whispered, "I do wish you'd warned me. You can't know how frightening it is, to those of us who lived through..." She did not finish.

Debbie Dreher came over, her steps dragging a bit; she was into the sixth month, when the baby grows fast. Her flower-print dress was faded nearly as gray as Peace Hope's. "Of course we must do something, Isabel, but please, nothing rash. If the angelbees ever find your radio they'll—"

It was too much to take anymore. She turned and strode up the aisle, avoiding the faces, and headed out the side door into the courtyard. The hot air enveloped her like a cloak, and a squirrel skipped away from her feet. The cicadas' hum rose and intensified.

There was one place to get away, one place where the elders never came. That place was the Wall.

III

ISABEL CUT THROUGH the cemetery, the rows of headstones, five times as many as the current population. She passed the earliest ones already leaning, and the little lamb that marked Vera's stillborn from the Death Year, then the later ones for Daniel's parents and Peace Hope's two brothers. Then she walked on through the stand of pines beyond. Dry needles crunched underfoot, and the shaded air was sweetly cool.

She came to the place where the strangeness began. The pines thinned out, and the few trunks that remained grew at a slight angle to the earth, all leaning back toward her in parallel, almost like the old headstones. Past the leaning pines, the forest gave out altogether, with just a few stunted bushes that straggled back as if crawling on the ground.

Now Isabel could feel the unmistakable pressure of the Wall, a larger version of the airwall enclosing the Pylon. It was as if an enormous hand were pushing her back, gently but steadily.

Isabel stopped and pulled a pair of mirrorshade glasses out of her overalls. The sun was coming in from the east, its ultraviolet rays unscreened by the Wall. Only directly above Gwynwood the Wall's upper dome enclosed a patch of ozone to filter the sun.

She walked on, another ten paces or so, the air pressure rising until her face went numb. Then taking care not to fall backward, she gradually sat herself down and stared through her mirrorshades, through the Wall.

The ground beneath the Wall itself was bare, sun-baked clay, an otherworldly sterile zone. Beyond, well outside, lay the hulks of dead trees, miles upon miles of charred deadland. But just at the threshold of deadland lay the skeletons.

The bones were not all human, of course. Isabel could spot parts of deer, and dogs, and raccoons, even a barn owl here and there among the scorched dry bones. One skull of a large dog happened to face her directly, its eye sockets shadowed dark, tilted just a bit to one side as if begging its last meal. Human or animal, the scattered skeletons lined every stretch of the Wall that imprisoned Gwynwood town.

It was hard for Isabel to comprehend that the Wall had not always stood there, and that the pines and farmlands and crowded towns had once covered Pennsylvania. Those who had lived before spoke of it and taught what the world had been before Doomsday. What was harder to speak of was what had come after.

One morning, the skies already filling with soot from distant firestorms, those residents of Gwynwood who had not fled town awoke to discover the Wall. The Wall was a tangible barrier that solid matter could not pass through, not even dust or flour. The dome of the Wall, some twenty miles across, cut an unearthly hole through the black clouds. Within the circle of the Wall, there was light and warmth. Outside, there was dark and cold. Nuclear winter.

Living things trapped outside quickly noticed the place of light within. From miles around came animals, birds, and people to press into the Wall, in vain. Only light could pass through, and sound. The elders rarely talked about that.

Outside the temperature fell to well below zero—just how far below, no one could say, but the corpses stayed frozen through the next planting season. When they thawed at last, there were no animal scavengers, and no birds. There were plants, but they shriveled in the radioactive rain. There were some flying insects; but, surprisingly, these vanished and were gone before Isabel was born. Marguerite said that the nuclear blasts had mopped up so much ozone from the upper atmosphere that the ultraviolet had blinded all sighted creatures. Microbes, millipedes, and a few hardy weeds inherited the world outside.

The Wall became a sort of terrarium, its upper atmosphere condensing into a round pancake cloud that rained upon the crops. Within the Wall, people were safe from ultraviolet and from dirty rain, but the soil still leaked poison. One year, the seepage into Gwynwood's farmland had killed a third of the town, and not a child that year was born alive. After that, they had listened when the Pylon warned Alice to destroy a crop of apples or potatoes.

It turned out that the angelbees had set up similar Walls scattered around the globe, seeming to sample the population in proportion to the number of survivors. Thus in Australia they set up a dozen of them totaling two hundred thousand people plus twice that number of sheep. The tip of South America came out well, too. North America had only three other known airwalls, one at Vista, a big town of two thousand on the West Coast, and two smaller ones in Canada. Asia had several, but Europe had none.

Wisps of something green poked up among the charcoal stumps beyond the skeletons. Outside the Walls, no human survivor had been seen, in all the years since the Death Year. No human could have survived the ultraviolet, let alone the radioactivity, dying of cancer before reproductive age. By now, though, the radiation would be down and the ozone would have recovered—if the angelbees had allowed it to do so.

Marguerite had tried to estimate the radiation levels that remained outside, and whether it was yet "safe." For Isabel, though, radiation was just another fact of life, like typhoid. The pioneers who had built America the first time risked typhoid and more. The time had come for new pioneers.

But still there was the Wall.

Off to Isabel's left, the Dreher kids, Miracle and his sisters, came out to play against the Wall. The game was to turn and run backward as far into the Wall as you could, then jump up and fly off for several yards. Faith and Charity squealed in chorus as they went airborne for a moment, then tumbled to the ground. Above their squeals rose a hollow wailing sound, the sound of the wind outside blowing in against the Wall, as if the voices of the dead rose to speak in some incomprehensible tongue.

Shunned by the elders, the threshold of the Wall had become a meeting place for the young. As Isabel expected, Sal and Deliverance Brown soon came strolling after her, with Daniel between them.

"Isabel!" called Sal. "Whatever possessed you? We can't just go visit the Pylon."

"Especially with Alice still sick." Deliverance ran to the little ones. "Faith, the sun's coming in; you'll get cancer.

Come back and sit in the shade with Teacher Daniel."

Isabel kept her back to them, and stared into the Wall. Daniel's reply was inaudible, but Sal added, "They know Alice is dying. I saw three angelbees floating over the Meetinghouse, waiting like—"

"Oh, hush, Sal," said Deliverance.

Peace Hope came over and dropped her crutches, letting her leg prostheses splay out as she supported herself on her gripper-hands. Her gray homespun skirt spread out over the grass. "'Where does thee come from, and where is thee going?'" she remarked, after Carroll's Red Queen. Peace Hope, who loved chess, kept the Red Queen in her breast pocket for luck because, though limbless, the "Queen" ran the fastest.

Isabel got up and moved back to sit with her friend beneath a pine tree.

"Whatever possessed thee?" Peace Hope's voice carried reproof and admiration.

"I was just witnessing to the Truth."

"But why did thee leave so abruptly?"

Isabel sighed, and she looked away again through the Wall, at the dog's skull that jutted at an angle from the pile. "I guess I've just had enough. Something happened last night." She saw again the sky as it had seemed to crack and peel away, draining the lifeblood of Earth. "Something's changed. I feel I don't belong here anymore." She thought of Daniel again. If only he could see her point of view. They had argued it for years; but now they were graduates without a future. It was time to act. "The point is, I'm ready to speak for myself. I'll strike out on my own if I have to."

"That's just what they're afraid of. They think thee has already joined the Underground. Carl Dreher was saying, thee is a danger to the town."

"That's just an excuse." Angrily Isabel pulled a grass blade and peeled it in half, then in half again. "The real danger is here." She tossed the bits of grass to the radioactive earth. "How many of us will make it to the next generation?"

"The deadland is only worse."

"Around here it is. But Mother says there must be places less contaminated, maybe down in Mexico. We could live there—if the angelbees would pull out the Wall and quit bleeding off our ozone."

"Everyone knows that," said Peace Hope. "That's why we're going to do something about it."

"You mean this afternoon. They'll just talk it to death. What we need is people to fight for freedom, like Harriet Tubman." The famed conductor of the Underground Railroad had actually gone on to command an army unit for the Union. As a child, Isabel had read Tubman's biography and imagined that Tubman was her ancestor.

"It is hard for us," said Peace Hope quietly. "We are law-abiding people."

Isabel raised her voice. "The old-time Quakers broke plenty of laws to free the slaves." She looked back to see whether Daniel had overheard. He smiled and walked over, and sat down next to her.

"Thee spoke well, after Worship," he said. "I don't agree with thee, about fighting the angelbees. But...these events need prayerful consideration." As if uneasy with himself, he got up abruptly and returned down the trail through the cemetery. Sal and Deliverance soon followed.

Perplexed, Isabel watched him leave.

Peace Hope said, "I agree with thee."

Isabel looked quickly at her. "You do?"

"We need to overcome the angelbees, that is true."

"You'll help me build the radio?"

"Of course. I wouldn't let thee get into any such scrape without me." Peace Hope's blue eyes twinkled beneath her sandy curls, and her body swayed slightly above her metal arms.

"We'll join the Underground!" Isabel whispered fiercely. "We'll form our own secret cell, with our own transmitter— Radio Free Gwynwood. We'll get Teacher Becca to join; who knows, she might be a member already." Becca, who had sent the electronics book in a hamper of vegetables; who had asked Isabel to come and see her again, for some new secret. Becca had once taught a stirring lesson about Independence Day. "We'll pledge 'our lives, our fortunes, and our sacred honor.'"

"Especially honor." Peace Hope added, "If we wish to

overcome an enemy, the first thing is to find out how they think. Maybe we should play chess with them."

Isabel waved her hand impatiently. "Maybe we can enlist Matthew to do experiments on them—and on the Wall. Maybe..." Suddenly she frowned. "Scatterbrain, I'm surprised at you. You're much too virtuous to get into something like this."

"Thee just doesn't read thy Bible. Try John 8:32."

Which read, as Isabel checked later, "Know the truth, and the truth will set you free."

IV

IN THE HEAT of the afternoon, Isabel was at the cistern again, hoisting up water for the sheep. She walked back past the house, noticing by the door three gallon jars of honey from Ruth Weiss's apiary, enough to last well into winter. That would be for delivering the baby. Isabel remembered suddenly the fan from the Scattergoods; she would try to get it fixed before heading over to the meeting about the angel-bees.

She entered the barn and sloshed the water into the trough, taking care to avoid loss. Immediately the four Suffolk ewes came running, their black legs pounding. "Meh-eh-eh," called Hepzibah, the bossy one. They bleated frantically, jostling one another to stick their necks in the trough. Isabel hugged their greasy woolly backs and scratched their necks, especially the Dorset hybrid lamb with spotted legs, whom she had raised from a bottle the Christmas before. The ram, and the two goats, and the remaining ewes straggled in.

Andrés returned to drop off the tree clippers. "The dwarf apples are getting old. Too many sports to be pruned out."

Isabel nodded. "You coming to the Scattergoods'?" Maybe the town would do something after all.

"Yes. Your mother will come, if she feels she can leave Alice."

Isabel winced. Poor Alice was now on oxygen upstairs. The sheep lapped noisily at the water, and the rustle of mice could be heard behind the wallboards. Isabel remembered her mother saying about Aaron Weiss, "We did all that medical science could do." Marguerite would be saying that again soon.

Then she thought of something and glanced at her father curiously. "What did you think, today, about that sermon of Matthew's?"

"Sermon? You call that a sermon? *No sabe ni la a.*"

His vehemence surprised her. "Why not?"

"The Tree of Life, that represents the cross of the crucifixion, foreshadowed at the Fall. That's what the priest says. You Americans know nothing about Christ." Then he relaxed and chuckled to himself. "Imagine, that I should sermonize like a priest."

Isabel took a deep breath, but knew better than to ask further about his past.

Just then, for no apparent reason, one ewe broke away and charged out of the barn, and the others stampeded after her. Andrés chuckled. "Sheep never change. Foolish as men."

The hands of the grandfather's clock stood at half-past four in the Scattergoods' sitting room. Some two dozen people had managed to come, seated in the straight-backed pine chairs Nahum had built years ago. A welcome current of air circulated from the fan in the window, which Isabel had fixed in time.

"We are gathered to consider prayerfully the events in our skies," Liza said carefully. Next to her sat Nahum, a man of rather pinched features who seemed to scowl perpetually. His gray-streaked hair was tied back, and he wore black every day. As a child Isabel had feared him, but he taught her a lot of good woodworking.

Carl Dreher cleared his throat. "What is there to say? The work of the angelbees is beyond our hands. Let's be thankful for what little bit of Earth the Wall preserved for us."

Debbie nodded and reached to retrieve Miracle, who had crawled halfway down from her lap. Faith and Charity were on the floor drawing with new crayons. Where had those come from, Isabel wondered suddenly. The monthly shipment from Sydney must have appeared at the Pylon through the cross-dimensional link, despite the absence of Alice. She remembered the spacecraft "leg" she had seen poking out of the fog, the night before. Was that the vehicle for transport of the shipment? she wondered. In any case, she must be sure to pick up the medicine box for her mother, and check the *Herald* for news of the Underground.

"Never," Anna Tran spoke up, with unusual vehemence. "I'll never, never be grateful for the Wall, till my dying day." Her dark Vietnamese eyes glared challenging at her neighbors. A three-year-old on Doomsday, Anna barely recollected the world before the Wall, but she had always been convinced that it must fall.

"The issue is survival," said Marguerite. "Let's face it: we can't make it from one generation to the next, sitting on this hot spot in the most bombed-out country on Earth. That's clear from our birthrate and death rate. If the angelbees keep blitzing our ozone, then they don't mean to pull out our Wall anytime soon."

Vera Brown, Deliverance's mother, spoke quietly. "There must be some way to clean things up. After all, this is our home." Vera had a pedigree that traced back to colonial times in Gwynwood.

"Of course there will be a way," said Carl. "Someday. All radiation decays. For goodness sake, Doctor Chase: What do you expect us to do?"

Marguerite did not reply, her lips shut tight, the muscles taut in her neck. Quiet in anger, she preferred to keep her dignity. Andrés put his arm around her. "Let's take a few pot-shots at the beasties," he suggested, with a wink at Isabel.

Carl half rose from his seat. "And have the whole town put to sleep again?" That was fifteen years before, when someone had popped several angelbees with a BB gun. That day, a strange fog had poured out of the Pylon so thick you could not see a hand in front of your face. Something in the fog put everyone to sleep. Isabel remembered awakening, dazed and parched.

"It only lasted three days," Andrés replied.

"What if next time it's permanent? Whole Wall-towns have vanished before."

Liza said quickly, "Let us consider Isabel's original proposal, which was to send a Committee of Concern to the Pylon. A responsible suggestion, I think."

Isabel blinked at being called "responsible." She stole a glance at Peace Hope, who grinned back and lifted her gripper-hand.

There were uneasy mutterings and shuffling of feet. Debbie said, "Only the Contact can talk to the Pylon."

"Only the Contact is 'spoken to,'" said Marguerite. "Anyone can go and stare at the Pylon, if it comes to that. If we stare long enough, who knows what may happen."

But others were still shaking their heads. "They'll just put you to sleep again, if they get annoyed enough," said Jim Pestlethwaite.

"This is an emergency," Marguerite insisted.

"How does thee know?" Nahum spoke sharply, and the others quieted. "How does thee know what our friends from the stars have done in the sky? How does thee know the spectacle of lights is their doing? How does thee know what God intends for our town, whether life or death?"

The room was still, except for the gentle hum of the fan. Isabel thought, only a Quaker as "plain" as Nahum could call the angelbees "friends."

"Of course I don't know," said Marguerite evenly. "I've given you my best professional diagnosis, that's all."

There was silence again.

Peace Hope said, "Surely, Father, we can say that we are frightened. Surely that is something we can 'tell' the Pylon."

"Of course, that is a proper concern." Nahum nodded. "All of us possess the gift of speech. To leave such a burden up to thy grandmother all these years was as ungodly as keeping a preacher in a steeplehouse."

There was a thought. How hard had anyone tried to make "contact," besides Alice?

"We can send people in pairs," Liza was saying. "A vigil around the clock. I'll take the first shift."

"I'll go, too," said Carl.

Matthew said, "I'll spell you in the morning."

"I will join thee," Daniel told Matthew.

"Then I'll go next," said Isabel quickly, "with Peace Hope." Maybe something would happen. Even if not, it would be a good excuse to inspect the Pylon at leisure.

Chairs squeaked on the floor as neighbors got up, to get their chores done before sundown. As Daniel crossed the room, he touched her shoulder lightly. Isabel caught his hand. He turned to look her full in the face, with a friendly smile.

A rush of warmth came over her. Then with a nod he left, and Isabel took a deep breath to collect herself.

Peace Hope moved her crutch forward. "Thee'll be staying for dinner, Isabel?"

"Thanks. Will you, Dad?"

Andrés shook his head. "Your mother won't bother to eat if I don't fix something."

"Then you can take home the medicine box from Sydney. There was one, wasn't there, Peace Hope?"

"Yes," said Peace Hope. "The whole shipment was there outside the Pylon as usual, just by the airwall. Carl picked it up for us."

"You checked it with the counter?"

"Yes, always." Usually the Sydney shipment was clean, but one time it had flipped the Geiger needle clear offscale.

"What about the return shipment?" Isabel asked.

"Carl just dropped it there, outside the airwall. We'll see what happens."

After dinner, Isabel took the *Sydney Herald* upstairs to read while Peace Hope worked at her desk. She yawned, realizing her exhaustion; she thought of Liza at the Pylon and wondered how that tireless woman would manage another night without sleep. Isabel herself needed sleep, but she was determined to get what she could out of the *Herald* before it was passed around the town. The dingy gray paper, printed on much-recycled pulp, would have to be returned next month else the subscription rate doubled.

LABOUR OUT screamed the headline. Beneath was a photo of a party rally, the streets jammed with bicycles and solar mopeds. Buried on an inside page was another escape attempt, an explosive blast through the section of airwall that spanned the Port Jackson Harbour. The Wall supposedly thinned out underwater, they said. Not thin enough, unfortunately.

What about the Underground? What about the little airwall around the Pylon; might that one be easier to breach than the outer Wall? Isabel decided to bring a shovel, for her shift with Peace Hope.

The back page of the *Herald* regularly featured the Taronga Zoo. Nine tenths of the Taronga collection survived nowhere else on Earth. This month, the keepers had gotten a nesting pair of bald eagles named George and Martha to produce a fledgling. Eventually they hoped to reintroduce the pair to the wild, right here in Gwynwood.

There was a full-page ad for "electrics." Sydney was

proud of being electrified, mostly solar. If Isabel saved another month's allowance, she might just get the solar cell she needed to amplify her receiver, if the prices did not go up . . .

The problem was that Gwynwood lacked goods for export. The harvest produced a surplus most years, but none of the local produce met Sydney's radiation limits. And they had no industry to speak of.

The town had come up with one salable commodity: hand-decorated stamps depicting native American scenes. The artist was Peace Hope, who drew and painted by holding the implements between her teeth and had shown an early artistic gift. Liza would spread the glue and stamp the perforations and make packages to order. They fetched outrageous prices, in Isabel's opinion, starting at ten Australian dollars for a half-inch portrait of a crested cardinal, on up to fifty for an old-fashioned Quaker "family scene" done in silhouettes to avoid blasphemy, each stamp having "Gwynwood, USA" penned in the corner.

Had the Scattergoods kept the money, they would have been richer than the entire town, several times over. In fact, they turned their earnings over to the Town Meeting, which then had to allocate funds. The biggest single allocation went to Marguerite for the hospital. So Isabel leafed through the medical ads, figuring that here at least were a few trinkets they might be able to buy.

There was a sale on hospital equipment. A fetal heart monitor, the cordless model, was marked down to $50.

Isabel looked up from the floor. "Look, Peace Hope: a fetal monitor. I've never seen one for under five hundred. We might manage the deliveries better."

Peace Hope was working on her stamp portraits, at her desk nestled beneath the slant of the roof. Her desk lamp, running on solar storage, threw jagged shadows across the room. As usual she had her thirty-year-old tape deck playing an ancient "I Love Lucy" soundtrack, about Lucy and Ricky hunting movie stars in Hollywood. The tape had so much hiss you could barely make out what Lucy was wailing about. It focused her concentration, Peace Hope claimed. She let the paint brush drop from her mouth and said, "A fetal monitor would be a good thing. It would bring Debbie some peace of mind." Debbie's son Miracle had suffered brain damage from a prolonged labor.

"The sensor is a miniature microwave transmitter. I could use it to test our clandestine radio."

"Good. I'll chip in my allowance, if need be." Peace Hope took up the paint brush between her lips and touched up the black face of a cardinal. On the wall above hung a framed engraving of the Scattergood family tree which traced Quaker ancestors back to seventeenth-century England. From the tape deck came Lucy's cry of "Ricky!" followed by some unintelligible imprecation.

"I wonder how Liza is doing at the Pylon," Isabel mused. "Do you suppose the Pylon will take any notice?"

"Only to stare back." Peace Hope's voice was muffled around the brush handle.

"We must get them to notice us." Isabel caught her fist in her palm. "Teacher Becca knows something. Will you come with me to see her tomorrow?"

"Mm-hm." After another brush stroke she added, "I still think we ought to play chess for them. No intelligent creature would pass up a game of chess."

"You and your chess. I'm going to try an experiment. Like digging a hole under the airwall." That could hardly be ignored.

The fluorescent bulb flickered, and the tape slowed to a drawl. Peace Hope flicked off the tape, and the lamp steadied again. "The charge is almost down. I have to get ready for bed, while I still have good light."

For Peace Hope, getting ready for bed was a complex operation. First she sat on her bed and got the front of her homespun dress unhooked, using teeth and gripper-hands, exposing the joint between false leg and leg stump. She dropped the clothes onto a shelf right next to the bed. With her grippers she flipped the clasp at each leg joint to release the ring clasp, and then the legs came off, revealing the stunted limb buds with which she had been born. With her teeth she flipped back her arm clasps, first the left, then the right. The left "arm" bounced on the floor with a hollow sound and rolled to the wall; the right one, a more sophisticated prosthesis with finer controls, she caught in her arm bud and set down more carefully on the shelf.

As she set the arm down next to her clothes, the Red Queen slipped out of the pocket and rolled under the bed. Isabel reached beneath the bed to retrieve the chess piece. As she did so, she spotted a paperback farther under and retrieved that also. "What's this? Is it any good?" New books were rare; she thought she had read all the Scattergoods' books by now.

The title was *Pirate's Flame*, slashed across the cover. Below was a picture of a woman on a burning ship, her head cast back, in the arms of a well-muscled black-haired man. The woman's dress, which was the same color as the flames on the ship, was half open below the neck.

"It is good," said Peace Hope. "I wish I could forget it, so I could read it again."

Isabel turned to the first page and read to herself: "...his hungry eyes devoured her neck, and her breasts, and he said, 'Beware, maiden, for I will carry you away with me across the sea!'"

The lamp sputtered out at last, the day's electricity spent. Out the window, in the darkening twilight, the ungodly orange of the angelbees' handiwork had reappeared.

"Put it back, please," Peace Hope added, "so Mom won't see."

"Scatterbrain, I'm surprised at you."

"Why shouldn't I? You're lucky, you've found a boy that you care for in this little town."

"Daniel doesn't care for me, though, not in that way."

"One never knows. Plain Friends take their time." Peace Hope added, "I'll need broader horizons to find the kind of boy for me."

Isabel looked at her, suspicious of the implication that her own tastes were provincial. "What kind of person do you like?"

"What I'd really like is someone like..." Peace Hope eyed a book on the shelf. "Stephen Hawking."

Stephen Hawking, the brilliant twentieth-century physicist who wrote *A Brief History of Time*. Isabel had unearthed the book from her mother's attic and given it to Peace Hope for Christmas. It stood out prominently on her shelf, its author pictured on the jacket in his wheelchair against a back-drop of stars.

"You're right: you won't find a Stephen Hawking in Gwynwood." Isabel lay back on the mattress and stared at the ceiling where cobwebs nested in the corner. "That's all the more reason for us to get out of here. To civilization—to Sydney. To the Uni..." Her eyelids fluttered and her head fell forward.

"My dad says that Sydney is more wicked than Babylon ...Isabel, thee looks tired. Would thee care to spend the night?"

She shook herself awake. "Better not; I have to milk the sheep. I'll borrow this, if you don't mind." She tucked the book into her overalls.

"Sure. Thanks for getting that fan done so fast. Take the lantern; there's little moonlight tonight."

"You're coming, tomorrow morning, to see Teacher Becca?"

"I'll come. Don't forget the vigil at the Pylon afterward."

That she would hardly forget. Isabel lit the candle between the glass panes of the lantern. She felt her way down the stairs and out the door, where she glared her defiance at the sky and at the angelbees that came out in greatest numbers at night. She swung the lantern as she walked, and an old rhyme came into her head:

> How many miles to Babylon?
> Three score miles and ten.
> Can you get there by candlelight?
> Yes, and back again.

V

BY MORNING THE air had cooled some. Puffs of cloud lined the upper ceiling of the Wall far above Gwynwood, shading the town. Outside, though, the sun still shone mercilessly upon the deadland.

At the Weisses' house, Isabel tied the horse's reins to the weatherworn picket fence, then she helped Peace Hope step down on her crutches. One of the older homes in Gwynwood, the main house had a solid stone foundation and gabled windows above. Becca lived in an attached apartment that had been built for her grandmother; she had preferred this partial independence, rather than share the main house with her brother's family. The construction of the apartment was simpler than the rest of the house, with aluminum siding and minimal trim. Isabel noted immediately the window Becca must have meant to be fixed, to the right of the door: its screen mesh bulged apart from the frame, and the old spline hung out, disintegrating.

"No problem," Isabel told Peace Hope. "We'll just stuff it back in the groove and replace the spline." She knocked on the apartment door.

"Come in," came a voice from inside.

Isabel opened the door and helped Peace Hope up the step. The room was darker than she had expected; of course, Becca would not need light. The curtains of the picture window were drawn to keep out the heat. Becca sat at an old rolltop desk, reading, her hand brushing across the rows of Braille. There was a shelf full of books which Becca had used to teach the children math and spelling. Isabel still winced to recall, years ago, one day that she had missed seven times eight.

Peace Hope said, "Good morning, Teacher Becca—oh!"

An angelbee appeared in the corner, glittering faintly as it circled, right in Becca's apartment. Isabel's mouth fell open, and she felt cold all over.

"Yes," said Becca, "we have an extra guest."

Isabel said wonderingly, "How can you tell?"

"I can hear it hum and feel the air as it rustles by. Angelbees seem to come very near me, as if they know I cannot see. It doesn't occur to them that I might have other senses. What do you make of that, Isabel?"

Isabel thought hard. Before she could answer, Becca added, as if to herself, "At least they do not chatter, which is better than I can say of some of us. Some who think I need company all day. This is such a small town."

Isabel was taken aback.

"We won't say another word, if thee'd rather," Peace Hope promised.

At that, Isabel made a frantic face, but Peace Hope ignored her. The angelbee loomed closer, reflecting shafts of light from between the curtains. Its eyespot was a black rounded disk with a hexagonal facet cut across the surface. In the center of the hexagon was a pupil wide enough to stick a finger in. Isabel had noticed before that not all angelbees looked exactly alike; in particular, some would have a perfectly rounded eyespot without the hexagonal facet. The smaller ones, and the ones just budding off from a parent, always had rounded eyespots.

The darkness of the room unnerved her. She pulled the curtain aside—

There were three more angelbees hovering just outside the window screen.

Isabel's hand froze, and her scalp prickled. Those angelbees hovered so close, almost as if they were...concerned. Concerned for the one inside?

"You need more light." Becca rose from the table. "I will fetch a candle for you."

"Oh no; please don't go to any trouble."

Becca moved slowly and deliberately to the sideboard. She took a candle from the drawer and stuck it in a crystal holder. Then she took out a kitchen match.

"Please let me—" Isabel bit her tongue, cursing herself inwardly.

Becca expertly lit the match. Her face with its hooded empty eyes sprung into focus.

The angelbee retreated to the far corner, rotating so its eyespot turned away, out of sight.

Isabel gasped, and Peace Hope stared.

"Our guest has taken flight?" asked Becca.

"The ones at the window left, too," noted Peace Hope.

"As if they thought you'd burn the house down," said Isabel.

"Curious." With the match Becca lit the candle and set it on the sideboard. "It seems that our...friends can't take the heat. Now why would that be, I wonder."

Isabel thought quickly. "They float in air; they're filled with hydrogen gas. Heat would cause the gas to expand, even burst into flame!"

"Excellent, Friend Isabel. I always knew you had a good head on your shoulders."

Isabel glowed at this praise. "How did you ever capture it?"

Shadows lined Becca's face in the candlelight. "As I told you, the angelbee was inspecting me, rather closely. It followed me inside, and I closed the door."

Peace Hope shook her blond hair out of her face. "What else does thee know about angelbees?"

Becca sat in silence for a bit. "Why do you ask?"

Isabel's pulse quickened. "We want to break through the Wall. We want to overthrow the angelbees and set Earth free of them."

"Freedom. A noble task. I commend your ambition."

"But thee must help us," said Peace Hope. "Thee knows things about the angelbees."

"And about the Underground," Isabel added hopefully. "How do we join?"

"As to that, you're already members."

"I mean the real Underground."

"What do you think 'underground resistance' means? Ordinary people taking things into their own hands, as you are doing."

"But there's an organized Underground."

"Organized for what? Setting explosives?" Becca shook her head. "There is much to be done first. Much to be learned."

"What else?" Peace Hope persisted.

"Everything else. We know the eyes of our masters, but

where are their limbs? Where are their mouths? What do they want of us?"

"I saw a limb," said Isabel. "A sticklike mechanical limb, jutting out of the cloud around the Pylon. It looked something like a leg of the lunar module, remember?" That was back in tenth grade.

"How curious. Now, they must have arms as well as legs."

"Maybe that's what they want us for," said Peace Hope. "For our arms. Like we keep horses, for their legs."

Isabel frowned. "Come on, Scatterbrain."

Becca asked, "Would you care to stay for some tea?"

"No thanks." There was cleaning to be done at the hospital, and planning for the Pylon that evening. Fire—might the Pylon be scared of fire, too? "I'll be back with fresh spline for the window." She opened the apartment door and held it for Peace Hope.

Peace Hope gasped. "Shut the door, silly!"

Isabel hesitated, perplexed. In that instant, the angelbee darted across the room and slipped out the door. It passed her head, so close that she heard the humming of the tiny wing flaps that vibrated beneath the sphere.

"Darn. I'm sorry, Teacher Becca." What an idiot thing to do; she felt worse than Grace Feltman. "I'll try and get it back here for you—"

Becca tensed suddenly. "Let it go, Isabel. These are the 'masters of the Earth,' remember? Indulgent though they may seem. You're a grown woman, now, but I still have to answer to your mother." Then she relaxed and leaned back in her chair. "Take care," she said in her quiet, ironic tone. "Take care, lest the catcher be caught."

At a quarter of five, Isabel had the horse hitched again, ready to pick up Peace Hope for their shift at the Pylon. She wondered briefly whether Daniel would have got any response from the Pylon. Probably not, no more than Liza had. She checked her supplies once more: the ladder, the tool kit, the shovel, and a stack of firewood. All she needed for her "experiments" on the Pylon.

Andrés came out with a covered basket. "I've brought you some dinner..." He stopped and stared at the ladder poking out of the carriage. "Belita, what is this? You are going to build a house, perhaps?"

"Never mind. Thanks for dinner, Dad."

"You can't scale an airwall with a ladder."

"Dad! Don't be silly, you'll just upset Mother." It was too late; already she saw her mother hurrying out to see her off.

Marguerite's glance took in the ladder, the shovel, the tool kit. She took a deep breath and spoke slowly. "Isabel, this is supposed to be a prayer vigil."

"Sure, we'll pray. Peace Hope is bringing the Bible." Isabel put a leg up to the driver's seat.

Marguerite caught her arm and looked full in her face. "For God's sake, Isabel, what are you up to?"

"Mother, don't be bearish. I'm late already."

"Do you want to get transported? You're not going anywhere with that shovel."

Isabel turned to her father. Andrés shook his head. "Your mother's right."

"You're the one who said we ought to shoot them," she retorted.

"I told you," her mother accused him. "Putting ideas in her head."

Andrés lost his temper. "Can I help it if the girl's verrückt?" At bad moments he fell into German, from his immigrant grandmother. This moment being especially bad, he stomped off without another word.

"You won't go with that shovel," Marguerite repeated.

"I won't go, then—and I'll never set foot in that church again, either."

"You have to go to Meeting, and you know why, too. We promised those—those outside the Wall." Suddenly her mother was close to tears. It shook Isabel to see that. "Outside the Wall," the skeletons were always there, though the elders never spoke of them.

"We've done our best by you, Isabel, the best we could. We've given you a good education; we've kept off talk of marriage. Please."

"What education? How can I go to college and become a doctor like you did?"

"You can take college classes right here. Why not? The basic subjects, at least."

"Really? How?"

"How do you think? We're all college-educated. I'll see to it," her mother promised.

Isabel considered this. College now, here in Gwynwood. It seemed too good to be true. She could attack the Pylon later on—after she had learned some more physics.

"All right." She tossed the shovel out of the carriage, then drove off.

Anna Tran's house was coming up on the right, then the road opened into the clearing, and the Pylon appeared up ahead. Isabel tugged at the reins. Jezebel snorted and tossed her head as she came to a halt. In back, Peace Hope pulled her bag of books up over her shoulder. She wore her usual gray Quaker dress, the Red Queen tucked discreetly in her pocket for good luck.

Across the grass came Daniel and Matthew to greet them. From the looks of it, they had been sitting around ten meters back from the airwall, an overly respectful distance, Isabel thought. As Daniel's eyes met hers, she thought suddenly of the pirate in the book and wondered whether Daniel could ever act that way. Startled at the idea, she shook her head and pulled herself up straight.

"Well?" she asked. "Any response?"

"Several angelbees hovered over us," Daniel replied. "Perhaps they were moved by our prayers." He seemed well pleased with the day he had spent.

"What about the return shipment to Sydney?" The medicines had to be paid for.

"It was gone, last night," Matthew said. Isabel smiled, thinking perhaps Matthew could teach them college physics. She looked at Matthew curiously, tempted to ask why he had spoken in Worship as he had, but she did not.

When the two men had left on their bikes, Isabel jumped back up to the driver's seat and urged the horse on toward the Pylon.

"Isabel?" Peace Hope called as the Pylon loomed close ahead. "Is this wise?"

"We want to get noticed, right?"

The horse whinnied and thrust up her head as she met the resistance of the airwall. Isabel stopped at last, got down and went to soothe the horse, stroking her mane. Then she helped Peace Hope down with her books, shaking her head slightly. "Scatterbrain, what good will all those old books do?"

"You'll see, silly. You're not the first person that ever wanted to break through walls."

The first thing Isabel intended was simply to observe. Scientists always started with observation, then worked from there. So Isabel leaned into the airwall and observed the Pylon.

The Pylon seemed shorter and wider at its base than it had from a distance. It sat upon a smooth gray platform of unknown substance, level with the earth surrounding it; at the edge of airwall, an odd visual effect blurred the demarcation between platform and grass. The Pylon's six sides, which by night appeared smooth white, by day showed a surface pattern of very pale colors, swirls of palest pink merging into orange and green. Isabel squinted and stared hard, trying to make out any symmetry in the pattern.

From behind she heard the flapping of pages. "The Book of Joshua," Peace Hope announced, and read:

"And it came to pass, when the people heard the sound of the trumpet, and the people shouted with a great shout, that the wall fell down flat, so that the people went up into the city, every man straight before him, and they took the city.

"And they utterly destroyed all that was in the city, both man and woman, young and old, and ox, and sheep, and ass, with the edge of the sword."

An uplifting tale, as usual. Even the poor sheep. How did good Quakers put up with that stuff, even if it was in the Bible?

"Scatterbrain, come here a minute and tell me if I'm crazy. What do you see, along the edge?" An oval path of pale green seemed to be shrinking, very slowly, until it pulled away from the edge between two surfaces, surrounded by the spreading of orange tint.

Peace Hope got up on her crutches and came to the airwall. "It's all shifting," she said at last. "Like when my colors get too thin and they dribble into the white." With her gripper-hand she took out a notepad and popped a pencil in her mouth. She deftly sketched the edge of the Pylon, copying the pattern on its face.

"Whatever could it be? I wonder if Teacher Matthew noticed." Isabel was getting a headache and she had to look away.

Peace Hope was reading now from Jeremiah: "'The wall of Babylon shall fall...'"

"So the Bible had it in for cities. We want to save cities, not wreck them. Listen—what do you think the 'Tree of Life' means?"

"The Tree of Life?"

"Teacher Matthew says it stands for power over death. My dad says it stands for Christ on the Cross."

"Christ lives within each of us, every creature that breathes."

"Really? Even the mice behind the walls, the ones we set traps for?"

"Even so."

"Even the angelbees?"

Peace Hope closed the Bible with a thud. "Perhaps Shakespeare would please thee better."

"I'm going to measure the Pylon: its height and width, its precise dimensions." Isabel returned to the carriage, where Jezebel was contentedly nibbling the grass, presumably at peace with the Christ within her. Isabel picked up the tape measure from her kit and dragged out the ladder. Behind her, Peace Hope read:

"O Wall, full often hast thou heard my moans
For parting my fair Pyramus and me.
My cherry lips have often kissed thy stones,
Thy stones with lime and hair knit up in thee."

"*Scatterbrain!* That stuff's even worse than the Bible. It's as bad as your *Pirate* book." Actually, Isabel thought the *Pirate* book was rather good. She stood the ladder just outside the airwall and peered across the top of the Pylon, trying to sight it in line with a tree across the field. A couple of angel-bees came sailing over, apparently to see what she was up to. Never mind—the fire would come later.

With much pacing and measuring from this tree and that, figuring and refiguring the geometry, she came up with a height of just under three meters, and a width, from edge to far edge, of one point eight. "That's a ratio of about one point six. What do you make of that?"

Peace Hope looked up from where she sat and stared, tilting her head to the side, then back. "It looks like the Golden Mean."

"The what?"

"Keep cutting off the biggest square, and the ratio of what's left stays the same. The Greeks used the Golden Mean. So did Leonardo."

"Uh-huh." Suddenly the Pylon felt closer, its creators more human. Isabel disliked that. "They're just fooling us."

Peace Hope opened another book. "'There was a wall. It did not look important. It was built of uncut rocks roughly mortared. An adult could look right over it, and even a child could climb it.'"

That was true of an airwall; even Miracle could climb the Wall. "That's from Le Guin."

"Sure, silly. Remember this part: 'Like all walls it was ambiguous, two-faced. What was inside it and what was outside it depended upon which side of it you were on.'"

Isabel blinked twice. Of course, the Pylon was inside its little airwall; and yet it was outside Gwynwood, in the sense that things passed outside there through some intangible doorway, like the neck of a Klein bottle. But could there be any sense in which Gwynwood was outside the outer Wall, and the rest of the universe was enclosed? Could the angel-bees be thought of, somehow, as prisoners of the universe? "What do they want from us," she muttered and recalled that Daniel had asked that very same question.

Isabel shook herself and looked at the sky. Twilight was falling, and the fireflies were coming out, the bright sparks swooping upward, then winking out for the descending flight. Above in the sky, the traces of orange fire were beginning to appear.

"They're at it again. Let's give them a taste of real fire." She dug out a patch of bare earth to avoid setting the dry grass on fire. Then she piled up wood and kindling, right there next to the airwall.

As flames leapt from the wood, three angelbees darted into the airwall with unnerving speed. Then, unaccountably, all three of them vanished.

"Look, quick! Did you see that? Where'd they go?"

Peace Hope was opening the dinner basket and arranging empanadas on two plates. She looked up apologetically. "I'm sorry, I wasn't looking, I—" She stopped. Her face froze, and her mouth hung open.

"What is it?"

"Look—in the Pylon."

An orange glow had appeared, in the side of the Pylon just facing the fire. The glow seemed to emanate from within, not from the surface, as if buried, deep within the Pylon. It was an image, she realized, a fuzzy mirror image of the fire she had created.

The angelbees were scared by her fire. Was the Pylon trying to scare her in return?

VI

IN THE HOSPITAL room upstairs, next to the birthing room where Ruth had delivered, lay Alice Scattergood.

The coverlet was folded back from Alice, her frail head propped up on two old pillows, the skin drawn into her cheeks. Beside her was a tray with a bowl of soup, unfinished.

Liza sat at the bedside, clasping Alice's hand. "I am sorry, my dear," she said in a low voice. "But we must know if what thee has seen resembles...what we have seen."

Isabel sat with Peace Hope, a few steps back from the bedside, while Marguerite hovered about the other side, watching Alice's heart rate trace out on the monitor. By now everyone knew, and many had seen, the image of the fire projected within the Pylon. Isabel had slept most of Tuesday, the day after her vigil. Then on Wednesday, Marguerite had given permission to approach Alice.

Alice's eyelids fluttered and shadows moved in the lines of her cheeks. "Thee sees, then. Thee sees, as well as I? That is good; I can feel at peace, at last."

"Not quite, dear mother," said Liza. "We have seen only something..."

"Something reflected," Isabel offered. "A sort of mirror image of our fire."

"The pictures were always lined in orange," Alice said. "It reminded me, somehow, of an old daguerreotype, etched in scarlet."

"Did the pictures move, Grandmother?" Peace Hope asked.

"Move?"

"Motion, like a motion picture," said Marguerite. "Like television, remember?" The angelbees forbade television as well as radio. Only the *Herald* was permitted, presumably under heavy censorship.

"No," said Alice, "just a still tableau, quite fuzzy. The most common picture was just a Sydney boy wrapping our monthly package in black plastic, for delivery. Of course, I can't say for certain he was from Sydney, but he was not one of us." Alice thought some more, then added, "The one I'll always remember was the figure of a handsome young man in a very well cut suit. He became thy husband, Friend Andrés."

Isabel looked away.

"The angelbees were always solicitous," Alice remembered. "They would come down so low that I could tickle them under the chins..." Her eyelids half closed, and her head sank back slightly.

"That's enough." Marguerite was at the door, her hand firmly on the doorknob.

They filed solemnly into the dim hallway. Peace Hope's chin nudged Isabel at her shoulder. "What we saw wasn't like that."

"No?"

"It wasn't just a picture."

"No, it had depth, like a hologram." Isabel had once seen a hologram, in a promo for Aussie football in the *Herald*.

"More than that—it *moved*, it flickered just like the flames; it was alive."

"Yet it was just a reflection of what we made. Not a message at all." Isabel shook her head, puzzled. "Or was it? What do you suppose would happen if we surrounded the Pylon with fire?"

Peace Hope opened her eyes wide. "Let us ask Mother what she thinks."

They caught Liza outside before she left. "Liza," asked Isabel, "what if we make a bonfire around the Pylon?"

Liza looked hard at her and stood still. "We must consider this...carefully."

By evening the word had spread, and everyone had a different fierce opinion on it. At dinner, Marguerite shook her head. "I'm bearish," she told Andrés. "What if the Pylon overloads somehow? What if it breaks down? What if the Sydney shipment stops?" No more vitamins, no more oxygen for Alice. "Yet we have to do something," Marguerite added. "We can't lie down and take it forever."

"Well, well." Andrés served up the corn, a dozen ears of it. He had spent all morning filling bushels of it, which Isabel had delivered around the town. "You Americans are so impatient. Only twenty years of solitude, and you're climbing the walls."

"It means our survival." Isabel ate her corn hungrily. If Liza agreed, and Anna Tran, and the Browns...

A frantic knocking sounded from the front door. Isabel hurried to open it. There was Faith Dreher, her pigtails askew, breathing heavily from a hard ride on her bike. "It's my sister," she gasped. "Charity's fallen off the swing, and her leg's twisted real bad."

Marguerite already had her kit in hand. "Remember to check Alice once an hour." She passed Isabel on her way out, adding as usual on such occasions, "Back in the saddle again."

The sun had just set, Thursday evening. Fireflies were winking on as they flew upward, then off again. The Pylon still wore its coat of shifting colors, now barely visible, fading soon to white.

The fire was to be set up in a broad circle around the Pylon, just out of reach of the miniature bubble of airwall that closed it. About two dozen people were gathered, while Liza directed the digging out of the grass and the placement of firewood. Not everyone was fully satisfied with the plan. "A waste of good firewood," muttered Vera Brown. "What if the wind whips it out of control?" someone asked. But soon the flames began to crackle and whoosh; black smoke rose, blowing westward, with an acrid odor of pine. Kim and Terri Tran cheered and laughed with typical preteen antics.

Isabel was exhausted from chopping and hauling wood. She sat down next to Peace Hope and watched the flames, and the fireflies winking across the lawn. She thought, with satisfaction, at last the town was taking a stand, if not so bold as Harriet Tubman's. Even Daniel was there, though Nahum had stayed home, saying he believed in Christian submission to the rulers of this world. Anna Tran and her children were there, sitting on a blanket with their thermoses. Andrés was poking the wood to get the flames coming higher. Marguerite was back at the hospital, taking a closer look at the Dreher girl's leg, which seemed to have worse than an ordinary fracture.

Within the Pylon, the mirrored flames came to life, leaping higher even than the actual flames outside the airwall. There was uneasy shifting of feet.

"We should get the kids home," someone murmured. "What will it do to us?"

Peace Hope said, "I never heard of angelbees hurting anyone, directly. Maybe they have a 'peace testimony,' as we do." The Quakers had an absolute testimony against killing of human beings.

"Sure, that's why the angelbees killed six billion in the Death Year."

Peace Hope closed her eyes. "Sometimes, Isabel, it's hard to have thee for a friend."

Isabel winced. "Come on, Scatterbrain. I just try to keep the record straight."

"Sure, silly." She rested her head on Isabel's shoulder, the nearest she could get to a real hug.

The sun was long gone. The black sky burned with the orange streaks that had filled it since Saturday. Isabel watched, until she felt something prickling on her leg. Several black ants had crawled up, for she had sat upon an anthill unaware.

She got up and approached Matthew Crofts, who was watching the Pylon intently through the flames. "Teacher Matthew, what do you think it's made of? To keep changing appearance so."

"I don't know. Liquid crystal surface, maybe. But there has to be more to it." Matthew pulled out a stick that burned at one end, and he stood to hold it aloft, above the main fire. Within the Pylon the image of the flame appeared. "Observe the size of that image, and its shape. It is larger, not just fuzzier. It is responding not to the visible spectrum, but to the infrared, including the cooler part of the flame we can't see." He dropped the stick back to the fire, and sparks flew up. "I wonder what else we can't see."

Then it happened: the puffs of fog appeared, blossoming, as if from nowhere, filling the hemisphere of the airwall. But the heat from the fire seemed to pass through the airwall, drawing off the fog. As the fog melted away, the spidery spacecraft appeared, surprisingly small and squat, with six black, jointed legs, each like the one leg Isabel had seen poking out of the cloud on the first night. The faces of the polyhedron alternated square and hexagonal, and there were angelbees sitting atop several of them.

The neighbors exchanged exclamations, and several rose to leave. But Peace Hope got out her pencil and fumbled for her pad in the darkness. Isabel got the pad out from her pocket for her. Peace Hope held the pad in her grippers, put the pencil between her teeth, and began sketching rapidly.

Aside from the soft hissing of the cloud substance, the craft made no sound, or at least none that could be heard above the crackle of the fire. Within the fiery circle, through the rising air, it was then at last that something else appeared in the Pylon. A luminous shape appeared within the hexagonal pyramid, not an angelbee, but a formless shape of red light. The light grew and spread, like the red heat around an electric burner, till it crystallized suddenly into a human form. A face in a bonnet, then arms and dress extending downward, as if an invisible hand had sketched it in. A flat, still figure, like a snapshot.

It was Alice Scattergood, the Contact, outlined in glowing red, standing within the Pylon.

Peace Hope gasped, and the pencil fell from her mouth. Isabel thought, A good thing Nahum was not here to see this "graven image" of his mother in the Pylon.

From beside the circle of fire, Liza rose to her feet. "Friend Alice is ill," her voice called above the crackling flames to the spacecraft. "That is why she has not been to the Pylon. Thee will have to speak with us."

The apparition did not change.

Then Liza did an extraordinary thing. She took a stick from the fire and raised the burning end far overhead, the sparks falling past her gray bonnet. "Our sky is burning." Her voice wavered with strain. "This is not a good thing. Thee must put a stop to it."

Abruptly the fog expanded out from the airwall, in a silent explosion, cloaking everyone. It was so thick that Isabel could see nothing but grayness. She tried to cry out, but she felt dizzy, and her head grew numb; everything seemed to echo from a distance. Her last thought was, the airwall was breached; *how*...

The next thing she knew, she was awakening with her head on the ground. She squinted and tried to pull herself up, though her arms felt heavy as if she were carrying pails of milk. Peace Hope and most of the others were still asleep, in odd positions as if they just dozed off. She heard a quiet clicking sound, the beads of her father's rosary as he sat on the blanket, staring pensively at the charred circle.

The fire was out, and the angelbee spacecraft and their apparition were gone.

The dawn was just edging over the horizon. There were stars yet, hanging in a strangely peaceful sky. Isabel thought a moment, then she remembered. The stars had not been seen at peace since the night she and Daniel went out to watch the Pylon.

"Dad—the sky is clear."

"So it is, Belita."

Liza came to join them, her skirt damp and wrinkled from the night spent on hard ground. "Can it be that our prayers were answered?"

"You're a brave woman," said Andrés.

"It could be chance," Liza reflected. "They may simply be done with their... work, for now."

"But the last time the sky burned, it went on for a full two weeks. Our fire worked, I'm sure it did." Isabel's spirits soared; she felt a sense of lightening inside, an excitement she had not had since the new lambs came in March. She tugged at Peace Hope's shoulder. "Wake up, Scatterbrain. Look what's happened."

Behind them, Anna and her daughters were getting up, and others were hurriedly packing their things to leave. The night's events had been more than they had counted on.

Peace Hope pulled herself up on her gripper-hands, and Isabel brushed the tousled hair from her friend's forehead. As she did so she noticed the sketch of the "spacecraft," crumpled from where Peace Hope had fallen across it. Isabel picked it up for a closer look.

The form of the little spacecraft fairly leapt off the page:

the six spiderlegs, each with a cuplike foot, and the polyhedral body, eight hexagonal faces alternating with six square faces. Upon each square face, Peace Hope had drawn a curious rounded scale with a hexagonal facet, something Isabel had not noticed at all. The detail was striking, for all of fifteen minutes' work.

Matthew stood by the charred remains of the fire, speaking with freckle-faced Jon Hubbard.

"Teacher Matthew, come look at this," called Isabel. "We got a custom portrait of our masters' spacecraft."

Jon looked pale and drawn, despite Matthew's reassurances. But he came over with Matthew for a glimpse of the spacecraft. His eyes actually brightened a bit. Peace Hope glowed to see how impressed he was. "Why, you can actually see it," said Jon, "just as if it came out in daytime. You must have touched it up a bit."

"I did not," said Peace Hope sharply. "I sketched it just as it was."

"That was well done, Peace Hope." Matthew studied the sketch intently. "Well done," he repeated. "Our friends love symmetry, and delicate construction. And yet...no sign of propulsion, or wings for lift. Do the angelbees sit inside?"

"They sat on top," said Peace Hope. "Four of them came off, before the fog rolled out."

"Do they always travel so," Matthew wondered, "through tunnels outside our universe?"

"The craft looks flimsy enough," said Isabel. "No wonder our masters don't want us to see it."

There was silence as everyone pondered the implications.

Jon's face twitched, then he broke away as if it were too much to bear.

"They are not our masters." Daniel spoke from behind her shoulder. "They just think they are."

Startled, Isabel turned to face him. She looked into his eyes, thinking if only he would tell her what he really meant by that, and other things.

Daniel returned her look, more intently than he usually did. Then his gaze fell, and he turned to Liza. "Thanks for guiding us, Aunt Liza. If it pleases thee, I'll be walking home."

He wanted her to follow, Isabel thought, though she could not say why. Her heart beat very fast. Hurriedly she folded up her blanket and tossed it in the carriage for her father to take home. Then she headed down the road, catching up with Daniel just past the Trans' house. They walked together, past the trail up Gwynwood Hill where they had climbed to watch the Pylon from afar.

"Why did you say that?" asked Isabel. "Are the angelbees not our masters?"

"They must answer to the same master that we do."

Isabel frowned. Overhead a jay squawked noisily, and the rising sun slanted through the pines. "I still don't believe angelbees have souls."

Daniel considered this. "I suppose it's hard enough to think humans have souls."

This remark caught her off guard. Before she could respond, Daniel added, "That was brave of thee, and of Aunt Liza, to reach out so."

"I'm glad the town agreed. We're showing some backbone at last."

"And yet..." His steps slowed. They turned onto the highway, stepping around the cracks, passing the boarded-up stores. The gas station still had a faded sign in the window, the upper part torn off, displaying the word "Cola" and an arm holding up a bottle to a vanished head.

"I hope we did not send the wrong message," Daniel concluded.

"What do you mean?"

"The message of fear and hatred."

"It only makes sense to hate them," she said, "like you would hate a cancer." When he did not respond, she added, "Even if they do have souls, it hardly matters if we hate them. We're in no position to hurt them."

"Is that so, that our hatred matters not?" Daniel half smiled. "If so, that's the virtue of powerlessness."

"But how are we to survive without power?" It was always like this; they agreed about nothing, yet there was no one else she wanted more to talk with.

As they approached the turn for the Scattergoods' house, their steps slowed. Isabel turned to face him. His eyes, though beautiful, had shadows beneath. "Your medicine is ready. I'll bring it over, this afternoon."

"Why, thanks. What shall I send back with thee? A sack of potatoes, I suppose, in return for the gift of life."

She looked away. "For that matter, it was Peace Hope's stamps that bought the medicine."

"So the gift goes around the circle." From his breast pocket, Daniel took a neatly folded handkerchief of homespun. "I thought thee might like this."

Isabel stared in surprise at the neatly sewn piece. The Scattergoods spun and wove all their linens, with enough left over to clothe half the town, and Daniel sewed all his own shirts. But the handkerchief had an embroidered border as well, a simple design, little six-pointed stars all along the edge. Isabel flushed, and her dark complexion turned chocolate. Without looking up, she managed to thank him. When at last she did look up, he had turned, his back receding up the road home.

VII

THAT WEEKEND, ISABEL found out what a bris was. The ritual for Ruth's son was performed at home, and somehow just about everyone in town managed to crowd in. The mood was festive, not only for the birth but also since the deadly streaking had been stopped in the sky. Becca directed the service, standing in for her lost brother, and Marguerite assisted with the circumcision. In her readings, Becca made much of the significance of the firstborn son, who now received his name, Benjamin. Becca commented on the absence of Jewish men to perform the rite, noting that during the captivity of the Hebrews in Egypt the men had similarly been in short supply, and that Moses' wife Zipporah had been called upon to perform circumcision in an emergency.

Afterward there was more good corn and beans and honeycakes than anyone could eat. Ruth's baby nursed quietly, gazing at his mother's face, where wisps of her tied-back hair strayed down. Grace hung over Ruth, begging to hold the baby again when he was done.

Isabel moved through the crowd, until she reached Becca. "How is your window screen holding up?"

"Excellent, thank you very much. I'll be sending you a special something, by and by."

Something about radios again, or the Underground perhaps. Isabel keenly looked forward to it. "Have you had any more... visitors?"

"Oh, they're still afraid of the heat. But they'll be back."

Vera Brown was listening in, so Isabel changed the subject. "What did you think of Teacher Matthew's sermon last Sunday?"

Becca said, "For a Christian, it wasn't bad."

Vera moved off again, toward Deliverance, who was chatting excitedly with Daniel.

"Matthew is a fine man," Becca added, "though he needn't be so apocalyptic about trees. The Tree of Life will outlive us. We have a saying: bear a child, write a book, and plant a tree."

She added, as if hearing Isabel's thought, "Not necessarily in that order."

Then Ruth hurried over, the baby consigned to other hands. "Isabel, would you spare a minute to come out to the apiary? The bees are giving trouble; they don't escape fast enough. You might be able to rig up a better frame."

Isabel followed Ruth outside, her curiosity piqued by this odd-sounding problem. Ruth gave her gloves and a net veil which came down over her head and shoulders. The beehives stood under an oak on the south side, stacks of white-painted wooden boxes carrying the vertical frames of honeycomb. Ruth lifted the hive cover and the bees could be seen, crawling over the hexagonal cells full of stored honey.

"The stacked boxes have no top or bottom," Ruth explained, "so the bees can pass easily between the brood chamber below and 'supers' of stored honey above. But to harvest the honey, you have to smoke the bees out of the supers. The problem is getting them to stay out." Ruth pointed to the division between the brood chamber and the first super. "You put a barrier in between, called an escape board, like this one." She picked up a wire-mesh panel with a two-inch hole in the center, framed to the horizontal dimensions of the hive. "Now the bees can escape the smoke through that hole, reaching the brood chamber, but not find their way back to the supers."

"That's clever," said Isabel.

"But they don't escape fast enough," said Ruth. "It takes more than a day, and without bees to fan the supers, the honeycombs will melt in the heat."

"More holes, maybe?"

"Then the bees will find their way back. There's another design, conical escape holes that funnel out. I saw it in the *Herald*."

"Sure, I'll give it a try." Mentally Isabel sized the frame, estimating the lumber she would need. Overhead she glimpsed a couple of angelbees hovering as if curious.

"The angelbees always come around," said Ruth. "All those little hexagons—anything six-sided fascinates them. But they don't bother the hives. The hives are doing fine, all except one that lost a queen. Its workers gave up, and the hive went to waxworms before we got it requeened. I'm still not sure that it will take. Aaron was so good with the bees." Ruth's face wrinkled, and she bit her lip. "Isabel?"

"Yes, Ruth?"

"You know Becca likes having you young people around."

"I try not to bother her overmuch," Isabel replied cautiously, recalling Becca's words about visitors.

"Never mind that, you hear? You come around, now. Becca needs more company; she just hasn't been the same since—" Ruth broke off. "She was so close to her brother. He had a gift with words, he could paint pictures for her. He was like her eyes. I'm worried that—" She turned away and pressed her hands to her forehead, then she patted Isabel's arm. "You come around, that's all."

"Sure I will, Ruth."

On the way home in the carriage, Marguerite shared the bad news about Charity. "I couldn't spoil the occasion, but— the fracture was not a hole in one."

"No?" Andrés observed. "Children knit bones fast."

"Not when there's osteoma."

Isabel lost her grip on the reins and had to lunge to retrieve them.

"I don't think it's metastasized," Marguerite went on. "But I think the leg will have to go."

"You're the doctor."

"Andrés, for God's sake, we have no facilities for major surgery. The child belongs in the..." The only hospital was upstairs.

"Could you not transport her to Sydney somehow? Maybe in the mailbag?"

"We tried that once before," Marguerite reminded him quietly. Humans were transported only to random destinations, and they never came back.

After the horse was unhitched and watered, Isabel rejoined her father in the sheep barn. He gave her his usual bear hug that swept her off her feet. After he set her down, she asked: "Dad, why don't we try to blow out the Wall, like they do in Sydney?"

Andrés shrugged and patted the back of Esmeralda, his favorite ewe. "For my village in Valdivia, when the darkness fell, it was just el destino, fate, you understand? For you Americans it was different. You invented the bomb in the first place."

"But we didn't start the war."

"Who is to blame: he who drops the match, or he who fills the barn with gasoline?"

"The Herald had a piece about how there couldn't have been enough bombs to trigger the Death Year. The angelbees must have dropped their own bombs."

Andrés looked up, as if trying to recollect something. "A professor once wrote a book to prove that the Germans never built gas chambers."

"Anyhow, why should that make us powerless? Where's the virtue in powerlessness? All we do is attend la ruca and hear sermons where nobody even agrees what's being spoken of."

"That's just the point. You see, Belita, all these trifles—a cross here, a star there—millions have killed for them, all in the name of religion or country. So, your elders made a promise, to the souls of los huesos." The bones, outside the Wall. "We promised that there would be no more conflicts, ever, and that the survivors would work together in everything, even matters of religion. Especially religion," he amended.

"But still nobody agrees on anything. Nahum Scattergood doesn't even go to Worship."

"Nahum is a Quaker; you should know him better than I."

"I'm not that kind of Quaker. Besides, I'm a Catholic, too."

"Not till we have a priest to baptize you. Perhaps someday someone will transport one."

VIII

THE NEXT DAY, following Meeting for Worship, Liza called on volunteers for a College Committee, to establish a curriculum for a Gwynwood College. Several elders offered to help, and everyone in Isabel's class signed up right away. Isabel was tremendously excited about it, although she could not imagine how it would be managed.

That evening her friends gathered at the Wall behind the cemetery, as they often did, to share music and talk about Sydney and, now, to wonder about a "college" for Gwynwood. What classes would be most important—history or physics, literature or the arts? What about all the dead languages? Isabel insisted on physics first.

Across Gwynwood Hill, the setting sun poked out from beneath the thick dark cloud bank that capped the town like a giant pancake. A hopeful sign, the clouds might mean that rain was due. Outside the Wall, the skies above the deadland remained clear in all directions. Rain had been scarce outside ever since the Death Year, due perhaps to the acceleration of the greenhouse effect from the carbon dioxide released by Doomsday's firestorms.

Isabel leaned back on the ground, breathing in the cool air with its scent of grass. Jon Hubbard was playing the guitar, and Peace Hope had a real knack for the harmonica, which she played using a special rubber attachment on her right gripper-hand. Sal rested her head on Jon's shoulder, looking quite sharp in her new blue dress with the lace trim. Deliverance had made the dress, learning to sew with Anna Tran, the town's best seamstress. Deliverance sang along with Daniel, her voice a rich soprano that always stood out during the hymns. It made Isabel feel self-conscious about her own deeper voice, which croaked by comparison, she was sure.

The sun touched Gwynwood Hill, shedding pink across the pines and upon *los huesos* outside the Wall. Overhead, the pancake cloud was darkening with turbulence, and fitful winds were lifting branches of the trees.

Deliverance looked up. "We'd better be getting home."

"Just one more song," Peace Hope insisted. "Who knows this one?" She began on the harmonica, but Jon's hands fell beside his guitar. Isabel did not recall the tune either, but Daniel began to sing:

> "Drink to me only with thine eyes,
> and I will pledge with mine,
> Or leave a kiss within the cup,
> and I'll not ask for wine.
> The thirst that from the soul
> doth rise, doth ask a drink divine,
> But might I of love's nectar sip,
> I would not change for thine."

Isabel wished she could hear his voice and see his eyes that way forever. But as they started on the second verse, lightning illuminated the forest and a thunderclap nearly deafened her. A second bolt of lightning hit, then a third. Right above them, an angelbee came ablaze in a ball of flame.

Isabel cried out and rushed to help Peace Hope away from the danger. Others screamed and fled back toward the Meetinghouse.

She looked back. The flames were still leaping in the air. "Daniel, wait. It might start a brushfire." With the wood so dry, they could ill afford a fire out of control.

But the rain fell at last, a downpour that drenched them to the skin. Clean, nourishing rain for the corn to drink, rain to fill the cistern again. The fireball from the ill-fated angelbee hissed and vanished in a cloud of steam.

It rained for three days. Though much needed, the rain made the barn a less pleasant place in the mornings, with the stench of manure. Mice scurried in the corners, and Isabel actually caught one alive. She named it Peewee, and made a cage for it out of chicken wire. She built an exercise wheel for Peewee; the mouse took to it and spent all night racing for miles. She helped with the corn harvest until she was exhausted, then started rereading The Dispossessed until she fell asleep.

The rain also prevented further attempts to test the Pylon by fire. Then the Town Meeting voted to forbid any further use of fire before the Pylon. Isabel was outraged, but most of the townspeople were too afraid of being put to sleep. They voted narrowly to allow attempts at "prayerful visitation," which Nahum spoke out for despite his objection to the circle of fire.

"So what do we do now?" Isabel wondered. The Lucy tape was creaking away as usual, and Peace Hope was penning outlines of finches and cardinals.

"Try the . . ." Peace Hope mumbled.

Isabel slipped the pen out of Peace Hope's mouth. "Please, Scatterbrain."

"Try the carrot, perhaps, instead of the stick. Find a gift they desire, as much as they hate fire."

Isabel snapped her fingers. "Hexagons! Hexagonal polyhedrons. Where's that sketch?"

She snatched up the sketch pad and flipped to the drawing of the "spacecraft," with its hexagonal facets. "How tall was that thing, do you think?"

"Half again as tall as me," said Peace Hope.

"With or without legs? Yours, I mean."

"With legs, silly."

Isabel went home to dig out old cardboard cartons from the attic and set to work with sliderule and compass to design a model, roughly lifesize, of the structure she had seen at the Pylon. While Andrés shook his head at her, in her garage workshop, Isabel pieced together the cardboard shell, first each half with a hexagon surrounded by three hexagons alternating with squares, then she fit the two halves together. "Legs" she tacked on, six of them, made of peeled birch branches.

"There," Isabel told Peace Hope at last. "Do you think that will appeal to their vanity?"

"It feeds thine, that is certain."

Isabel turned on her, furious, until she saw Peace Hope laughing at her. "You're just jealous of another artist."

They carted the construction out to the Pylon, as close to the airwall as they could manage. They camped out for the night, to see what would happen. Nothing did.

The next morning, they left the construction sitting in the grass and they departed, Isabel to the corn harvest and Peace Hope to her stamps; it was gluing-and-cutting day. The morning after, the structure had vanished.

"They accepted our gift," Peace Hope mused. "I wonder..."

"So where does that leave us?" Isabel demanded.

"There's always, thee knows, the Trojan Horse."

That was a twist. To hide herself inside the cardboard box and...Isabel felt her hair stand on end. Slowly she shook her head. "I admit, I haven't the guts for that."

"Of course not, silly. How foolish of me to suggest such a thing."

Still, Isabel felt that she had failed her pledge of life, fortune, and sacred honor. If she ever did find the Sydney Underground, whatever would they say?

The Scattergoods were impressed by the "gift," and even Nahum commented favorably. After some thought, Daniel decided to resume occasional nighttime vigils at the Pylon. Isabel was pleased, although privately she doubted it would do any good.

That afternoon, Jon Hubbard stopped by the Chase house to deliver a covered basket from Becca. Instead of garden vegetables, the basket contained an ancient shortwave radio receiver, its case worn and rusted; it must have lain in a closet for years.

Isabel was beside herself. She hooked the cord up to the generator and twiddled the dials.

Nothing happened. She pried the case open, to test connections with her voltmeter. The problem was revealed: several empty clips betrayed the loss of circuit elements, presumably cannibalized for some other use. She tried to guess the original circuitry, inserting transistors and capacitors from her plywood board, but it was no good; the speaker was dead as the deadland.

Undaunted, Isabel set the receiver on her workbench for further tinkering and went upstairs for her daily scrubdown of the hospital. Her mother was still keeping watch on Alice, and she had prepared a letter to Sydney regarding Charity's leg.

* * *

The Gwynwood College opened in the third week of September, after the main crop was in. At first, the "college" classes looked just like an extension of the one-room grammar school, run by Teacher Becca in the Weisses' basement, beneath portraits of the two school heroes: Helen Keller, a Special who had made good, and John Dickinson, a colonial Quaker who had opposed the War of Independence. But some of the college classes were to meet in the homes of the teachers, away from the distracting younger ones. It was hardly the Sydney Uni, but Isabel felt very proud, determined to excel and to quiet the murmurs that there were more crucial tasks than book learning.

Isabel and Peace Hope had carried on a scholastic duel as far back as she could remember. In history, Peace Hope got back papers with lots of admiring red "Goods" in the margin, whereas Isabel's papers got more cross-outs and shocked question marks. Latin went better, as did Braille and signing; but science was Isabel's forte. Isabel chose physics, and Peace Hope joined her just to prove there was not something she could not do. Matthew Crofts agreed to teach it, out at the Browns' house where he had lived since the Death Year. The six students shared *College Physics* by Miller, the book Isabel's mother had used.

Peace Hope's choice was a second year of French. "French," Isabel grumbled, having had her fill of Latin, "another dead language. Why bother; to speak with the dead behind the Wall?"

Peace Hope said, "I want to read *Tristan and Isolde.*"

So now here they were at French again, along with Daniel and Jon and Teacher Debbie. Debbie's eyes were sunken, and Isabel felt sorry for her, knowing she had bleeding with her pregnancy, *placenta previa*—she would have to look that up. But the class looked even worse than Isabel had expected. Instead of *Tristan*, they were reading a children's tale called *Le Petit Prince*. The Little Prince was a Special, Isabel decided, although not as bad off as Grace Feltman, since he managed to fend for himself alone on his own little planet. His planet was inhabited by sheep, like Australia. To escape his planet, he had harnessed a flock of migrating birds.

The illustrations were indifferent; Peace Hope could have done much better. But the picture of the Little Prince sailing off behind the migrating birds did interest Isabel. It was not so much more farfetched than some of her own ideas for escaping the Wall. Of course, all the migratory birds had died off in the Death Year. Hummingbirds, for instance, legendary for their tininess, were extinct. Still, local birds might carry messages, at least, if not people. Could they fly through the upper Wall, though Sydney's airplanes could not?

What about angelbees? Angelbees just melted through airwalls, somehow. Could you harness angelbees to penetrate the Wall?

Isabel and Peace Hope paid another call on Teacher Becca, to apprise her of their progress. The fate of the cardboard "spaceship" excited her interest, even more so than Isabel had expected. Becca demanded to know every detail, from its precise dimensions to the placement of its "legs."

"But what about the angelbees?" Isabel asked at last. "What do you think? Could they be captured somehow? The airwall always seems to melt before them, automatically. They must emit some kind of signal." Another question for Teacher Matthew, after next physics class. "Perhaps we could shove an angelbee through, and follow through the hole."

"No," said Peace Hope. "Why would these 'masters of Earth' let us get away with such a thing?"

"I wonder." Becca seemed to be talking to herself as she sat in her chair pulled at an angle from the desk. "The angelbees are our masters, and yet, not, somehow. But Peace Hope is right: I warn you, Isabel."

"Yes, but, Teacher Becca, you caught one, and nothing happened to you."

Suddenly Becca gripped the edge of the desk as if in pain. "Of course...yes, nothing happened. But that was different. The little friend came of its own accord, of its desire to see me. I merely encouraged it to stay awhile." She seemed to be trying to convince herself.

"Is thee all right, Teacher Becca?"

"Yes, of course." Becca was her usual crisp self again. "Isabel, you might consider this: Our friends have accepted a gift from you, have they not? Wait to see what they may offer in return."

IX

BY SUNDAY THE rain cloud had cleared, though in the Meetinghouse the odor of damp earth lingered. Isabel was sitting next to Peace Hope. She thought of how Alice yet clung to life, and how little Charity was confined to bed now, with a bone that would not heal. She scratched at an arm, then made herself stop, and felt a quick spasm of fear. Epithelioma was rarely malignant, she told herself. Still, what if her mother was wrong?

She had looked up "placenta previa" in the obstetrics text. It meant that the placenta, the baby's organ of nourishment, had grown over the cervical opening, obstructing the passage for birth. It also meant that, without surgery, Debbie would not survive.

She took a deep breath and tried to center, giving Peace Hope a nudge to stop clicking her grippers.

But Peace Hope nudged back, and nodded off to the right.

Isabel made an indignant face. It was highly incorrect to point or stare during silent worship.

Peace Hope nodded again, and this time, Isabel followed her gaze.

It was a stranger.

There was no doubt about it: a strange man sat on the back bench to the right, next to Anna Tran. A stranger in the Gwynwood Meetinghouse; a stranger, from beyond the Wall.

A transportee? But why no advance warning? Angelbees made very deliberate decisions and gave good warning, most of the time. But then, Alice had just missed her second appointment with the Pylon. Maybe this was a warning: Do not ignore us.

Transportees had to have done something very bad, for their neighbors to leave them to the angelbees. But the only transportee ever received by tiny Gwynwood was her father, and he had turned out well enough, whatever he had done before.

Isabel tried but could not take her eyes off the stranger. A muscular Caucasian, he was tanned coffee-brown, square face and thick jaw, hair straw blond. Age, going on thirty, she guessed. Unlike her father, he had not thought to wear his best suit for the trip. His shirtsleeves were rolled back, revealing what unmistakably was a tattooed snake, dark blue, twining up his left arm.

Nobody in Gwynwood ever had a tattoo. Isabel had seen it only in pictures, in old *National Geographic* magazines.

As he sat there with his arms crossed, suddenly the man winked. He actually winked at her.

Isabel was scandalized. She looked down immediately, feeling heat rush into her face, and for the remainder of the period of silence she studied the worn toes of her shoes.

At the rise of Worship, the stranger stood up, and Liza announced him: Keith Moran, M.D., from the City of Sydney.

"A doctor!" said Isabel. "A modern city doctor."

"An Australian!" Peace Hope exclaimed, adding in a hoarse whisper, "I wonder what he knows about the Underground!"

During social hour amid the teacups, Keith Moran related his story to a rapt audience. "All I know is, I awoke there, alone outside your Pylon, at midnight, in the pouring rain." He pronounced it "ruh-een." "I found a dirt road full of muck and trudged on till I came upon this house, where Mrs. Tran opened the door. So I said in what passes for Chinese, 'Where am I? Is it the wet season?' "

Several chuckled.

"I hate to guess what Mrs. Tran thought of me, soaked to the skin with my pockets bulging with suspicious ampules."

"You're a godsend," called Marguerite. "What's your training?"

"Just got my M.D. at the Uni," he said. "It's like this: A while back, we were hearing bad news from transportees about health standards out in the bush. Most of you do without doctors at all. So Parliament got this bright idea to help out: let the space cockies transport new M.D.s, at random of course, just like the pickpockets. The devil of it is, we get picked at random, too. We have to sign the bloody paper to matriculate; then at graduation, there's a lottery, and it's 'Sydney or the bush.' " He shrugged. "I got the bush."

"You'll stay at our place," Marguerite insisted.

Isabel was beside herself. "Oh, Dad, isn't it fantastic? Another transportee, just like you."

"*Una buena historia*," muttered Andrés as he leaned against the wall, his face dark. He distrusted this Dr. Moran.

For Keith's first dinner at their home, Andrés cooked the empanadas so spicy that they burned in Isabel's mouth. But Keith ate everything with relish, and he had a great time recounting tales of the City, including actions of the Underground which had not made it into the foreign edition. "Those dills at the *Herald* are scared to death," he said. "Wouldn't dream of offending the space cockies."

Marguerite nodded politely and expressed no overt interest, though she listened keenly, Isabel thought. "And your professional interests? Surgery, did you say?"

"Plastic surgery was my aim. But when my number came up, I took a crash course in parasitology. More relevant to the bush—no offense meant." He tasted the milk, and hesitated.

"Goat's milk," said Marguerite. "Our cows didn't last the Death Year."

"No worries. What is your illustrious background, Dr. Chase?"

"Kenyon College, then Jefferson School of Medicine, in Philadelphia." Marguerite had pointed out the places once for Isabel, in the old road atlas.

"I'll bet your dad was a doctor, too, eh? Family tradition?"

"Hardly. Dad was a Vietnam vet who turned Quaker and made a career of pouring blood onto missile tubes."

Keith laughed. "A lot of good that did. Lucrative, too, I imagine."

"It hardly mattered, as Mother was a Philadelphia lawyer."

"So how'd you end up here on D-day?"

Marguerite swallowed, and her voice went lower. "I nearly didn't. I worked at a clinic in Nicaragua, run by the American Friends Service Committee. I came back to Gwynwood for a vacation with my parents. That's where I was, on that day."

There was a pause. A line crossed before the time after

"that day," a line as invisible and inviolable as the Wall itself. Andrés stared grimly at the table.

"And you, Andrés?" asked Keith.

"Born in Valdivia," Andrés said without looking up. "Mother was German. Probably the only Germans left are in Chile."

Marguerite added, "Andrés knows corn and sheep like no one else does. I don't think we'd have made it through the lean years without him."

Andrés caught Isabel's eye, and she knew he would guess the question in it. His face softened. "Of course, Keith *amigo*, I did not come here the same way you did." Deliberately he put on a thick accent. "In my town, there was a girl known far and wide for her beauty; 'Bianca the beautiful' they called her, and she belonged to the heavens, not this Earth. One of many rivals for her hand, I was challenged to a duel. My rival was slain, and I alas..."

Isabel glared at him. *"Buena historia!"*

Everyone laughed, except Isabel.

"And your family, in Sydney," Marguerite said to Keith. "How sad for them."

"I don't have much family. My parents died of radiation sickness shortly after D-day. I grew up in an orphanage run by the Sisters." He paused, then added, "Lifespan's improving, you know. Down Under, that is; you folks up north caught it worse than we did. At any rate, now that I'm here, I'd better get to work. I'd like to look at your hospital, first off."

Marguerite nodded. "It's right upstairs."

Keith's face changed. In the City, a hospital would not be found on the second story of an old Quaker mansion.

"What exactly did you bring?" Marguerite asked. "Not to press, but you did mention..."

For answer, Keith reached into his pocket. Onto the table he spread a handful of sealed ampules. "Antibiotic producers. Tetracycline, penicillin, gentamycin—these bacteria are engineered to make them all. It was the easiest thing to carry, and all you need's a good micro lab to maintain them."

"Antibiotic producers?" Marguerite was astounded. If true, Isabel guessed, they would never run out of antibiotics again. "But the patents on those strains; the cost is prohibitive. The town's budget for the year won't cover them."

"No worries; Parliament—" He caught the eye of Andrés and changed his mind. "The truth is, I filched them. Figured if I had to lose their bloody lottery, I'd get some of my own back."

Andrés grinned. "That's better, my friend. See, you are a pickpocket after all."

After dinner, Peace Hope showed up with her portfolio. Having toured the hospital upstairs, Keith was resting out on the porch, a tumbler of iced tea next to the lawn chair. His open collar revealed a cross on a chain, like Isabel's father. He rubbed his fingers on the muscle of his upper arm, and his eyes seemed to have a faraway haggard look.

"Don't suppose you'd have a pot of beer?" he asked Isabel.

"The Drehers make beer."

He was puffing on a cigarette, another novelty for Gwynwood. As Isabel spoke, he removed the cigarette and tapped out sparks over the porch rail. "My last pack. Which way to the milkbar? That is, the deli? The grocery?"

Isabel was puzzled. Then she remembered. "The 'grocery' is boarded up. Since before I was born," she added, recalling the number of times she had biked past the faded sign. "You might try to get them by mail, once you get your allowance."

"Allowance?" Keith laughed. "From whom?"

"From the town. You'll get paid for your work, too—in potatoes, probably. You can't export those."

Keith shuddered. "Don't remind me." Sydney had a stricter radiation standard, which Gwynwood could not afford. With a shrug, he dropped the cigarette and ground it beneath his heel.

"Peace Hope earns all our foreign exchange," said Isabel proudly, giving her a nudge.

Keith nodded politely. "G'day, Miss. I don't believe we've met."

"Peace Hope Scattergood," said Isabel. "The artist. She does our stamps."

"Stamps? You mean you're 'Gwynwood, USA'? Well, I'll be darned. A dear friend of mine collects them. Pleased to meet you, Miss Scattergood." He stood up and extended his hand.

Peace Hope reddened and averted her eyes. She had never

met anyone who did not know her condition.

"Beg yours, no harm meant."

"She draws with her teeth," Isabel explained. "Dr. Moran, have you ever seen an angelbee spacecraft?"

"What's that? Never. I can't say that anyone has."

"We have."

"What? You're having me on."

Isabel nodded at Peace Hope, who still looked like she wished she were somewhere else. She reluctantly let Isabel take the portfolio and open it to her sketch of the spacecraft.

For a second or two he stared. Then he grasped the picture and held it out to the fading sunlight, eyes squinting, the blue snake rippling on his arm. "This is real? Not fancified at all?"

Peace Hope's head came up. "Of course it's *real*. Mom and Dad don't let me draw any way else."

"They're plain Friends," Isabel explained, but he was not listening.

"Was it daytime?"

"No, past midnight."

"Where'd the light come from?"

"The fire, of course."

"Fire?"

"The bonfire," said Isabel. "We made a bonfire, to protest the destruction of the ozone."

"The skystreaking, yes; that's one theory for it."

"The angelbees wouldn't come out near the fire. But they came on their spacecraft, to put us to sleep."

Keith looked puzzled. "Space cockies wouldn't be caught dead near a fire. And they short out anything electric."

"They gave us a good fifteen minutes," said Isabel. "Right next to the Pylon, too."

He laughed. "That you could never manage in Sydney. Our Pylon's kept under twenty-four-hour guard."

"By the angelbees?"

"No, by act of Parliament. To avoid bloody fool incidents that get the city put to sleep for a week."

"We're not supposed to, either. Only the Contact sees the visions in the Pylon, but she is ill."

"Contact? Visions in the Pylon?" Keith seemed to be thinking to himself. "I've heard of such, from transportees.

Never in Sydney, though. The Pylon's covered with thick fog within its airwall, all the time. The angelbees must think we're too dangerous, and they're too right." Keith looked at the sketch again, then he looked at Peace Hope. "Draw me something: that bird over there." He pointed to a cardinal in the maple tree.

"That wouldn't be fair; I've done a hundred cardinals."

"Well do the tree, then."

Peace Hope got out a pencil, and for the next ten minutes she scratched away at her pad. A tree took shape, each pencil stroke a branch at just the right angle, each branch shaded in real as life.

Keith looked it over. "Okay, I'm sold." Keith looked again at the sketch of the spaceship. "Those legs—and those little hexagonal things on the sides. How odd. I wonder where the door is."

"Doesn't it look flimsy?" Isabel asked. "Has anyone ever managed to blow one up?"

"Isabel!" Peace Hope was scandalized.

"I've never heard of a spacecraft like that," said Keith. "The angelbees, now, they pop like balloons."

"Does thee know, is it true that they do not take life in return?" Peace Hope was convinced that the angelbees had a "peace testimony," as Quakers did.

Keith shook his head. "It's hard to know what logic the space cockies follow. Maybe they think we're wild animals who just don't know any better."

"You must be a member of the Underground!" Isabel exclaimed at last.

He laughed. "Not I. I just keep up with things."

"But I read the paper; I've never heard anything like that, aside from the escape attempt in Port Jackson."

"That was too big to hush, even for the foreign edition."

"Well, you can join us then: we're the Gwynwood Underground."

Keith did not smile. He seemed to hesitate.

"It's just us two, so far," Isabel admitted. "But we mean business. We've pledged our lives, our fortunes, and our sacred honor."

"I see. In that case, I'll tell you what. I'll join your Underground, if you promise to help me out here. See, I'm new to the bush; I need to learn the laws of the tribe."

"The tribe?"

"Your town. Rules and regs, especially the unwritten ones. Life-style, you understand?" He seemed to mean something specific, just what, Isabel could not guess.

"Don't wink during Worship," Peace Hope offered. "And call me 'friend,' not 'Miss,' since I'm a plain Friend. And don't spend thy allowance on cigarettes, lest the town vote to cut it."

"That's the idea," said Keith with enthusiasm.

"Don't worry," said Isabel. "If you're ever in real trouble, we'll warn you before they send a Committee of Concern."

"Well then, Friends." Keith raised his iced tea, then said with a wink, "Lives, fortunes, and honor—here's to Free Gwynwood."

Isabel found herself echoing her mother—this Keith was a godsend. Yet it was the angelbees who had sent him.

And Becca had said, the angelbees would send her a "gift" in return for hers. Could this be it? For just a moment, her flesh turned cold.

X

THE SEPTEMBER *HERALD,* which had arrived with Keith, was headlined, SKY BURNS FIVE DAYS. That reportedly was two days shorter than the shortest such episode on record. The paper speculated that there was barely any ozone left to get rid of. But no one knew for sure how much ozone there was outside. Isabel wondered if their vigil had made the difference.

There was no follow-up on the blast at the Wall. The zoo column featured the two-year-old gorilla Bin-Bin, who had just learned to spell out, "Want to play football." The science column offered a clue to the nature of airwalls. It involved a distortion of the twenty-third dimension, based on a fifth force giving rise to hypercharge... Teacher Matthew might help with this.

In the hospital, Keith soon made his reputation. He changed Daniel's medicine, and Daniel was looking better. He prescribed chemotherapy for Charity Dreher and said she might not lose the leg. Soon he was a frequent visitor at the Drehers, bringing back gallons of home brew. Nahum Scattergood built a shed out behind the hospital to house an expanded micro lab for the new strains. Isabel spent hours streaking plates and inoculating fermentation vats of the life-saving bacteria.

She finally got up the courage to ask Keith about the cancerous spots on her arm. At first he got very excited and insisted on a biopsy to make sure that it was not something worse. But it turned out to be just epithelioma after all, to be kept in check by burning them off once a year as Marguerite had prescribed.

Her father still treated Keith coolly, and Isabel wondered about this. "What do most transportees get sent for?" she asked Keith.

"Oh, anything from pickpocket to mass murder, depending on the town."

"Why have we never got sent more than two?"

"Probably because you never send any. You're one of the smaller Wall-towns. Most Wall-towns your size have gone quietly extinct since D-day. Beg yours," he added, seeing her startled look. So that was what had become of the vanished towns: attrition through disease and crop failure. Her mother was right, they were in trouble for sure.

"How would we go about transporting someone?" asked Isabel.

"You leave a man chained outside the Pylon overnight. He's gone in the morning."

Isabel shuddered. "I can't imagine doing that to anybody."

Keith shrugged. "Some get sent out more than once. It's one way the Underground spreads." He paused, then added, "Not all of them end up on Earth, though."

"What do you mean?"

"One fellow claimed he came back from a bizarre place where the universe doubled back on itself. Said he felt like a bloody lab rat."

"You mean, the angelbees did experiments on him?"

"Something like that. Another fellow said he'd escaped during transport and managed to find his way to the Hive itself. One bomb could knock it out, he said, and all the Walls would vanish."

So there was room for hope, then. Isabel redoubled her efforts to get Becca's radio working. One day she actually managed to get sound out of the speakers, a crackling static that sounded the same across all channels. She was so excited that she ran upstairs immediately to show Keith. To her annoyance, he laughed, seeming less than impressed. "It's Radio Free Gwynwood, all right. You'll burst us out of our bubble, yet. When you do, I'll take you back to Sydney and give you a tour of the Cross. We'll watch the poofs at Les Girls."

Undeterred, Isabel counted down the days till the next Sydney shipment, when the fetal monitor was due to arrive. Then she would have a radio frequency source to test her receiver.

In physics class, they were learning about black holes. Teacher Matthew said that if you could stand next to a black hole, you could look to the side and see the back of your own head, from light spiraling into the vortex of space-time like a marble spiraling down a funnel. Isabel grasped this right away, but Daniel and Jon looked puzzled. They would probably stop by later to get help from her. After class, Isabel stayed to ask Matthew about hypercharge.

"Hypercharge would be a force that acts something like gravity, only it would be repulsive, not attractive," Matthew explained. "Its existence requires the assumption of an extra dimension, outside space and time."

"Could it explain the pressure of an airwall?"

Matthew's eyes rolled around, as they tended to do when he was thinking something through. "It is hard to guess what would generate such a force. But something must happen outside three-space, to account for the transfer of matter between two pylons."

"Could the universe fold over on itself, in this extra dimension?"

"It could happen. It could work something like the black hole, although the forces would come out differently. Try this—" He pulled a book from his shelf, a Heinlein collection. "Here's a story about getting trapped in an extra dimension."

She read the title of the story, "And He Built a Crooked House." "Thanks," she said. "Five dimensions are bad enough, but the *Herald* says there are twenty-three dimensions."

"That's speculation. Physicists had such a theory, once, to account for the known particles. But all that work ceased on Doomsday." Matthew looked away, and his hand toyed absently with a bit of chalk at the blackboard.

Then she recalled his sermon in the Meetinghouse, and she thought, If she did not ask him now, she never would. "Matthew, why did you say that in the Meetinghouse—I mean, the Church—about Doomsday?"

"What did I say?"

"You said we deserved what we got from the angelbees. You said that humans were not meant to have power over life and death, and that science only made things worse."

For a moment Matthew eyed her keenly, then he shut his eyes and pressed his hands up over his face and wrinkled forehead. "At Alamogordo, the day before the first test of a nuclear device, Fermi calculated that the explosion might ig-

nite the atmosphere, perhaps incinerating all life on Earth.
His colleagues were furious; they recalculated, and the test
went ahead." He pointed his chalk at her. "For the first time
in history, the world's existence hung on a calculation.
Should any mortal hold such power?"

"But science does lots of good things. Science cures ill-
ness. Should we go back to the Middle Ages, when they
burned witches?"

"We almost did." He smiled, but it was a tired smile. "I'm
just a chemist, not a historian. As a scientist, I blame the scientists who built the bombs. As a historian, I would blame
history, 'the march of folly.' As a Christian, I blame Christian-
ity for its failure." Her teacher's eyes fixed hers with a sudden
intensity. "Isabel, think of this. Let's say those angelbees
really did jam the radar on both sides with false signals, as
we've been told. *Suppose both sides had chosen not to respond?*"

Matthew looked at her expectantly, but she found nothing
to say. "If only somehow," he added, "we humans had mas-
tered the simple rule, 'What is hurtful to thee, do not to thy
neighbor.' That's all I should have said, Isabel."

While physics was her best class, French was even worse
than Isabel had expected. Not that it was hard, with her background in Spanish. The Little Prince was busy visiting little
planets. Isabel had already figured out that the law of gravitation would rule out those little planets with their little volcanoes, but Teacher Debbie did not seem concerned about that.
The third little planet the Little Prince visited was inhabited
by a man surrounded by bottles, half of them full and half
empty.

"*Que fais-tu là?*" the Little Prince asked.

"I drink," said the man.

"Why do you drink?"

"To forget."

"To forget what?"

"To forget that I am ashamed."

"Ashamed of what?"

"Ashamed of drinking!"

Isabel decided that the author, like his protagonist, belonged in the category of Grace Feltman. She glanced surreptitiously at Daniel, whose head was buried in his book while Deliverance recited and translated for the class. Hidden behind her own book, she signed the word for "stupid" to Peace Hope, knocking her S hand against her forehead. But Peace Hope ignored her. Peace Hope was insulted because Jon and Daniel always came to Isabel for help with physics homework, never to her, although she was nearly as good at it.

Isabel recalled the faded portraits of Helen Keller and John Dickinson in Teacher Becca's schoolroom. She sighed and decided to be virtuous.

"You have to tell Jon you can't keep coming over," Isabel told Daniel after class. "It's not fair. Tell him I'm too busy with the hospital extension. Peace Hope can help you both."

"Why not tell him yourself," Daniel suggested.

Isabel looked away. "It will hurt his feelings if I tell him."

Daniel did not answer right away.

"It's not my fault!" she burst out suddenly. "I can't help it if I was born with arms and legs and not somebody else."

At that Daniel actually cracked a smile and started to say something, but thought better of it. "I'll talk to Jon." As he left, Isabel felt mad at herself rather than virtuous; it was always that way with him.

Daniel was still keeping a vigil at the Pylon two or three nights a week. One night Isabel stopped to sit with him. The embroidered handkerchief was tucked in the bib of her overalls. From the trees surrounding the field came the insistent hum of cicadas. Twilight was deepening, but Daniel had not made a fire in the charred circle around the Pylon. *"Like all walls, it was ambiguous, two-faced..."* The angelbees came hovering just above their heads, turning their shiny black eyespots. Isabel thought she might just touch one, but they always managed to bob up out of reach. She consoled herself by scooping a late-summer firefly in her palm, where its bulbous abdomen came aglow with yellow light, then darkened again.

The light of fireflies was actually cold, she recalled. Their bodies emitted light at a well-defined wavelength, without the heat of incandescence. How would angelbees react to a "cold" light source? Would they be able to see it at all?

Daniel spoke quietly, yet it startled her, out of the stillness. "What do they fear about fire, I wonder. Is it just the physical danger? Surely that's too simple."

Isabel sighed. "Perhaps they're just simpletons, like le Petit Prince."

For such advanced creatures, angelbees had precious little room for brains. It made no sense, but then, nothing did. She felt Daniel's nearness and wondered whether he would let her hold his hand. Tentatively she slipped her fingers across his, and she felt a gentle tug in return. She breathed in deeply.

Daniel said thoughtfully, "They don't feel like 'masters,' do they..."

"They don't put up with being shot."

"...more like curious children."

It occurred to her that the "punishment," the three days of blinding fog, had come from the Pylon, not directly from the angelbees themselves. So had the "visions."

Was it possible that the humans had yet to see their true masters?

Isabel was plucking squash from the garden one evening when she saw Liza dismount her horse and step briskly to the front door. The harvest had been better than expected, so far, with enough rain to save the squash and pumpkins, although the tomatoes had some kind of blight.

Liza seemed in a hurry. Was someone sick at the Scattergoods'? Isabel picked up her bucket of squash and returned to the house.

Liza was speaking with Isabel's parents in the hallway, something about Becca. They turned, and the three of them faced Isabel, eyeing her oddly.

"Becca has disappeared," Liza said. "Daniel found her Bible outside the Pylon, with the note inside." She handed Isabel a slip of paper.

Isabel's hand shook as she read. "Dear Ruth: They gave me eyes. All of you are beautiful; you shine like stars. But I must go away with them. I know you will not understand, but please forgive. I will try to return, but I can't say when. Please give Isabel the candle box, and give Benjamin another kiss for me. Love, Becca."

At first Isabel could not look up from the paper. Then her forehead was ringing, and cold seemed to reach to her toes.

"It's not your doing, Isabel," Liza was saying kindly. "This is ... a shock to us all. But this box ... we had a faint hope that you, perhaps, could tell us something."

She forced her eyes to look up. Liza was holding an oblong wooden box, the one from which Becca had taken the candles, the day she had trapped the angelbee.

Isabel opened the box. It contained several tall white candles, plus assorted smaller ones, some down nearly to the base. There was a box of kitchen matches, and an old cameo pin. Beneath the candles was an object which she could not identify. Hexagonal in shape, slightly smaller than her palm, its black surface was rounded and shiny. At the center was a hole, about half an inch in diameter. She turned it over; the obverse was flat, like the backing of a cheap imitation stone, although the piece looked rather large for costume jewelry.

None of it held any message for her, that she could see. All she could think was, somehow, the catcher had been caught.

XI

THE TOWN WAS stunned. Death was an everyday reality, but this abrupt disappearance, with the mysterious intervention of the angelbees, was unheard of. Keith was as astonished as anyone, for in Sydney the angelbees kept a far greater distance from humans than they did in Gwynwood.

"Why is that?" Isabel insisted. "Why do they treat us differently from the City? You must tell us; you joined our Underground, remember?" She still suspected he knew a lot more than he was telling.

"Sorry, mate." He gave her shoulder a pat. "Wish I could say more. Come to think of it though, primate watchers have always done the same."

"What do you mean?"

"You know, the Jane Goodall types. One tribe of chimps they'd feed bananas by hand; another lot they'd watch by hidden camera."

Isabel thought this over, then froze again. "You think they took Becca to a zoo? Oh my God, no." She turned away, unable to stop the tears anymore. She remembered all the questions Becca had asked, about the spacecraft replica, about the angelbees; if only she had guessed where it would lead.

"Now, you can't think that." Keith put his arm around her, the way her father did. "Look here: she chose to go, right? Maybe they took her to see the 'Queen,' eh?"

Liza called an emergency Town Meeting in the Meetinghouse.

"We've got to get her back," said Marguerite. "She's not well." Becca's card in the file listed an abdominal tumor, slow-growing, inoperable. Isabel winced and shut her eyes.

"How, that's the problem," murmured Carl, his voice subdued.

Anna said, "The circle of fire worked before."

"But the note said she chose to go." Ruth's voice was shaking. "The note said they fixed her eyes. Maybe they promised to make her well, too."

"Did she really write the note?" someone asked. "Did she know what she was doing?" There was the unspoken question, was Becca out of her senses; had "they" taken over her mind, somehow? Could it happen to others?

Ruth said, "The Pylon might explain to Alice."

Liza nodded. "If she could go. If she could be brought, at the next new moon. Could it be done?" She turned to Marguerite.

"Yes," the doctor said quietly. "If Alice's condition is stable, it could be done."

In the end, everyone offered support for Ruth and her son. Isabel promised to clean house and mind the bees twice a week. Daniel offered to take on Becca's classes; since the children knew him from the Sunday class, it would ease the transition. He insisted his health could take the strain, with Keith's new medicine. For the future, the Pestlethwaites let it be known they wouldn't mind moving out of their own home, which needed an unaffordable roof job, to move in with Ruth. The move would make economic sense, saving firewood for the town as a whole. But the loss of yet another house was a chilling reminder of their population decline.

Afterward, Peace Hope nudged Isabel. "The note didn't say they fixed her eyes, it just said they gave her eyes. Maybe they gave her prosthetic eyes."

Isabel blinked, then shook her head. "Who knows? Look, Scatterbrain, she must have left some kind of message in that box. I'll bring it over, tonight, when it's too dark for apple picking."

Isabel sat on the carpet in Peace Hope's bedroom. She picked the candles out, one by one. "No message that I can see."

"Thee might not see it," Peace Hope reminded her.

"Of course—she would have inscribed it, in Braille." Isabel turned the candles over again, feeling them carefully with the tips of her fingers. Peace Hope took up a candle, rolling it against her cheek. But when all the candles were done, still they found nothing. Only the cameo and the odd hexagonal piece were left.

"The cameo was hers from Aaron," Isabel said, "Ruth told

me. The other piece Ruth didn't recognize. She said Becca liked to collect odd bits of things."

Peace Hope leaned over and stared at the hexagonal piece. "I'm sure I've seen something like that before. Would thee please fetch my sketch pad?"

Isabel grabbed the sketch pad and flipped through the first couple of pages. There were sketches of the Pylon, from their first visit, and sketches of angelbees. One large angelbee had a daughter cell budding off; the eyespot of the parent had a flat hexagonal facet, as if a slice had been cut off. The pupil of the eye was a hole right at the center of the facet. "That's it!" Isabel shouted. "This piece would fit right into the eyespot of an angelbee, hole and all." She picked up the object and poked her finger through its hole.

"Let me see."

Isabel passed it to her. Peace Hope sat against her bed, holding the piece between her grippers.

"It has to be, don't you think?" Isabel sat on the floor, arms clasped around her legs, chin resting on one knee. "It must have fallen off the eyespot, like a discarded bit of insect shell."

Peace Hope studied the object. "Or it could be one of those hex scales from the spaceship. They were about that size."

Isabel was taken aback. She flipped farther through the sketch pad, till she reached the spacecraft, whose replica she had constructed. Each of the square sides had a small hexagon penciled in, a detail Isabel had forgotten. "But—they can't be the same thing. Why would the angelbees decorate their spaceship with discarded eyespot scales?"

"I wonder what it's made of." Peace Hope flexed her gripper, and touched the object to the tip of her tongue. "It tastes ceramic. Ouch!" The scale dropped. "It zapped me, like an electric shock. Practically burned my tongue off." She rolled her tongue with a pained expression.

Isabel felt her flesh tighten. She retrieved the scale, and returned it to the candle box, her hands shaking. "What if it's something they want back?"

"I don't think so. They've got plenty more."

"That hardly makes it any better!"

A distant look came into Peace Hope's eyes. Absently she picked up her crutch and raised herself to sit at her desk, then she took a pen between her teeth, bending to dip the tip in the ink.

"Scatterbrain, you can't just *draw* at a time like this!"

"Shh; it helps me concentrate." Deftly she penned the outline of a baobab tree, a scene copied from *Le Petit Prince*. First the trunk, then the ridiculously cumbersome roots, strangling a planet impossibly small to support a tree, according to *College Physics*.

Isabel watched until she could stand it no longer. "Of all things, why that stuff? Your own originals are so much better."

Peace Hope let the pen fall. "The narrator was a pilot, not an artist. One has to start bad, to get to be good." She looked up. "Becca must have learned something about the scale. Maybe she figured out what it was for."

"What if it's to do with the Wall? A control device?" That would be too much to hope for.

"I wonder what the town will think of it."

"We can't tell them," said Isabel quickly. "They'll just take it away. They'll make us give it up, at the Pylon."

"It doesn't seem right, not to tell them." Peace Hope's eyelids wrinkled around her blue eyes.

"It's a secret for the Underground," Isabel insisted. "Remember, you pledged. I will tell Keith; he's in the Underground."

Isabel rode her bike home, the headlight pulsing in the darkness in rhythm with her pedaling feet, the cool air whipping past her face, a sign of autumn. As she reached her home, she caught sight of a lone angelbee high among the branches of the chestnut tree. For an instant she was convinced it had followed her home. But then, angelbees were everywhere, she reminded herself.

When Keith heard about the "scale," he reacted with alarm. "A piece of hardware, maybe off their spaceship? With live electronics in it? Fair go, mate. The space cockies will catch up with you, and there'll be hell to pay."

"Oh, come on. Nothing's happened, yet. If it does, what's a

bit of fog? Keith, you joined our Underground, yet you won't tell us one thing, not even about radio contact. You pledged your sacred honor."

He flinched and looked away, the muscles of his upper arm tightening beneath the tattooed snake. "All right then," he said quietly. "I'll tell you something. If you want to pick up something of interest on your shortwave, try a thousand megahertz."

A thousand megahertz; that was well outside her present range. Divided into the speed of light, that meant a wavelength of thirty centimeters, much shorter than she expected for long-distance transmission. She would have some fixing up to do, when the new parts arrived from Sydney.

XII

THERE WERE MANY days to pass yet before the next new moon. Daniel obtained from Ruth a picture of Teacher Becca, which he brought to show the Pylon when he kept vigil there at night. Isabel's mother warned him that, with his added burden of teaching the grammar school, he needed to conserve his strength.

The apples were coming in thick, some to be packed away in the cellar, others sent to the Browns for canning. At night Isabel did her homework until her study lamp ran out, then she fussed over her seven mice; Peewee had delivered a litter within two weeks of captivity. She built a second cage to enable separation of the sexes.

At last she got a chance to read the Heinlein story which Teacher Matthew had given her. In the story, some people got stuck in a "tesseract," a four-dimensional house built of eight cubical rooms. The rooms were folded into one another in the fourth dimension, so that each appeared to be adjacent to four others, plus one beneath the floor and one above the ceiling. You could run forever in an apparently straight line, from one room to the next; or you could run forever upstairs, or downstairs. Either way, you would always come up upon your own tracks again, like Piglet chasing the Woozle in *Winnie the Pooh*. If all the doors were open for four rooms in a row, you could look through them all to see the back of your own head. The thought made her queasy. She hoped that Becca had not ended up in a tesseract. If only Alice could manage to communicate something at the next new moon.

In the micro lab, enough cloned ampicillin and tetracycline had been grown and tested to be put to use. At first Marguerite was reluctant to try it, for what if toxic impurities remained? But when Miracle's strep throat failed to respond to the batch from Sydney, she prescribed the home-grown antibiotic instead. Almost overnight he was better, ready to run out and climb the Wall again.

"Not surprising," said Keith. "There's little quality control on the stuff they ship abroad."

Isabel was shocked. "I must say, Keith, this city of yours sounds more and more wicked, to me."

"As wicked as Babylon. But we have our share of Bible bashers, too. I'm Catholic, myself."

Isabel nodded, recalling the cross that he wore. "You should tell Dad. Dad's been looking for a priest. Are you a priest?"

At that, he started to laugh, and he laughed so hard he could not stop. "Sorry, mate," he managed to say at last. "If you ever find one, though, let me know."

In the second week of October, Alice refused her oxygen. There were hurried consultations between Marguerite and Liza. "Thee must tell her," Liza insisted sternly, as if she thought it was the doctor's fault somehow. "Thee must tell her it's all right."

"I did tell her." Marguerite was tired, and her hair was showing the first few wisps of gray. But her eyes flashed, alert as ever. "I told her we can afford it, we won't have to cut the children's vitamins or any such thing. But she knows our resources are limited. I've told her; what else can I say?" It worried her sick, Isabel knew, because at night Marguerite could not sleep, and she heard the sounds of her steps thudding up and down the stairs.

Liza went in and spoke with Alice alone, then she fetched Nahum and Peace Hope to see her, and Grace, too. Alice had always been especially fond of Grace, and had spent many hours talking with her as a child.

In the end Alice accepted the oxygen again, but it was too late, or perhaps it would have made no difference. On the sixteenth of October, Alice Scattergood died.

She was buried the next day, a day that dawned crisp and clear, one of those days when one could see every needle of the pine trees in sharp outline. Everyone in Gwynwood came by the cemetery to drop a wildflower on the mounded earth, or to whisper a prayer perhaps. After the others had left, Isabel stayed on with Peace Hope and her family. Pensively she brushed the arms of her sweater of plain Dorset wool which Alice herself had spun and knitted long ago for the doctor when Peace Hope was delivered. It gave her a tingling sensation to think how the fingers that had knitted that sweater now rested cold underground.

Among the pines, at least twenty angelbees hovered owlishly, each eyespeck rotating slowly around its globe. They seemed almost expectant, as if they did not quite believe that Alice was dead and would stay dead, like the sentries at the tomb of Christ. There were always one or two angelbees at a funeral, presumably more at this one because Alice had been their Contact. Isabel felt sorry for the Scattergoods; what an intrusion on their grief. But Liza and even Nahum stood by stoically, not deigning to notice. They must have prepared themselves for this. Afterward she walked on, slowly, past the familiar headstones: Vera's husband, Grace's parents, Daniel's parents, Aaron Weiss... It seemed to her that she knew more faces among the dead than the living.

Beyond the leaning headstones the pines shriveled away before that other place of death, the Wall. The bones beyond the Wall were exposed, some half buried by sand and weeds. Most were scattered, but a few complete human skeletons could be spotted, the ribs neatly parallel, the arms and legs crumpled in, like fetal position. Isabel found herself wondering why nobody had given them decent burial. But, of course, there had been no one left outside to do so; only the voice of the wind against the Wall, keening in its dead language.

How on Earth would the angelbees pick their next Contact? How had Alice been picked in the first place? No one seemed to remember. Andrés claimed to know. "The angel Gabriel will appear to the chosen one," he told her.

Isabel pretended not to hear. She asked Keith, but of course he had no idea since there was no Contact in Sydney.

In the cemetery most of the angelbees had departed, but one or two continued to hover above the grave. The new moon was approaching, but Alice would not be there at the Pylon to seek word from Becca. There was talk of starting another bonfire at the Pylon. The monthly shipment from Sydney appeared as usual, and Daniel picked it up. Isabel rushed over to the Scattergoods' place to see what had come.

To her delight, the new parts for the radio were there, as well as the fetal heart monitor. "We're in luck, Scatterbrain!

We'll get the radio working, and get to test it, too." Before hurrying back to her workshop, she skimmed the *Herald*. Still nothing new on that blast at the harbour. The Taronga Zoo featured its bottle-nosed dolphins, alive nowhere else in the world.

Outside Isabel's garage workshop, a gentle rain fell all day, the raindrops trickling down the windowpanes. The mice scampered contentedly in their two cages. Isabel pulled out the pieces to the fetal monitor and matched them to the instructions. The printer unit would sit on a shelf, but the two sensor disks for contractions and fetal heart rate would be taped to the woman in labor. The printer and sensors beamed microwaves at each other, so there were no connection cords to restrict the mother.

Within twenty minutes she had the instrument hooked up and a signal trailing across the display, with jagged squiggles appearing whenever she tapped one of the sensors. Now she would be able to test whether her radio could pick up the signals, too.

Marguerite was pleased to see the monitor working. "I'll try it out at Debbie's next visit." After some thought, she added, "It's still going to have to be a cesarean."

"A cesarean? We've never done one of those."

"Keith has fresh training in surgery. You'd better start calling in the blood donors. Starting next week, we'll need as many pints on hand as we can manage."

There was a cold spell. Isabel's fingers were so numb she could barely turn a screwdriver. No longer could she sleep out in the garage; she had to move her bedclothes back upstairs, along with *College Physics* and the rest of her books. Peewee's family came, too, and they all slept on top of one another in a big ball of fur. The second floor was dead quiet with the windows closed, and the grating of Peewee's wheel was enough to wake her early in the morning.

In her workshop she spent hours tinkering with connections. She turned on the fetal monitor for a signal, but no sound broke the static from the tiny speaker box. It gave her a start to hear Peace Hope at the garage door call over, "Hey, silly. How's it going?"

"Um," she mumbled, a clip in her mouth. "Hand me that pliers, will you?"

Peace Hope lurched forward, laid down a crutch, and picked up the pliers in her metal gripper. "Guess what? *Le Petit Prince* just arrived on his seventh planet —Earth."

Isabel knew this was meant to annoy her, as her grade had slipped on that last test. Between the bees, and the hospital chores, she hardly had time to study. "He can take *un viaje a Marte* for all I care."

After another hour's work, the hiss and static gave way to a clear tone. The tone went off and on as she flicked the switch of the transmitter.

"*We've done it!*" Isabel threw her arms around Peace Hope, who nearly lost her balance. "We've really done it. We just have to hope it will work at Keith's frequency."

"What exactly will you find on that frequency, did he say?"

Isabel shook her head. "Keith is too cagey. Never mind, Peace Hope: Radio Free Gwynwood is in business."

The tone from the monitor came steadily clearer as she worked on the receiver, but still only hiss came from the band where Keith had said she would find something "interesting." Then one day, after she replaced the battery and moved the antenna, she thought she had something—something different. Something not just background hiss. It was a sort of squeal that rose and fell at odd intervals. Definitely not a voice; but then maybe the signal was coded?

Isabel went to fetch Keith, but he was upstairs in the hospital with Marguerite, learning a test for giardia that he had not covered in medical school. She ran back down to the garage.

She found that she could move the antenna different ways to get the best signal. In fact, the signal seemed to have a rather precise direction. That was suspicious. Could the source of the signal be quite close—perhaps here in Gwynwood?

The whole rig would not fit on her bicycle, so she dumped it into the carriage, then she set off to collect Peace Hope.

With Peace Hope adjusting the antenna, they rode up the street in the direction pointed by the antenna, and the squealing got a little clearer. Then the noise seemed to drift away; they had to retrace a bit, and then back, until at last Peace Hope suggested they turn up the road to the Meetinghouse. That road was winding, but on balance the noise still increased.

They rode up, passing the old abandoned burned-down house, then on all the way to the Meetinghouse. The noise was suddenly very loud indeed.

Isabel felt the hairs prickle behind her neck. She reined in the horse. The building was still, its log walls musty, spotted with fungus in little fan shapes. Above the tar-paper roof, the sky was clear except for wisps of cirrus overhead in the height of the Wall's dome.

Peace Hope said, "What's the matter, silly? Got cold feet?"

"You see where we're at?"

"Maybe the Underground escaped here in secret, and dug a hole beneath the Meetinghouse. It would be the best place to hide. Like 'The Purloined Letter.'"

The source of the noise was close by. But the Underground, here? It made no sense. Thirty centimeters—for some reason, that wavelength...

Isabel lifted the reins, and Jezebel plodded on slowly. They passed the Meetinghouse, then moved slowly toward the cemetery.

She snatched the reins so hard the horse whinnied. "Turn it off! Turn it off, for Christ's sake!"

Above the cemetery hovered a single angelbee, still watching the grave of Alice. Thirty centimeters was about the span of an angelbee, a good size for an "antenna."

The signal was coming from the angelbee, watching and transmitting to someone, somewhere.

She cornered Keith afterward. "Why didn't you tell me it was angelbees?"

Keith said, "Well, why didn't you tell me you'd picked up a signal before you ran off after it? Of all the bloody fool things to do."

"You should have told me what it was I'd be picking up.

What did you expect I'd do when I found it—go pray in the Meetinghouse?"

"It's true," he admitted. "We doctors should know better." Keith looked pensively out over the porch rail and put two fingers to his lips, as if smoking an invisible cigarette; he had taken Peace Hope's advice.

"Radio wave transmission—how on Earth do they manage *that*?" Isabel exclaimed. "I always thought angelbees were, well, like animals."

"Plenty of animals have organs that sense an electric field, like the bill of a platypus. Besides, remember, these 'animals' have technology far beyond ours. Maybe they all have electrical implants."

"They sure don't look that smart; they act so dumb most of the time. Anyway, now they know about my radio. What am I going to do?"

"The best thing to do would be to leave it out by the Pylon, and let the angelbees dispose of it."

"But to give up my radio, after all that work."

"You can build another one, out of my allowance."

At that she felt ashamed, knowing how badly Keith missed the City, and how pitifully little his allowance bought. "I already spent Peace Hope's, as well as mine. I can't just take yours."

"Why not? We're all in the Underground together. We pledged our fortunes, remember?"

Isabel squeezed his arm. "Thanks for the offer, anyhow. You're a real friend, Keith."

But there was no way she would give up her radio so easily. She had not seen any angelbees at the house yet, so how would they know where to find the radio? She would hide it in her room upstairs, in a bottom drawer beneath her winter clothes. Another thought: She would keep a candle burning, to scare them away.

As she was opening the drawer, she caught sight of Becca's candle box lying on the dresser. She stopped with a sudden thought. Opening the box, she took out the hexagonal scale and set it on the dresser. She turned on the radio and tuned it to Keith's frequency.

The faint tone returned, from the angelbee in the cemetery,

nothing more. She tried other frequencies, but still nothing. Disappointed, she picked up the scale to return it to the box.

A screech jabbed her ears, as soon as she touched the scale. She dropped it and covered her ears. Instantly the noise stopped, though her head was still throbbing.

She turned down the volume, then cautiously reached for the scale again. All it needed was a touch to set off its signal, somehow. It was communicating—with angelbees, somewhere. The angelbees knew, every time she held the object in her palm.

XIII

NOW THERE WERE angelbees hovering over the Chases' house, first two, then four or five, slipping through the red and yellow foliage of the taller trees. At night they ventured closer to her window, and she imagined them laughing at her, like the witches in *Macbeth*.

"Isabel." It was after dinner. Marguerite faced her, her chafed hands clasped upon the table, the muscles taut in her neck. "You know this can't go on."

"What do you mean?" said Isabel.

Andrés was regarding her gravely. Keith looked down at his hands.

"You know," her mother repeated. "The radio. It's got to go."

"What's a few angelbees? Nothing's happened, yet."

"But it *will* happen, sooner or later. They'll come over in a cloud, put us to sleep, and take what they want. I can't have that, at the hospital."

How would they take it, she wondered, vaguely picturing the angelbees with their spacecraft-thing. They did not even have arms.

"I'll hide it in the barn."

"That's even worse. They won't know where to look for it. You tell her," Marguerite appealed to Keith.

Keith looked up. "It might be all right. If there's no sign of a transmitter, they may just go away after a while."

Isabel stared at her plate. She had told no one about the signal from the scale, and now she felt extremely uncomfortable.

The next day, Isabel was scrubbing the hospital rooms when she heard a knock on the front door. Marguerite was out examining Charity, Andrés was out in the orchard, and Keith was back in the micro lab. So she hurriedly rinsed her hands and went downstairs to get the door.

Liza stood outside, in her gray Quaker dress and bonnet.

With her were Vera and Ruth, who was carrying Benjamin asleep in a sling from her shoulder.

"Isabel, we have a concern for thee," Liza said. "I hope this is not a bad time."

"Of course not. Please come in; sorry about the ammonia." With a sinking feeling, she realized what it was: a Committee of Concern, from the Town Meeting.

The three women settled themselves in the sitting room, while Isabel started the kettle for some tea.

"Is thee enjoying the new college classes?" Liza called to her.

"Yes, very much. Though sometimes I wish we could go further in the book. In physics, that is." Isabel got out the spoons, and hunted for unchipped cups and saucers.

"Teacher Matthew says he has never seen such promising work from the students as this year."

Isabel's face grew warm, but she said nothing. When she sat down, she looked up at Ruth. "Is the honey flow doing well this year?"

"The flow has been good," said Ruth. "We're several gallons ahead of last year. The Geiger count's not too bad." Some years the bees managed to find their way to the spring behind the old Feltman place, where all the flowers were contaminated. "You've been a big help," Ruth answered her. "The new escape board works much better, and your help with the harvesting has eased things for me."

Isabel nodded. She had learned to tell brood cells from honey cells, and the overbuilt queen cells that meant a colony was about to swarm away, and the signs of waxworm in the comb. Now the main task would be to winterize the hives so the bees could keep themselves warm until spring.

"Becca enjoyed your company," said Ruth. "She did, so much. I wanted you to know that."

"I know." Isabel swallowed hard. This was going to be worse than she had thought.

"Poor Becca," murmured Vera. "You see, Isabel, that's just the point. That's what concerns us about you."

Isabel blinked. "You mean, you think that I—that it was my—"

"No," said Liza. "Thee is not to blame. We worry, though, that a similar fate may befall thee."

She returned Liza's look, but could find nothing to say. Outside the autumn wind gathered strength, and the tree limbs could be heard knocking together. In Ruth's arms the baby yawned in his sleep, wrinkling his tightly shut eyelids as he stretched, then lay still again.

Vera stirred her tea. "Of course, we all want to do something about that Wall. But really, what use is it to flout the rules for nothing?" She meant the radio.

Isabel looked hard at Liza. "You stood up to the Pylon." She would always remember that night, Liza in black from head to foot, raising the burning stick from the fire.

Liza nodded. "So I did."

"Of course she did," said Vera. "Liza is Town Clerk, and besides, her child is full grown. Whereas—"

"Yes, that is so," Liza interposed gently.

"So what should I do?"

There was silence again.

Vera said, "We must put the town's welfare first, Isabel."

"Don't I do enough for the town? I barely have time to study for my tests."

Ruth leaned forward and extended her arm to clasp Isabel's hand. "Isabel, I don't care about the town; I'm worried for you. I can't think of losing you, too, do you understand?" Her voice shook.

"I put away the radio," Isabel forced herself to say. "Keith said it would be okay."

Silence again.

"You want me to leave it at the Pylon."

"We knew you'd understand," said Vera.

Liza put down her teacup. "I think we've given Friend Isabel enough to think on and reach her own decision. Now, Ruth, thee'll be wanting to get the baby home."

As the committee members departed, Vera lingered a little. At the door she turned and whispered quickly, "Isabel, it's time you thought about your future. My Sal and Deliverance both will be engaged to young men by Christmas, only don't breathe a word. Now, with your brains, I suppose you're bored with the younger men; have you ever thought of someone like Matthew, perhaps? I know he's very partial to you." She patted Isabel's arm and departed.

* * *

When her mother returned, Isabel faced her accusingly. "You put them up to it, didn't you?"

"The town is worried," said Marguerite. "You attend Town Meetings; you know what goes on."

"I thought you said I could finish college before getting married."

"What?" Her mother looked up sharply. "They weren't supposed to get into that."

"Vera did, afterward. How can I ever go back to physics class after... what she said about Matthew?" She found herself shaking, and tears came. She liked Matthew intensely, as a teacher; to think of him in another way was unbearably unsettling.

Marguerite closed her eyes. "That woman. I should have known."

"But what am I to do?"

"I'm sorry about this, truly. As for Matthew, think no more of it; that's all in Vera's head. Matthew will never marry again, not since Janet —" She cut herself off. The shell of Matthew's old house still stood, just outside the Wall where it crossed Peachtree Court. That was why he lived with the Browns now.

"Not that he hasn't felt the pressure, too," Marguerite continued. "Especially since men are in short supply, in your generation." Marguerite sighed and fell into a chair, putting her feet up on the coffee table, something she had long ago forbade Isabel to do. Having a second doctor had not meant any less work, it turned out; it only meant that everyone expected house calls. "You know, in medical terms, Vera's dead right."

"But life is more than medicine. I want to marry when I'm good and ready, just the right person. You know, like Hermia and Helena," she added, referring to Shakespeare's heroines.

"Well said. The trouble is, we educated you for civilization, not for survival. Not that you don't do your part. But there's no arguing with mortality."

"Why did you have only one child?"

"I nearly died, with you. I hemorrhaged, and nobody else knew what to do. They couldn't afford to lose me."

Isabel looked away.

"You might make things easier if you at least look like you're, well, socially interested. Wear a skirt to Meeting, at least. Then they'll feel better."

"You still promise they can't make me get married?" she asked suspiciously.

Her mother gave a wry smile. "Of course not. For better or worse, this is still a Christian town."

That evening, Isabel packed the radio into the carriage and drove out to leave it at the Pylon. A couple of angelbees watched her owlishly against the sky, which was banked with pink-lined clouds in a brilliant sunset, the kind of sunset the Little Prince would have loved. Isabel watched the angelbees guiltily, and she hoped they could not read her mind, as some feared they had read Becca's. The radio she gave up was missing a number of essential parts, the ones hard to obtain from Sydney. She planned to take Keith up on his offer to help build a new one.

XIV

FOR WORSHIP, THE second Sunday of November, Isabel assembled an outfit of some clothes from her mother's college days. A navy skirt, calf-length, with a faded print blouse and dark winter panty hose completed the picture. She then decided her hair needed a trim. Keith offered to oblige, insisting that he was an expert stylist. Keith took a great deal of amusement in her project. "'Struth, you look sharp enough for a night out at the Whale!" he said, meaning the famous Sydney Opera House.

Isabel felt self-conscious throughout the worship service, convinced that everyone must be staring at her. Afterward, she braced herself for the remarks.

"How nice you look," said Debbie sincerely. Her face had developed brown blotches, but she was basically well, the baby gaining on schedule despite her blood loss. "Que vous êtes belle!"

Isabel looked away, abashed at this quote from The Little Prince, complimenting his rose. "Thanks," she murmured, adding, "we have four pints of blood on hand, so far."

"Thank you," Debbie whispered.

Jon approached her with a lot of questions about gravitation and planetary motions. She answered politely, but wished Peace Hope would have stayed.

Deliverance stopped by, with Daniel in tow. "Isabel, could you use some more clothes? Would you like me to do you a wool skirt for winter?" Deliverance had become an accomplished seamstress, and now Daniel, too, was learning to sew with Anna Tran. "We've got this new dye, maroon, that the wool picks up fine. The A-line is in right now, in Sydney." Daniel's hand was clasped in hers, and Deliverance swung his arm back and forth. She had just completed a new suit for him.

Isabel said, "I'll bet Daniel could sew it just as well."

Daniel said, returning her look with a smile, "I'm just a novice."

Deliverance laughed. "Oh, Daniel picks up at the needle, quick as that." She pulled him away, her woolen skirt swishing around.

Isabel muttered, "'Get you gone, you canker blossom.'" Before she could slip away, Grace stepped in front of her, smiling broadly.

"See, I learn sign word!" Grace placed her open right hand in the crook of her left arm, cradling her right arm with her left, then rocked her arms back and forth.

"Very good. Is that . . . 'doll'?"

Grace shook her head vigorously.

"No? Is it . . . 'baby'?"

"Yes! My baby!"

Keith caught her arm at last. "Quit being the life of the party. The horse is waiting."

On the way out, Isabel noticed an angelbee floating discreetly above the tar-paper roof. It had to be the same one she had seen at home that morning, because it had a daughter cell growing out the side, at just the same stage of development. She was convinced that it had been following her, for the past week if not longer.

That afternoon Isabel picked apples, just about the last of the crop. The branches of the aging dwarfs bowed so low that some of the limbs brushed the ground, and she had to stoop for the ripe apples one after another, the ones with just a touch of pink on one side. Pluck, and the branch swooped back with a rustle, and her sack swelled full until her back ached, and it was time to unload into the wagon below.

As Isabel reached up again to the uppermost branches, a cool wind on her forehead brought welcome relief. She paused to bite into one particularly ripe fruit, and its sharp, sweet taste brought a shock of pleasure after hours of exertion. The crunch of the apple and the wind in the leaves were the only sounds stirring Gwynwood, it seemed, as she looked out on the patchwork farmlands, sheltered by Gwynwood Hill to the north, rimmed to the south by the deadland.

Her eye caught a movement, someone coming along the

path where the orchard gave out. It was her father, striding at
his usual measured pace, herding the sheep. For the moment
the sight plunged her back into childhood, when her earliest
image of God was just that: a man in an apron of tools, un-
hurried, striding across His creation. That was so long ago;
she had long since discarded any tangible picture of God, although she had not admitted so to anyone but Peace Hope.
Still, the force of it shook her for a moment.

Andrés came off the path at last and approached the
wagon by the tree. Isabel tossed away her apple core, wiping
her hands on her overalls.

"The generator's out again," he told her.

"And you've spent the whole morning on it, without calling me? You should know better by now."

"Watch out, Belita; who taught you to hold a wrench, eh?"
He punched her arm. Then his face changed, and Isabel could
see he had something else on his mind to say. "You know, we
don't often talk anymore."

"No?" She half smiled. Suddenly she wondered, Would
he ask if she believed in God? But no, her father would
never ask a thing like that. He probably guessed what she
thought, anyway.

"Our friend Keith Moran; he's a good doctor, no?"

"And a very good person." It vexed her that her father still
kept a distance from Keith.

"Of course, he's a very good man." Her father looked away,
clasping his hands as if trying to wring the words out of them.
"I know you've rather taken to him. I just don't want to see
your feelings hurt, before it goes too far."

"You think I—and Keith?" Astonished, Isabel shook her
head. "He's a friend, he's—" She started to say "a member of
our Underground."

"That is good. I hadn't seen young Daniel around much
lately."

"Well, Daniel is busy with the school." Still, she felt a
pang inside, fearing that for some reason Daniel was slipping
away from her. "But why do you think Keith would hurt my
feelings?"

"He would not return your feelings. He is, I think, a lover
of men."

Isabel paused to figure this out. She knew little about love between men, aside from occasional references in the *Herald*. She thought of the scene in *Moby Dick* where the narrator finds himself sharing a bed with a cannibal. "A lover of men? But how do you know that, about Keith?"

Andrés looked away. "One knows."

"What do you mean? You shouldn't just say a thing like that."

"Such a person seeks others, you understand."

"You mean—he thinks you are, too? Did he fall in love with you?"

"No, by God." Andrés's face swelled and reddened, and his look was wild, like a stranger. "What do you think I once killed a man for, if not for saying that?"

At first Isabel could not comprehend him; then she felt herself shaking all over. Then she broke away and stumbled back to the trunk of the apple tree, steadying herself against the rough bark.

"God knows I'm sorry," said Andrés behind her, quietly again. "You always wanted to know, didn't you? Maybe it's about time."

"But...I don't understand." She started to cry and let it go for a minute or so, then forced herself to stop. She turned around to face him again, her back to the tree as if for support. "It is time. I want to know."

Andrés looked helpless. "How can I say? One's youth is a dangerous time."

"But to kill someone—how could you do that?"

"You've never lived outside the Wall, in a country of eight million. People are like grains of sand."

"But still...what is wrong with 'loving a man'?"

Andrés seemed to draw into himself for a while. Then he said slowly, "You are fortunate you will never know. What I knew, outside, was this: To kill a man, though wrong, might be honorable, but to love a man, no matter how right, was shame."

"But you're a Christian. Christ would have said that love is right."

"Yes. It is easier to listen to Christ within this Wall."

For some reason Isabel recalled her Underground pledge

of honor, then the schoolroom portrait of John Dickinson, the man who would not kill to free the Colonies. Was he trying to warn her of that, too? "Is it different then, here, in Gwynwood? I mean—you wouldn't do it again?"

"How can I say for sure? Don't fool yourself: no one, not even a Friend, can say for sure."

"Well I wouldn't. I would never kill a person. An angelbee, maybe. Don't tell me that's wrong." Her pulse raced at having said it.

Andrés laughed and slapped his hands on his overalls. "You have much company, then. What has every righteous man always said? Do you think my grandmother would have left Germany if they had considered her a person?"

Isabel said nothing for a bit, gazing past him. She could not help trying to visualize it; her father, striking someone in some blurred sort of movement, the body falling and fading into a skeleton, its skull staring out at her like those beyond the Wall. "Does Mother know?"

"You mean, why did she marry such an evil fellow? That, you should ask her," Andrés said quietly.

XV

ISABEL COULD NOT bring herself to ask her mother about what her father had said, but she did tell Peace Hope after physics class. They were standing outside the Browns' house by the horses.

Peace Hope considered the news. "So that's how it happened, after all."

"Is that all you can say? When my father's a murderer?"

"Well, thee always suspected so. Why else would he not tell?"

"But that was just imagination," Isabel insisted. "This is a fact."

"A fact thee has lived with, without knowing. Does it make such a difference now?"

Above them a slight breeze stirred the branches of the trees, and a few dried leaves fluttered down. The old black walnut tree had already lost its leaves; its bare limbs pierced the sky, like a Hindu deity with a thousand arms. The angelbee that had been following Isabel floated high above, along with its daughter cell, which by now had budded off on its own.

"Do you think it runs in the genes?"

"I should think so. We all bear the mark of Cain."

"Even Daniel? Even your dad?"

"My dad says that before Doomsday everyone was a murderer. Everyone paid taxes to build the bombs."

"Taxes?" Taxes, she recalled, were something like the town allowance in reverse. "Why would everybody pay taxes for such a wicked thing?"

"It was the law. My dad says he refused to pay; he worked for himself, as a carpenter, and he gave the 'tax' to charity instead. When they found out, they took his car, and would have taken the house, too, only it was in Grandmother Alice's name. They gave him thirty days in jail."

"Jail! Not your dad." The thought of prim Nahum Scattergood in jail lightened her heart considerably.

* * *

In November the Sydney shipment did not arrive after
the new moon, nor the day after. For three days anxiety
mounted, casting a shadow over preparations for Thanksgiving. Isabel knew they needed the medicines, and the
special sutures for Debbie's operation. What could have happened? Were the angelbees angry at Gwynwood? Did they
still think Alice was alive? How could a new Contact be
established?

On the morning of the fourth day, the shipment came at
last. Half the orders were unfilled, and the newspaper told
the tale. There had been another breakout attempt at the Sydney Wall in the harbour, a much bigger explosive this time.
The Wall appeared to have focused the blast back in some
way, such that a major segment of the waterfront was leveled.
People were still trying to dig out, and things would take a
while to get back on schedule.

Isabel read the story with mixed admiration and disquiet.
Of course, no one could have expected the Wall to do that,
but still—she tried to visualize half of Gwynwood blown
away at once. Certainly her own Underground would not risk
such a thing.

She borrowed the paper to show Keith. Keith gripped the
paper hard, and his face turned white as he read the headline.
"Not the waterfront. For God's sake, what a bloody fool thing
to do. Did they list the casualties?" He fumbled through the
pages.

Isabel watched sympathetically. "You must know all those
people."

"Not half. But my friend lives there. I must get in touch
with him, straightaway. But the mail will take months." Keith
seemed to be talking to himself.

"Someone you loved very much?" Isabel asked timidly.

"Yes. Though it scarcely matters now, does it." Keith relaxed his arm, and the paper fell to his side. Looking away,
he put his fingers to his lips, as if holding the invisible cigarette.

"Is it true that it's a hard thing? Loving a man, I
mean."

Keith looked at her, and his face changed. "Bloody hell,"
he said in a low voice. "So your dad let on, then."

"Dad meant no harm. He just—"

"No harm meant—that's what they all say, the 'breeders.' Why do you suppose they threw me to the bush?"

"What do you mean? You said there was a lottery."

"Your chance goes up tenfold if you're not a breeder, or if you're Catholic; and I'm both."

Isabel absorbed this in silence.

"And you can tell your dad I did not filch the gene strains. It's a government program, probably one of the few decent acts Parliament ever passed." Keith crossed his arms and looked away again. "I suppose I'd better take off, now, hadn't I. Get myself transported elsewhere in a hurry."

"What do you mean?"

"Well, once your Bible bashers find out, I'm finished, right?"

"But—but why? We can't possibly do without you at the hospital. Besides, you pledged to join our Underground."

"The Underground, yes." The word took on a chilling tone. "I hope you see, now, why I never joined the real Underground. What a lot of hotheads. All breeders, too; why didn't they blast their own neighborhood?"

Isabel wondered what to make of it. She and Peace Hope would never try anything so dangerous. She winced to think that Keith had never taken their Underground seriously after all. But then, what had they accomplished so far: a radio that she had to give up, and a hexagonal device left behind by some angelbee.

To her dismay, Peace Hope reacted much the way Keith did. "Friend Isabel," Peace Hope solemnly announced after French class, "I must tell thee that, after very prayerful consideration, I feel compelled to withdraw from the Underground."

"Oh, Scatterbrain, how could you? After all we've been through? Besides, you promised."

"It's a sinful thing to withdraw a pledge," Peace Hope agreed. "But I've come to see that it was a worse sin to join in the first place."

"It's not fair," Isabel objected. "I've done nothing wrong, have I?"

"Not yet, thee hasn't. But the road has its destination."

"Your folks have been at you."

"They have not, indeed," said Peace Hope with a rare flash of anger.

Isabel's patience ran out. "So go ahead and quit then; I'll just have to carry on alone."

For the next day or so, Isabel spoke barely a word to anyone. At night she got out her radio components and the circuit diagram and looked them over by candlelight, but it was depressing to think of starting over from scratch. Besides, what was the use? What if there was no real Underground out here, in America? The nearest Wall-town was Vista, out on the West Coast. There had never, ever, been living people sighted in the deadland.

The cooking for Thanksgiving went on, all the pies and the stuffed squash, the *pastels* of corn and peppers, and the goat's milk cheeses. When the day came, everyone gathered at the Scattergoods' for a community feast. Isabel served the soups and stews for a while. May and Amanda Pestlethwaite came by, their fingers flashing; they had grown so over the summer, she realized. *What to eat?* she signed, her finger brushing down across the left hand, then her right fingers together moving toward her mouth and back.

Both girls pointed their right thumb and fingertips down into the left hand, twisting back and forth like a cookie cutter.

Isabel knew it was not yet time for cookies. She reached down the table and fetched a couple of corn muffins. May signed a quick *Thanks*, then hurried after Amanda, whose mouth was already stuffed.

When she finally got to her own turn, she faced the ordeal of her annual turkey serving. She enjoyed the taste, and her mother said that occasional meat was good for her, but she hated the thought of the lambs and chicks that were raised so clearly to be slaughtered. She had always thought, if the biblical Abraham were really so foolish as to consent to feed his own son to some God, then why had he not done so and spared the poor ram.

Jon was serving the turkey, a major item from the Hubbards' farm. He beamed at her and served her twice as much as she could eat. Isabel was conscious of her dress outfit again; she felt like pulling down the hem. "Will you come over this afternoon," Jon asked, "and see what a lot of corn we got stored for the winter? The dry spell barely hurt at all."

Isabel caught Peace Hope's eye, but her friend quickly turned away, blond curls swooping round her head. Peace Hope was still annoyed that the boys would never notice her.

At last Isabel sat down, her plate filled with corn bread and black bean pie, and Anna Tran's stir-fry, a delicious vegetarian recipe from her Buddhist mother. Keith came over to join her; since their angry exchange, he had redoubled his efforts to be friendly. "Poor Isabel, to be chased by lovely young men you don't want. Others should be so lucky."

Isabel tried to ignore him. She did not yet want to forgive him for insulting the Underground.

"Perhaps you prefer your two admirers in the trees," Keith added, referring to the angelbees that tailed her. "I sympathize. At least they're not breeders."

She glared at him. She considered several good curses in Spanish and one in German. Then she laughed, and kept laughing, until she noticed an ant crawling up her leg and brushed it off. For some reason a flood of fear came over her; the sense that, somehow, the angelbees were crawling into her life and there was no escape. Ants, too, were social insects, and much more bothersome than honeybees. "I still can't see it, though," Isabel told him, trying to shrug off her fear. "Why should the angelbees bother with me? So stupid," she said, knocking her S hand against her forehead.

"I agree," said Keith. "They're not completely brainless; but, smart enough to run a planet? Now that I see them, here, close up, like Jane Goodall giving us bananas—it doesn't add up."

Isabel leaned back on her elbows. "They're like bees in a hive, isn't that right? Workers tending a Queen. Maybe the Queen is the intelligent one?"

"Bees, okay; but where are their keepers?"

The hair rose on the back of her scalp. "The Pylon. There must be something, or someone, inside..."

Keith shrugged. "Who knows? All our guesses are no more than the gropings of blind men about an elephant. The space

cockies aren't exactly bees, any more than they're exactly
angels."

"Then we need better guesses." There was one place to
hunt for clues: her mother's attic, where all the old books
were stored. Those books had solved many a puzzle before.

XVI

THE ATTIC SMELLED musty but dry, except for one shrunken puddle beneath a cracked slate, which Isabel dreaded climbing out to fix, lest others crack, too. The light from her candle made the shadows dance wildly. She coughed from the dust, and her groping hands soon came away blackened. Outside the wind whistled, and she rubbed her arms to keep warm.

Her mother's books were packed away in unmarked cartons. One box was full of paperbacks, from Dickens to De Lillo; another, volumes of the *New England Journal of Medicine*, dating from the late nineties. That seemed closer; she heaved the box down, and checked underneath.

She was in luck. College texts: *Psychology, Microeconomics, History of Modern Europe,* and finally *Life: The Science of Biology*. She thumbed through the yellowed pages of *Life*: photosynthesis, chromosomes, monera, protista. Taxonomy and phylogeny: there were ciliates, fungal hyphae, nematodes and annelids, bryophytes and brontosaurs... Were angelbees saprophytes or parasites? Did they have a genetic code? Did they exhibit kin selection?

If angelbees reproduced by budding, then why on Earth would they need a "queen"?

Bewildered, she shook her head. It was hard to believe one planet could have held so many life forms, each so complex in form and function. It would take her a thousand years to think through it all.

She started in on arthropods, and got through trilobites and crustaceans. When she had enough she closed the book with a thud, nearly jarring out her candle flame, then moved to another box. These turned out to be old children's books, most of which she herself had read once. Many were about biology, too, her mother's childhood passion. *Microbe Hunters*, about picking scum from your teeth and watching the little animals wiggle under a lens. A storybook about a girl who shrank to the size of an ant and helped the ants milk their aphids; that one, she could see, all right. A guide to the human body, with the circulatory system illustrated in vivid color, arteries scarlet and veins blue. What kind of circulation did angelbees have? Her eyes swam and her head throbbed, but she read on into the night.

From downstairs came a faint tapping on the door. A call for the doctors?

Isabel picked up her candle and crept downstairs, the shadows swinging around her. The floorboards chilled her feet through the worn soles of her slippers; there was no heat downstairs at night. She opened the front door, and the wind swept in.

Daniel stood on the step. "It's you," he sighed, slightly out of breath. "I hoped it would be you."

"Daniel! Whatever are you doing here? Come on in, for goodness sake. We can stir up the kitchen fire."

They raked up the embers and managed to get enough going to keep their hands warm at least. They sat together on the hearth, not quite touching. For just a moment Isabel felt light-headed, but then she caught herself. What had he come for? She looked at Daniel expectantly.

"They chose me as Contact."

Isabel blinked. "They?"

"The Pylon."

She caught a hand to her mouth. "Daniel, what happened?"

"I went to sit outside the Pylon, as I had so many times before. I thought this would be my last time; it's getting too cold at night." He stopped.

"What happened then?" she ventured.

Daniel kneaded his forehead and stared into the fire. "The Pylon filled with reddish light. Then I saw...Alice. Like a still photograph. And then her shape sort of blurred and changed; and then it was me."

Her scalp prickled at the thought of it. With a tentative gesture she pressed his arm. "Somebody has to be Contact, Daniel. Someone has to do it."

"But why me? I'm young; I'm not an elder."

Taken aback, she nearly observed that he sure sounded like an elder most of the time. "They would pick someone young, so they don't have to change too often. They don't like change, do they?"

Daniel said nothing.

"What happened then?" she asked. "What did you see next? They must have lots of messages for us; it's been so long."

"I can't say. I ran away."

"You ran away? But why?"

"Isabel, don't you understand?" He turned and looked at her for the first time. "I can't do it; I refuse. It's not right, don't you see? We are called to witness to one another, as equals in the Light of Truth. No power on Earth can justly single out one above another."

Isabel swallowed. There seemed to be nothing left to say. "Why did you come ... here?" she asked at last, hesitantly.

Daniel looked away again. "I just wanted you to know, that's all."

Then it occurred to her. "You've joined the Underground, haven't you. After Keith and Peace Hope quit." She shook her head wonderingly. "You joined in a big way, too. Making a radio is nothing compared to—" She stopped as she thought of something else. "Are you really sure you must refuse? After all, you might do more good by going along, by using the chance to spy them out."

"Do you understand nothing? Don't you see; it's not a question of rebellion, but of obedience." With a twist of his head, Daniel rose from the hearth and left as abruptly as he had come.

XVII

THE COLD, HARD benches were filling with neighbors as the town met to take up Daniel's refusal to act as Contact. Miracle Dreher squealed as he ran along behind a back bench, running back now and then to tease his sister Faith; Charity was still confined to bed. Their parents sat up front; Debbie looked exhausted. Everyone seemed to be there: the Browns, the Weisses, the Scattergoods except for Nahum. Isabel did not sit with the Scattergoods because Daniel was unaccountably angry with her again, and she was still mad at Peace Hope for quitting the Underground.

Keith shook his head. "I can't make this out, mate."

Isabel herself was still amazed at what Daniel had done. She remembered last summer, that night on the hill, as he told her that people had to earn their freedom. But how? Why did he always reject her own way, and always come back again?

"Daniel is a plain Friend," Isabel tried to explain. "They're extra strict. Quakers think that everybody is exactly equal in God's sight. That's why they don't have preachers. So they aren't about to let the angelbees set one up, either."

"But his grandmother Alice was a plain Friend too."

"I guess he had a different revelation."

Keith shook his head. "Your tribal superstitions confound me."

Isabel bridled at this. "At least he had the nerve to stand up for something—which is better than some of us."

"Too right."

"Anyway, why should the angelbees only talk to one of us?"

"If they're a 'hive,' maybe they have only one collective consciousness. Why should 'it' try to address the whole quarrelsome lot of us?"

The room hushed as Liza rose to speak. "I wish to speak for myself and Nahum in supporting the stand our nephew has taken. Daniel has chosen to witness to the Light of Truth.

This decision was his and his alone to make, but it must also be said that Daniel well knows the grief it caused his grandmother to serve our masters in this way. We ask the town to understand and support him in this time of trial."

There was some muttering, then Carl Dreher arose. "I wouldn't want to go against anybody's conscience, but I have to point out that the town has a lot at stake here. The angelbees have to reach us in their own way, and most of the time it's to our benefit: climate forecasts and so on. Doesn't the Apostle Paul instruct us to obey our earthly rulers, whoever they may be? 'Every person must submit to the supreme authorities. The existing authorities are instituted by God.'"

Several heads nodded, but Isabel was annoyed. Existing authorities, indeed. The devil take Carl and his sermons.

Matthew asked, "What happens, then, when the rulers act against the Lord? The disciple Peter told his jailors, 'We must obey God rather than men.' Such obedience requires a special leading, of course, to know that one has heard God's voice. I for one feel compelled to trust in Daniel. Let one who disagrees follow his or her own leading to act as Contact."

"But the angelbees chose Daniel," said Carl. "How can we refuse? Besides, Scripture tells us exactly what happened when 'the rulers made common cause against the Lord.' The temple was destroyed, and the dead were exposed in their graves. Isn't that what became of us, too, in our own generation? Our fathers ruled falsely; we have the Wall as witness to that. Today's rulers may not be perfect, but they were sent by God to save our lives."

Just then, Vera came between the benches and tapped Marguerite on the shoulder to whisper something. Marguerite nodded, then told Isabel, "Debbie's bleeding. We have to go."

Debbie lay in the bed in the birthing room, breathing quietly. Vera was adjusting the pillow, and Carl sat at the bedside holding her hand, his wooden chair creaking slightly as he leaned forward. The floorboards were still icy; the electric heater was just beginning to take the edge off the cold. The fetal monitor read the baby's heartbeat at a steady one-fifty, no problems there. Isabel watched, then got up and stepped out to get fresh towels for Debbie.

In the hallway, Marguerite whispered to Keith, "She's got to deliver, now. She'll need a unit of blood soon."

"Too right," Keith agreed. "Let's go: the IV, the sutures, the ether—"

"Not ether. She's six weeks early; ether might endanger the baby."

"The baby won't survive anyhow, under these conditions."

Marguerite gripped his arm. "Thirty-four weeks—that baby will live, you hear?"

Keith returned her stare, then looked away. "You've got no caudal or epidural agents. Nor the equipment; we've discussed this."

"There's lidocaine."

Keith put his fingers to his lips, an invisible cigarette, then exhaled slowly. "Lidocaine in the abdominal wall. It's been done, but it still hurts like hell."

The thought of abdominal surgery with only local anesthesia made Isabel feel nauseated, and slightly faint.

"You ask Debbie," Marguerite told Keith.

Keith reentered the birthing room.

"Start the IV," Marguerite told Isabel. "Give her the first unit of blood now." Then she called through the doorway, "Vera, please fetch us water from the cistern. We'll need cold water, heated water, and wash water." Fortunately the cistern was full.

While Isabel inserted Debbie's IV, Keith wheeled in the operating table, which Nahum had built specially for the hospital many years before. Isabel's skin tightened involuntarily; the sight of that table brought back difficult memories, especially of Aaron's last days.

Vera returned, carrying three pails of water. "Good," said Marguerite. "Isabel, get that basin to ninety-eight degrees and keep adjusting it, hear?"

"Yes, Mom." She poured together hot and cold, squinting at the thermometer until it read correctly. This basin would serve to warm the newborn.

Marguerite was passing out the surgical gowns and gloves

and counting the suture packs. Isabel stared at the pile of sutures as if it were a heap of gold. She had never seen so many catgut sutures used at once.

"The autoclave must be done," called Marguerite.

Vera went out to fetch the sterile instruments from the autoclave. Keith and Carl lifted Debbie onto the operating table, then they moved the bed to the wall to make more room. Marguerite set up a curtain crosswise over Debbie to shelter the operating area. Debbie's face was pale, and her eyelids fluttered rapidly. But her look was steady, and she nodded to Carl as she held his hand.

The smell of stale blood was becoming noticeable. Isabel looked at the window, although they probably could not afford to open it and lose the heat.

There were angelbees outside—not just one or two, but a cluster of them, perhaps a dozen of the floating moons. Why so many? Did they know that something would be different about this birth?

Vera returned with the instruments wrapped in towels. Keith tried to open them, but then he snapped his gloves off. "It's no good; my fingers are bloody ice." He plunged his hands in the pail of hot water. When he was done, Isabel checked the thermometer in the baby basin and added some more hot water.

"Check her blood pressure one more time," Marguerite ordered.

Isabel applied the cuff to Debbie's arm. The readings were a bit low, but in range.

Already Keith was wiping the skin, toward the base of the uterus. "A low transverse cut is best," he muttered. "Let's hope the placenta's not anterior." If the placenta lay too far forward, and he cut into it, Debbie would bleed to death.

Marguerite was applying the anesthetic. "You should be getting numb now, Debbie. The baby will come out real fast. Afterward, for the stitching up, we'll give you ether."

Debbie nodded. Carl's fingers were red beneath her clenched hand.

"Relax, as best you can," Marguerite advised quietly. "Your breathing should help." To Isabel, she added, "Ready to strip and clamp the placenta?"

Isabel nodded. This part she had done before, for the birth of Benjamin Weiss. While Keith would do the cutting and stitching, her mother and she would handle the newborn as usual.

The blade entered the skin. It sounded rather like Anna Tran snipping denim for her sewing. It made Isabel's hair stand on end to see skin being cut that way. Beneath Keith's fingers she mopped up the trickle of blood, while Debbie's breaths came shorter and faster to manage the pain which the anesthetic did not completely cover.

"Keep breathing; you can manage." Carl's voice sounded higher than usual.

When the abdominal wall was opened, Debbie cried out several times. Then, quicker than Isabel had anticipated, a miniature person was dangling from between Keith's fingers, the tiniest baby she had ever seen. She grasped the cord and stripped the extra blood back to the baby, then clamped twice and snipped.

"You've got a daughter." Marguerite took the baby, syringing out her nose and mouth. Debbie was weeping softly, relieved but still in considerable pain.

But the baby was silent. Her mouth and eyes were closed, and her limbs hung limp.

"Breathe, will you." Marguerite suctioned the nose and mouth, then massaged her face and chest. Then she plunged her into the waiting basin of warm water.

The tiny face grimaced and choked, then emitted a squeaking cry, and the arms and legs flew out straight. Her color started to pink up, though her fingers were still blue. Isabel stared, transfixed; it was almost as if a dead person had come awake.

"She's beautiful," cried Vera. "I've never seen such a lovely newborn."

It was true, her head was perfectly round, not misshapen from travel through the birth canal. Her arms and neck had deep folds filled in with white vernix, but the surface of her skin was smooth without a blemish. Que vous êtes belle. Carl came over and touched her hand; the tiny fingers grabbed tight the tip of his own.

"Sutures, please," called Keith.

Isabel hurried back to the operating table where Debbie was being sewn up, asleep now under ether.

"She's barely four pounds," Marguerite estimated, still supporting the baby's head with her hand.

"She won't maintain temperature," said Keith as he tied the sutures. "You could keep her in the plate incubator from the lab."

"You could keep her taped to Debbie's chest all day," Marguerite suggested to Carl. "She'll be kept warm, and convenient for nursing too."

"Debbie will have to watch this incision," Keith warned. Isabel continued to hand him the sutures.

When the operation was done, Isabel stole away again to see the baby, now asleep wrapped in blankets while Carl held her. "Her head is so round," Carl mused. The shiny hairless scalp was almost as round as an angelbee. The fontanel, the diamond-shaped patch of skin where the skull plates had not yet fused beneath, was larger than usual due to prematurity; at just the right angle, you could see the skin move up and down with the heartbeat.

Then Isabel saw something not quite right. There was a small spot, at the crown, where the skin had failed to close. The spot was white, like the bones beyond the Wall.

"Mom, look at this. Is that the bare skull?"

Her mother turned to speak; but Carl snatched the bundle away. "I don't care what it is, do you hear?" His voice was unnaturally high, and his face had gone white. "Whatever's wrong—you *won't kill her.*"

Vera, too, was staring at Marguerite, her mouth open, her eyelids fluttering with terror. Isabel looked from one to another, completely bewildered. What had she said? Why would they expect such a thing of her mother?

"The baby's fine," Marguerite insisted soothingly, "just fine. The scalp will close in time, there'll be a bald spot, you won't even notice. For God's sake, Carl."

The room was cleaned out, and Debbie was sleeping with her baby. Marguerite stopped and rubbed her forehead. "You'd better turn in, Isabel."

Isabel looked up. "Mother, why did Carl...say that? Why would he think such a thing?"

Marguerite sank into a chair. Her shoulders drooped, but her eyes were alert again. "He was worried sick; one always is. It was all right this time, thank God."

"But what if it wasn't 'all right'?"

She paused, withdrawn in thought. "Perhaps I go further than I should. Certainly further than I was trained. But, God knows, we have so many defects since the Death Year. The minor ones, like Benjamin's heart murmur, we cope with. The severe ones—we haven't the funds nor the staff to maintain them."

"But you're a Quaker. You can't just..."

"What would you do with a baby born without a cerebral cortex? Or its spine open halfway down? Or a heart defect that would kill it within a year?"

"But how would you *know* that? You're only a doctor; how would you know for sure?" She thought of the tiny graves in the cemetery, supposedly stillborn.

Marguerite shook her head slowly. "Somebody has to decide. I've always prayed it wouldn't be me. Now at least Keith is here, so it will no longer be me alone."

"What about Peace Hope?" Isabel shook uncontrollably. "Would you have killed her?"

Marguerite hesitated, and Isabel remembered, who else had delivered Peace Hope, after all? "I—I thought of it." Marguerite swallowed, and her throat constricted. "Just a knob of a head with a trunk, like a clothespin doll; who wouldn't have thought of it? But then her eyes—I looked at her, and she looked back, do you see? She must have been the most alert newborn I've ever seen."

"But you thought of it."

"What do you think it's like to be a doctor? Wasn't Keith ready to write off that baby to save Debbie?"

"*You wanted to kill Peace Hope! You're a murderer, just like Dad!*" With a choked sob, she pounded downstairs, grabbed her jacket and bicycle and headed outside.

Isabel huddled with Peace Hope under the blanket in Peace Hope's bed, the air cold enough to freeze the drinking water in the pitcher. The candle on the desk sent bizarre shadows bouncing over the walls, and the odor of beeswax came over in waves. Isabel swallowed, her tongue swollen from sobbing. Her head ached from exhaustion, but she knew she could not sleep.

Peace Hope sighed. "Poor Dr. Chase. I always wondered what it must be like."

"But she tried to kill you. Don't you hear what I'm saying?"

"It might have been better if she had."

Startled, Isabel turned her head beneath the blanket. "You can't say that, Scatterbrain. You can't really mean it." She thought uneasily, it was hard to imagine life without arms and legs. Yet it was even harder to imagine life in Gwynwood without Peace Hope.

"No, I don't really. Not most of the time, anyway." Peace Hope smiled briefly, and her head turned out of the shadow. "How did your mother take it, when you found out?"

"Oh, I don't know." Isabel had not really thought about this. "She's still a murderer."

"Well I don't know. That's a bit simple, I think."

"It's the truth." But Isabel was beginning to think she did not quite know what the truth was anymore. She pressed her hand over her aching forehead. What would Keith say, she wondered. Marguerite seemed to think that Keith would do the same, that he, too, could take a life and call it kindness. That was not how it was supposed to be. The "milk of human kindness" was supposed to prevent murder, not excuse it. She remembered Teacher Becca in high school, reading aloud from *Macbeth* and from *Midsummer Night's Dream*, making the voices of witches and fairies come alive. Her eyes filled with tears again.

"The truth is, your mother saved the baby," said Peace Hope. "A good thing it came out okay. I'll bet your mother sure is relieved."

She winced. In fact, Marguerite must be worried sick after Isabel had run off into the night. She would not get to sleep, and she needed sleep after the ordeal of that operation.

Isabel turned over and buried her face in the pillow, but it was no use. "I guess I'd better go home."

* * *

The moon waxed nearly full above the house as Isabel pulled up on her bicycle, the headlamp sending its pulsing light across the familiar drive. The house was dark. Several angelbees still hovered outside the room where Debbie had given birth. Isabel paused at the sight of the hateful creatures, thinking that with inhuman blindness they had caused the Earth to be poisoned, cursing the birthdays of all who came after.

Upstairs her room was empty and quiet except for Peewee's wheel. Outside the closed window she could see her two followers, one angelbee, then another, their eyespots staring toward her. One of them was close to the window, much closer than usual. It was the daughter cell, the one with the rounded eyespot.

As Isabel caught her breath, an idea came to her. Quietly she closed the bedroom door. She turned on her fluorescent study lamp, which would not scare them off because its light was mostly "cold." Then she went to the window and pushed it up, with some effort as it had been closed since summer. Then she stepped aside.

Slowly but surely, the angelbee meandered toward the window and moved inside. Isabel rushed back to the window and slammed it shut again.

The angelbee floated before her dresser unhurriedly, rotating its eyespot down. It seemed not to care to stay away from her; in fact, it moved toward her, until its eyespot nearly touched her nose. She raised both hands and brought them together. The tips of her fingers caught the bright globe.

Its surface felt dry and taut as a drumhead; she had the sense of something trembling beneath her fingers. With a surge of anger, Isabel pressed her hands inward as hard as she could.

Her hands collapsed in. There was a flash; a wave of pain burned across her face and hands. She screamed and fell to the floor, holding her face in her hands. Before her eyes all was blank, not the black of night, but an empty grayness, like the face of a granite tombstone before it was chiseled.

"*Light, turn on the light!*" Isabel screamed. "Please, a light!"

She heard the door open, and voices, and hands reached her; her father, her mother, somewhere nearby.

"A light—please, somebody..."

"But the light is on," her father's voice told her.

XVIII

ISABEL SAT IN the examination room, where Marguerite
and Keith had spent hours examining her eyes, pushing,
probing, shining lights which she could not see.

"Flash blindness usually recovers within hours," said
Marguerite out of the grayness. Isabel figured it must be mid-
day by now, although she could not bring herself to ask.

"That's not it at all," said Keith, his voice coming from
farther off. "Her skin shows no sign of superficial burns.
Some substance from within the punctured angelbee must
have poisoned her retina."

At the sound of that, Isabel felt a cold shock, and her head
reeled.

"You don't know for sure yet," Marguerite said quickly.
Keith did not say more.

"There must be other cases?" Isabel asked, trying to re-
cover her calm. "Surely it's happened before?"

"Not to my knowledge," said Keith. "I never heard of anyone who grabbed a space cockie barehanded. When somebody pops one with a rifle, the sleep-fog pours out of the
Pylon until it fills the city. After three days people start waking up, but the fog takes weeks to dissipate completely."

"The angelbees never kill humans?"

"Not directly. You get traffic accidents in the fog; people
get run over by bikes."

"My eyes," Isabel said. "Why retaliate against eyes?"

"Angelbees act like eyes," said Marguerite abruptly.
"Looking, spying; but they never touch us."

"Maybe they are just eyes," said Isabel. "Maybe they take
off their arms and legs, like Peace Hope, and leave them inside their spacecraft."

"Eye for an eye—that's a good one," said Keith with a
chuckle. "Nobody's ever looked inside a spacecraft and come
back to tell what's there. I can see it, arms and legs stacked
neatly in a row—"

"No—the spacecraft-thing is itself the arms and legs!" Isabel exclaimed. "Angelbees and it, in radio contact, just like

the fetal monitor with its sensor." The idea mushroomed in her mind, exploding with possibility. Was the "spacecraft" really an organism, something like a crustacean with an exoskeleton? One of those spiders in the *Life* book had looked like a lunar module. The new picture of Earth's masters came into focus: not a myriad of legless angelbees, but a few central "keepers" with invisible tentacles of radio waves...

Everything was still invisible to Isabel, she recalled again with a shock. "How are the tests coming out? Did you find what's the matter yet?"

There was silence. For an instant Isabel panicked, thinking, what if she had lost her hearing, too?

Marguerite said, "The tests are done for now, Isabel."

The tests were done, and there was no answer. She might be blind forever, for the rest of her life. Blind like Becca.

Isabel groped her way back to her bedroom, running her hand along the walls. Then she ran her hand across the worn old coverlet onto the grainy wood of the bedstead. Warmth suffused her arm, and she knew it must be sunlight from the window. How odd it was to feel her body set firmly in her old, familiar room, while within her head her mind spun helplessly in blank emptiness.

Suddenly she squeezed her eyelids shut. If only it would get darker, that would mean that at least some light had been getting in. But the grayness did not change. The inaccessibility of dark was nearly as appalling as the absence of light.

Her eyes relaxed again, and a few tears came out. Then she rose and felt along the windowsill until she hit the dresser opposite the bed. The bottom drawer hid the old candle box that Becca had left her, with its unanswered questions. The angelbees had given Becca her sight, not taken it away. To see people, after all those years; no wonder Becca had written, "You all shine like stars."

And yet, she had gone away with the angelbees. Why? And why had the angelbees, or their "keepers," taken her?

The floorboards vibrated as someone ascended the stairs and entered Isabel's room. "It's me," came Marguerite's voice out of the grayness.

"More tests?" Isabel asked hopefully.

"Sorry," Marguerite whispered. "Ruth stopped by to give

you this. She said you're welcome to others, too, from Becca's room. Until you get better, of course."

Isabel's hand fell upon a book with a Braille title, *The Torah*, the first five books of the Bible. *English Bible*.

She felt her way back to the bed and sat down with the book, starting with Genesis. She was out of practice at Braille, and it took her some time to remember all the three-by-two dot symbols. The translation was unfamiliar to her, neither *New English* nor *King James*. "God said, 'Let there be an expanse in the midst of the water...'" Isabel had always pictured the biblical sky as a solid vault, like a cathedral dome above the Earth, not as an open expanse. As her fingers laboriously picked out the words, her attention wandered. She wondered about the angelbees and their exoskeletal keepers. Why had they ever come here from the sky? What were they getting from Earth?

Later that afternoon her mother knocked on the door again. "Peace Hope is downstairs. She wants to know if you can have visitors."

"Goodness, yes. What do you think I am, contagious?"

So Peace Hope came upstairs, her crutches thumping methodically on the stairs. Isabel could hear her coming across the floor; then suddenly Peace Hope's cheek rested against hers, her chin leaning on her shoulder.

Isabel hugged her hard and started to cry, and kept on crying until she was exhausted and her eyelids felt swollen. At last she let go of Peace Hope, sat up on the bed and pushed back her hair. "The worst thing is, I can't even tell what I look like. How do I know if my hair's combed straight? I probably look worse than Grace."

"Thee looks the same as ever," said Peace Hope. "Like a Spanish aristocrat."

"I'd rather be a campesino. The Spaniards were slavers, just like the angelbees."

There was a pause. "Is the baby doing well?" Peace Hope asked.

"Fine. She's down the hall with Debbie; take a look." She shuddered at the word.

"Even the angelbees must have been impressed. They're still watching at the window."

Isabel frowned. "My window?"

"Oh no; the birthing room."

The birthing room was empty now. It made no sense.

Then she remembered something else. "The Town Meeting last night. Whatever happened?"

"We adjourned without a decision. We're to reconvene this evening." Peace Hope paused, then added, "My mother thinks that thy...injury will have some effect."

"Sure it will. You'll all say, see what comes of standing up to angelbees. Scatterbrain, listen: the angelbees are just eyes." Isabel grew excited again, remembering. "Just eyes—that spacecraft is really their other half, their 'arms and legs.'"

"That could be. We know there must be something more than angelbees. But why would their body parts evolve in two pieces? Could they have replaced one part with a machine? That spacecraft still looks mechanical, to me."

"So does an insect. Perhaps the keeper with the arms and legs evolved separately from the angelbees, and they came together in symbiosis. Like ants and aphids: ants milk the aphids for food. But the aphids aren't social, like the ants; they reproduce by 'parthenogenesis'. Angelbees reproduce by budding, so why would they need a Hive? It's their keepers that need the Hive."

Peace Hope considered this. "If these keepers are the arms and legs, I wonder where the brain is."

"The keepers could have brains. Or the brain could be decentralized throughout the colony." Isabel shook her head; it was too complicated to think about. "Oh well. Maybe I'm not quite a murderer, after all." She half smiled. An eye for an eye—Keith was right at that. She asked guardedly, "Does Daniel know...what happened?"

"When Daniel heard," said Peace Hope, "he was very angry indeed."

"Angry at me?"

"Not at thee, I think. He said to me, 'Thee sees, I was right to refuse.'"

Isabel let out a long sigh and squeezed her eyelids shut again, but they could not shut out the grayness. "He picked a fine time to join the Underground, with you and Keith quitting and me knocked out of action."

"We didn't really quit. We just stepped back for a bit. Thee knows, Quakers were always revolutionary. The early Friends used to denounce wicked preachers for removing God from the sight of ordinary men and women. They got so excited over it, they ran naked in the streets."

"Is that right? I'll bet that's what your dad did when they put the cross up on the 'steeplehouse.'"

Peace Hope laughed. "I'll bet he did. Isabel, will thee come to the Meeting tonight?"

"No way. I'm not about to show up like this, so Sal and Deliverance can smirk in front of me. How can I go to class now?"

"I copied out some text for you in Braille—"

"Really? Physics?"

"I started on that, but I have to figure out how to do the equations. This is from Le Petit Prince."

"Oh."

"We're almost done with it in French class," Peace Hope added hurriedly, "the Little Prince is just about to leave Earth and go home to his own little planet. Teacher Debbie said we can try Tristan, then."

After Peace Hope left, Isabel fingered her way through the lines of French that Peace Hope had punched in painstakingly with a Braille tool. The Little Prince had just found a well in the middle of the desert; a likely idea, about as likely as most of his adventures. The narrator, instead of getting his plane fixed like any sensible aviator, was helping the Little Prince to get a drink of water from the well, and this led him to muse about his youth during Christmas time. Here or there was a word Isabel did not know, but she could work it out. Most of French was just mutant Spanish, after all: "la lumière de l'arbre de Noël," had to be la luz del árbol de Navidad, the light of the Christmas tree.

It occurred to Isabel that Christmas was less than a month off, and she might not see the lights this year. She shuddered and pressed her finger again through Peace Hope's text, until she reached an unfamiliar word, aveugle. Les yeux sont aveugles. "The eyes are..." Blind? It had to be, although it looked nothing like the Spanish ciego.

Aveugle was better, she liked the sound of it, somehow; it conveyed the horror of not being able to see. But what was this? Had the Little Prince gone blind in a chapter she had missed? "*Les yeux sont aveugles. Il faut chercher avec le coeur,*" one must seek with the heart.

A knock at the door startled her.

"Yes, Mom?"

"It's Daniel, to see you."

She felt warm in the face, then suddenly cold, until she thought she would pass out. "No," she managed to say. "I mean, I can't make it downstairs." She could not bear to have him see her this way.

"Of course. He'll understand."

"Wait, Mom. Tell him that—" She swallowed, turning over a decision in her mind. "I guess what I'm trying to say is—I want to be there tonight at the Town Meeting."

XIX

THE INTERIOR OF the Meetinghouse was a confusion of voices and children's cries. Isabel navigated the aisle gradually between her parents, until they found her a seat.

As Town Clerk, Liza opened the Meeting, which was to take up Daniel's refusal to serve as Contact. Almost immediately Carl's voice was heard. "Some of us have pursued a suggestion from last night," he said. "Remember, we considered offering the Pylon a substitute Contact, a youngster of age and character comparable to Daniel. I would like to put forward the name of one who would be willing to serve: Deliverance Brown."

"Deliverance!" Isabel whispered at her father. "That ignorant wretch. *No sabe ni la a.*"

Andrés chuckled. "What does Carl think we need, a vestal virgin? The gods do not take substitutes."

In the meantime, Deliverance was assuring the Meeting that she would accept this duty, and Vera was saying how proud she would be of her daughter.

"Thank thee for thy offer," Liza said to Deliverance. "Nevertheless, I believe some of us wish to discuss first the accident that has befallen one of us."

There was dead silence. Isabel imagined that all heads had turned to look at her. "Dad, can I—can I say something?"

"Yes, go ahead. Stand up so they hear."

She stood. It was odd to speak into blankness, yet in a sense easier not to see all those eyes. "The angelbees are just ...eyes," she croaked. "That is what I think. That is why they ...retaliated against my eyesight." She went on quickly, "Somehow, we have to get the Pylon to reveal its hands, and its brain. Somehow..." She had no way of telling how her words were received or comprehended. Feeling dizzy, she managed to sit down.

"Yes, Anna," called Liza.

"It was more than an eye for an eye." Anna's voice was indignant. "It was *two* eyes for one. Maybe let's shoot out ten of theirs and see how they like it. What's a few days of fog?"

There was a chorus of "Amen," and a muttered, "Can't let them get away with this."

Perplexed, Isabel had not expected this reaction. A heated argument ensued between those who wanted a substitute Contact, and others who wanted to start shooting angelbees. To her chagrin, Isabel found herself agreeing with Carl and Vera.

"Calm, Friends, please." Liza's voice grew, with a rare note of strain. "We may have missed a central point of Friend Isabel's mishap. It seems that at first the angelbee actually approached her, seeking some kind of contact, in an exceptionally direct manner. Is this not so?"

"Yes," Isabel admitted, "it seemed so." In retrospect.

"It may be that these angelbees, or the creatures to whom these 'eyes' belong, are at last seeking more open contact with us. This may be a time for a group of us to approach the Pylon together. We could join Daniel in visiting the Pylon at the next new moon."

There was a pause while people thought this over.

"I would consent to Aunt Liza's plan," said Daniel.

"I won't," called someone else. "Not unless Isabel gets better."

The Meeting closed after prolonged discussion, having finally agreed to Liza's plan to approach the Pylon as a group. That night Isabel slept fitfully, with dreams whose waking was terrible because she could see in sleep so clearly what she could not see awake. The next day brought no relief to her eyes. She made herself go downstairs and began to get around better by herself, creeping along the walls. She held and smelled the scent of the tall beeswax candles that Debbie had sent to the doctors, for delivering Patience. But feeding herself was the worst; she could never tell what was on her plate, and spooning cereal for breakfast was impossible.

"You've eaten little, Belita." Her father's voice was low and tentative, as if he had volumes he could not speak.

Isabel tried to figure out where to push the spoon. "I can't stand it, making a mess that I can't even see."

"You're managing all right."

Isabel gave up on the spoon and squeezed her eyes shut to see if it would get darker. It did not.

"How are you feeling this morning?" he asked.

Isabel sighed. "I feel like I've lived a thousand years in a day."

"So you have."

Tears rose in her eyes again, but she forced them back. Then she felt her way to the sitting room. She had left her reading there, the Braille Bible and *Le Petit Prince*. It was hard to believe she had no work to be getting after today, nothing to do but read. That was what a real college was supposed to be like.

"Can I help you with anything, Belita?"

"Thanks, Dad; I'll be okay. You go look after those sheep. Make sure they get their foot-rot medicine." She opened to the final chapter of Genesis. "If you run into Ruth, you might ask her to drop off some more Braille books. Anything will do; I'll go crazy reading the Bible all day."

She heard the door close as he left. From outside, the autumn wind sighed and rattled the last of the brittle leaves. She read for over an hour, until her fingertips ached from scraping across all the tiny dots.

A knock came from the door. Isabel got up and felt her way down the hall, past the open passage to the kitchen, coming to an abrupt halt at the outer door. She patted the door panels until her hand fell upon the door handle and opened it. The door pulled back, and the November wind blew in. "Who's there?" she called.

The visitor hesitated. "It's me," said Daniel. "Sorry—I'll leave, if thee'd rather."

"No, no." A wave of heat came over her, but she kept her composure. "Come in, please."

There were footsteps on the doorsill, and the door closed. Daniel's arm slid under hers to help her back to the sitting room. She sank back into the old sofa, then she felt the cushion sink as he sat next to her.

"What happened to thy hands?" Daniel asked.

Isabel looked automatically at her hands. She felt the sore fingertips; the pain worsened, and something moist came

away on her thumbs. "I'm not used to reading Braille. Goodness, I must look like Lady Macbeth."

"I'll get you a cloth." Daniel arose, then returned with a
cloth moistened with cistern water.

As Isabel soothed her fingers, the silence lengthened in
the grayness between her and Daniel, and she had a sudden
need to fill it with words. "You know, even normal eyes are
blind throughout most of the spectrum. The spectrum spans
everything, from radio wave and microwave on the long
end, through infrared, through visible; then there's ultraviolet, and X rays, and gamma rays, the shortest and deadliest
of all. Our eyes see just a tiny slice of it: red through green
through violet, all sandwiched into the slot between infrared and ultraviolet. Of course animal eyes have different
ranges; honeybees can't see red, but they see ultraviolet.
Some flowers that look white to us look bright colored to
them."

"And the angelbees are eyes that see infrared," said Daniel. "Eyes, perhaps, that serve some greater creature."

His voice was so beautiful, even more so than when she
could see him. It was almost worth the blindness to be able to
hear him this way.

"Thanks for coming, last night," Daniel added. "Thy rea-
soning was helpful. I feel that I know the creatures better
now."

"You don't...blame me then, for what I did?"

"It was unfortunate, but understandable. Of course, thee
was afraid."

In fact, she had felt anger more than fear. "I still hate
them," she said honestly. "I can't help it."

"Hate is the first step. Afterward comes understanding."

Isabel turned, and she found herself squinting at him, in
vain. "How do we get there? How do you suppose we're to
'earn our freedom'? Didn't the slaves have to fight for it?"

"There are different kinds of freedom. The reason the
Quakers freed their slaves was because the condition of slavery prevented obedience to the Light."

"So you think we are free enough, just because we're free
to worship in the Meetinghouse?"

"The Meetinghouse is not essential to worship. It's just a

convenient reminder. Every moment of life must be an act of worship. Otherwise, we're as dead as those beyond the Wall."

Her fingers gripped the sofa, and pain shot up through them. It was too unsettling to think of all those moments, hating angelbees, hating Carl Dreher sometimes, even hating her own parents when they fell short of perfection. Human beings—the product of a billion years of evolution, still capable of hatred and murder.

"It's too hard, Daniel," she exclaimed. "Why can't it be enough, just striving to live?" She thought of the determined green weeds out in the deadland, pushing up among the charred tree trunks.

"There's nothing wrong with striving to live. The angelbees never interfered with that, either."

"Then why did they come in the first place to touch off Armageddon? Why do they still keep us behind airwalls and burn off our ozone?"

Daniel was quiet. The pause lengthened, and the wind whistled outside. The scent of pine came from the fireplace. "I don't have an answer. If I did, if I felt called, then it would be much easier. Do you know the story of the Quaker who came to a very wicked city and was much troubled by its wickedness. When he could stand it no longer, he began to preach in the main square about the wickedness of the city. So the people promptly locked him in jail. In jail, he prayed to thank the Lord for setting him free."

"Well, our town isn't that wicked. There's no jail to put you in."

"No. No, there is no jail, here. Not in Gwynwood."

For some reason this made her uneasy. What sort of jail could he be thinking of? Did he want to get transported? "Daniel, what did you come here for?"

"I came . . . to see thee. Isn't that enough?"

"You ignored me for weeks. I thought you didn't like me anymore."

"No, that's impossible." His voice became lower, full of hurt. "If anything, I thought I might like you too well."

That puzzled her. "Why, Daniel?"

He said slowly, "It wouldn't be right. Dr. Chase said I might not live past thirty."

"But you're doing better on Keith's medicine."

"Better, for now. I still need to get to Sydney for a bone-marrow transplant."

"Anyway, who can ever be sure to live past thirty? I'll probably get melanoma by then."

To this Daniel said nothing.

She added, "You still have to marry somebody and have kids. If you die, you know they'll be looked after."

"The Specials are children enough, for me."

"So that's why you came back to me, is it—because I'm Special now?" Isabel was indignant. "Well, is it?"

"It's true." Daniel's voice was muffled, so she could barely hear. "I wished that you would be less 'perfect,' too, so I would have a right to ask."

"But—but that's silly. I only wished that you could be well."

"I know. But I can't help wishing dark things sometimes."

"Even you? No matter how many Specials you teach?"

"The darkness lives in all of us," Daniel said, steadier now. "When I forget, I need only face the souls behind the Wall."

"But we can't help them now. Nobody can."

"Our grandfathers could have, or our great-grandfathers."

"They didn't know what was coming."

"They had eyes to see and ears to hear. Our eyes and ears are theirs." The cushion lifted as Daniel stood up. "I think I'd best be going, to prepare the noon class."

She reached out to him, and he clasped her arm firmly.

"I'll come again, every day," he promised.

Isabel withdrew her arm. "I don't need charity, just because I'm Special."

"I'll come anyway if you get better."

She nodded, and some of the bitterness subsided. A sense of peace crept over her, as if a window had opened to another place. It was perhaps the first honest conversation they had ever shared.

XX

THE NEXT FEW days brought a stream of visitors. Peace Hope came by to play chess, and Daniel came back at four o'clock when he was done teaching the little ones. Ruth brought more Braille books for Isabel, Vera came to pray for her, and Matthew came to help her catch up on physics, painfully awkward though that was. Isabel, hating to be pitied, almost wished they would all stay away, except for Peace Hope and Daniel. Each morning Marguerite examined her eyes again, and for three days there was no change.

On the fourth day of December, while her mother was looking at her retina, a flicker of something appeared out of the fog. Isabel gasped. "I *saw* something; I know I did."

Marguerite brought the instrument close to Isabel's eyeball and set the switch on and off. The flicker of light came and went as she did so.

By the end of the week, her sight had recovered to the point that she could distinguish the faces around the dinner table. As Isabel's eyesight improved, she was milking the goats again and sorting apples from the second crop, and in the repair shop tacking insulation into the winterized frames of Ruth Weiss's beehives. She went back to physics and French class, although the reading gave her a headache. Daniel still came to visit every day.

One afternoon Keith had something to show her. "Where do you think this came from?"

It was a disk of rock crystal, a handbreadth across, polished smooth in the form of a lens, except for one jagged edge that had broken off. From the intact edges hung folds of tough membranous material. As Isabel turned it over in her palm, her scalp prickled. "It's from an angelbee? Not the one I..."

"Too right, mate; it's the one you popped. I found some pieces of it, mortal remains you might say, scattered on the floor. Did you know how the infrared eye works? A professor at the Uni figured it out. Look." He held up the lens. "A space cockie grows its lens out of rock salt, which transmits far infrared—that includes body heat radiation. Now to detect that radiation, there's a retina of sorts along the inner back side of the hydrogen balloon."

He held out another fragment of membrane, which felt something like a snakeskin, stretched out between his fingers. "This 'retina' is coated with pigmented sensory cells—they act like microscopic thermometers. They detect the image focused by the lens. The outer surface, however, is reflective, to avoid incident radiation." He turned the membrane over. Its other side reflected iridescently, with thousands of tiny scales that Isabel could see when she held it up to her eye.

"A giant eyeball full of methane and hydrogen."

"Mostly hydrogen," said Keith. "Methane absorbs some infrared."

"But the radio signals," said Isabel. "How do the angelbees transmit their signal?" She recalled that penetrating signal her receiver had picked up from the angelbee out in the graveyard.

"That's more of a mystery," Keith admitted. "At the Uni they found crystals of magnetite in the eyespot, rather like those found in pigeon brains. However the signal generator works, it must be contained in this thingo here." From his pocket he held out a brown fragment of chitinous stuff that looked like the same material as Becca's hexagonal scale. One surface, presumably that which faced the angelbee, was flat, whereas the outer surface was rounded like a breadloaf. In between there were supporting braces forming channels, presumably some sort of circulatory system. The outer surface had a flattened region that cut off at an obtuse angle, possibly a fragment of the hexagonal facet cut into it. "The scale would fit right there," Isabel decided.

"Right. I picked this up, too." Keith fished from his pocket a hexagonal scale with a pupil hole. A corner was crushed and broken off; otherwise, it looked just like the one in the candle box.

Isabel clapped a hand to her mouth. "It's a transmitter! The angelbees—they'll know, every time you touch it."

"I doubt it, mate. The space cockie it belonged to is dead."

He fitted the scale neatly into the broken corner of the eye-spot.

"Then it must have been the daughter I hit," Isabel observed, "since I still have the scale from the parent. The parent may still be around. Have you seen it?"

Keith shook his head. "Not a trace."

That was a relief. And yet, Isabel found herself vaguely disappointed; she almost missed her two followers. She kept watching for the parent, and one evening, she thought she glimpsed it hovering above the oak tree uphill, like Banquo's ghost to haunt her, but it did not come near. Isabel thought of the polyhedral keepers that lay in wait behind it and its sisters, coordinating their invisible tentacles across the landscape of Gwynwood. And yet, it was hard to think of angelbees as totally lacking individuality. Were they really just body parts, "obligate symbionts," or might they be able to exist on their own?

After physics class, Isabel showed Matthew the fragments that Keith had picked up from the angelbee eye. The lens caught his interest. "This could focus infrared," he said, turning the object over in his palm, "though the resolution would never be as good as ours in the visible."

"Couldn't the angelbees see our visible range, too?"

"I don't think so."

"Why not? Salt transmits visible light."

"The optics would be completely different. Remember how a prism spreads out the bent light rays at different wavelengths? To 'see' body heat, we're talking nine microns, a twentyfold increase in wavelength. I'd guess the angelbee's range of wavelength, like ours, is less than twofold; say, five to ten microns."

Isabel considered this. "In that case, how do they see in the daytime, when everything warms up?"

"The contrast would be lower, that's all. The sun itself would be barely noticeable."

"But sunlight is *warm;* you can feel it."

"That's due to absorption of visible light, converted to heat in your skin. That is how you start a fire with a glass lens. Sunlight peaks in the visible; beyond four microns, direct solar radiation is swamped by ambient heat emission.

You wouldn't see much shadow, either; you would see relative amounts of glow. Think of a stained-glass window, with glass panes of varying brightness: that's how it might look. At night, the contrast would be spectacular. People would literally glow like stars."

Isabel stared in shock. "That is what Becca wrote—*people shine like stars!* Do you see, they gave her infrared eyes." The terrible memories came back, and she had to sit down to steady herself. Why had the angelbees taken Becca—and why had she chosen to go? "It must be," she whispered.

"There's nothing you can do," Matthew said gently.

"Yes we can. We can demand Becca back, at the Pylon."

"She said she chose to go."

"I don't understand any of it. Why would they give her infrared eyes? As an experiment? Out of a guilty conscience? I think they've got no conscience at all. Why do they keep burning our sky?"

"That's a good question." Matthew rolled his eyes around. "I've always wondered why they bother. It would be so much simpler to inject nitrogen oxides into the upper atmosphere, as the bombs did. Instead, what they're doing looks like some kind of electrical discharge, which is more likely to create ozone than to destroy it."

"But the *Sydney Herald* says—" She recalled that Keith's opinion of the *Herald* was little better than Nahum's.

"I'm sure the *Herald's* right, Isabel. It's outside my field entirely."

Still, the seed of doubt was sown. Isabel felt frustrated. It was hopeless: the more she learned, the less she knew.

XXI

NOW THAT DANIEL was coming to visit every day, Isabel found she could think of little else. All morning she looked forward to his coming, and after he left she spent the evening reliving what they had said and done. Some days they walked out a bit in the orchard, but it was too cold to walk far. Daniel was always very proper; the *Pirate* book did not seem to apply at all.

In mid-December there was a warm spell, a bit of Indian summer. One day, Isabel set out on her bicycle at three-thirty to catch Daniel before he left home. A mild breeze ruffled her jacket. The ground had unfrozen and glistened wet in the dirt road, perhaps the last reminder of summer before the snow came. As the gables of the Scattergood house appeared through the tree branches, which were bare now but for a few crinkled brown leaves, Isabel's heart beat faster. She got off the bike, banged the kickstand hard, and tried to compose herself at the door.

Grace Feltman came to the door with her usual exaggerated grin. At Isabel's request, she stumbled off, calling, "Dan-iel!"

Daniel came to the door. He did not seem surprised to see her.

Isabel shifted her feet on the step. "I thought we might ride out for a picnic on the hill. This may be the last warm weather we get." She tried to keep the tension out of her voice.

Daniel said, "I'll get my bike." With a nod, he turned and went down to the garage.

A thrill of elation coursed through her veins. As she sped off beside him, the late-afternoon sun gleamed through the branches, a bluejay flew upward with a raucous shriek, and a rabbit tore off into the bushes, flashing its white puff tail. The light in the trees seemed to sparkle as it played across the branches. It seemed as if every piece of the day was in perfect place.

They stopped at the bank of the road across from the Trans' house where the trail winded upward into the pines. Isabel skipped uphill rapidly, breathing deeply the scent of the pines, her feet bouncing on the thick carpet of needle leaves. At the summit of Gwynwood Hill the cliff overlooked the Pylon, now inert except for its pale, shifting colors, casting a long shadow back toward the hill. She stopped and leaned into a birch trunk to catch her breath, wincing as a branch dug into her back.

Daniel came up and passed her, stepping over a log that had fallen across the path since last August. He stopped and looked out into the valley. He seemed not to notice her, watching the Pylon as if he could penetrate its secrets from afar.

Isabel rested in quiet, scraping her sole against the tree bark, until she could hold back no longer. She stepped forward tentatively over the log, and the crunch of pine needles underfoot seemed suddenly very loud. Reaching Daniel from behind, she raised her hand and caught him on the shoulder. She pulled him around and kissed him, hard, holding him so he could not break away. Then she felt his hands behind her shoulder blades, returning her embrace, and her head swam.

But then he withdrew and held her at arm's length. She read the familiar "no" in his eyes.

An unexpected bitterness welled up. "What's wrong with you?" she demanded. "Is it only broken things you can love?"

"In God's name, no. How could thee think so?" His voice was strange, a voice she had never heard before. "It's just that I long for thee too much. More than one should, for any one person. 'If this be death . . . I would woo death everlasting.'"

Isabel blinked at this, a little scared despite herself. "It's not too much for me. What else can you love, if not one person?"

He pulled her close and kissed her again, this time so hard it hurt. He drew her in at the waist as well; then they sank back into the grass and lay together for a long while, until the sun turned red and touched the horizon, spilling rays of blood across the far deadland.

When at last they drew apart, Isabel found the top buttons of her blouse had popped.

"I'm sorry," said Daniel. "I'll sew them back on for you."

"It's all right, really."

"Isabel," he said with a trace of impatience. "Thee is good at giving gifts, but thee has to learn to receive as well."

She smiled. "Well in that case, Friend, thee'll have to give me thy shirt to wear home." Hearing no objection, she undid the rest of the buttons and exchanged the blouse for his shirt, which fit a bit loose but well enough. Daniel folded the blouse neatly and tucked it into his knapsack.

"Thee'll have to explain," Isabel added, "what a hot day it was, to go shirtless."

XXII

THE NEXT FEW days passed like a dream. Wherever she went she felt Daniel in her thoughts, as if he breathed just behind her shoulder. Yet when they met together, she would freeze, thinking it was impossible; he could not really have accepted her, it was all a mistake. So each time they embraced again it was almost like new, like the first time, like Christmas morning every day. "*La lumière de l'arbre de Noël...*"

A dusting of snow appeared one morning, enough to scrape up a snowball or two. The temperature took a serious dive, and at home the family had to huddle around the wood stove. Peewee and her children slept on top of one another in a great ball of fur, snug in the corner of the cage. Surface-to-volume ratio, conserving body heat, thought Isabel, recalling the lesson out of *College Physics*.

One afternoon she went out with Daniel to cut Christmas trees, one each for the Scattergood and Garcia-Chase households. They picked two well-proportioned Scotch pines from behind the Meetinghouse, sawed them off and hauled them onto the carriages. In the meantime they carried on an old debate about the Quaker colonial hero, John Dickinson. "I still don't see why he refused to help the war effort," Isabel insisted. "He could have at least run an ambulance or something. What should the colonists have done—accept British rule forever?" She pulled the ropes tight around the tree, securing it in the carriage.

"John Dickinson considered himself an Englishman," said Daniel. "He had grievances against the Crown. He led the economic fight against taxation and essentially won, well before Independence Day."

"But King George was a tyrant. If we had all followed Dickinson, we'd be ruled by tyrants to this day."

"At least they would be human tyrants." Daniel smiled briefly. "Human tyrants always fall. It is God's will." He rested his arm upon the cut trunk and looked across at her.

Their eyes met for a long moment. "Thee knows I can't take this much longer, Isabel. Will we be married?"

"Oh yes!" She threw her arms around him and they hugged tight, awkwardly with their bulky jackets squeezed between. "But not for a while, yet," she added. "I want to finish college first."

Daniel looked down as if he had something difficult to say. "I know, I want to finish college, too. The trouble is, if we're to have children, it may as well be now, while I'm still here to help thee raise them."

The sense of his words chilled her. She had never looked at it that way before. She felt slightly sick. "You can't think like that, Daniel. We'll get you to Sydney...somehow."

There had to be a way. If someone destroyed the Hive of the angelbees, Keith had said, then the Walls would fall. But where was this Hive; and how was it to be stormed? There was no God to come out with a miracle and throw down the Walls.

The words came back: *"Like all walls, it was ambiguous, two-faced..."* The little airwall around the Pylon was somehow the real way out. She would have to find out how.

On the Friday before Christmas, the night of the December new moon, the townspeople gathered around the Pylon. The sun had set an hour before, and snow was falling thickly in huge fluffy flakes. The Scattergoods were there, including Nahum, and the Browns, wrapped up in blankets to keep warm. Anna Tran was there, but Carl and Debbie were home with the children and baby Patience. It was a hard time for the Drehers, for Charity was still bedridden, and she needed special tests which the doctors upstairs could not provide.

Isabel squeezed Daniel's gloved hand, and watched the snow fall around the airwall of the Pylon. It was curious to watch the flakes falling directly above it part and veer outward, descending along the shape of the airwall. The same thing still happened above the outer Wall, too. An enormous rampart of snow would accumulate above the skeletons, twenty feet of solid whiteness, enclosing Gwynwood like the wall of Jericho. The snow that fell here, inside, came entirely from water condensed beneath the outer Wall's dome.

Around the Pylon, its unearthly platform was bare, while the blanket of snow thickened outside. The black plastic package for Sydney, full of Peace Hope's stamps and orders for medicines, sat in the snow at right leaning into the air-wall.

A few angelbees hovered, watching the people; unlike the earlier gathering at the Pylon, there was no fire to scare them away. One of them veered alongside the airwall, then it casually penetrated the curve of falling snow.

Isabel frowned and squinted at the spot where the angel-bee had entered the Pylon's domain. In its wake, the angelbee had left behind a disturbance in the trajectory of the falling snowflakes. Some of the flakes were actually falling straight downward, through the airwall, to land upon the smooth platform supporting the Pylon. For a minute or so, Isabel watched the flakes trickle in, until they vanished, their invisible entrance presumably closed off.

She blinked and rubbed her eyes, wondering if she had imagined it. But there on the platform lay a scattering of snowflakes, already melting into dark wet spots. The Pylon's domain must be warmer than outside. In fact, it could be an entirely other place, like Alice's Looking-glass Land, connected to this place at the interface of the airwall.

The angelbee meanwhile appeared to be retracing its path, to come out through the airwall once more. Isabel watched intently to see whether the snowflakes would penetrate again.

At the airwall, on its way out, the angelbee vanished. This time no snowflakes got through.

"Daniel! That angelbee just disappeared—instead of coming out here. It must have gone somewhere—some other 'here,' where there's no snow. A Looking-glass Land, connected to 'here,' at the airwall."

Daniel nodded but said nothing. She knew he was tense, awaiting the appearance within the Pylon. Beyond the tree-tops the last traces of sunlight faded away, leaving only the stuffy blackness of snow-filled sky. The cold deepened, and Isabel stepped up and down to keep warm. There was no telling whether anything would happen, since Daniel was not alone. The snow tapered off, and the clouds parted overhead revealing a pair of stars.

The kernel of redness appeared in the Pylon, insulated at first, like a honeybee larva curled up in its cell.

There were gasps from the people gathered, and hasty whisperings. "Let's be silent," warned Liza.

The red glow grew until it filled the Pylon. A pattern emerged, of oval shapes against a mottled background. Isabel peered at it, trying to figure out what it was. Behind her came questioning whispers.

"They're honeybees," said Liza.

Of course: now she could see the striped bees on a comb. In a minute or so, the picture shifted; there appeared to be flowers, with worker bees gathering nectar. There were several shifts more, each a still view of bees in one activity or another. Bees were a favorite subject of the Pylon's visions, Alice had said. It had never been quite clear what message, if any, the bees were intended to represent. Did the angelbees (or their keepers) see themselves as solicitous workers, tending their human brood?

An apple tree appeared, with no sign of bees. It was an older tree; Isabel recognized the thick crooked side branch that bent so low its foliage brushed the ground. It was at the far end of the orchard, near the spring.

The picture changed: flames of a bonfire, not unlike the fires that had surrounded the Pylon on the night of the witness against the burning sky. Then it changed again, back to apple trees, a view of the same area by the spring, at a slightly different angle. The pictures shifted, back and forth, twice more.

"The apples must be hot." Marguerite's voice was unsteady. "The trees nearest the spring must have picked up hot water from underground. I thought they tested okay, but we'll have to run the counter over every bushel."

Liza said, "I think this means that we should burn the crop."

"Burn and starve?" Marguerite said bitterly. "By official standards, everything we eat should be condemned."

Before anyone could answer, there was something different in the Pylon. It was something flat and angular, a machine of some sort, although the details were blurred. Then it changed, to an image of the Pylon itself. The Pylon's image had another Pylon within, and so on, like a mirror trick.

"That one Alice saw before," Liza remembered. "When we had to give up things."

Carl said, "Yes, that was years ago. All those radios and TV sets."

"It's not my radio," Isabel said quickly. Her radio was long gone.

The machine reappeared, at a different angle. Isabel clapped a hand to her mouth. "It's the fetal monitor!"

"Goodness," said Vera, "no wonder so many angelbees were pestering us the night Patience was born."

"It can't be," Marguerite insisted. "The fetal monitor was for sale, right in the paper."

"No wonder it was marked down," said Keith in a tone of disgust. "Sorry, I should have guessed. Its frequency must interfere with the bloody space cockies."

The Pylon-within-a-Pylon reappeared, then the machines returned once again. People shook their heads, and someone muttered, "We ought to get our money back."

There were gasps of surprise, and Isabel clutched Daniel's arm. *It was Becca Weiss.*

Becca was standing quietly in her familiar denim skirt, her hair tied back as usual. There was no sign of alteration in her sightless eyes, the lids half closed.

"Where *is* she?" someone demanded. The background was indistinct; for that matter, it could have been a picture of her in Gwynwood from any time before she had disappeared. It was almost unbearable to watch her image, as though she were really there and could somehow step out of the Pylon.

In a minute the ruddy image was gone. In its place stood a pair of deer, two young does, grazing in a field. Then there was a flock of birds in an oak tree; then a possum on the ground, sniffing with its pointed nose; then a hexagonal patterning, what looked like larval brood cells of a honeycomb. Becca reappeared, so did other birds, and some kind of frog, and even a sheep.

Isabel looked to Liza, whose face could barely be made out

in the darkness. But Liza had no clue to their meaning. Even Alice had never reported such visions.

"Those birds," Marguerite observed. "Scarlet tanagers, I could have sworn. But they're extinct, here."

"The tree frogs, too," someone else added.

There were more scenes, including several more of brood combs. Then abruptly the Pylon went blank. In another minute, its outline became blurred as billows of fog swirled around it, growing within the airwall.

Andrés grabbed her arm. "Get out, for Christ's sake. Before the *verdammt'* fog puts us to sleep."

Everyone made a hasty retreat, recalling what had happened on the night of the bonfire. Isabel left with reluctance, thinking what on Earth could the keepers have done with Becca to connect her with birds, sheep, and extinct tree frogs. And where were her infrared eyes?

That airwall—there was a way to get through. And she, Isabel, was going to do it.

XXIII

ON SATURDAY MORNING, the black package had been replaced as usual by one from Sydney. At the Scattergoods', Isabel perused the pages of the *Herald*, along with Daniel and Peace Hope, and Teacher Matthew and several others, all eager for the latest city news. The harbour area was being rebuilt. There was a suspect in the case, still at large, a leader of an Underground group known as the Shades. The Shades had claimed responsibility for the blast at the Wall. The name of the suspect was Dirk Brendan, a transportee from Vista, the Wall-town on America's West Coast. A blurred photograph was published, of a fair-haired man wearing mirrorshades. Isabel studied the photograph with interest, poor though it was. She had never seen an Underground man in the paper before. Their activities were getting too big to ignore.

Isabel exchanged pages with Matthew, who had been looking at the science column. "This should interest you," Matthew said, "on medical thermography for detection of cancers."

"That sounds like something the hospital could use." She looked up at him. "How did you like those 'visions' in the Pylon? What sort of technology could possibly make them?"

"Actually, they didn't impress me much." He flipped the page over. "Why only still shots? Any video set can do better. I guess you didn't grow up with television."

Isabel recalled watching a video screen of some sort, once when she was small, before the angelbees had claimed them all. "Well, they must think we're rather primitive. Simple stuff is good enough for us chimps."

"Or else they're just not used to working with visible light. Suppose we had to design an infrared TV set..." Matthew shook his head. "It shouldn't be that hard. They've had twenty years at least."

"They must be a decadent race."

"No Yankee ingenuity." He grinned at her, and she was

glad to see him cheerful for a change, less withdrawn into his own thoughts.

Then it flashed into her head, her own bit of ingenuity from the night before: a way to get in at the Pylon, by plunging in after an angelbee. If only there were a way to get the "hole" to stay open...

Absently she dropped the newspaper and stood up, turning over ideas in her head. As she turned to leave the sitting room, Daniel caught her arm. "Where is thee going, Isabel?"

She turned to face him. He knew so well when she was cooking up something. "I'm going to take another look at the Pylon."

"I'll come with thee."

She said more quietly, "I intend to break into the Pylon."

"I'll come."

With a deep breath, she said, "All right, then. *Vamos.*"

The crust of the snow sparkled in the sunlight in the field where the Pylon stood. Boot prints crisscrossed the area, and several folding chairs were left over from the night before. The Pylon was no longer quite the sacred place it had been for so long.

It was impossible to get the carriage through the snow, so Isabel had trudged out with the coil of rope over her arm, with an old skillet tied to one end for weight. Daniel had carried it part of the way; even so, now her shoulder was sore. She massaged it, hoping it would not affect the aim of her throw.

"What now?" asked Daniel.

"We wait for angelbees." There were none in sight, so far. Isabel inspected the airwall closely. Around its perimeter, the snow had melted back a few inches. Inside, the otherworldly platform gleamed like polished metal.

"Surely they'll stop us," Daniel said. "How could they not? I think it's unwise, Isabel."

"We'll be off again before they get us. They're always slow to react." Unwise he might say, yet Daniel would follow her nonetheless, just as he had on that night in August when the skystreaking began.

She set down the coil of rope a few feet from the perimeter. Then she swung the skillet overhead a few times, testing her arm.

Daniel in the meantime had sat in one of the folding chairs and was reading from *Le Petit Prince;* their final exam was Monday. Isabel dropped the skillet to rest, and she stepped back to read over his shoulder. It was near the ending, the part that made least sense of all. The Little Prince, sitting atop an old ruined stone wall, was conversing with a golden snake that reared its head from the sand. He was asking the snake for a deadly bite; and, somehow, his death was to carry him back to his own little planet with his baobabs, his three volcanoes, and his one beloved rose.

Isabel shook her head and looked up toward the Pylon. The angelbees had come at last; two, she counted, then a third one, hovering overhead. "There, Daniel, they've come to snoop on us. Come on, you can help me out now."

"Don't we have to wait till one of them crosses the airwall?"

"We'll give them some encouragement." Isabel tied the other end of the rope to a chair leg, and she pounded the chair into the earth to anchor it. Then she took out a box of matches. "When I give the word, you light the match. It's a good bet those angelbees will take fright and scoot right out the airwall."

Daniel looked uneasy. "We don't want to hurt them."

"No, silly. Just give them a quick scare, that's all. We can't wait all day."

He looked away. A wisp of hair strayed gently beneath his hat, lifting in the breeze. But his mouth was set in that stern way.

"It's just a match," Isabel said quietly. "Like lighting a candle. Remember, we have to find Becca."

His face wrinkled in anxious lines. Reluctantly he took the matchbox.

Isabel picked up the skillet with the rope trailing behind. An angelbee sailed lazily overhead, a little too fast to manage. She would wait for one that moved a bit more slowly. At last another one came, closer, so close that the sun glinting off its surface made her eyes squint. "Okay, ready—now."

A crackling sound; behind her, the match was lit. Above her head, the angelbee moved through the airwall. It hung inside briefly, then its form became a black disk that shrank away to nothing.

With all her strength, Isabel heaved the skillet upward, into the spot where the angelbee had disappeared.

The skillet paused in midair and seemed to hang there for just a moment. Then it fell inside with a clatter, upon the platform. Behind it, the rope had uncoiled and flowed up through the unseen hole. Then it slowed, and the upper stretch sank a bit, still suspended as if by some magic thread.

"It's through! We've poked a hole!"

"No." Daniel grabbed her arm. "Isabel, let's keep away from—whatever it is. It must be dangerous."

But Isabel pulled away from him. "It's just a hole. The angelbees go back and forth all the time..." How big was the hole? It was flexible enough; she could pull the rope down and sideways, and the suspended stretch moved along the airwall.

She stepped slowly into the airwall, feeling its pressure, then she moved her arm alongside the stretch of rope. Along the rope, the pressure lessened. Then, quite without warning, the airwall gave way, and she stumbled to the foot of the Pylon. Her mouth gaped open as she stared upon the smooth surface with its pale, swirling colors, just within reach. She raised an arm but did not dare to touch.

"Isabel!" From behind her Daniel was calling. "Isabel, does thee hear me? For the love of God, please come back."

"It's okay, I'm coming."

Isabel grabbed the rope again, and retraced her path, this time feeling the pressure in. For a moment, there was panic; she could be trapped in here...

And then there was dark. In an instant day turned to night as Isabel tumbled forward onto the floor of a dimly lit corridor. The air was full of a mist that cut off her vision beyond a few paces. No snow, no Daniel; only her own shadow, cast from a light source somewhere behind her.

Isabel cried out. She turned, and found that she stumbled for some reason, unable to keep her balance; she felt as if she had lost half her weight.

There was the Pylon. It had stood there behind her, and

the light came from within the circle of its airwall; its platform was a gleaming disk set in the dark floor. Its only source of light was Earth's sunlight. The skillet still lay there, its rope seemingly cut off at the perimeter.

The sight of this familiar object calmed her and helped get her brain working again. Of course, that was how the angelbees had done it the night before: first they crossed into the Pylon's domain, then they turned and came out somewhere else. It was just like Heinlein's tesseract story, where the two universes came together at an "edge," and you could go either way.

She reached for the end of the rope, the airwall pressing back on her. At last she grasped the rope and pulled it toward her. The skillet grated across the platform. When its handle reached her hand, the airwall gave way. She plunged through, turned and escaped back into the sunlit snow.

Daniel threw his arms around her and held her so hard it hurt.

"I got in," she gasped. "I found the other place."

"Thee got out again, that's the main thing."

"It was a dark corridor, and my feet felt light. Maybe it was their Hive, in the satellite! Maybe there are other pylons down the corridor..."

Daniel pointed behind her. "Look."

The fog was creeping into the airwall from all sides. Someone inside had noticed something amiss.

"Run for it." The two of them ran to the road as fast as they could, stomping through the snow. When Isabel at last dared look back, the fog remained largely confined to the airwall, only a few puffs escaping.

"My dad will be mad at the loss of that rope," said Isabel.

"He was lucky not to lose a great deal more."

Isabel bit her lip and said nothing. Perhaps it was crazy to follow the angelbees and their keepers into their own place. There had to be a way to do so, without getting caught, some way to creep inside unnoticed, like mice behind the barn walls.

That afternoon Isabel spent in the microbiology lab with Keith, processing vats of bacteria making ampicillin and erythromycin. The filtrate containing the antibiotics went straight onto the columns for concentration. It was a taxing job, and by evening Isabel was barely awake enough to read.

Sometime after sundown, there came a knock on the door. It was Terri Tran, her straight black hair cropped short around her face, so serious as she delivered her message. "My mom says you'd better come quick," said Terri. "There's a message for you in the Pylon."

"But—why? How do you know it's for me?"

"Mom says come *now*."

In the Pylon, as Isabel's family looked on with the Scattergoods and the Trans, ruddy images flashed, one after another. The first was simply Isabel herself, with Daniel, a red-tinted "snapshot" that could have come from anywhere. The second was the image of the nested pylons, one within another within another, *ad infinitum*. The two scenes alternated ceaselessly, just as they had for the fetal monitor.

XXIV

THE NEXT MORNING was the last Sunday before Christmas. The temperature had dropped below freezing, and in the Meetinghouse the window cracks were stuffed with rags, and the fire was crackling in the wood stove. Isabel wore a pair of jeans under her skirt and a jacket of her mother's that predated Doomsday. Debbie held up the woolen-wrapped bundle that was baby Patience, while Miracle and Charity and Faith wore hand-knit sweaters and scarves. Charity's little cardigan had been worn by the Tran boy the year before, handed down by most of the Gwynwood children before that. The Pestlethwaite twins had not gotten new boots this year; they had layers of thick stockings stretched over their shoes.

During the time of silence, all that Isabel could think of was the ominous message in the Pylon. That she and Daniel must be "given up" to the angelbees, like a forbidden radio—surely the town could not consent to such a thing.

And yet, the town had never before refused a request of the Pylon. Would they do so now? At what cost?

With a shudder she gripped the cold wood of the bench, then she flexed her fingers to keep them from getting stiff.

What would Daniel say, she wondered. It was she who had dragged him into this. Nonetheless, he seemed to have taken the news calmly. She recalled the story he had told before, of the Quaker who was thrown in prison and thanked the Lord for setting him free. Quakers had always said, there exists a law higher than the law of man. Was that true of the angelbees as well?

The programmed service began, and Carl led the singing of the Advent carol:

"O come, O come, Emmanuel,
And ransom captive Israel,
That mourns in lonely exile here
Until the Son of God appear."

It was sung every Christmas, and Isabel knew the alto part by heart. But now she found herself choking over the words. Would this be the last Christmas she would ever see?

After the service, Liza opened an emergency Meeting to deal with the crisis. The mood was somber; no one felt confident to say what should be done.

Anna ventured a suggestion. "What if we ignore the Pylon? Let the two youngsters keep safe at home."

There was silence as everyone pondered this thought.

Keith slowly shook his head. "I doubt we'd get away with it. One way or another, the space cockies will get what they want. People have disappeared before."

"How?" Anna asked. "Can angelbees drag them from their homes?"

There was silence again. Isabel thought of the polyhedral creature that Peace Hope had drawn. It had legs, but no sign of grasping arms.

Carl Dreher rose to speak at last. "What can we say? What recourse do we have? We can pray for the two youngsters, as we did for Becca, but beyond that—" He shook his head. "I know this sounds hard, but at least this time we know that we ourselves brought on the wrath of our masters."

At that, Isabel felt bad again; that "we" was really just herself, endangering the whole town. But then her mother rose so swiftly that Isabel jumped in her seat. "Is that all you have to say?" Marguerite demanded. "Do you love our masters so well?"

Carl's brows knit and he reddened. "They are kind masters, on the whole," he said a little louder. "Perhaps kinder than we deserve."

"What good is it to have kind masters, if we remain slaves?" Marguerite's chest heaved with agitation. "I know what's at stake. They can cut us off from Sydney; they can hunt the entire town. But what will become of us, if we never take a stand? The next generation will never have known life without angelbees. The generation after will know no history, only legends. Then, if our masters ever desert us, how shall we do without them?"

At that everyone seemed to want to speak at once. Debbie tried to stand, but Miracle tugged at her skirt, overexcited by the fuss. "Mommy, there's only one God," his voice piped with six-year-old literalness. "That's what Teacher Daniel says. God is big and strong. God can do anything, just like the angelbees."

Daniel turned pale and squeezed Isabel's hand again. That was not exactly what he taught, Isabel suspected. In a burst of comprehension she saw why he refused to become Contact. It gave her a cold feeling in the pit of her stomach. Her mother was right, she knew; they had accepted the angelbees, and they depended on them more deeply with every passing year, every spring that the Pylon told when to plant the crops. But would the children grow up thinking angelbees were God?

Liza said meditatively, "It's true, is it not. The angelbees have become our gods, our angels. For our grandchildren, angelbees may be the only gods they know. That was the fear that haunted Alice before she died."

"I say, what choice do we have?" Carl insisted. "We're trapped; we're as helpless as animals in a cage. What can we do—blast a hole through the Wall?"

"No," called out Keith. "Don't try that nonsense, please. Whatever you do, please don't leave a heap of casualties for us poor doctors to clean up."

Daniel said, "I will go. I asked for it, and I'll take the consequences."

Isabel's heart pounded. "I'll go, too," she called out.

"No." Anna Tran glared from one to the other. "You can't think of just giving up. Who will my children have to live with, if not yours? I've a mind to throw a cover over that Pylon and ignore its silly visions."

After that, everyone wanted to talk at once and little more was accomplished. The Meeting broke up as people dispersed to finish digging out from the snow and prepare for Christmas. Isabel was still too stunned to think of anything, even getting out the tinsel garlands for the hallway. The vision in the Pylon reappeared that night, and the next, Anna reported.

"What do you think?" Isabel asked Keith hopefully. "Maybe if we stay away, they'll forget about us?"

Keith shook his head. "Not bloody likely. They'll get you,

one way or another, by the next new moon."

"But how?"

"It's not clear. I told you, they keep their distance from Sydney; it's too populous. I only know what the transportees have to say."

Isabel pondered her fate. "Maybe I should ask for 'last rites' before it happens."

Keith chuckled. "There's a thought. Seriously, though, I'm sure they'll treat you well. They treat us all so very well, don't they—and at what expense. If only we knew what for." He looked past her with sudden intensity.

"That doesn't mean they'll treat me and Daniel well. Maybe they picked us as specimens to dissect."

"No, surely not. For that, they wait for deaths, I think. They've been rumored to take fresh bodies now and then."

Isabel stared in horror, thinking of the angelbees that had waited above the grave of Alice.

"Come, Isabel. Stop thinking that way, eh? It's nearly Christmas. Try to cheer up, if only for the sake of your poor mom."

Reluctantly she half smiled. "Right. Thanks a lot, Keith."

She tried to console herself by watching the Christmas tree, whose lights seemed extra precious this year. She unpacked the creche from the attic and set it up as usual, fingering all the lovely animal figures. The exquisite hand-carved set had been bought in Italy by her grandmother. There were sheep, oxen, asses, camels, even chickens. She always wondered, though, why so many animals would have welcomed the birth of the Christ child. Christ had done little for them.

Every year, the challenge was to come up with something new in the way of gifts or cards, something better than jars of honey tied with ribbons. This year, Isabel came up with microbial Christmas cards. She streaked red Serratia cultures onto green-tinted agar, forming the words "Merry Christmas," then dried the grown plates in the oven. The agar popped out of the plates in shiny disks, almost like miniature stained-glass windows. Everyone was much amused, except her father.

"Bacteria belong in the barn," grumbled Andrés on Christmas morning, "not in my clean house."

"But bacteria work for us," Isabel reminded him. "They make our antibiotics now."

"Bacteria make antibiotics? What will we see next, I wonder." Then he stopped and hugged her fiercely. "I'm sorry, Belita; it's just too much to bear."

Isabel fled before the tears came. Later she spent a quiet hour with Daniel, walking through the snow. The trees hung with ice that sparkled, and their heavy boughs drooped almost to the ground.

"I've been thinking, Daniel." She kept her eyes on her feet as she walked, not daring to look at him. "Perhaps we ought to get married after all. It may be the last chance we get."

"I hope that's not the only reason."

She stopped in her tracks. "Of course not," she told him indignantly.

Daniel drew her in for a kiss. "I'm forever grateful," he said with a smile. "I could not have held out much longer. At least thee has saved me from a life of sin!"

XXV

THE WEDDING PLANS were quickly arranged. Isabel had worried that her parents, and the Scattergoods, might object to the unseemly haste, but to her surprise everyone was immediately enthusiastic. The service would be held the Saturday after New Year's. Sal and Jon, too, announced a Christmas engagement, although they would be married next spring.

Peace Hope came over to congratulate her. Up in Isabel's room, she took off her arms and legs and bounced on the bed, just like the old days. "Thee is so lucky, Isabel."

"Lucky? To be married till the next new moon—then what?"

"Well, at this rate that's longer than I'll ever be."

"Oh, Scatterbrain." Isabel stroked Peace Hope's long blond hair. "Someday, you'll find your Stephen Hawking out there."

"Yes, but how?" Peace Hope stared at her with sudden intensity. "Isabel, would thee give me the eyespot scale?"

Isabel blinked and sat back. "You know it's too dangerous."

"But I want it. I want to try, at least, to discover its power. It must hold the key to our freedom; thee knows that. Thee must pass it on to me, as Becca did to thee."

Aghast, Isabel did not know what to say.

"Why should I not?" Peace Hope went on quickly. "Suppose they go after me; why not? They have a peace testimony, I'm sure of it."

"I can't," she blurted. "Scatterbrain, I'm sorry. Daniel would never forgive me."

Peace Hope looked away again. Then she looked back, her face once more the picture of sunshine. "Thee's as good as a mother, Isabel."

This odd compliment warmed her heart, yet it left her somehow disquieted. With all her own happiness, she ached to think how little she could do for her friend.

* * *

It was agreed that after the wedding Isabel would move out to the Scattergoods' where she and Daniel would have Grandmother Alice's old rooms until they fixed up a place of their own. It made sense, as the Chases' house with the hospital upstairs had gotten a bit crowded since Keith moved in.

Out in the barn, her last morning for milking, Isabel brought the mouse cage and set it down in the straw. With Andrés and the wide-eyed sheep looking on, Isabel ceremoniously opened the cage door.

The mice did not notice right away. Isabel rattled the cage a bit until they came alive and slipped out one by one. They disappeared into the barn walls, all but Peewee herself, who showed no interest in leaving. Isabel had to pick her out of the cage and set her down. Peewee's nose wiggled a lot as she sniffed her new surroundings. Then she crept back into her cage and crawled back into her nest of shredded paper.

"Let her be," murmured Andrés. "I'll look after her."

This was a surprise. Her father was hardly one for pets, believing that animals should earn their keep one way or another.

"Dad, it won't be that bad," she reassured him with a hug. "I'm only moving just up the road." She winced, hoping somehow that would be true.

The wedding took place on Tuesday morning, conducted in the manner of Friends. The dress, from her grandmother's wedding, was an inch short on Isabel, and a bit discolored from age, but still it looked striking compared to everyday jeans and homespun. Daniel had also come up with a suit that looked remarkably good. The couple waited outside in the foyer as the rest of the town took seats. Isabel shivered despite a double layer of stockings beneath her dress.

When everyone else was seated, the couple walked in. The benches had been arranged traditionally, with four sets of rows facing inward. The couple was to sit together in the central reserved place. Isabel sat, without looking at Daniel but intensely aware of him next to her. Her eyes glanced over the facing rows across to where the Scattergoods were seated. Beside Liza sat Nahum Scattergood, here in the "steeplehouse" for the first time since it was erected after Doomsday. Isabel swallowed hard, realizing how strongly Nahum must feel to come and support them here.

The Quaker tradition was for the couple to sit in silence until the moment of inspiration, when they rose and recited the vows to each other. No clergyman was present, of course, just as for regular silent worship; or, as Liza used to say, everyone present was a minister. Sal had once laughed and said that if Quakers did it that way, it was a wonder any of them ever went through with a marriage. Acutely self-conscious, Isabel could appreciate this point as the next few minutes stretched and lengthened. She stole a glance at the side table, where the wedding certificate that Peace Hope had lettered would soon be signed by all present.

At last Daniel gripped her hand, and they both rose. Daniel said, "In the presence of God and these our friends, I, Daniel Jacoby, take thee, Isabel Garcia-Chase, to be my wife, promising with Divine assistance to be unto thee a loving and faithful husband so long as we both shall live."

Isabel swallowed, wondering, would she get it all right? "In the presence of God and these our friends," she began, in a voice that sounded unlike her own, "I, Isabel Garcia-Chase, take thee, Daniel Jacoby, to be my husband, promising with Divine assistance to be unto thee a loving and faithful wife so long as we both shall live."

They exchanged rings. The rings were a matching pair of gold bands, left to Daniel by his parents, who had known he could never afford to buy his own. It gave her pause for thought, how after all these years, somehow, the dead still looked after the living.

XXVI

FOR ISABEL, ONE of the nicest things about married life was waking up to find Daniel's arm across her and the sunlight streaming through his hair. It reminded her again of that bizarre scene in Melville when the narrator shared a bed with a friendly cannibal; the incongruity of it made her laugh to herself.

Otherwise, her daily routine changed rather less than she expected. She had always spent half her time at the Scattergoods' anyway. Except for the milking, most of her chores remained the same: mopping the hospital floors, making up the medicines and diagnostics, and fixing whatever came into her workshop. She considered moving her workshop but decided it was not worth the trouble.

The Pylon was still flashing its message every night about herself and Daniel. After several difficult Meetings, the town agreed to implement Anna's proposal. Anna stitched together an immense cover out of old sheets and burlap. It took several people to pull the cover up over the airwall around the Pylon. Once up, it hung there like the cap of an overgrown mushroom.

Isabel was skeptical of this device. The cloth used was probably not opaque to the far infrared, and besides, she thought, it would only disappear the next day.

In fact, however, the cover remained in place for several days. This raised her hopes enough to start talking with Daniel about what it would take to fix up one of the abandoned houses in the spring. Every household in Gwynwood would contribute a month's allowance to the project.

Then in mid-January, a few days before the new moon, the angelbees reappeared, following the two of them as if keeping them in sight lest they escape.

Isabel watched the angelbees apprehensively, with Daniel's comforting arm around her. Slowly she shook her head. "I just can't figure it out. What do they expect of us?"

"They want to transport us," Daniel said.

"And if we refuse? If we just don't show up at the Pylon? The keepers don't even have arms to drag us off."

Isabel returned to the attic with the books, reading until the candles melted away and her fingers turned to ice. She reread the ant story, then returned to the biology text to dig out more about symbiosis. There were birds that picked ticks off of rhinoceri; a tree that fed and housed ants who protected it from predation; algae that fed fungi, and others that lived inside coral. Most bizarre was *Mixotricha*, a mixed-up protozoan that lived inside termite guts. *Mixotricha* had bacteria living within itself to digest all the cellulose from the wood the termite ate, thereby feeding both protozoan and termite host. To get about inside the termite, *Mixotricha* had long spiral bacteria attached to its surface which rotated to propel the protozoan.

It turned out that even human cells and their mitochondria had evolved from symbionts. When Isabel read that, she dropped the book and coughed at the cloud of dust it raised. The next day she took a break to see Peace Hope.

"You know, Scatterbrain, I don't think I believe half of what's in those books. They make less sense than the *Herald*."

Peace Hope, who had tired of cardinals, was penning extinct hummingbirds on her stamps. The first shipment had sold well, and she had orders for a dozen more. Maybe the Pestlethwaite girls could finally get new boots. "I feel the same. That is why I always return to the Bible."

"You mean Jael and Sisera?" Isabel shook her head. "I don't trust a word in print."

"Then thee agrees with Plato."

"I agree with me, and that's all. Seeing is believing; I'll never see mitochondria, that's for sure. If only I could figure out how..." How Becca had learned to see—if she had. Isabel pulled the eyespot scale out of her pocket.

Peace Hope gasped, "The signal! They'll know—"

"So what? They already know where to find me." She glanced out the window, where half a dozen angelbees crowded to peer inside. Then she turned the scale over in her palm, fingering its smooth surface, poking her index finger through the pupil hole.

"Isabel, before anything happens..."

"What?"

"Thee must leave it with me."

"The scale?" Isabel took in a sharp breath. "I told you. You'll end up like me."

"Maybe not. Maybe I'll learn something. I'll read those books, too; there must be something true in them. Thee knows, the scale is the key to what Becca found out."

"And what became of Becca? Is she 'extinct' like the tree frogs?"

"They gave Becca eyes. The worst they can do is give me arms and legs."

Isabel looked away. Slowly she turned the scale over once more, then she set it down upon Peace Hope's shelf next to the Red Queen. Unexpectedly, the act released a flood of fear inside her. She felt certain, now, something really was going to happen to her at the next new moon.

"Oh, Isabel—I'm so frightened for thee." Peace Hope rubbed her eyes with the shell of her gripper-arm. "I'm so sorry, I can't help it. If they take thee and Daniel away, like Becca, how will I ever know what happened? 'Le mouton oui ou non a-t-il mangé la fleur?'" Would the Little Prince's rose survive his sheep, or not?

Isabel hugged her tight. "It's all my fault. I just wanted so badly to get us out of here, out to civilization. I tried so hard."

"If you do go, will you get them to send us back a message? Send a picture of a sheep in the Pylon, if you're okay."

"I'm going nowhere without a fight, that's for sure." Isabel sat up straight. "I won't give myself up at the Pylon. Let's see what they can do about that."

Her friends offered support in their own characteristic ways. Keith insisted that she stock up for a trip, just as he had when he got transported. Vials of antibiotics, analgesics, contraceptives, and Daniel's anemia medicine went into her pockets. She did not ask what would happen when they ran out.

"There's just one thing more." Keith took a small pillbox from his pocket. It contained two tablets. "One for you and one for Daniel. Final friends."

It took her a moment to figure out what he meant.

"Are you *serious?*"

"Absolutely. They were for me, originally, in case I found the bush just too much to bear. But it suits me fine now, thanks mainly to you and your mom and dad."

"I see," she whispered. Her lip twitched. "You and Mother. Are all you doctors murderers then, in the end?"

"*Pace*, Hippocrates. What else could one do for the dying after D-Day?"

Isabel shuddered. "I won't give up that easily. How about matches? That's the one thing angelbees are afraid of."

"Have this." Keith pulled out a metal object the size of a fat pencil. It took a minute for Isabel to recognize it as a cigarette lighter. Keith had not smoked since the day he arrived in Gwynwood.

Matthew paid a call on Isabel, and they spoke for some minutes about her science classes over the years. It seemed to her that he had something on his mind to tell her.

"You know," he said abruptly, "I've been thinking about the airwall, that night when the snowflakes were falling through." He sounded puzzled. "It's rather odd that no one ever noticed that before, in twenty years."

"Nobody ever looked before, besides Alice. She wasn't exactly one for scientific curiosity."

"That's not quite fair to Alice. Besides, you weren't the first to watch the Pylon from afar with binoculars. I did, more than once."

Isabel's scalp prickled. She did not know what to say.

"If snow could penetrate behind angelbees, all these years," he went on, "why not insects? Why hasn't the deadland been recolonized?"

"The deadland is poisoned. Things can't live out there."

"That was true only the first five years or so. Maybe for humans, it would still be true. But the grasses out there— they're flourishing, not limping along like the first few years."

The Pylon had let the snow fall through its airwall, deliberately, so that she would see. It had enticed her to enter its Looking-glass Land.

The new moon fell on a Sunday. Isabel tried not to feel self-conscious as she sat in the Meetinghouse, everyone knowing that this might be the last worship meeting she would ever see. She rubbed her hands to keep them warm and listened to the crackle of the wood stove. At least the fire kept out the angelbees, who kept their watch on her and Daniel from outside the window.

After the time of silence, Debbie Dreher read a passage from Martin Luther King, as was customary each year on the Sunday nearest King's birthday. The passage she read described the power of Christian love to overcome oppression. The word King had used to name this power was *agapē*, from the classical Greek, a dead language they had not yet studied in Gwynwood. Debbie concluded by saying she hoped that King's message might yet be of help to the prisoners of Gwynwood. Isabel listened respectfully, though she doubted that *agapē* would have any meaning for non-human oppressors.

Unexpectedly, Nahum Scattergood rose to speak. "I am moved to recall a story from my grandfather," Nahum began, his voice familiar yet unheard before in this Meetinghouse. "My grandfather was born into a large family on a farm during the Depression of the nineteen thirties. One day a knock came at the door, and the man of the house went to answer, rocking a baby in his arms to soothe it while the women were fixing dinner. The door opened, and there stood a stranger with a shotgun, demanding all the money in the house.

"The man of the house said, of course, the stranger could have what he wanted, but he'd have to hold the baby while the man went to fetch it and, meantime, wouldn't he stay for dinner? Of course, the stranger had to put down his gun to hold the baby. It turned out the stranger was a farmer fallen on hard times, and after dinner the Scattergood family discussed how they could lend him some stock to tide him over. To drive home the story, my grandfather liked to end saying, 'And I myself was that baby.'"

Nahum added, "Today let us hope that if we must give up our young ones to an unknown power, God's purpose may likewise be fulfilled."

That night, instead of going out to the Pylon, Isabel and Daniel huddled at home with the Scattergoods. Isabel's parents waited with her, leaving Keith to look after the hospital.

They kept the fire blazing in the fireplace, and candles all over, to ward off angelbees.

Around midnight, the front-door knocker clanged loudly. It was Anna with her two children, both wide-eyed with terror. "The Pylon's gone crazy," Anna said. "There's a thick fog pouring out of it in all directions. I had to warn you."

"It will blanket the whole town," suggested Liza, "as it did before." That had happened the time when the angelbee was shot down.

"I don't like it," said Anna. "The fog's so thick, it even creeps into the house. What if it puts us to sleep again?"

Daniel said, "We should give ourselves up now. We can't endanger the town."

"No," insisted Anna. "Your loss is the greater danger! Hide—in the cellar. How can they find you there?"

So the two of them went down into the cellar, with Isabel's parents, while the others kept watch above. The freezing cold penetrated to their skin, even through their sweaters and jackets. They huddled together in the darkness, avoiding lanterns that would attract notice. Isabel could not say how long they waited there, but as she slipped out of consciousness, she had a vision of the skeletons beyond the Wall on a starless night, rising up to stand, their fingers wearing wedding rings for which they had no heirs. They greeted her thus: *"You who sought our land for so long, welcome to the realm of the cold and the dark."*

XXVII

ISABEL'S EYELIDS OPENED. She squinted as drops of perspiration flowed into them. There was a bright light from somewhere. Slowly she pushed herself up on an elbow, and pulled feebly at the zipper of her jacket, for she was much too warm. She peeled off her sweaters and boots, and felt a chill as her accumulated perspiration evaporated. The epitheliomas on her arm itched terribly. She dropped her things onto the surface beneath her, a pinkish, waxy material. The surface extended several paces to a wall, built of the same waxy stuff. Six such walls surrounded her, with a low roof above.

The shock of it overwhelmed her. She stifled a scream, her hand clawing at her mouth. "Daniel?" she called hoarsely.

Daniel lay nearby, just beginning to stir. She hurried to pull off his hat and unzip his jacket, for he, too, was drenched with sweat. Her fingers were shaking still, but she was getting her senses back. "For God's sake, how'd we get here? Where are we?"

In one of the walls a round window was cut crudely into the pink stuff, about half a foot thick. Outside was maple foliage within arm's reach, and birds were singing a medley of different calls. The smell was of spring grass, with a faint whiff of skunk. Was she still in Gwynwood, somewhere? But it was winter, after all. Had she lain here for months, or years, like Rip Van Winkle?

She looked at her watch, an heirloom from her great-grandmother. The hands stood at eight-thirty. The date read January nineteenth. That encouraged her a bit though it did not rule out time dilation.

"Where are we?" she said again. She rummaged in her pocket and fished out the compass. The needle spun around and around as she tilted it, finding no horizontal direction. When held vertical, however, it registered a strong upward bias.

The hair pricked on her scalp. "Maybe we're not on Earth."

Daniel's eyes widened. He leaned toward her and touched her shoulder. "But where else could we be?"

"Who knows? Wherever their Hive is, maybe." She remembered the red satellite tracking across the sky.

For just a moment a hint of fear crossed Daniel's face. Then he looked at the floor and scraped it, as if puzzled.

"What is this stuff, do you think?" Isabel pounded the floor once, then harder, and her palm left a definite dent. With her fingernails she dug up curls of the stuff, and found that with kneading it turned soft and slightly sticky in her fingers. Not bad, she thought; if the whole prison were made of that stuff, she would be out in no time. But then, this "cell" with its window was already open. It could not be that easy.

Something flew in the window and buzzed right in her face, like a large bumblebee. Alarmed, Isabel threw up her arm reflexively, but the thing buzzed out as quickly as it came, alighting on a tree branch just outside the window. Isabel got up and looked outside.

It was not a bee, but a tiny bird, the smallest adult bird she had ever seen. It had a dark coat and head, with a white collar, and an exceptionally long needlelike beak. As its head tilted and caught the light, the dark patch below the beak turned bright scarlet. "Daniel—it's a hummingbird. But they're extinct..."

There were trees: maple, black walnut, a sassafras with its lobular asymmetrical leaves. Birds hovered everywhere: cardinals, bluejays, and a number of others that Isabel had never seen before.

Daniel came to stand at her elbow. "The angelbees must have collected them, before Doomsday."

There were no angelbees in sight. A pair of deer bounded across the woods, and a raccoon came out from behind the oak tree, its black-masked head sniffing deliberately at the ground. It disappeared into a patch of sunflowers. Behind the sunflowers there appeared to be other patches of vegetation in orderly array, like a garden.

Isabel leaned out of the window and craned her neck upward...

The sky took her breath away. Pale colors of every hue swirled across the sky, as if all of Peace Hope's paints had upset and dribbled down the pallet. Mauve and violet and bluish green, yellows and golds, in huge arcs that swept and faded across the sky. Higher up, toward the zenith, the colors faded into white, no distinct sun but a diffuse white light too brilliant to stare at, merging with the pulsating sky.

Daniel came to look out beside her. He gripped her arm with a sudden fierceness, as if in dread of the inexplicable. Isabel felt her skin tighten all over. This was not a natural place, no matter how much "nature" there was.

The cell had no door, so Isabel cautiously climbed out the window and peered around. Several more pink waxen cells were stacked alongside there, like a honeycomb, each cell with its one round window. She peaked in the window of the one next door to her right, but there was no sign of occupancy.

Beyond the garden patches extended a level forest. How far did the forest extend, she wondered. Would they eventually run up against an airwall?

Daniel came out behind her and took her hand. With a rush of gratitude she squeezed hard. How ghastly it would be to find oneself in the midst of this strangeness all alone. She found herself thinking, perhaps the whole of Gwynwood no longer existed. For her and Daniel, it might as well no longer exist.

They took a few tentative steps away from their cell, toward the garden patches, where Isabel saw ripening corn as well as pea vines. As they went the sky above faded into a uniform tint of green-brown. Squinting at the sky, Isabel crouched defensively. "A storm coming on?"

But the gray-green was not the color of any storm cloud she had ever seen. The air was still and quiet, except for the birds. The temperature was moderate, with no sign of impending change.

Her attention turned to the garden. Ahead of her rose a neat plot of corn, about ten yards across, the stalks tall with brown tassels. The plot was not square, but cut off to either side at an obtuse angle. Next to the plot was a bare path dotted with curious animal droppings, dark green, more compact than horse dung. There was an adjacent plot also of corn, only the green shoots about a foot high as they would be earlier in the season.

Isabel frowned. What season was this, anyway? Spring, summer, or fall?

She walked the path between the young corn and the ripening corn, until the path between them forked, forming a Y, with a plot of pea vines extending ahead of her. She turned back to survey the corn patches again. "Angelbees like nothing but hexagons," she told Daniel as he approached.

"Perhaps," he said. "They must think we like nothing but squares."

They walked on together down the zigzag patch among the hexagonal plots, having to choose right or left each time the path forked. The arrangement would drive any human gardener nuts, Isabel thought. Soybeans in their hairy pods, ripe tomatoes leaning over, young cabbages just getting started—how to keep track of it all? It would be easy to get lost among these paths, which one could never see to the end. Isabel was beginning to worry when abruptly the path opened into a clearing with the forest of pines beyond. Three deer grazed calmly, undisturbed. What kept them out of those tidy plots? she wondered.

For that matter, how had she and Daniel gotten here? How had the angelbees gotten them out of the cellar?

Daniel said, "Is that water running, somewhere?"

She listened. Beneath the birdsongs came a faint rushing, lapping sound, the sound of a fountain or waterfall. She walked through the forest in the direction of the rushing sound. The sound grew into a burbling and splashing, and there it was: a gush of water rose from a cleft rock, falling endlessly into a pool which let out into a stream that coursed across their path, muddying into marshland off to the right. In the pool, black minnows darted beneath the surface, and a school of pollywogs huddled at the edge. The bank was thick with tiger lilies, columbine, and coneflowers. There were insects flitting from the water's surface to the bank, dragonflies, horseflies, even fireflies with their little pink tail ends. And butterflies two inches across, some mottled orange and black, others black with white vertical bands and blue spots along the edge. She had never seen those before, except in pictures.

Daniel scooped up a handful of water and drank. "It's very good."

Isabel winced, thinking of giardia and strontium-ninety and other nasty things the stream might harbor. But then, this was no natural stream. She peered critically at the water gushing from the rock. "For plumbing, it'll do."

Daniel blinked as if startled from another thought. "Yes, of course. Plumbing. Someone has gone to a lot of trouble for us."

"Zookeepers always do." A cage was a cage, no matter how well gilded.

It was then that an angelbee appeared from among the trees, just overhead. Isabel's pulse quickened, and she gripped Daniel's hand again. "There's the keeper." Or a zoo visitor, perhaps. A sightseer, to gawk at Bin-Bin the gorilla playing football.

The angelbee came down just within reach. It had a rounded eyespot, not the kind with the flat hexagonal face. After hovering for a moment, it moved slowly back among the trees, as if beckoning the two humans to follow.

Isabel and Daniel crossed the stream by stepping from one mossy stone to the next. Then they followed the angelbee, pausing only to let a skunk pass at its leisurely pace. Isabel wrinkled her nose; an overabundance of skunk was one thing she could have done without.

The trees gave way at last to a grassy clearing, about an acre in size. The sky was playing tricks again; from gray-green it had slid into a sort of peach color, like the walls of their cell.

In the middle of the clearing stood a pylon, similar to the Gwynwood Pylon, only smaller, barely taller than Isabel. Like the one at home, this pylon was covered with the palest of colors migrating across its surface. The sky had looked like that before, a giant version of a Pylon...Something odd was going on here, if only she could fit it together.

Isabel moved closer, and she felt the rising pressure of an airwall, just like the Pylon back home.

Daniel stopped and caught her arm. "We mustn't stay here."

"Why not? What more can they do to us?"

Daniel grabbed her arm. "Isabel, look."

Behind them stood a keeper, in broad daylight. Its polyhedral shape, about as tall as herself, was a shiny dark brown, like the material of the hexagonal scales. Its black, double-jointed legs moved up and down as the creature slowly advanced. From the underside of the body came puffs of water vapor, bathing its surface and leaving behind a foggy trail.

Something caught Isabel's eye, in the grass ahead of the creature, something that moved. It had a long, sleek green body, as thick as Isabel's leg, and it slid its length through the grass like a snake. Its body disappeared, then reappeared unnervingly out of the grass several feet closer to her. At one point it briefly raised its upper end, an eyeless head whose mouth was stuffed with half-chewed vegetation.

"Look—another one." Daniel pointed off to the right, where another green-sheathed body was busy coiling itself up a tree. It snapped off a two-inch-thick branch and proceeded to munch away at the leaves while holding the branch entwined within its coils.

Isabel screamed and sprinted past the airwalled pylon, pulling Daniel after her. How many of the snake-things were there? Were the two humans surrounded? There was a path into the woods beyond, narrow like a deer trail. She plunged into the forest, half choking on sobs of terror.

In what seemed a very short time, they came upon another cluster of pink honeycombed structures, similar to the one from which they had started. Isabel reached the waxen wall of the honeycomb and stopped to rest, still shaking all over. The sky overhead had its coat of pale colors, as before.

"It's all right," said Daniel reassuringly. "I think we've lost them."

"For now. What repulsive beasts those were. I never heard of those in Gwynwood, even before Doomsday."

"At least they're vegetarian."

"They could be omnivores." She flinched, recalling the picture in Le Petit Prince of the boa constrictor that had consumed an elephant. But these were eyeless vegetarian boas, somehow associated with keepers...

Then it dawned on her. "That's how they got us out of the cellar." She imagined those immense snakes coiling around the sleeping bodies, dragging them out of the cellar. For a moment she felt she would lose control of her senses.

Daniel was trying to tell her something. "These little pink houses," he said. "Who lives in them? Perhaps we're not alone."

Isabel nodded. She managed to steady herself enough to creep along the side of the waxen structure until she reached an open window, similar to the window she and Daniel had climbed out of when they awoke. She felt embarrassed to just peek into somebody's window like that.

But the cell was empty, as far as she could see, just six

walls with another window across the way, and a rather low ceiling. It might as well have been an abandoned storefront along the old highway.

Disappointed, they moved along to the next cell. Daniel called out, "Is anyone home? We need help; we ask to speak with thee." He peeked cautiously into the window and gasped with surprise.

Their own jackets and sweaters lay there in a heap, just inside the far window.

"We must have come around in a circle," Daniel said.

"But we didn't come out this window. We went out *that* window, straight ahead—and we've been heading straight ever since. I don't get that badly lost..." Isabel's eyes widened. "It's a tesseract, that's what it is! They've got us trapped in an extra dimension, so no matter how far we run, we return from behind. Keith knew someone that happened to—but *he came back.*" There had to be a way out again. She clapped her hands in delight. Her terror was forgotten; instead, here was an elegant problem to solve.

Daniel twisted his head as if trying to imagine it. "A tesseract is square, isn't it? Eight cubes collapsed into one? Our horizon looks round to me."

"Then it's not a cube, it's a sphere with an extra dimension, a hypersphere. How would that work? Suppose we were ants, traveling along the surface of a sphere. No matter which direction we went, we'd always come back round where we started. We could see our starting point, too, because the light rays would curve along the sphere."

Daniel frowned, perplexed.

"The trouble is," Isabel went on, "we actually exist in three dimensions; the sphere is in a dimension outside us. So what about 'up' or 'down'? Shouldn't that be like an ant trail, too? What happens when we look up?" Isabel looked up. She certainly could not see herself and Daniel in the pale, multi-colored sky. But that might only mean that the hypersphere had a distortion, that it was not a perfect sphere...

Daniel said, "That doesn't make sense, about *seeing* your starting point. What if there's something in the way, to block the light? There's bound to be something—"

"That's it! *It's the pylon,*" she cried. "The little pylon must be directly opposite this place, on the equator of the hyper-sphere. If the 'sky' fills half the hypersphere, and the 'earth' fills the lower half, then there must be some place exactly opposite us, along the 'horizon,' where all the curving light rays intersect. That place is the pylon. So no matter where we look up from here, in the sky, we see light rays coming from the pylon. And when we're at the pylon, we see pinkish light coming from the walls of these cells. In between, everything reflects gray-green, from forest or garden somewhere."

"All right, you don't have to shout," said Daniel. "But then, where does the 'sun' fit in?"

"There is no ordinary sun. There must be an artificial light source, filtering in through the extra dimension."

Daniel shook his head. "What happens when you go straight up? Do you eventually start coming down again?"

Isabel considered this. "The surface of the ground must actually be the inner surface of a spherical shell. The pylon lies directly opposite us, across the interior. Its reflected light rays all curve around toward us—that is why its image fills our entire view of the 'sky.'"

"Then why can't we see the land curving all around us?"

"Because the curvature is all in the extra dimension, when you're on the ground surface. The two-dimensional ants would see no curvature along the ground, just an infinite re-peating view. But if they were flying ants, if they could fly up along the upper shell of the sphere, then they might see—"

Twigs snapped behind them, and there came a rustle of leaves. Isabel and Daniel grabbed each other's arm and turned.

From out of the woods stepped Becca Weiss. Becca wore a familiar blue print dress, faded from many washings. Her eyelids were closed, and upon each eyelid adhered a hexago-nal scale.

XXVIII

"ISABEL," BECCA SPOKE, in a voice that seemed to creak from disuse. "And Daniel, too. To see you, at last. I never imagined it would be like this, to see; that you would glow like angels."

Isabel stood as if transfixed. She wanted to cry out, to hug Becca tight—*but those eyes.*

Daniel said at last, "We missed thee so, Teacher Becca. The children still ask for thee. Every day I begged God to keep thee safe."

"Prayers are tricky things," Becca returned tartly. "I prayed to see you again; was it right that it came out so?"

"Oh, Becca, I'm sorry," said Isabel, choking back a sob. "You warned us, but how could I stop? Becca—tell us about your eyes."

Becca raised her hand to her right eye and removed the scale. A reddened area remained on her eyelid where the hexagonal shape had rested as if some kind of pressure had held it in place. "The scale tells my brain what the angelbee sees. How, I can't say."

Suddenly Isabel was aware of the two angelbees hovering overhead, observing her and Daniel. She had grown so accustomed to their surveillance, she barely noticed angelbees anymore. But these two creatures, now, were actually linked to Becca. She gaped at them in astonishment.

"You may try, if you like." Becca offered her the scale.

Isabel eyed the scale with caution. "Will it hurt?"

"Not at all. Please, try it," Becca insisted. "I want you to see that it's true."

Isabel looked at Daniel, who nodded encouragingly. Then she accepted the scale. Her hand shook so that she nearly dropped it. At last, very carefully, she applied the object to her closed eyelid. It stuck with a gentle suction. It did not hurt, but she could not see anything, either.

"Do you see?" Becca asked intently.

"I don't think so, I—" A flicker of light came into her closed eye, then disappeared. "There is something. It's not distinct."

"You can imagine what it felt like for me, to see even that, after years of darkness! It takes the scale about twelve hours to adjust to a new eye. Then you'll see everything."

But Isabel removed the scale to return it. "I wouldn't want to keep this from you."

"Thanks, but never mind. There are newborn angelbees all over the place; you can always get a new scale to pop out for you."

"Is that how you got them in the first place?"

"Yes. You remember how the angelbees used to cozy up to me. One day, when I was pressing together some lumps of beeswax to melt into candles, an angelbee dropped that little scale right there on the table. I played with it out of curiosity; goodness knows why I put it on my eyelid, an ironic attempt to imitate the angelbee, I suppose. The gardener, of course, is plastered all over with scales. It can command at least half a dozen eyes at once."

"The gardener?"

"It maintains the place, here. You'll run into it soon enough."

Daniel observed quietly, "I think we already have."

"Excellent. But—why, you must be starved. Forgive me; instead of eyes, I should be offering food and drink. Please come." Becca turned, and the two angelbees followed above her. She led Isabel and Daniel to her own cell, at the far end of the row of hexagons. The interior walls had hollow niches dug in where Becca had stored berries and apples, nuts, carrots, and even milk in crude containers shaped from the same wax that the walls were made of. "The sheep are tame enough to be milked," Becca explained. "I only wish I could make a fire to cook things. I tried, but it frightened off my eyes."

Isabel hesitated, then realized Becca meant the angelbees. "We'll take care of that for you."

Daniel added, "We should keep a fire burning at all times, to save on matches and lighter fluid."

Becca's hand lifted, and the tendons stood out in her

wrist. "Be careful, please. The wax melts."

"Of course, Teacher Becca," Daniel promised. "We'll set up a fireplace outside, at a distance."

"Do take some breakfast first," Becca insisted. "I must do well by your parents."

Isabel bit her lip against her painful thoughts, accepting the offer of milk with raspberries. She discovered she was indeed ravenous with hunger.

Daniel said proudly, "We are married now. We plan to fix up our own house in the spring."

There would be no spring here, thought Isabel, though the "setting up house" would come sooner than planned. What a fix they were in.

"I guessed as much," observed Becca, "from your rings. My best wishes. I always knew you two would make a good pair, and now you even look well matched. What other news? How is Ruth, and my little Benjamin? Did she save the queenless hive? Did Debbie have her baby?"

So as they ate their breakfast from Becca's wax cups and spoons, they filled her in on baby Patience and all the children Daniel had been teaching, and Keith, of course, the most interesting new arrival in Gwynwood. It was hard to remember now that the Aussie doctor had not simply grown up with all of them. Isabel rubbed her eyes but made herself go on, answering all of Becca's questions about home. All the while it was at the tip of her tongue to ask Becca the real questions—the questions everyone in Gwynwood had pondered after Becca's departure. But somehow every time she glimpsed those two scales on Becca's closed eyelids, she held back, dreading what nameless strangeness she might uncover.

After breakfast she and Daniel went out to gather stones to build a fireplace with a makeshift roasting oven. They fueled the fire with fallen branches which smoked a lot but worked well enough to roast cobs of corn from one of the hexagonal garden plots and chestnuts gathered from the tree. The meal took most of the day to prepare, but at the end, as Isabel bit into the crisp corn, she felt she had never enjoyed food so much.

Above in the sky, the light was fading, though there was no real sunset. The colors from the pylon faded to gray, a hazy darkness without a moon or stars. All sorts of animals came out, crossing right by the three humans as they dined outside Becca's cell. There were raccoons foraging, lizards and peeper toads, even a mother possum laden with her brood. In the distance several different kinds of owl calls could be heard above the singing of the tree frogs.

"Does it stay that loud?" Isabel wondered how she would ever get to sleep.

"The night life is impressive," Becca admitted. "What a lively place old Earth must have been before Doomsday."

"It is beautiful," said Daniel. "It's like a Garden of Eden."

"Complete with snakes," Isabel recalled, and a chill went down to her toes. "But *these* snakes were never found on old Earth." She had seen no more of them since morning, but she could scarcely forget them.

Becca nodded. "You must be meaning the 'goatsnakes.' I call them that because, like goats, they'll eat anything."

"*Anything?*"

"Anything vegetable," Becca reassured her. "I've never seen them capture so much as a mouse. They follow the gardener at night, munching the edges of the plots to keep them trim. They do all the heavy work for the gardener."

The "gardener," Isabel realized, must be what she and Daniel called a keeper. "The goatsnakes must be radio controlled by the gardener, like the angelbees." Isabel paused, then forced herself to ask. "Becca, why? Why didn't you tell us in Gwynwood about the angelbees? Why did you...go away?"

Becca waited as if gathering her thoughts. "When I first... *saw* things, in my eyes, I thought I'd gone mad. Yet it was a madness I longed for—can you understand that? I kept trying it in secret. By the time I figured out how the angelbees worked, the secrecy had become a habit." Becca swallowed. "I began to wonder what people would think. Most of our good neighbors hate the creatures so. Would they have thought me possessed?"

Isabel bit her lip and looked away.

"Surely not, Teacher Becca," whispered Daniel.

"The angelbees showed me things in the Pylon," Becca added. "Much more than Alice ever saw, I'm certain. Living pictures, moving and breathing, as if they might step out upon the ground. One day they began to show pictures of myself, entering the Pylon, going away, to a place that looked like heaven. The pictures were insistent."

There was silence for a long while. The grass outside the waxen cells was thick with fireflies, winking on and swooping upward.

"I visited your mother," Becca added, "for a pain that I had, a dull persistent pain in the abdomen."

"I know," Isabel whispered.

"Your mother was honest about what she could do—and what she couldn't. I thought to myself, Perhaps these advanced creatures can do something more for me."

Isabel swallowed once. She nearly fainted as memories of Becca's brother Aaron flooded back, his last days in the hospital, when even the opioids no longer quelled his pain. Becca had lived through that too. "Did they...help you, then?" Isabel managed to ask.

"It's no matter, really."

"I packed some codeine tablets, before the new moon, once it became clear that—"

Becca turned on her, and both angelbees hovered close. "Did you really?"

Isabel got up to fetch her the painkiller. There was enough to last six weeks perhaps, if taken sparingly.

When she returned, she gathered the courage to ask one last question. "Teacher Becca...what did the angelbees want you for?"

Becca faced her thoughtfully. "That is what I have spent my time here trying to figure out."

XXIX

EXHAUSTED BY THE day's food gathering, Isabel fell asleep more quickly than she expected. She awoke in the early morning to the sound of raindrops pattering on the leaves outside. She looked over at Daniel, still asleep beneath his winter coat which served well enough as a blanket. His face, with his eyes shut beneath the wisps of hair on his forehead, seemed to her at that moment indescribable. She whispered a German expression of her father's, "so fein."

From outside came the cry of a sheep, "Mah-ah, mah-ah." Isabel quietly pulled herself up onto the windowsill and let herself through. The rain had stopped, but the damp grass soaked her feet. The woods were full of birds extinct on Earth—finches, blackbirds, orioles, all calling an in unimaginable variety of songs. She followed the sound of the sheep to just outside Becca's cell. Becca was milking the sheep, capturing the spray of milk into a pail fashioned of wax. The fleece of the ewe was thick and knotted, as if it had never been shorn.

"The sheep run wild here," said Becca, "but this one, Hannaleh, is quite friendly. Even the deer will come up to my window at times."

Hannaleh was nibbling contentedly at some corncobs piled against the wall of Becca's cell. After the milking was done, the ewe bolted away for no apparent reason, as sheep were apt to do. Isabel felt oddly reassured. She had missed the sheep, since her marriage.

"I will see if I can tame another one," said Isabel. "We'll be needing more milk now."

"The flock can usually be found down by the river."

"Yes," said Isabel, remembering, "the fountain in the pool on the way to the little pylon."

"Any way you go, it leads to the pylon. I'll take you there later. You'll see amazing things in the pylon."

After breakfast, Isabel and Daniel took stock of their resources. Isabel laid out on the floor her boxes of matches and cigarette lighter, her useless compass, her old Swiss army knife with its multiple blades, her first-aid kit and pharmaceuticals. At the last minute she had stuffed one book in her jacket, the biography of Harriet Tubman, with its portrait of the bold slave-rescuer in her flowing skirt, a rifle clutched in her hands.

Daniel had packed a sewing kit, a bar of soap, and of course a Bible. He frowned at one item in Isabel's store, a bottle containing two pills marked simply, "Death." "Shouldn't the label be more specific?" he asked. "What use is this medicine?"

"It's in case the keepers torture us or perform experiments on us. Keith didn't say what it is, and I didn't ask."

He stared at her in shock. "That would be evil in the sight of God. I'll dispose of this...poison, and that's the end of it." He reached for the bottle, but Isabel caught it first.

"You'll do no such thing! Daniel, I have to know it's there, or else I can't go on." The terror of the unknown flooded over her again, this hypersphere with its horrid goatsnakes lurking about. Nausea rose in her throat. "Promise, Daniel," she said hoarsely. "Promise you'll let it be."

Her breathing slowed to normal. After what seemed forever, Daniel said, "Thee must promise thee'll never use it."

"I won't use it, I promise." What was a promise? Could God see into a hypersphere?

They had to get out of this place, back to Gwynwood, and out to Sydney where Daniel and Becca could get help for their illnesses. But how? Freedom seemed more remote than ever, now...

Somehow there had to be a way to turn the airwalls inside out.

The angelbees. Becca not only saw through their eyes; she controlled them. Surely she could follow one through the airwall.

Later they shared their more practical items with Becca, who was particularly delighted to see the soap. They also compared calendar notes, and found that the two newcomers were only a day off from Becca's own records scratched into the wall of her cell. That was a relief to know.

"I'll show you around the garden today," said Becca. "And you must return to the pylon tonight. You'll see the most amazing things."

"Becca," Isabel asked cautiously. "Did you ever try to steer your angelbees through the airwall, just to take a look?"

"That's dangerous," said Becca flatly. "You'll only get in trouble. Your mother would never forgive me."

Irritated, she dropped the subject. She gazed about the treetops, wondering whether a stray angelbee might trust her enough to wander down. Then she followed Becca down the zigzag rows between the garden plots kept trim by the goatsnakes. Isabel kicked one of the flat green animal droppings in the path. "Do the goatsnakes leave these?" she guessed.

Becca nodded. "They make good fertilizer, I suppose."

Daniel observed, as he had before, "Someone has gone to a lot of trouble for us."

Why, Isabel wondered. What did the keeper-gardeners want from the humans? Could their freedom be bought?

Daniel spent some hours working at the fireplace again, trying to get it waterproof somehow, so they would not use up all their matches. He carved some wax out of the wall of an empty cell and fashioned a cover out of it, but of course it melted in the heat of the flames. Meanwhile Isabel dug up potatoes from a garden patch and gathered wild strawberries from the woods. She wondered how she would ever manage to plan her escape, if it took them all day just to prepare dinner.

In the evening, just as the "sun" was going dim, they set out with Becca and her angelbees to visit the pylon.

When they reached the pylon, it was dark. There were two or three other angelbees lurking about, in addition to Becca's. There was the nightly uproar of tree frogs, crickets, and various owls.

"Look, there," exclaimed Becca, pointing to the pylon. "The gardener is standing there, within the pylon. Two goatsnakes are slithering around. When I raise my hand, see— one of the goatsnakes rears up and bends its head forward imitating my arm. It's munching on some sort of vegetation; I told you, goatsnakes will eat anything."

The pylon was dark. Daniel clutched Isabel's hand, distressed. For a moment, it crossed Isabel's mind that Becca might have gone mad. But then of course, she realized, Becca was seeing with angelbee eyes, and the pylon was designed to show infrared. Dependent on the visible, she and Daniel were the ones who were blind.

XXX

THE EMBERS OF Daniel's fire went out again overnight, quenched by the rain that fell during the same early hours as it had the night before. According to Becca, it rained about the same every night, at about the same time.

So they tried to set up a fire in one of the unoccupied cells, as distant as possible from Becca's cell so as not to frighten off her angelbees. As the flames rose, the pile of sticks sank gradually into the melting wax of the floor. That gave Isabel another idea: the heat-softened wax could be used to fashion more cups and plates for herself and Daniel. She dug up some of the wax with her knife and started to shape it, taking it outside again to avoid the smoke, for there was no chimney.

The wax proved easy to mold into any shape. She had just finished shaping two drinking glasses and was about to go and dig out some more wax when she noticed an angelbee just a few feet away watching her.

It seemed to take a close interest in what she was doing with the wax. Isabel crumpled one of the drinking glasses into a ball, and she held it out toward the angelbee. The silvery globe descended closer, so close that she heard its winglets humming. She blinked at its brightness. Its eyespot faced her, almost within reach. The eyespot was smoothly round; its hexagonal scale had yet to come off.

Isabel's heart pounded fast. She was very careful, remembering the last time; she could ill afford to lose her sight again. She stepped forward and tentatively touched the eyespot with her hand.

There was an audible snap, and something fell to the ground. A flat facet was now cut into the eyespot. Isabel looked down and picked up the fallen scale.

She placed it on her left eyelid with her eye closed, just as she had done with Becca's scale before. As it gently adhered, the angelbee retreated to the trees, startled, perhaps, by the influx of unfamiliar signals. For now, Isabel could see little in her eye, but she would put up with this temporary handicap if it brought her one step closer to escape.

As she completed two dinner plates out of softened wax, Daniel returned with some vegetables for dinner. He stared in surprise at her eye. "Is this wise?" he asked. "Might it not damage your own retina in some way?"

"We have to take some risk, or we'll never get out of here." She spoke sharply, then changed the subject. "Daniel, what are we going to do about our clothes? I can't stand another day without a wash, it itches all over."

"We have one bar of soap."

"That won't go far on clothes."

"I remember one year," said Daniel, "when we ran out of soap, we used wood ash."

"That's worth a try."

They scooped up ashes from the dead fire outside and packed them into their clothes, which they soaked and rinsed in the pool with the fountain, where they both enjoyed a good bath as well. Afterward, since they had no change of clothes, they wrung them out as best they could and put them back on again. The shirts were dingy gray, but at least they smelled better.

In the meantime, Isabel was beginning to see flickers of something in her left eye. She closed her right eye to concentrate better. As she lay in the "sunlight" to dry her clothes, she managed to capture the image of a tree, glimmering red against an unexpectedly dim sky. The spectrum of the sunlight must be similar to that of Earth's actual sun, which radiated low amounts of far infrared.

The trees and foliage all glimmered various shades of infrared. Occasional bright spots swooped across; these, she realized, were birds. It was as if all the lights on a Christmas tree had miraculously come alive. Then, quite unnervingly, she suddenly saw...herself. Herself, and yet not herself, for her body shone like a statue of glass red-hot from the glassblower's flame. She caught her hand in her mouth, and as she did so, the glowing statue did the same, with the right hand, not the left, as would her image in a mirror.

Startled, her right eye flew open again. She peeled the scale off her left and cautiously tested her own vision again, for despite her brave words she cared to keep her own eye-sight. In fact, after a few minutes she could see as well as ever. The angelbees hovered a few feet above her shoulder waiting expectantly. So she replaced the scale, closed her right eye, and lay back in the grass.

She spent the rest of the afternoon touring the hyper-sphere through the glimmering vision of her angelbee. She found that by concentrating she could direct the angelbee to glide ahead and to turn in its path. It sailed above the dull orange canopy of trees, passing over the honeycomb pattern of cells. One of the cells was strikingly white, brighter than anything she had seen so far; that must be where they had started the fire earlier in the day. As the angelbee rose higher, the forest and the ground below seemed to rear up-ward all around, like the sides of a giant teacup. There was no clear horizon; the distant regions faded into the sky above, where they must meet to complete the inner surface of the sphere.

"Daniel, you've got to try this," she told him at last. "It's the most beautiful thing I ever saw. You should see your-self."

His face turned dramatically bright infrared as he blushed, extra heat rays emanating from his cheeks and forehead. "To-morrow," he said guardedly. "It's time to be getting dinner ready."

Isabel walked slowly back toward the outdoor cooking oven, preoccupied with the extraordinary view from her new eye. She gathered up fresh kindling wood and, without think-ing, she lit a match.

Above the match, her angelbee saw a screaming blotch of white, much larger than the flame seen by her own eye. The infrared flame actually appeared to engulf her hand. Startled, Isabel cried out and dropped the match. The view dipped and rose with dizzying swiftness as her angelbee broke free of her mental control and headed upward, away from the danger.

Daniel hurried over. "Is thee safe?"

Isabel had pulled the scale from her eye, which was squinting now as the pupil readjusted to daylight. "I forgot, of course, the angelbee won't tolerate flame. The temperature of the flame is so high that even the surrounding hot air looks blinding white. For a moment I thought my hand—" She shuddered. "Why would angelbees have evolved infrared vision, instead of the same visible range as ours? This infrared is so sensitive."

"It must have been an advantage in their habitat. Where did they evolve? A swamp, I suppose."

"A swamp, where the heat of the soil might indicate rich areas of methane production. Also, I bet there was fog all the time, which would have limited the visibility in our range of the spectrum." The angelbees, and their keepers, certainly were partial to water vapor. That time when she had tumbled across the airwall at the Gwynwood Pylon, the other-dimensional corridor had been filled with a dense mist.

After the meal was cooked, the two of them left the fire to eat their dinner with Becca. Isabel replaced the scale on her eye. As the sky's extra-dimensional light source turned off and the foliage gave up its heat, the night forest became a light show of animals. Wherever she looked with her angelbee eye, the animals shone brilliantly against the dim background of underbrush and tree branches. A pair of young owls on a branch, tilting their hooked beaks. Raccoons, three or four of them, foraging in the underbrush, and another skunk doing the same, trailed by three tiny ones. And mice in the hundreds, popping in and out of burrows, their shapes lighting and disappearing like fireflies; remembering Peewee, she shed tears of homesickness. All of them, all warm-blooded creatures, were living stars in the night sky.

They were finishing dinner when something happened to the sky above the honeycomb, something only Isabel's angelbee could see. Enormous concentric rings of reddish tint appeared, centering far overhead. The rings were not perfectly round, but fluctuated in shape, perhaps bent by imperfections in the hypersphere. They were all gradually closing in toward the center, while new ones appeared at the perimeter. The contrast, between her left eye that "saw" and her right that saw only dark, took her breath away.

Becca said, "It's a summons." There was a touch of excitement in her voice. "The pylon always has visions, but tonight they will be exceptionally communicative." She added, as an afterthought, "Pick up a piece of wall-wax before we go."

* * *

As they approached the pylon, Isabel sent her angelbee soaring ahead to peer down upon the six-sided pyramid. Within its sides, an infrared pattern of concentric circles appeared. The circles faced upward, so they would appear to be flat in the sky across from the opposite point on the hypersphere, at the comb of cells where Isabel had watched before.

Then abruptly the circles disappeared. In their place, as Isabel's angelbee looked down, was an enormous human eyeball, seemingly alive. The lid of the eyeball blinked twice.

Isabel stumbled in her tracks, and Daniel had to help her up. Becca laughed. "My dear, you've just exchanged an eye for an eye! But wait, this is only the beginning."

While Isabel tried to explain to Daniel this disconcerting vision, Becca had walked up to the airwall. She held out to the pylon a piece of wall-wax, which glowed slightly infrared from the warmth of her hand.

The pylon returned a formless lump of infrared glow.

Next, Becca split the lump in three. Three lumps of infrared appeared.

"I see." Isabel took out her own piece of wax and shaped the letter A. A letter A appeared in the pylon.

"That's useless, unfortunately," Becca said. "It understands some English but it won't actually *speak* it, unless..." She paused as if a thought had occurred to her.

Isabel meanwhile had shaped a crude stick figure of a human. At first the pylon simply returned a five-pointed star. She frowned, then tried to improve the head and feet.

A keeper-shape appeared, not a lifelike image but a stylized representation; the polyhedron was unmistakable. Above it were six angelbees in a row and, below, three goatsnakes.

"A keeper," Isabel exclaimed, "with all its eyes and arms! I shaped a human, and it returned a keeper."

Daniel commented with quiet amusement, "An *I* for a thou. All right, thee has convinced me it's worth it."

"Try to shape a pylon next," Becca insisted suddenly. "You must: this is very important. It worked for me, but only the first time..."

With a nod, Isabel crumpled the wax in her palm. She pressed six sides into it, pulling out the tip to form a pyramid. She set the pyramid on her palm.

In the pylon, a pattern of horizontal bars appeared, fuzzy and shifting. Then abruptly, there was a figure of a woman. The figure moved and spoke but was flat, like a movie, not three dimensional, like the other infrared images she had just seen. The woman was a stranger, Caucasian features with doll-like curls, wearing an old-fashioned dress with a scoop neckline, early twentieth century, perhaps. She stood gesticulating toward the right. Then a second figure appeared, a man with arched eyebrows and a rather well-fed look, in a suit with his hair slicked down like Andrés's. The couple appeared to engage in some foolish antics, though it was hard to tell without voices. "Is that meant as a comment about us?"

"No, no," said Becca. "Wait."

After some further antics, the pair of characters abruptly disappeared. There appeared a large heart shape, like a valentine, containing letters in script: *I Love Lucy*.

"Daniel—It's *I Love Lucy!*" Her hair stood on end. "How on Earth—did they pull that out of my head?" She had never seen the video before. From Peace Hope's sound track, she had always imagined the couple wearing overalls, like herself and Daniel.

"It's television, you see," said Becca. "The pylon is like infrared television in three dimensions."

"But why *Lucy*? How'd they read my mind?"

"No," Becca insisted, "they don't read minds. There must be more *I Love Lucy* out in space than any other show from the early days of broadcast. This is my theory: I think the early TV broadcasts were the first sign of intelligence on our planet that the gardeners picked up, way out in space. The scene you just saw was the same one they showed me—the first time I shaped a pylon."

"The first human signal—the first pylon," said Isabel.

"That's right," said Becca.

"So once they found us, they closed in for the kill." *Veni, vidi, vici,* except that *vidi* came first.

"Not exactly. They came, and they waited; that's all we can say," said Becca.

"But why?"

"Why indeed," Becca wondered. "Why all these gardens; what is it to them?"

A thought came to her. "Becca...I'm going to light a match."

Becca was silent. "You're right. We need to try this, but my 'eyes' won't stand the heat. I will go home now; you let me know what happens."

After she left, Daniel turned to Isabel. "Won't your angelbees fly off, too?"

"Stand here," Isabel directed him, "just by this side of the match. So the pylon sees the flame, but my angelbee doesn't." She pulled out a match, struck it, and heard it hiss as it came alight.

The pylon went dark. For a moment, her angelbee saw nothing in the pylon. Then a faint figure began to appear; a human shape but—

It was a skeleton. A female skeleton, with narrow shoulders and broad pelvis. It was lying in a crouched position, like some of those behind the Wall. Below the rib cage, cupped in the pelvis, was a tiny curled up skeleton of a baby, a fetus it must be, small as a squirrel. A pregnant skeleton.

The skeleton grew brighter, much brighter than the figure before. Suddenly the angelbee turned away, and the landscape seemed to whirl around. Isabel gasped and ripped the scale from her forehead, dropping the match.

"God forgive us," Daniel exclaimed.

In the pylon, the image was so intense that it shone with red heat now, even to the human eye.

XXXI

THE NEXT MORNING over breakfast, Isabel told Becca what she had seen.

"A remarkable response," said Becca. "If that is what they think of fire it's certainly frightening enough."

"But why *that* image in particular?" Isabel thought of the skeletons behind the Wall. "Was it meant as a warning to us?"

"Not necessarily. Remember, the pylon's responses are reciprocal. You showed fire; the pylon tried to communicate to you what fire means to *them*, the gardeners."

"Why should they fear fire so much?" Isabel wondered. "The keepers are far too advanced; they must have had their own Prometheus long ago."

Daniel said, "Their Queen would be the counterpart to a pregnant mother. Perhaps they think fire is a danger to their Queen."

"I wonder," said Becca slowly, her two angelbees circling quietly overhead. "I wonder whether perhaps their thinking is more...symbolic. Perhaps the fire reminds them of some problem of their own. Perhaps not unlike some of ours."

Isabel asked, "What do you mean?"

"It's curious, isn't it. The gardeners tend us along with a virtual Noah's ark of other creatures that would have gone extinct without their care. Why, I wonder; why so much trouble over endangered species? Humans never gave a thought to the dodo bird or the passenger pigeon. We invented 'endangered species' only once we realized that our own headed the list."

As Isabel thought this over she felt a slight prickling at the back of her neck.

"Surely not," said Daniel. "The gardener, even the goat-snakes; they seem so peaceful."

"So would the attendants at the Taronga Zoo."

"In that case," Daniel asked, "what do they expect of us, the three of us, kept here? Why isolate us from other people?"

Isabel remembered the release program at the Taronga Zoo. "Sometimes the zookeepers train a few breeding pairs for release in the wild, that would be like Daniel and me. But this hypersphere is nothing like the deadland outside the Wall. Everything's tended for us."

"Exactly," said Becca. "Primitive survival is the last thing any of us survivors need to learn. But . . . there might be something else. Something we have yet to find."

"Why don't they just tell us?" But Isabel already knew the answer to that. The Taronga zookeepers couldn't just tell George and Martha to hunt and sink their eagle claws into wild mice and squirrels. The knowledge of survival had to well up out of the creatures' own deepest instincts.

Daniel said at last, "It always saddens me, all our preoccupation with survival. Will we never get beyond that to something better? Or will our generation be the last to remember?"

"It certainly won't be the first," said Becca. "Remember the words of Chief Seattle, as his people gave up their ancestral lands to enter the reservation: 'It is the end of living and the beginning of survival.'"

Survival took up most of their energies over the next few days. Daniel managed at last to keep a small fire going inside the cell at the far end; he took care to get up and check it once or twice at night. While they were saving on matches now, still there was a never-ending supply of firewood to be collected, an arduous job with only Isabel's pocket knife. Their diet was a change from what they were used to, and Isabel seemed to have chronic indigestion. She suspected giardia in the water; if only they had a pan to boil water, and the unpasteurized sheep milk.

With her angelbee eye, she explored the hypersphere. She followed the stream from its source where the fountain sprang up out of the rock to its ending in a bog full of skunk cabbage, a place where the angelbees came for refueling. The stream seemed to trace an equatorial line about halfway around the hypersphere, presumably from the highest to lowest points of "elevation." About three quarters of the land was forest, mostly conifers, with patches of hickory, oak, and locust.

Once, her angelbee came across the keeper in an empty

garden patch. Becca said she had never seen more than one keeper-gardener at a time, although she suspected that different ones took shifts. This one had all its goatsnakes and angelbees in attendance. The angelbees, like Becca's angelbees, each had a curious feature that human eyes could not detect: a pattern of six bright dots evenly spaced around the outer edge of the eyespot. The infrared dots winked on and off in a pattern she could not decipher, though it reminded her of Braille. Was this how a keeper "talked"? Or could it be that angelbees had their own means of communication, perhaps independent even of their keepers?

One of the goatsnakes was burrowing through the soil of the garden patch, presumably turning it over to prepare for some kind of planting. After a while the keeper moved just outside the patch, where it stopped. What was it waiting for?

A bright streak appeared in the branches of a tree that overhung the garden patch. Isabel tried to send her angelbee closer, but it refused, keeping a cautious distance. Within the tree, whose canopy was largely transparent to infrared, a goatsnake had entwined its midsection around the upper trunk. Its head and neck wielded a cylindrical implement that emitted the bright streak, a beam of some form of energy. The beam sliced through the overhanging branches like butter. The branches fell into the garden patch where another goatsnake set to hauling them away.

Isabel stared long and hard at the cylinder with its energy beam. What a useful tool that would be—and even a weapon. If only she could get hold of one.

Daniel managed to acquire an angelbee as Isabel had done, by attracting it with a shaped ball of wax. Now he could join Isabel, exploring the world of infrared.

"Isn't it lovely?" she said. "It looks like a different planet." Of course, it was not even a planet, she reminded herself. For all they knew, they could be light-years away from Earth by now. Perhaps all her family had long ago aged and died. She suppressed tears.

Daniel gently touched the shiny scale on his eyes as if puzzled. "It reminds me that nearly everything we see through our human eyes is reflected light, not light which emanates intrinsically from the thing itself. I wonder whether angelbees, and their keepers, have a world view that differs from ours because they perceive things by their own light."

Isabel shook her head. "I couldn't begin to guess. Daniel have you figured out what the angelbees are doing with those six blinking dots? Can you control the pattern or yours?"

Daniel tried and Isabel tried, but neither could "will" the eyespots to change their lighting pattern.

"Eventually we'll get it to work," insisted Isabel. "I'm sure it just takes focusing one's brain the right way."

"I wonder whether it's safe to keep controlling them like this."

"It seems okay. Becca's done it for months."

"I meant, safe for the angelbees. *Tu es responsable pou toujours de ce que tu as apprivoisé.*"

"Of course, you're responsible for what you tame. Haven' you ever raised a lamb on a bottle?"

"No, I haven't," said Daniel. "Actually I've never ha much to do with animals. I was sickly as a child, and Aun Liza was always afraid I'd catch something."

"That's silly." But Isabel was reminded of his blood defi ciency, and she felt a touch of fear. "How are you doing now Is your medicine still working?"

"I feel fine, most days, so long as I get enough sleep."

They had to get back home, she reminded herself. "Danie. I've been thinking. I don't think those keepers are training u for anything. Instead, I think they've just put us here like on reservation: a place to keep us alive while they take the rest o us off the Earth for good."

"Why would they do such a thing?"

"Because they want to reshape the Earth, to remake i climate to something that suits them better but excludes u Turn it all into a foggy swamp."

"It could be," he admitted, "but we've no reason to think so."

"It makes sense to me. The point is," she added, "we can just sit here, letting them do what they want to us. We have t fight back. Above all, we've got to escape our cage."

Daniel's lips tightened. "What does thee have in mind?"

"The airwall around the pylon. It's the one exit." The ai

wall enclosed their hypersphere as surely as it enclosed the world outside.

"The keepers will come after us."

"Perhaps not. It's daytime, remember. Even the pylon will be asleep."

Daniel looked very reluctant, but she knew he would follow. She jogged down the wooden path to the pylon, her angelbee soaring ahead of her.

The pylon itself was blank except for its usual shifting colors; even her angelbee saw nothing more than surface swirls of infrared. Remembering her adventure with the rope and skillet at the Gwynwood Pylon, Isabel walked cautiously toward the airwall until its pressure was palpable. Then she brought her angelbee down, just a couple of feet ahead of her, and willed it forward. As it went, the wall pressure receded and she could walk another step toward the pylon.

The angelbee vanished. Its vision was gone and a rough invisible hand shoved Isabel back. She fell, hitting the back of her head. As she tried to pick herself up, nausea rose in her throat. She turned over, trying to get her bearings.

"Isabel? Is thee hurt?" Daniel asked anxiously.

"Not badly." Her head and side were throbbing with dull pain. She stretched and let Daniel help her to stand. "I can't see a thing. What happened to that angelbee?" She touched the scale on her eyelid. It seemed to be in place.

Suddenly the vista reappeared: the brilliant shapes of birds and grass over the clearing, the dull red outline of the pylon. "There, my angelbee came back. It must have returned through the airwall."

"Take care," said Daniel. "That was a bad fall."

"I'm fine. I'm going to try again, keeping the angelbee closer this time." She brought the angelbee down, just above her forehead. This time it crossed just into the pylon's domain, without disappearing. Very slowly, she inched toward the invisible wall, pressing ahead one step, then another. Then abruptly she fell forward, catching herself just in time to meet the ground with her hands.

Her ears popped, as if the air pressure had dropped. Her own eyes saw misted darkness; but her angelbee saw a corridor ahead, outside the airwall, which now enclosed her. She was turned around face-to-back, like the last time she had crossed an airwall at the Gwynwood Pylon.

Carefully she followed her angelbee out into the corridor.

She was chilled, and she hugged her arms for warmth. The ground beneath her was not the grassy clearing in the woods. It was a floor similar to the platform of the pylon. At either side, a metallic wall rose at an obtuse angle, then folded inward halfway up toward the ceiling, forming a hexagonal corridor, through which her infrared eye saw clearly despite the mist. Along the obtuse lower walls of the corridor ran rows of panels glowing infrared—at just the right height and angle, she thought, to be pressed by a keeper's foot.

She got up, keeping her balance with difficulty, as half her weight seemed to have fallen away. Was this the degree of gravity keepers were used to on their own planet?

She willed her angelbee to turn, slowly above her head. There was the pylon behind her, as if it, too, had been transported instantaneously to the corridor. A cry of surprise escaped her. There stood Daniel, a moving shape of infrared contained within the pylon, waving at her frantically. By contrast, the pylon her own eye saw was completely dark.

"Daniel?' she called, but he could not hear her. She waved back, then signed, *I see you,* waving her hand forward and back before her eyes.

Daniel signed back the same way, adding *too,* his hand with the index fingers extended tapping together twice. Then his hands opened into *fives,* and the flat palms moved downward in waves: *Fear.* He added, *Come back now,* emphatically, thrusting both hands forward with the palms up.

Wait, she signed back, for her curiosity was inescapable. She sent her angelbee floating slowly around the pylon, and as it did so, Daniel's image vanished off the side, the view within rotating until the entire circuit around the pylon had been covered. So that was how the keepers watched her and Daniel through the pylon. But where were the keepers? Was this their Hive? She picked herself up, shivering, and resolved to bring her winter coat next time. The keepers must prefer a cooler climate.

She sent the angelbee off, slowly, down the corridor. Other angelbees appeared, flashing their six-dotted code. Surely the

keepers would have spotted her by now. But they were slow
to react, and there was no sign of them yet, nor of their goatsnakes.

Ahead in the corridor stood something luminous, exactly
what she could not tell; the resolution of her angelbee was far
from twenty-twenty. As she hovered closer, though, the shape
became clear: It was another pylon.

This new pylon, too, contained visions of infrared within.
As her angelbee circled around it, she made out trees, exotic
trees with cascading branches of giant leaves and birds with
enormous beaks, the like of which had never been seen in
Gwynwood. This was a different kind of habitat altogether,
another house of the "zoo."

A keeper appeared to her own eye, looming out of the fog,
its spindly legs rising up and down.

She had let her angelbee loiter for far too long; now how
could she call it back in time to flee back to Eden? Immediately she willed it to return, down the corridor, but it came
slowly, much too slowly.

Through her angelbee, she saw that goatsnakes were slink-
ing beside the keeper. Isabel's mouth opened, but she was too
frightened to scream. Her angelbee watched from a distance, a
distance that narrowed too slowly. The keeper lifted one of its
legs to a panel on the wall. Something made a hissing sound,
the sound of an invisible gas escaping. The sleep-gas enveloped her until she lost consciousness.

She awoke in the sunlight of the hypersphere, the pinkish
sky overhead. Daniel was holding her hand and speaking to
her, trying to get her awake. She rolled over and pushed herself up on her elbows. "I'm all right," she said groggily.
"What... what happened?" She looked up at him question-
ingly.

Daniel's expression was oddly wooden. "I saw it all, this
time." He stopped as if he couldn't go on. "The goatsnake
carried thee out."

"Oh, God, I'm sorry, Daniel—" she tried to hug him, but
he would not respond.

"What if thee had never come back?" Daniel demanded.
"What if thee was dead? What was I to do? Thee might think
of that, for once."

"Of course I think of that. I said I was sorry." His anger bewildered and frightened her.

"Thee must promise never to try that again."

"But, Daniel—how else are we to get out of here?"

"Never mind that. Our keepers will let us know their intentions in good time."

"But what if it's too late? What if your medicine runs out? What will *I* do then?"

"Never mind. Thee must promise."

"All right," she sighed, "I promise." For now.

XXXII

ISABEL WONDERED ABOUT the airwall, and how she might slip by the keepers. At times she found herself wondering whether she might slip past Daniel as well, to try again. She immediately felt remorse, for it had never before occurred to her to deceive him.

She talked often with Becca, who could never hear enough about home, all the children in her class, and of course Ruth and little Benjamin. The baby had just been sitting up and starting to say "Ah-bah," before Isabel had left. It embarrassed her that she remembered little more, for she took little notice of infants once they were safely born, aside from giving them DPT shots at checkup time.

"And how were the beehives getting on?" Becca inquired. "The honey flow was a good one? Are you sure the new queen took?"

One of the hives had had to be requeened because the old queen had died, and for some reason no new queen cells were made. So they had ordered a new queen from Sydney, the Italian variety, and she had taken well.

"Of course, the Italian queens are the hardiest," Becca assured her.

"Still," said Isabel, "you would think all the worker bees would instinctively recognize and destroy any queen of alien ancestry. Once the queen takes, the old workers are a dead breed, and they don't even know it."

"It's a miracle," Becca agreed. "Their nurturing instincts must surpass the call of the genes. They come from the tribe of Rachel and Leah."

Isabel thought again how the angelbees had watched over the beehives, presumably directed by their keepers. A thought came to her about the pylon. "Becca—do you suppose it's the Queen of the keepers who 'talks' to us through the pylon?"

"I would not be surprised," said Becca. "The keepers themselves never seem to take notice of us."

"Except when we try to escape," Isabel noted ruefully. "Have you found out much else from the pylon since you came here? What does the Queen look like?"

Becca considered this, as if trying to explain. The shiny scales on her eyelids twinkled in the light from the cell window. Keith had said, "They took her to see the Queen." Tears of homesickness filled Isabel's eyes, and she rubbed them out. "It's hard," Becca said at last, "I'm not used to describing the look of things. Come see for yourself."

So the three of them paid another visit to the pylon. Night had fallen, and a number of bats flitted across the clearing, their silhouettes black to human eyes, brilliant orange to the eye of Isabel's angelbee. For the pylon, Becca shaped a piece of wax into something like a Venus figurine, with a tiny "baby" that could be placed in and out of the pregnant belly. Presumably the pylon would return an image of the "Queen" which gave birth to keepers.

In the pylon appeared an enormous many-legged creature, at first glance resembling a giant centipede, or perhaps a Chinese dragon. The head of the creature was bulbous, without recognizable features. The rest of the body was composed of angular segments with spiderlegs, almost as if a line of keeper-shaped polyhedrons had been squashed together. The segments appeared more clearly articulated toward the end of the tail; in fact, the final segment looked just like a keeper, down to the hexagonal facets for angelbee scales to attach. As she watched, the keeper split off from the tail end. It stretched its sticklike legs feebly, then took a tentative first step.

"Why, the keepers bud off just like the angelbees do," Isabel exclaimed. "This creature is their Queen."

"She looks nothing like a honeybee queen," said Daniel.

"Of course not, but the point is, her body is structured for reproduction, unlike that of the keepers. Keepers are like worker bees; they can't reproduce. Only the Queen can generate new keepers." She paused. "I wonder what their generation time is. Becca, do you know?"

"That I can't tell you. Angelbees bud off every month or so; I can see on yours a swelling at the side, where the bud is taking shape."

"The keepers must take longer than that. Let's ask."

"Based on what unit of time?" Becca asked. "That is what gave me trouble. The keepers would not think in Earth years."

"They certainly know the lunar cycle." For the next hour, Isabel shaped figures to establish the lunar phases. Becca contributed a binary code that she had worked out. Then they tried to offer the human "generation time," combining Becca's Venus figure with two to the eighth power of lunar cycles, or about twenty years. But the numbers the pylon returned were much too large—around two to the thirteenth or fourteenth power, in lunar units, which meant about a thousand years.

Isabel shook her head. "That can't be right."

"Perhaps that's not generation time but lifespan," Becca suggested. "Perhaps they, or their Queen, live for a thousand years."

They paused to ponder this.

Daniel said at last, "The sequoias lived for a thousand years. I wonder what it feels like. Perhaps that is why keepers move so slowly. Perhaps we seem like buzzing insects, to them."

"I wonder," said Isabel. "If that is how they live . . . how do they die?"

"Isabel," Daniel warned.

Before he could stop her, Isabel had shaped a polyhedral keeper in her hand; then she squeezed and crumpled it between her fingers, the pieces falling to the ground.

In the pylon, there was a flash so bright that it sent her angelbee spinning out of control. By the time she got it back, a mushroom cloud filled the image of the pylon in three dimensions, rings of cloud expanding through the upper atmosphere, so real that her hair stood on end. Then she realized—that was how humans died, not keepers. She had shown a keeper, and the pylon returned the equivalent, about humans.

Daniel grabbed her arm. "Thee'll never learn."

"But, Daniel, I just want to figure things out."

"Not that way. We're going home."

* * *

Isabel arranged herself in her well-worn sleeping place, a mat of sassafras leaves piled into a depression in the floor where the warmth of her body had gradually melted the floor down. She watched Daniel trimming his beard with the pocket knife, by the light of a crude candle with a wick made from fleece. She rather liked his beard; it made her desire him even more. "Daniel, it still puzzles me, what the pylon said..." she paused, hesitating to anger him again, but he looked up encouragingly. "I only showed one keeper dying, but the pylon showed how a whole lot of humans got killed at once. Does that make sense, one for many?"

"That makes sense to me. Cain's first act led inevitably to man's last. The end of living began with Cain."

"That's a depressing view. You'd agree with the astronomers who say the reason we never heard from extraterrestrials is that any race bright enough to send radio messages soon blows itself up."

"So, thee thinks that intellect is our problem?" He smiled at her ironically.

"Extremes of any sort are a liability, in terms of evolution. Extreme intellect may be as bad for us as extreme physical size was for the dinosaurs."

Daniel faced her sternly. "God works through all of us, intelligent or not. Intelligence gives us the choice between life or death. 'Choose life, that you and your children may live.' The keepers lived to hear our radio signals. I believe they found a different path. They came here to help us, in the first place. They never started our war—that was just a sheep painted black on one side. They're not destroying our ozone; they're trying to replenish it, with electrical discharge, as Teacher Matthew says. And someday, when our Earth is habitable again, they'll release us; but not before we've learned to treat it right."

She blinked at him. The candle flame shifted, and half his face was in shadow again. "You mean, they came here across all those light-years just to help us out?" She shook her head. "What do they get out of it?"

"That's just the point. What do they get out of us? Why would they have bothered to come here just to destroy Earth?"

Isabel had no ready answer.

"They must have learned to save themselves from their own worst instincts," Daniel said. "Perhaps this is the key to survival: learning to help others without gain for oneself."

It was late, and Isabel felt her mind going numb. The part about the ozone was almost certainly true. But what were the keepers: guilty preservers, as Becca had suggested, or were they Daniel's enlightened altruists?

She closed her eyes and lay down in her sleeping place. She tried to sleep, but her stomach felt worse than usual. Her breasts ached from lying against the hard floor, so she turned on her back, but still she felt sick. She heard the nightly rain patter on the roof, and the chorus of birds that began at dawn.

At last it was too much; she got herself up and managed to reach over the window ledge just in time to empty her stomach outside.

Daniel got up and put his arm around her, trying to comfort her. "Will none of these medicines help?"

"I've tried all the antibiotics, except the giardia medicine. It's got rather bad side effects." Wearily she groped through the pill bottles until she found the right one. She flicked the cigarette lighter for a quick look at the label. Among the warnings, she read, "not to be taken by pregnant women."

She went cold all over. The bottle slipped from her hand. "Daniel, I haven't bled for two months.".

"Thee's been under stress."

"I know but . . . I don't think that's it." Her breasts felt sore all the time, and her clothes were tight at the waist.

"But thee has been taking the pills." Daniel's voice rose, and he held her tighter, afraid now.

"The pills must be no good. Mother rarely prescribes them; it's hard to know. Like those bad antibiotics we got from Sydney. No quality control out in the bush." She buried her head in his shoulder, and a sob rose in her throat. Unless they escaped, she would have to face childbirth here, without even the Gwynwood hospital.

XXXIII

THE NEXT DAY Isabel lay inside her cell, weak and despondent. She thought about pregnancy and childbirth with no doctor, no extra blood, not even boiled water. All she could see ahead was months of a nightmare, most likely to end in a painful death. She cried without stopping, until she could barely speak. Daniel tried to console her, but she pushed him away, overcome with her grief and anger, as the weight of her whole situation seemed to crash down upon her.

At last she grew calm enough to think again. She wiped her face with her hands. "Let me be," she told Daniel. "I want to be alone."

"Is thee certain, thee will be all right?" The pain in his voice was heartbreaking.

She shuddered, but she could not bear to look at him. "Just for a while, let me be."

He left, climbing out the window. Outside a bluejay was calling, and a tree branch swayed from the weight of a squirrel. The sunlight came through the window, shining upon the eyespot scale that she had put off for the night. But none of these things were worth another thought, now.

For the first time she seriously considered that final means of escape, the two white tablets that Keith had sent with her. But then, Daniel would remain here to grieve, alone with Becca, who was dying of cancer and never said a word about it.

One of Becca's angelbees appeared in the window, then Becca herself with the two scales on her eyes. Isabel looked up at her, feeling a bit sheepish.

"Congratulations," Becca said.

"For what?" she replied indignantly.

"For nature's greatest gift. To create a new human being—it's the power of a god. That's why men invented Adam and Abraham, to take it away from us."

Isabel squinted suspiciously, wondering if her old teacher

was poking fun at her. "I'll never get that far. I can't even keep food down; I'll starve."

"Eat the way Ruth did," Becca suggested. "Like this hummingbird out here."

Isabel got herself up and leaned out through the window, her stomach still complaining though it was quite empty. A hummingbird was visiting a flower, dipping its beak deep within the nectar and pulling out, the tongue flicking rapidly. All day the tiny bird would hover from one flower to the next, feeding ceaselessly to keep its wings going at such a rate that they actually hummed.

"That's right," said Isabel, recalling her mother's instructions on Ruth's card in the file. "Eat a little at a time to keep just enough in your stomach." Debbie, too, used to eat the same way, a little at a time throughout the day, even snacking during Worship and late at night, to keep her digestion balanced under the stress of the hormones.

Isabel's practical sense came back to her: this was just another disaster to overcome, like the typhoid epidemic when she was ten, when they had to burn all the bed linens and disinfect whole houses, and even so Daniel's parents had died. It might not be such a disaster after all; the first year after Doomsday had been bad, when all the babies were lost, but since then four out of five survived birth.

The main thing was for her to keep herself in shape, like the primitives who delivered out in the field, since there would be no help to push the baby out. That afternoon Isabel staked out a jogging trail, down the path to the pylon and back around the other way, crossing the stream, in a longitudinal circle around the inside-out planet. She found she actually felt better while she was running. Lap after lap, the circular forest passed beneath her feet, like the rungs of Peewee's exercise wheel. She wondered about Peewee, and whether her father was still taking care of the little mouse. Of course he would be; what other remembrance did he have? That and a couple of faded crayon drawings from her childhood, still tacked on the wall upstairs...

Afterward a swim in the fountain pool soothed her won-

derfully, almost letting her forget the unsettled feeling in her
stomach.

That evening Daniel cooked a special dinner of stuffed
squash and berry pudding. Isabel reminded herself that she
would have to tame another ewe for milking, since her diet
would demand extra.

Later she put a cup of roast cornnuts by her sleeping
place, to calm her digestion before morning. As she was
combing out her hair before bedtime, Daniel watched her
with an anxious look. She frowned back at him, shadowed in
the candlelight. "What's wrong?"

"Will thee . . . forgive me?"

"For what?"

"For getting us into this mess."

"Oh for goodness sake." She put down the comb with a
sigh. "As if it's your fault. Look, you always wanted to be a
father." Illustrations from the obstetrics manual pierced her
mind—ectopic pregnancy, placenta previa, toxemia—but she
bid them vanish, useless as it was. She reached out to Daniel
for comfort. He returned her embrace hungrily, kissing her
forehead, her lips, the nape of her neck. They pulled off their
clothes, clumsily in their haste, and for a while nothing else
existed but their own passionate universe of each other.

When they came to rest again, the candle had drowned in
its pool of wax, and the darkness was full. Isabel listened to
the cicadas and the owls outside.

An image from the pylon came back to her: the glowing skeleton, with the tiny fetus curled up behind the ribs.
Her heart raced suddenly, and she gripped Daniel's arm
hard.

"What is it?"

"That—that message, the skeleton. It seemed like a warning, it must have been."

Daniel pulled his fingers through her hair. "That is an ancient fear, the death of the mother and child. It's a fear we
have faced since the first Adam and Eve." He paused, then
added reflectively, "As a warning, it could mean many things.
It could remind us that eternity might have an ending."

An ending. How many bits of eternity had already met an

ending, outside the Walls, and in the Gwynwood graveyard? Yet her own life with Daniel, so longed for, was just beginning. "*Drink to me only with thine eyes...*"

She squeezed her eyes shut until she thought her head would burst. "It's too much, Daniel. If there is a God, He must be a very bad joker."

Daniel's face turned toward her. In the dark she could not see him, but she ran her fingers down his chest, feeling the soft hair uncovered, vulnerable. He, too, was alone, she realized suddenly; alone, away from the Scattergoods, the spiritual support of Gwynwood that enveloped one continually, shielding one from the hollow-eyed gaze of the skeletons outside the Wall. Isabel raised herself on her elbow and faced him through the darkness. "What do you think?"

"About what?"

"About God. Do you believe?"

"Yes," said Daniel. "I've yet to see a bit of creation unmarked by God's fingerprint."

"Even the Wall? Even this place?"

"Even so."

Isabel was silent, somehow disappointed. She remembered Andrés with his rosary, and the words he had taught her: "*I believe in the Father, and in the Son...*" "Well I don't believe a thing," she announced, renouncing her Catholic heritage as well as that of the Friends. "Maybe God was alive for Moses, but He died long before me."

Her words entered the silence. No walls caved in.

"Indeed?" Daniel's voice was quiet, with a note of curiosity. "What does this unbelief mean for you? Is everything permitted? Would you lie, cheat, steal?"

"Good heavens, no." Murder, maybe, for a good cause. But she could not make herself say it aloud.

"No? Why not?"

"Well..." Why not, indeed. "Look, you still have to do right, no matter who's watching or not."

Daniel absorbed this; then he tossed his head back with a burst of laughter. "So you obey God even though He's dead. God says, 'Would that men forsook Me, if only they kept My law.'"

"Who said that?"

"An ancient rabbi, interpreting the book of Jeremiah."

"Well, it's the only sensible word about God I ever heard. Those rabbis knew a thing or two." Then she remembered that her father had a Jewish grandmother, the one who had emigrated because the Germans did not consider her a person. "I should have known I was a Jew."

XXXIV

THE NEXT DAY, Isabel told Becca of her discovery that she was a Jew. Becca, who was busy puzzling over the calendar scratched on the wall of her cell, seemed less impressed than she had expected. "You don't have enough troubles, you want to be Jewish?"

Isabel was disappointed. "Isn't there anything special I ought to do?"

"There are the ten commandments. There are the holy days." Becca looked again at the calendar. "If you like, you can help me celebrate Passover next week. I think the Nisan full moon falls on April first, appropriately enough for us."

"Passover? That's when the slaves came out of Egypt?"

"Z'man cheruteynu, the season of our freedom."

Isabel liked the story of Moses. Harriet Tubman had been called "the Moses of her people."

"If you'd like to do a mitzvah," Becca added, "you could give me some more of that medicine of yours."

Isabel swallowed hard, turning away from the stare of Becca's angelbees. "That was my last, I'm sorry," she whispered.

Without the painkillers, Becca was more alert, but at what cost could only be guessed. She spent a lot of time sweeping out her cell for her Passover: "cleaning out the chametz," the imagined crumbs of leavened food. For the seder, the ritual meal on the eve of Passover, Isabel dipped long candles, using chunks of wall-wax melted around the fire and threads unraveled from her shirt for wicks.

In the absence of a table, the settings for the seder had to be made on the floor of Becca's cell, which she had immaculately cleaned. For the symbol of the Pesach lamb, Daniel roasted a red beet dug out of the garden, which Becca assured them was an accepted vegetarian substitute. Juice was pressed out of apples to serve for wine. Corn cakes served for matzah, dandelion greens for bitter herbs, and for the eggs a roasted potato. Becca wrung her hands over this, and over the absence of salt in the water for dipping. "It won't be authentic," she muttered.

"Will it not count if it's not authentic?" asked Isabel.

Becca looked up sharply. "Of course it will count. Does God expect of us the impossible? Besides, among Americans it's traditional to be unauthentic, and to complain about it."

Isabel blinked and said nothing more.

After the artificial twilight was gone, the candles were lit and Isabel sat with Daniel and Becca around the seder place settings, including the fourth one for the absent Elijah. Crickets sang outside, and moths came in to flit among the candle flames. Becca had put aside her eyespot scales for the occasion, knowing that the angelbees would only be scared off by the flames. Besides, she said, she had done the seder sightless for years; it felt part of the tradition, for her.

Becca poured the first cup of fermented apple juice. "'And there was evening and there was morning, the sixth day...'" So began the service, in the first mythic Garden where's God's creation began. Following the prayers and the breaking of the *afikomen*, she lifted the platter and began the story of Passover. "'This is the bread of poverty which our forefathers ate in the land of Egypt. Let all who are hungry enter and eat; let all who are needy come to our Passover feast. This year we are here; next year may we be in the Land of Israel. This year we are slaves; next year may we be free men and women.'"

She set down the platter and looked up at Isabel and Daniel. "Remind me, which of you is the younger?"

"I am," said Daniel, who was younger by six months.

"Then you can read the four questions." Becca pointed to the wall, next to the "calendar," where she had scratched in several lines of writing.

Daniel read out the questions, beginning with, "Why is this night different from all other nights of the year?" Becca then retold how the Hebrews had entered Egypt as guests and been turned into slaves, until their God chose to set them free. Through Moses, God had asked that his people be allowed to go out and worship Him. As Pharaoh refused, ten times, the ten plagues were sent. To symbolize the ten plagues, each participant dipped a finger in the fermented apple juice ten times. Despite Isabel's best intentions, she could not help but feel a little foolish, coming from her Quaker background which was sparing of ritual. This practice felt even odder than Andrés saying prayers over his rosary.

The ritual foods were shared. The maror, bitter herbs, represented the bitterness of slavery, Becca said. The haroset, a paste of chopped apple and walnuts, symbolized the mortar used by the Hebrews to assemble bricks into walls for their masters. The paste was sweet, Becca said, because of the sweetness of slavery.

Sweetness of slavery? Isabel frowned at the plate of haroset. Whatever could be sweet about slavery? To be polite, she let herself taste the tiniest bit of haroset on her plate.

After the seder meal was done and they were clearing the plates away, Isabel did ask, "What was the point of calling slavery sweet?"

Becca turned on her, her face in critical lines, just like the old days in the basement schoolroom. "Why did you not ask before? What is the purpose of the entire ritual, if not to teach the young about freedom?"

"I know well enough what freedom is. That's why I don't understand why you call slavery sweet?"

"What do you know about freedom?" demanded Becca. "You were born a slave—both of you." Daniel nodded in agreement.

That was true, Isabel realized. She and Daniel were the first to be born and survive within the Wall. She grew uncomfortable, wondering what kind of argument she had got herself into. "But we have our history. We know what freedom was, and we know we want it back."

"Nonsense," said Becca. "You owe your very existence to the intervention of our masters. Your entire life consists of haroset." Becca turned and took a broom of tied twigs to sweep the floor.

"The Hebrews understood freedom little better," said Daniel, coming to Isabel's defense.

"Of course," said Becca. "The Hebrews came to Egypt in the first place and put themselves under Pharaoh, because they were starving; because life in Egypt was sweet. Once they became slaves, what did they do about it? Even Moses was useless, at first; he killed an Egyptian, then had to flee. It took a woman to teach Moses freedom," she added, waving a finger at Daniel. "That was his wife, Zipporah, who bore him a child and renewed the covenant. That had to happen, before Moses could become God's instrument to free his people." She set the broom aside. "Maybe when your own child comes, then you'll learn how to be free."

Isabel reddened at this remark. Just the opposite, she thought: How could she ever fight the keepers with a baby on her hands?

Daniel said, "Freedom has to be reborn in each generation. We do have our history to remind us."

"Yes," said Becca. "That's why Liza put those pictures up on the wall, for those of you who need to see."

"Pictures?" said Isabel. "You mean John Dickinson and Helen Keller?" She had never thought of them as heroes of freedom, but of peace and handicap.

"John Dickinson was a patriot," Daniel said. "He authored the declaration of the Stamp Act Congress and led the boycott of British tea."

"And then refused to vote for independence," added Isabel.

"Independence," repeated Becca. "Does freedom mean independence? What did American independence mean before Doomsday, when my watch came from Hong Kong, my blouse from Malaysia, and my heating oil from the Persian Gulf? Independence," she muttered. "Interdependence. The Earth is round...as far as you walk, you come back to where you started..."

Becca began to sway on her feet, and Daniel helped her sit down. It had been a long day for her, and Isabel recalled with pain how ill she was. "You need your sleep, Teacher Becca."

The two of them left Becca to sleep. They walked arm in arm outside, Daniel carrying a candle lit from the fire. Isabel looked up into the starless "sky," and thought how Harriet "Moses" Tubman had escaped to Canada with only the North Star as her guide. As they reached the window of their cell, Isabel's steps slowed and her heart beat faster. She released Daniel's arm and took the eyespot scale from her pocket.

"I'm going," said Isabel. "Back to the pylon. This time, I will escape."

"Escape where?" Daniel asked. "To another hypersphere?"

"I'll find other folks, somewhere, and we'll join forces to fight our way out."

Daniel held the candle up to her, and the shadows wove a jagged pattern across his eyes. "What does thee mean, Isabel?"

"I mean that with enough of us together, we might overpower the goatsnakes and capture their energy cylinders. We could use the cylinders to defend ourselves while we find the way out of the Hive."

"Isabel, thee doesn't know what thee is saying. That is precisely the kind of thinking that left us humans in Gwynwood, surrounded by skeletons. There are different kinds of freedom; remember Helen Keller? What did freedom mean to her?"

Helen Keller, as a Special Child blind and deaf, had had to be trained like a wild animal before her teacher had taught her to speak through the touch of fingers. Isabel frowned. "That's not our problem. What does freedom mean to us?"

"Freedom means obedience to God," said Daniel quietly. "No more, and no less. God set the Hebrews free only after they were kept from worshiping Him."

"Harriet Tubman prayed to God without ceasing. In the end, she took up a rifle for the Union."

"A brave woman. And yet, in a sense the Civil War postponed true emancipation a hundred years. The Quaker abolitionists knew better."

"How could they know? Those Quakers were never slaves. They were all white, like you."

Daniel's face darkened, and for a moment he could not speak. "Thee is wrong, Isabel. I was born a slave, as surely as thee. And when I hear God's word, I promise thee, I will go."

XXXV

OVER THE NEXT few days, Isabel tried to make her way into the Hive through the other-dimensional gate of the pylon, but each time the keeper overcame her with sleep and the goatsnakes carried her out again. After several attempts, the sleep-fog began pouring out of the airwall even as she came near.

There had to be some way to evade the keeper. A torch would scare off its angelbees, but it would scare off her own angelbees as well, leaving her without assistance to penetrate the airwall. For the moment, she was at a loss.

As April passed, Isabel's morning sickness lessened and her waist thickened appreciably. Daniel let out the seams of her overalls so she could still ease them on. She began to feel overly warm all the time, as if spring were turning into summer, but Daniel and Becca felt no change. The little inside-out planet enclosed a drop of eternal springtime. The garden was always full, for as one patch of corn died off another patch ripened.

Isabel chafed at the ease of it, how they took for granted their sustenance from their masters. "It's *haroset*," she said: "How are we to demand freedom, while we enjoy the fruits of slavery?"

She started to clear some plots of her own and planted seeds of zucchinis and sunflowers and tomatoes. Unfortunately the birds and rabbits attacked her plots with enthusiasm, though they stayed away from what the keepers had sown. Daniel joined her, plowing and sowing, and rising before dawn to scare off the robins. It was a small start, but it gave them something to do and at least a taste of independence. Through Isabel's mind flashed the recollection of Grace Feltman, driving home alone in the horse cart. Even poor Grace needed to feel independent about something.

Becca watched with admiration, but she did not join their efforts. "You may be right but—somehow—I have my doubts.

The gardeners know perfectly well that we can provide for ourselves, on Earth. These are not the gifts we must refuse. We have yet to meet the snake with the apple."

"On the contrary," Isabel exclaimed, "we've got too many snakes with too many apples."

"Perhaps." The scales twinkled on the lids of Becca's eyes, which were dark and sunken underneath, for her pain robbed her of sleep. "At any rate, something has happened to our pylon. It won't 'talk' as it used to."

"Not at all?"

Becca hesitated, "Go and see for yourself."

Isabel had not been to the pylon since the night she realized she was pregnant. So after dinner she put the scale on her eye, gave it a couple hours to adjust, then set out down the glowing path through the forest.

The pylon was not completely dark. It showed a single vision, over and over, the same one it had shown last: the nuclear mushroom cloud, erupting and boiling up into the stratosphere. Sometimes it was a groundburst, at other times an airborne fireball that reached to touch the ground, or occasionally a burst from underwater, spreading its fingers of lethal foam across the sea. But nothing else would appear within the six-sided pyramid, no matter what shapes of softened wax Isabel raised before it.

She felt her stomach turn over and her hair stand on end. Something had to be wrong, but what? Were they still upset with her for shaping the "keeper" and crumbling it in her hand? Had her gardening attempts displeased them? Or was there something else afoot, something she could not know about, outside the hypersphere?

She set her jaw hard. "If you're trying to scare us, it won't work," she said aloud. But the sound of her voice rang flat and empty in the unearthly darkness.

Since the pylon would not answer, Isabel took to following the keeper-gardener at night on its rounds through the zigzag rows of squash and corn. But neither the polyhedral body, nor its floating angelbees, would take notice of her. Isabel had failed so far to figure out the six-dotted code of the angelbees. She trained herself to wear two scales at once, one on each eye, as Becca did; it took a while to sort out the images from each. She discovered then that when one angel-bee turned to face another, the play of dots winking around the eyespot intensified, only to disappear when the angelbees were alone. So it seemed that the floating eyeballs could talk to each other. A sign of some autonomy, perhaps?

The goatsnakes, by contrast, appeared fully subservient to their keeper, feeding it regurgitated vegetable matter at the "mouth" on the keeper's underside, and performing various gardening tasks, pruning the foliage and sprinkling seed for new vegetables. She envied them their powerful tools, those cylinders with the bladeless saws that the goatsnakes wielded, entwined in their coils. She watched closely, in case they might drop one and leave it behind. Perhaps she might use it to take the keeper hostage and force her way out of the hypersphere.

As the fetus grew, Isabel found herself needing extra hours of sleep, and the pace of her jogging slowed. Still she kept it up, ten laps a day round the hypersphere, the sweat rolling down her forehead until it stung her eyes. She had to give up some of her extra gardening, but she continued to milk the sheep, gather nuts, and keep the fire going.

One night in June, as Isabel was trying to get to sleep, she felt something move inside her belly. She turned restlessly to the other side, but it moved again.

She tapped Daniel's shoulder. "It moved, Daniel."

"What's that?"

"The baby. It moved."

"Is that good?"

"Of course, silly. It means it's growing on schedule. Here, feel it." She placed his hand over the spot where it had moved, but just then the buried creature chose to be still.

The fetus grew rapidly, and by the end of the month scarcely an hour passed without the sensation of its head or its foot pushing outward. As Isabel jogged, the little one, too, seemed to be jogging inside; sometimes, when one leg pushed too far out to the side, she had to push it back in. All night she could feel it stretching and tumbling within the waters of its own inside-out planet.

Now that the baby's presence was so palpable, Isabel almost felt as if it had been born already. She decided to assume it was a girl and think of it as "she" from then on. Since "she" would need clothes and diapers, it was time to get things in order. Daniel cut up the snowsuits into diapers, and Isabel sheared enough fleece from Hannaleh and the other tame ewe to line a sleeping place.

Becca offered to help, but her condition had taken a turn for the worse. She was losing weight, and she spent most of her time lying inside her cell. At night she could be heard moaning quietly. Isabel ransacked her medicine collection one last time, but all the painkillers and sedatives were gone.

Daniel said, "I will read to her at night, until she falls asleep." He took up the Bible, one of the two books they had brought.

Isabel turned on him suddenly. "What about yourself? How's your anemia medicine holding up?"

"I've got another two weeks' worth."

"Then you'll have to conserve your strength, too. I'll do the reading."

"But thee needs sleep, for the baby to grow."

"You're the one who will have to deliver it."

He turned white, then sat very still, until the color returned to his cheeks. He swallowed once, then nodded. "I know. I just try not to think about it."

They hugged each other hard. "Let me try to escape again," Isabel whispered fiercely. "There's got to be a way back. I'll explore that corridor again—"

"No. It's not safe," Daniel warned. "If they put thee out again with that sleep-gas, it might harm the baby."

"Then you have to go."

For the first time, Daniel seriously considered this. "I still believe we are here for a purpose," he said. "We must find out what that is."

"What purpose? Look what's happening to Becca; what's the purpose in that? Even the keepers must see, now, how ill she is. How could they be so cruel as to keep her here?"

He thought this over for some minutes. From outside, a barn owl called twice. "All right, I'll try. After Becca's asleep." He climbed out the window with his Bible to read to her. As he went, Isabel thought again of Aaron Weiss in his last days in the hospital the year before. Now, how long did his sister have left?

XXXVI

DANIEL TRIED, BUT he had no more success than Isabel at evading the keeper at the pylon. In the meantime, as the nights passed, Becca seemed to enjoy Daniel's reading, and she passed more easily into sleep. When Isabel's turn came, she offered *Harriet Tubman* instead of the Bible, and Becca assented without comment. She read from the beginning, of Tubman's girlhood on the plantation, how she grew up in a slave cabin and was sent out to a mistress who whipped her nearly to death for leaving dust on the furniture.

Becca shook her head. "It's always hard to believe how foolish people can be."

Isabel looked up thoughtfully. "That is true. That is why I always had trouble with the Bible. Even the prophets sometimes acted so foolish."

Becca lay still except for her face, flushed with fever, her cheeks sunken and her skin withering as if she had aged another ten years. Her emaciation made the swelling of her tumor more pronounced, like a grotesque mockery of Isabel's pregnancy, though Isabel felt ashamed to see it that way.

"What else is the Bible for," Becca said, "if not foolish people? If people were wise, they'd have no need of the Bible."

"But in the Bible, even God looks foolish. Why would He tell Abraham to kill his own child?"

"That's a hard one, isn't it. Men have always been ready to devour their own offspring, like Chronos. All the Abrahams, sending their sons off to all the wars, all in the name of one God or another."

The bitterness in her teacher's voice stunned Isabel, and she wished she had held her tongue. Then to her amazement, a tear seeped out beneath Becca's eyelids and rolled down her cheek.

"And yet," Becca added more slowly, "there must be some

truth in Abraham. We must value God's law above all, even the security of our children. Had our mothers and fathers obeyed the ten commandments, instead of making missiles for 'defense' of their children, perhaps we wouldn't be here today."

She stopped to swallow, and Isabel lifted a cup of water to her lips. "The truth is," Becca went on, "we never learn. After Doomsday, all the parents of Gwynwood made a pact to spare their children the details of the Death Year. Life was hard enough, they said, in the early years, so why add this extra burden? We even left out of the seder the reading from *Night*, about Elie Wiesel's first night in camp, lest the children ask questions about that other 'first night.'" She added, as if to herself, "Perhaps we were not so far wrong. Even Wiesel kept silence, first, for many years. Children need time to grow, to learn joy. But you are grown, now, you and Daniel, and the others; you, the firstborn within the Wall." Becca raised her right hand, slowly, as if it took all her strength. "When you return, you remind them. You tell them, the time has come for things to be told and known."

"Yes, Becca." Isabel's voice was hoarse, barely recognizable as her own. Beneath her fingers the pages of her book were damp and tearstained.

Daniel tried several times to break out of the hypersphere, but got no farther than Isabel had done. In the meantime, as Becca worsened, she seemed to lose touch with the outer world, failing to respond when Isabel or Daniel spoke. Her head twisted from side to side, and she moaned in pain, continually, day and night. The two of them nursed her in turn, trying to keep her comfortable and clean.

"Isabel," Daniel said one night at dinner, "thee has not been eating very much."

"I'm not hungry."

"But the baby needs food."

"I know." She recalled from the charts that she ought to be eating twice what she used to. She felt ashamed to suggest that they move their dining place away from the honeycomb of cells, where Becca's cries could not be heard.

"Thee is overtired," Daniel said. "Thee needs to keep up

thy strength. I will nurse Becca alone from now on."

She did not refuse. She sat like a stone, the heat of her face relieved slightly by a gentle breeze, as much wind as they ever had in the hypersphere. Overhead the bats swooped after insects, and tree frogs and crickets competed for a hearing. Then a thought came to her, unbidden, and her heart beat faster. "Daniel . . . there is one last thing we could offer her."

Daniel put his plate down and faced her. "She's still alive. Who knows what will happen. The keepers may yet see that she is sick, and decide to return her."

"Even if they did, what could we do for her? The cancer must have spread everywhere by now, even to her brain. There's nothing to be done in Gwynwood, probably not even in Sydney."

"Doctors can be wrong."

Isabel felt her face grow warm, but she went on. "What do you think Becca herself would want? What if she thinks differently?"

Daniel thought this over. "All of Earth's great religions," he began slowly, "maintain this one law: 'What is hurtful to thee, do not to thy neighbor.'"

"And isn't it hurtful to her, to withhold her one last comfort?" Isabel got up from where she sat. "Let her choose. I will ask her."

Daniel rose swiftly, and his hand gripped her wrist. "Thee will not tell her. Thee must promise."

Startled, Isabel looked down at his hand on her arm, which held so hard that it actually hurt.

Daniel looked down, too. He seemed surprised at himself. He released her hand, saying quietly, "The madness is in me, too."

For a while they both stood there, looking away from each other, not speaking, but listening. From the forest outside a barn owl called, its muffled note swooping upward. Then she remembered her mother agonizing over the defective babies, and how she herself had fled from that choice. Her spirits fell, lower than she had ever felt before. "I suppose," said Isabel at last, reflectively, "the real Garden of Eden had no hospitals either. This is what it was really like. No wonder they ate the apple."

"The fruit of knowledge, of knowing and sharing another human soul." Daniel nodded. "The fruit of compassion. Perhaps that was what angered God, that we might love a fellow human better than Him."

Three days later, they awoke to silence. There was no sound from Becca's cell, and to Isabel even the birdsongs seemed muted.

When they approached Becca's cell, they found the windows completely sealed off, filled in with wax. Isabel cried and beat the window with her palms, and made a halfhearted attempt to dig through, in case Becca was still alive. But she knew it was pointless. Either Becca had died in the night, or else the keepers had taken matters into their own hands.

Isabel stood up, gingerly as the baby's limbs poked her insides, then she put the scales on her eyes and headed down the path to the pylon.

The pylon was unresponsive as before, still caught in its endless loop of fireballs, one after another. Isabel went up to it, pressing into the airwall as far as she could, then raised her arm and pounded the air with her fist. "Let us go, do you hear!" she shouted. "You're killing us all. I won't go on; I won't eat your *haroset*."

She took Keith's cigarette lighter from her pocket and clicked on the flame. Her two angelbees beat a quick retreat to the treetops, watching from a distance her own glowing form, arm outstretched holding the piercing flame, the pylon repeating its mindless apocalypse.

After a minute or so the lighter flame sputtered and died, its fuel finally spent. Her matches, too, were nearly done. She would have to watch the home fire now with extra care.

XXXVII

THEY TRIED TO mourn for Becca, as appropriately as they could. Daniel recited what little he recalled of the Hebrew *kaddish*, then he and Isabel spent some time in reflection on the many things their teacher had shared with them over the years, from the alphabet to Shakespeare, to the angelbees. Isabel remembered the scale in the candle box, which she had passed on to Peace Hope. She wondered whether her friend had ever figured out its use, or had the poor angelbee given up its futile pursuit?

And poor Becca, why had the keepers taken her into the hypersphere? Had they gained whatever it was they sought? What more did they expect now from her bereaved companions?

At night, Isabel redoubled her pursuit of the keeper in the garden. She grew bolder, approaching almost within arm's reach of the goatsnakes. It occurred to her: What if she tried to snatch a cylinder from a goatsnake's coils?

One night, a goatsnake was using its cylinder to slice off the limbs of a diseased maple at the edge of the garden, while the polyhedral keeper supervised nearby, squatting on its six spiderlegs. Isabel sent her angelbee to watch up close. The energy beam from the cylinder appeared bright white to her infrared eyesight, but not quite bright enough to scare off the angelbee. A high-pitched whine could be heard as each branch parted like butter, and below the underbrush crackled as the energy beam reached momentarily to the ground.

The goatsnake slithered down the trunk with its cylinder and paused to browse on the underbrush, its neck swelling as lumps of greenery were swallowed. Then it returned to the base of the tree and aimed its cylinder to bring down the trunk.

The keeper must have expected the trunk to fall forward into the forest. Instead, it teetered backward toward the garden. The goatsnake dropped its cylinder and vanished in an instant, but the more ponderous keeper was slow to react. As the trunk fell, it crashed down at the side of the keeper, pinning two of its legs.

Through her own two angelbees, Isabel watched, her mouth open in surprise. The keeper lay still; the cylinder lay beside the tree stump, inert. Two glowing goatsnakes lay in the underbrush, quivering, as if registering pain or shock. The keeper's angelbees were nowhere to be seen.

The cylinder. Isabel eyed it, her heart pounding so hard she could barely think. She stepped forward slowly, the leaves crackling beneath her feet, ready to flee in a moment. But there was no sign of any other keepers coming to the rescue.

She reached for the cylinder cautiously, uncertain as to which end projected the energy beam. As she picked it up she held it at arm's length, horizontal across her path, so that neither end pointed back toward her. At one end she noticed a band glowing faintly, encircling the cylinder. With her right hand she grasped the glowing band, which felt slightly warm to her touch. As she gripped harder, a sudden spattering of dirt erupted to her left.

She dropped the cylinder and stepped back, choking in the dust that had been raised. Then she realized what had happened: the beam had turned on, from the left end. More confident now, she retrieved the cylinder and practiced turning it on and off by squeezing the banded end, while aiming the opposite end into the underbrush.

The keeper; what was it up to? She turned quickly, but the keeper still lay there, its legs pinned down.

Now was her chance, she realized. She could mow down the creature, and its goatsnakes, too, just as surely as it had taken Becca's life. For once, she could strike back at her captors.

Yet, as she raised the cylinder, her stomach sickened at the thought. Somehow the broken creature before her seemed less an enemy than a wounded animal, an animal capable of feeling. She had never even brought herself to slaughter a lamb, much less a creature such as this. She had watched it for too long not to think of it as thou.

Her arm swung down, and she half turned to go. But the

memory of the stricken creature would follow her. The keeper would lie there in pain, for how long she could not guess. It would suffer there, just as Becca had suffered. Yet no amount of its suffering could ever bring Becca back to her again.

A flood of tears welled up unexpectedly. She sat down and let herself cry for some time, crying in a way that she had not been able to cry for Becca before, for her loss as well as her own helplessness and her fears for her future.

When at last her tears subsided, she breathed deeply and took another look at the fallen tree that pinned the keeper down. She aimed the cylinder to slice through the trunk at intervals, just by the side of the keeper, until there remained one segment small enough for her to lift off.

As she removed the tree trunk from the keeper's legs, it occurred to her that when the keeper recovered it might want its cylinder back. So she ran off with her find, intending to make good use of it as quickly as possible.

With the cylinder she chopped firewood, several weeks' worth, until she was exhausted and Daniel took over. It occurred to her that the beam might slice stone as well as wood; indeed it did, albeit more slowly. So, with some practice, she sculpted cooking pots out of stone, hollowing them out with brief bursts from the cylinder.

The next day Daniel used the biggest pot to cook up a thick vegetable stew, the first they had tasted in months. The first spoonful brought back to Isabel memories of her father and the spicy stews he used to make. For an instant she saw her mother and father across from her at the table as they had sat for so many years.

The keeper did not return for its cylinder. Daniel insisted that she return with him to the fallen tree, to see what had happened and offer further assistance if needed. But the keeper and its goatsnakes were gone, presumably either recovered or hauled off by others.

That evening, Isabel's angelbee saw in the sky a curious pattern of infrared that she recalled from her earliest days in the hypersphere. It was the pattern of concentric rings, extending across the whole sky, collapsing gradually inward to the zenith while new rings formed above the horizon. "That's from the pylon," she reminded Daniel. "Remember, before, when it was 'talking' to Becca, and to us; the pattern of rings was in the pylon, and we could see it across the sky from here. Maybe the pylon is ready to talk again."

"It's worth a try," Daniel agreed.

The pylon glowed with its concentric zebra rings, just as it had on the first night that Becca had brought her out with her angelbee eye. Isabel sent her angelbee racing ahead to face the hexagonal pyramid. As it approached, the giant human eyeball reappeared, displacing the pattern of rings. The eyeball stared back at her angelbee and blinked twice.

"It's back again!" Isabel clapped and shouted to Daniel. "The pylon's talking. Maybe at last we'll find out how to escape." She fingered a lump of wax in her pocket and thought of all the questions she wanted to ask. Her steps slowed as she approached the airwall.

The outsized eyeball faded away. In its place stood an image of the Queen of the keepers, its bulbous head trailed by the segments of keeperlike polyhedrons, each of which would someday bud off as a newborn keeper. The image was a still portrait, not alive with motion, but it was much sharper in detail than the stylized figure Isabel had seen before, when she had held up a wax-model of an expectant mother.

"That is for thee," said Daniel, arriving at her side. "They must know that thee is a mother now."

The Queen had huge mandibles curving up under its head, which she had not noticed in the earlier image. Were the mandibles for eating or for fighting, she wondered. Among honeybees, the Queen was a relentless killer, rarely permitting a sister queen to share the same hive.

"Where is the drone?" Daniel wondered. "There must be a male somewhere."

"Maybe keeper Queens self-fertilize, or maybe they're asexual, like the angelbees." Without sex, only mutation would provide genetic diversity. She wondered whether mutation ever interfered with the symbiosis of the keepers and their angelbees and goatsnakes. It was hard to imagine a keeper getting along by itself; even for feeding it required the stuff regurgitated by its goatsnakes. But the angelbees often ranged far from their keepers, and they talked among themselves with their Braille-like code of winking dots.

The image of the Queen was fading slowly. Nothing remained, at last, except for the domelike structure that had housed the creature. The dome was a geodesic patchwork of hexagons and other polygonal shapes. The structure remained there, unchanging, for some time.

Puzzled, Isabel shifted from one foot to the other. Now in her eighth month, the baby had reached a size that made any position uncomfortable within a short time. Finally she shrugged and began to shape the wax from her pocket into a flat slab. She shaped a wall with a door cut out and swung it back and forth at the "hinges." Surely the keepers knew the purpose of human doors. If only they would let her know what they required of her, to unlock their own.

The dome from the Queen faded away. Now the pylon showed a flat floor leading into a hexagonal corridor.

Isabel frowned. "That looks like the place in the extra dimension, the Looking-glass Land where I went inside before." She sent her angelbees around the pylon, and the view rotated, showing a second corridor running in the opposite direction from the first. Her pulse quickened. "Daniel—what if they're inviting us inside?"

"Thee can't be sure," he warned. "They didn't like it one bit, the other times we've tried."

"But it's different now. They know us better; they must like the fact that I helped the keeper who got hurt."

"That was well done," Daniel agreed. "But still—it's too dangerous. Let's wait until the baby is born before we try that again."

"The point is, I want the baby born in Gwynwood, not here, if I can help it." She shuddered despite herself. "Look, let's just step inside next to the pylon and let our angelbees do some exploring down the corridor."

They stepped in through the breach in the airwall generated by Isabel's angelbee. This time, they stayed just within the pylon's domain, the in-between place that switched between two places. No keepers appeared. With a scale cupping each eyelid, Isabel kept one angelbee hovering at her shoulder to look out for keepers, then let the other one venture through the airwall to explore the corridor.

The keepers did not seem to mind. As her angelbee and Daniel's floated on, they soon discovered a network of corridors, linking airwalled pylons throughout the Hive. Not all the pylons contained views of Edenic gardens. One appeared to be the main square of a town full of little huts with thatched roofs. Another pylon actually seemed to stand within a building of some sort, with crude unfinished walls, perhaps made of concrete.

Did all of these little pylons connect to hyperspheres, she wondered; or did some of them return to Earth?

XXXVIII

OVER THE NEXT week, Isabel and Daniel sent their angelbees to explore the Hive, while keeping themselves to the relative safety of the pylon's domain. All the while, the baby seemed to swim around inside her like a goldfish in a bowl, active day and night. Her size had increased so fast that she could not get on her overalls; Daniel had to cut a deep slit down the back, where an opening would be least immodest. But, aside from needing extra sleep, Isabel felt well, much better than she had in the early months.

One afternoon, as their angelbees roamed the mist-filled corridors, they came upon a pylon whose view set her heartbeat racing. There was the grassy clearing, and the oak trees beyond—surely the trunk with the big crook in it was the one just past Anna Tran's house? As Isabel's angelbee circled round the pylon, the view rotated around the clearing. Then, unexpectedly, a person appeared in view.

It was Peace Hope, seated in the grass with her crutches to the side. She was playing chess with herself as she contemplated the Pylon.

"*Peace Hope!*" Isabel shouted involuntarily, though she knew it was useless. Peace Hope had been looking out for her, trying to reach her, all this time; and there was the way back home to Gwynwood.

"Wait here," exclaimed Daniel. "I'll bring help." He stepped through the airwall and made a dash down the corridor.

Isabel tried to follow, but the airwall held her in. Quickly she directed the other angelbee at her shoulder to slip through. She ran as fast as she could down the corridor, stumbling with the unaccustomed drop in gravity. Daniel had already vanished from sight, trying to outrun any keepers with their goatsnakes. The fog chilled her, but at least her second angelbee above her shoulder enabled her to see her way ahead.

As an opening to the branch corridor came up, she

paused, trying to remember if this was the turn her exploring angelbee had taken to the Gwynwood Pylon.

Something grabbed her from behind, across her chest and smothering her scream. A goatsnake, she thought as she struggled to free herself. Her eyes opened, and the two scales popped off, leaving her lost in the fog.

But the flesh that her fingers sank into wore a shirtsleeve, distinctly human: a human arm.

"What is it, Dirk?" came a harsh whisper, an Aussie accent. Two burning torches loomed out of the fog.

"It's a girl, can't you see?" The man holding her had a deep voice, American, with a slurred edge. "Let's get the hell out of here."

"Not another girl," said the Aussie.

"You watch it, you dags," came an indignant female voice. "Look at her, she's preggo. Bob, you watch yourself."

"A preggo girl," Bob amended with a note of exasperation.

"Cut that shit." Dirk shoved her to the wall and forced her through a narrow crevice. She gasped as her belly scraped through.

The place behind the wall looked nothing like the corridor outside. Jagged structures jutted out at various angles, and one had to step carefully over the uneven flooring. Fortunately the fog seemed to lessen, so that the torches were more effective than they had been out in the corridor. But that was little comfort to Isabel as she was dragged along with the four or five strangers. At one point an obstruction blocked their path, and Dirk lifted a keeper's cylinder. Its beam played upon the obstruction, which quickly smoldered away. To her amazement, she saw that all the strangers wore cylinders slung across their backs. How had they obtained so many?

"Halt," called Dirk at last. "Time to take stock. Everybody make it?" Dirk leaned into the wall, breathing heavily. Bob and three other men ranged around him. The woman, a petite figure with curly brown hair, smiled encouragingly at Isabel, but the effect was odd with her eyes covered by mirrorshades. The four men wore mirrorshades, too, poking out through their tangled hair and beards, including Dirk whose long hair shone sandy-colored in the wavering torchlight.

Then she remembered: Dirk Brendan, the transportee from

Vista, leader of the Shades, in the Underground. The Shades had tried to blast through Sydney's outer Wall, but instead had leveled half of Paddington, where Keith's lover lived. Now here they were, in the very heart of the Hive, prowling the home of the Earth's overlords like mice behind a barn wall—or like waxworms in a honeycomb.

Isabel found her voice. "You can't do this to me. I've got to get back before—" She winced as pain shot through the arm twisted behind her back.

"We've no time to lose," Dirk said, "before the rovers catch up. Get moving."

The Shades scrambled on down the uneven passageway, dragging Isabel with them. At last they went out again into the corridor, their torches lighting up the fog. Another pylon appeared, glowing within its airwall.

"Halt," shouted Dirk. "I don't like the looks of it. Face masks, quick."

Something resembling surgical masks came down over their heads, covering their mouths and noses. The woman thrust one onto Isabel.

"A snake!" Someone screamed. There was a blue flash from a cylinder and a sickening stench in the air. "Got it all right, but look out for the rovers."

A keeper appeared, its six legs moving up and down a bit faster than usual. A second keeper arrived from the other side of the pylon. Dirk aimed his cylinder at the near one. The polyhedral body vaporized, leaving behind only a sort of skeleton, interlocking plates of "bone" that had extended at right angles to the faces of the polyhedron. Then the skeleton, too, blackened and crumbled away.

Within a few seconds, it seemed, the keepers were demolished and their goatsnakes nowhere to be seen.

"Bob, keep an eye out for the rovers. Everyone else—hunt for their rayguns."

The torches swung back and forth in a hasty search of the floor where the goatsnakes might have left cylinders.

Dirk shoved Isabel toward the pylon. "Get inside, we'll be safe." He aimed his cylinder at the airwall, and the hemisphere sizzled all over with jagged sparks. "That should do it." Still pulling Isabel, he and the woman walked straight through. After a few seconds, a lush forest appeared outside. Another burst from the cylinder, and they all walked out.

Isabel recognized the greenish sky as the sign of a hypersphere. But the air was hotter than where she came from, and the foliage was entirely foreign, trees with wispy green crowns and dense impenetrable grasses below. Something shrieked raucously as it flew overhead, while brightly colored parrots stood out in the branches.

They hiked down a path through the trees, arriving at a fortress wall built of jagged stone blocks. The cut surface of the blocks had the fused look of stone sliced by the beam of a keeper's cylinder. A thick wooden door swung back, revealing a campfire surrounded by several more men and women in mirrorshades, and a great heap of cylinders in one corner. There was a smell of burnt meat, and some kind of animal carcass hung from a pole.

"Hullo, we've got a new recruit," called Dirk. "The girl's name is—" He stopped and looked at her inquiringly.

"Isabel Garcia-Chase," she said in a small voice.

"Welcome to the Front. Get her some shades, Meg, and put her through orientation. We've got a raid tonight."

Isabel was too dazed to respond. Meg, the woman who had come with them from outside, beckoned Isabel to join her, offering a seat on a blanket. "My name's Megan Connelly," she said. "I know, we seem rough at first, but then we've got a rough job to do. Here, have some shades."

Isabel shook her head at the mirrored sunglasses in Megan's hand.

"You've got to," insisted Megan, placing them on her face. "Otherwise the space cockies will read your mind, from the temperature of your eyeballs."

Taken aback, Isabel blinked at her. It sounded like something the Herald would think up. "Look, Megan, I've had enough of this. You just dragged me here and—"

"Shh, before they hear; Dirk has a short fuse. See here, hon, it's your duty to join us. We're the Liberation Front, the leading edge of the Underground."

"Well, it's not my kind of Underground."

"We're the best. We're the only unit to penetrate the Hive. We actually got sent here, to this space-warped prison, because we were such a serious threat. But we turned the tables on them. We captured their weapons and found our way out. We've cleaned out a dozen rovers' nests so far. We're committed to the liberation of the human race. To do that, we have one ultimate objective: to destroy the Queen."

"The Queen?"

Megan turned her head, and her eyelashes appeared behind her glasses. "Look, the rest of the party's back. How many guns?" she called.

The men who had stayed behind to search the floor were entering the fortress wall. Bob held aloft a cylinder. "Only one lousy raygun. You'd think they'd know better by now." Laughter greeted this remark.

"Meg, get the barbie on," someone called out.

Megan got up. "Supper's early, since there's a raid tonight. Come on, you can help out."

The mention of supper reminded Isabel that she was starving, and that her unborn child needed nourishment. She followed Megan past the pile of cylinders to the cooking area, her mind racing. How could she slip out of here unnoticed? How would she ever find her way back without her angelbees? She fought down a sense of panic. Megan commenced cutting up meat and skewering it on a long stick. Warily Isabel picked up a scrap of red meat and looked it over. "What is it?"

"Wallaby. We had good mutton, the first few weeks, until the sheep ran out. Now we're down to roos and wombats." Megan pushed several pieces down the skewer. "Dirk says if we run out, we might have to raid the China town again for provisions. It's just down the hall, isn't that weird? I don't like the idea, but—we've got a rough job to do."

"If you do get the Queen," Isabel ventured, "what do you suppose the—the rovers will do about it?"

Overhearing her, Bob called, "The rovers are nothing, Izzy. Come, we'll explain." He and Dirk were studying something on a large wrinkled piece of paper.

Dirk said, "The Queen is everything. All the rovers, cockies, and snakes exist solely to serve the Queen. It's the ultimate statist system."

"And when the Queen goes, the rest falls apart." Bob's fingers mimed an explosion.

Isabel approached, noting that the paper appeared to be a map of some sort. "Why do you think they came here?" she asked curiously. "Why did they come, if only to destroy Earth?"

"To destroy us, not Earth," said Bob. "To settle our planet. Because they had already nuked their own planet beyond repair."

Dirk said, "Nukes are nothing to them. They blew their own planet to bits using space-warp, the same technology that built this inside-out prison." His hand rose, gesturing about the hypersphere. "They came here to nuke us out so they could resettle Earth."

Isabel digested this. The logic was chillingly plausible. The keepers would have kept a few Earth creatures, out of remorse, like Indians on a reservation.

She turned to Bob. "So what exactly are you trying to do?"

"Clean out the Queen's nest." Bob pointed to the map. Isabel saw what appeared to be the outline of corridors through the Hive, with many X's and scribbled notations. "Here are the main rovers' nests—here, and here," said Bob, pointing to the map, his beard nodding up and down. "The X's mark where we've cleaned out the nests already. Look how all the nests seem to cluster around this one spot. That's where the Queen's nest must be. We know what it looks like: it's a special cell, built like a geodesic dome, like this." He sketched a pattern of hexagonal roof tiles, extending down and around to form a dome.

"But—I don't understand. How do you 'clean them out'?"

"Simple. Just go in and burn them. Then pick up all their rayguns and clear out, before help comes with the sleep-gas. Occasionally they snare a few of us; that's why we need new recruits." Bob looked up at her reflectively. "You're a good looker, you know that?"

Isabel stepped back warily.

"Bob, como on," called Megan. "It's her first night, and she's preggo."

Bob shrugged and turned his back, while others joined him in planning the foray into the Hive. The sky darkened, and the cries of animals grew louder around the fortress, a cacophony of foreign croaks and whistles. Isabel tried to eat but could barely manage a bite. As she crouched on the blanket, she felt something attached to her foot. It was a black sucking thing the size of her thumb.

"Just a ground leech. You never saw one? Where're you from?" Megan applied a flame to its head to burn the leech off. She tossed it in the fire; a burst of sparks cascaded down.

"Gwynwood. Gwynwood, USA." The remembered phrase leapt off of Peace Hope's stamp into her fevered brain. Peace Hope was out there, still, somewhere; somewhere, out of this valley of the shadow of death. And Daniel might have reached home by now...

Her wits came back into focus again. She cleared her throat and looked earnestly up at the woman. Megan's glasses mirrored twin images of the flames of the campfire. "Megan, do you see—I know what you're trying to do, but I can't help you. My husband is sick and my people are dying. I have to get back home."

"We're all dying," said Megan. "Poisoned by the bloody space cockies."

Isabel shuddered, wondering whether Daniel was right, or was Dirk? Then a thought occurred to her. "Do they—the snakes—do they ever burn you, with those cylinders?"

"No, they're too slow moving. They can't aim well enough. Instead, they put us to sleep and do creepy experiments on us."

"Really? Like what?"

"How should I know? They'd never show me."

Isabel pondered this. "What do you suppose will happen, after you clean them out and get the Queen? Your friends are just the sort to start building missiles again."

Megan shook her head. "That was all a myth, you see. All that stuff about humans having nuclear missiles—does it make sense to you? Why would we nuke our own planet? It's a myth made up by the government, to trap us in guilt and dependency. To keep us from rebelling. But it won't succeed. When the space cockies are gone, there will be no more nation-states: just free men and women, protecting their own."

Isabel absorbed this recital in startled silence.

"Are you really married?" Megan asked suddenly. "Can I see your ring?"

Isabel shook herself out of her thoughts to look at Megan.

Then she removed her wedding band and held it out to her. "It's from Daniel's folks, actually. See their initials and wedding date, May sixth, twenty-oh-three."

"I mean your diamond."

"Daniel's mom was a plain Friend. She didn't wear diamonds."

"Oh," said Megan, disappointed. She turned the ring over a few times, then returned it to Isabel. "What's it like to have a baby inside? Does it know when you're patting it like that?"

Isabel realized that she had been stroking her belly without thinking, a habit she had acquired. She flushed slightly. "I don't know. She kicks back sometimes, I think."

"Is it kicking now?"

"Yes. You can feel her, right here."

"Can I really?"

"Sure."

Megan leaned over and tentatively touched Isabel's overalls stretched taut over her belly. Isabel guided her hand to the spot where the left leg was kicking now and then with an insistent thump. About half a minute passed. Then Megan's lips parted as if startled. "Wow, that was a sharp one. That must hurt bad."

"Not really. It's comforting, actually; it means the baby's okay."

"That's some pushy kid you've got in there. You put up with that for nine months?"

"She only started kicking about the fifth month. She's due in another month."

Abruptly Megan sat up. "You can't have it born here. There's nobody to deliver it."

"That's right," agreed Isabel, suddenly hopeful. "You see, that's why I have to get home."

"We'll take you to the China town."

"There won't be time. The labor may take less than fifteen minutes." This was unlikely, but not impossible.

Megan considered this. "They'll make me deliver it." She took off her mirrorshades and rubbed a hand down her face. Her dark eyes were surrounded by tired wrinkles; she looked suddenly ten years older.

"It's very tricky," Isabel assured her. "If you don't loop the cord over the head just right, it gets caught around the neck, and the baby slowly strangles to death. Then it gets caught halfway out, and the mother bleeds to death."

Megan grimaced. "Those dags, recruiting a girl who's preggo."

"So you see, I really do have to go now." Isabel started to get up.

"Sit down, hon. You'll get nowhere past the guards. Besides, they'll kill me if I let you go."

Her hopes dashed, Isabel sank back on the blanket and closed her eyes. Above her some night creature called and chattered from its perch on the stone wall.

"Rovers!" From somewhere came a hoarse shout.

Megan leapt to her feet. "We're under attack! And we're shorthanded; Dirk's out on a raid." She tossed Isabel a cylinder. "Pull on your mask and man the back lookout, right up these steps. You see snakes or rovers—burn them." With that she ran off.

The campground inside the wall was a confusion of masked people running and shouting. From the top of the wall, blue streaks aimed down toward outside, presumably at keepers and their goatsnakes. Isabel searched the wall with her eyes, seeking the nearest exit. She spied a dark crack behind the kitchen area; perhaps she might slip out there.

With an effort, Isabel just barely managed to scrape through the crack. Now the problem was to find her way back down the path to the pylon. But in the dark she had no idea where the path began. Furthermore, the familiar fog from the keepers was growing in, canceling what little visibility there was. The best she could do was to creep out away from the fortress, wading through the tall grasses where she might escape the notice of both Shades and keepers until morning.

XXXIX

THE PINK FLOOR of wax lay beneath Isabel's fingers as she awoke, just as on that first morning that she had arrived in the hypersphere. She looked up into Daniel's face, his eyelids fluttering anxiously. "Isabel, is thee all right? And the baby?"

Isabel winced. "She's still kicking." The goatsnakes must have brought her back again, she realized. That was thoughtful of them, under fire from those dreadful Shades.

Daniel let out a long sigh. "They took so much longer to return thee. I thought perhaps thee had escaped after all. At least," he added, his voice faltering, "I tried to think that."

She shuddered, and she hugged him fiercely. "No, I got caught."

"Was thee hurt? Did the keepers put thee to sleep?"

"Not keepers—the Shades. They're people, but they've infested the Hive like wax worms." She recounted her frightening capture, and how the strangers had dragged her off without the least consideration. "They kill everything in sight," she told him. "Not just keepers; all their sheep, too, and all those poor wallabies hung up on meat hooks." She shuddered. "I'll never eat meat again."

Daniel shook his head. "What was the purpose of this madness?"

"To find and destroy the Queen. To set us all free."

"But the keepers saved us all and put back our ozone. Did thee tell them?"

"They said the Queen brought the keepers here to live after they blew up their own planet. We're just Indians on a reservation, after all."

Daniel looked away, and he thought about this for some time. Outside the window a hummingbird swooped down and up in its dance of courtship. "That could be so," he said gently. "It is hard to know for certain what we see. We humans have always seen in the universe a mirror of our selves."

Isabel realized suddenly that she was famished. She reached for a cupful of blueberries from the ledge on the wall. The sweet juice of the berries crushed between her teeth reassured her immensely. "Thank God I got out of that mess safe."

"If only I had known," said Daniel. "I hope Peace Hope stays home."

Isabel looked up hopefully. "Did you ever reach her at the Gwynwood Pylon?"

"I ran down the corridor as best I could; it's hard when the gravity drops off like that, it felt like my feet would fly away. I did reach the little airwall, the one that opens into Gwynwood. But there—" Daniel stopped.

"What happened?"

"The keepers were waiting."

"Oh my God." Isabel covered her face in her hands.

"I got through the airwall," Daniel added. "The keepers are slow to react, and they seem reluctant to send their goatsnakes after someone awake. I made it into the Pylon's domain, just in time for Peace Hope to see me. She—she looked surprised," he said with half a smile. "But then sleep-fog closed in, and I lost consciousness."

"Then she *saw* you—with the scales on your eyes! She'll know how to *see*." Isabel patted his arm. "That was well done, Daniel. You're a fine member of the Gwynwood Underground. The real Underground," she emphasized.

His cheeks colored. "I'm sorry, now, for her sake. At least they didn't ship her out here. I hope she keeps safe."

"She'll do what she has to, like we did. You took your stand, once," Isabel reminded him. It seemed only yesterday that Daniel had appeared at her door out of the cold, having just refused the summons of the Pylon. "So what now," she wondered. "We know where Gwynwood is; but how to get there?" She frowned, thinking it over. "The keepers were there waiting for you."

"With all their goatsnakes and angelbees."

"Angelbees—they watch us all the time. In fact, our own angelbees must be broadcasting signals all the time, telling the keepers where we are." It had never occurred to her that their "gift" of angelbee vision was also a source of control for the keepers, like the radio transmitters used by humans to tag animals in the wild.

"Well," said Daniel, "at least we learned something."

"We always do," Isabel observed wryly. "All the same, we're back to square one."

For Isabel the hopelessness of escape was beginning to sink in at last. Any chance that her baby might yet be born in Gwynwood now seemed remote. She found that she had to face the fact, now, on a deeper level than she had allowed herself before. A sense of panic welled up, which she tried to repress, buried beneath the common sense needed to survive from day to day.

By the end of the eighth month, she was beginning to feel contractions, like a waistband slowly tightening, then relaxing. "Practice contractions," her mother would have called them. When she jogged down the path around the hypersphere, the contractions grew stronger. It was time to start the breathing exercises, what she could recall of them.

One morning her belly had settled distinctly lower, the baby clearly headed for its exit. She felt immediately more comfortable, and her breathing came easier as the baby pressed less upon her diaphragm. Only one problem: as she felt around for its position, she was increasingly certain that the big round head was tucked upward while the sharp feet were kicking downward, toward the birth canal. A breech birth was in store. That meant extra complications, of the sort she had described to Megan.

Isabel tried the exercise that Ruth had done to coax the baby to turn around. The idea was to lie on one's back, with the pelvis propped up, so that the womb lay just about horizontal and the baby could swim round more freely. It was not a comfortable position, with all that weight pressing onto the diaphragm again, but she set herself up in this position for ten minutes each morning and evening. She did this every day for five days. Still the baby's head pressed upward, locked tight as ever.

Isabel grew depressed. A normal birth would be risky enough, but the chances that Daniel could successfully midwife a breech birth without assistance looked slim. What would happen if the baby got stuck halfway, with its head inside and suffocating? What if the baby came out but the afterbirth didn't, and Isabel bled to death? She had put aside such thoughts before, but now there were too many grim possibilities to avoid them all.

It was too much to face, the thought of hours, even days, of agony, with almost certain death in the end. Daniel would have to go through it, too. In the end, he would be left alone, and he himself would not last more than a year or so, with his anemia untreated. All the while he would blame himself for her death, no matter what she said or did.

She thought again of the two tablets Keith had left her, final friends. She had not thought of them since Becca died. What would have been right for Becca was just as right for her. Like the Little Prince asking the golden snake for the mortal bite that would take him home...

It might be better for her to go now, to spare herself and Daniel this last horror. Daniel would not appreciate it, perhaps, but that could not be helped. If she went alone into one of the empty cells, and took the tablet there, then the keeper would seal her up overnight. Daniel would never have to watch her die, as he had watched Becca. Then, if he changed his mind, one last tablet would remain.

When Daniel was out gathering corn and firewood, Isabel hunted through the medical supplies for the pill bottle. It was not where she remembered, but after some frantic searching she found it. Her hands trembled as she opened the bottle.

There were not two tablets, only one. Someone had taken the second.

It could only have been Becca, whose angelbees had eyed Isabel's supplies and knew where everything was. That explained how Becca had died so abruptly at the end. She must have removed the tablet early on, then saved it until the last, until she could stand it no longer.

Isabel felt shock, relief, mixed oddly with a sense of resentment that Becca had had to steal it, that she could not ask. Becca had always been so proud of doing things her own way. And courageous; she had endured weeks of agony without hope, all the while with the passage to death at hand.

Now Isabel felt almost ashamed of herself, for she was not nearly as badly off as Becca had been. Isabel, after all, was healthy enough at present, merely terrified of the future.

She began to cry quietly, and she kept on for a long while, until Daniel came and found her there. She did not even bother to close the pill bottle. Daniel said nothing but stayed with her, holding her close, until she was capable of speaking once more.

"Why should I go through with it?" Isabel asked. "Why should I prefer a slow death to a quick one?"

"It's thy choice," he said in a low voice, more subdued than she had ever heard him. "I know I can't stop thee."

"We'll all be dying, soon enough." Her voice still shook with sobbing.

"People have been dying for a long time."

Isabel turned and looked him full in the face. "What if I die, but the baby lives? What will you do about it?"

"Try to raise it, I suppose."

"How? What will you feed it?"

A hint of annoyance wrinkled his lip. "I'll try the milk from the sheep."

"That won't do, the baby will only spit it back up. It will only prolong her starvation."

"Isabel, please don't talk this way; what use is it?"

"What will you do? I just want to know, that's all. Will you make the baby live, or not?"

Daniel looked away, the lines of his face softened, vulnerable. "Thee is cruel, Isabel."

"Truth is cruel." She felt a gleam of triumph. "What kind of God would leave us such an impossible choice? What kind of God would torture babies?"

"Who is thee to ask? Didn't thee kill a harmless angelbee? Didn't thy grandparents build the death that piled the skeletons around the Wall?" He sounded confident again. "So many choices we have, and so often we choose death. Yet, the choice is not impossible just because we can't see the right answer. Of course, earthquakes happen; but God gives us the tools of compassion, to aid the victims, and reason, to learn to predict earthquakes, if we apply ourselves. So often it turns out that the right choice exists, only we need to look a little

harder. Why should we expect any more of God than this, the
chance to seek the right answer?"

"Do you think you deserve your own fate?"

"Certainly, I've chosen evil so many times. I even wished
evil over you. A year ago I would have preferred that you had
been born like Peace Hope, if I could have claimed you then."

"But then," said Isabel wonderingly, "I only wanted you."
If even someone as good as Daniel could be so blind, then
what hope was there for intelligent life in the universe? No
wonder all of them, even the keepers perhaps, ended up with
a Doomsday.

Oddly enough, Daniel smiled. For some reason he looked
just like Keith, castaway from his City, stamping out his last
cigarette.

XL

TWO DAYS LATER, Isabel awoke feeling somehow "rearranged" inside. Something sharp jabbed toward her left side, and the pressure had eased over her bladder. She felt herself carefully, trying to locate the head and rump again. No doubt about it: the baby had "turned," its head now locked into the birth canal.

It was as if the sun had broken through the clouds. Isabel felt a surge of energy, a new strength in every muscle. One way or another, the baby was coming out. It would be all right; it *would* be all right, she decided.

The contractions were coming more often now, and they lasted longer. They still did not hurt at all, only made her breathe a little faster and woke her at night. Her belly seemed to dip lower each day, as if it would eventually fall over onto the ground. Jogging became too awkward, as the motions pulled and stretched at her skin. She walked instead, keeping up her imitation of Peewee, treading the circular path. When she was not walking or eating, she dozed, catching up on her lack of sleep at night. In the evening she sat before the fire, resting her head on Daniel's shoulder while he stroked her hair.

"Isn't it time we thought about names?" Daniel asked.

"I don't know," said Isabel. "Ruth waited until the eighth day afterward."

"Consolation, that would be a nice name."

Isabel glared at him. Not one of those virtue names for a child of hers. "I want biblical names: Jael for a girl, or Sisera for a boy."

One afternoon on her daily walk, something burst, and a gush of water splattered her feet. Startled, she cried out, then realized what it was. The membrane of the amnion had ruptured, releasing most of the fluid surrounding the baby. Usually this did not happen until labor was in progress. But she thought she had another two weeks to go.

She continued her walk, feeling distinctly more comfortable, less "tight" than before, but worried. If labor did not commence soon after rupture, the chance of infection would rise.

Her worry did not last long. By the time she returned to her cell, the contractions were coming in waves, rising to a dull ache and receding, every ten minutes. She stood outside and braced herself against the wall until each squeeze was past, then paced back and forth to relax herself.

Daniel returned from the garden. "Why didn't thee call?" He touched her shoulder lightly.

Isabel pulled away, trying to concentrate. "Here, take the watch."

He took the watch to time the contractions, then stirred up the fire beneath the stone pot, the one she had hewn with the keeper's cylinder.

"We'll need sterile rags," said Isabel, "and also the pen knife. And remember, you have to press the cord between your fingers, stripping back toward the baby, before you tie it off and cut."

"Yes, I know." Daniel took off his shirt and tore it in three sections, then put them in the pot of water with the knife.

Isabel saw this happen dimly, as if from far away. As the day wore on, the sky deepened through artificial twilight to starless black, but for Isabel the whole world was contained inside, with the steady waiting, the rise of pain, then subsiding into waiting again. With each one she found herself thinking, I can't go on with it, I will go mad if I have to climb that mountain of pain one more time. Yet afterward she would doze off even as she stood there, until the rising ache woke her again. Over and over the contractions rose and subsided, while Daniel counted the minutes in between. They were supposed to get steadily closer and stronger, but the interval seemed to hover forever between six to ten minutes.

Abruptly she felt an urge to push out this thing inside. Her legs buckled under as she fought to relax. "It's too early," she cried hoarsely, her mouth dry from hard breathing. She slid herself down, resting her back outside the cell.

"It's been seven hours," Daniel said as he stuffed her winter jacket behind her to cushion her back and a sterile cloth behind her legs.

Seven hours—it felt as if it had just begun. Still, it might not be ready. What if the cervix were not yet fully dilated? If she pushed then, the womb would split like a melon and she would be done for certain. Daniel would not know how to tell if she were ready, even if he could get under to see. For just an instant her eyes focused on him, his face etched harshly by the firelight.

She resisted the first few waves of pushing, breathing so hard her tongue was dry and swollen. Now she no longer dozed, she was alert, almost too alert, as if she had to get up and run again. At last she did try to get up, but a sharp pain dug into her pelvis, unlike the contractions before. Something was getting in the way of her legs. "Daniel—am I all right?"

"Keep going," he said, pressing her drawn-up knee. "I think that's the top of the head just appearing."

Then she pushed as hard as she could, though it seemed rationally impossible, like trying to squeeze one's foot into a hand-me-down shoe two sizes too small. It hurt harder than anything, as if someone were scraping her insides out. She thought, I'll die for sure; even if I live, I'll never enjoy loving again.

A cry came, or rather an indignant shriek. There was little Jael or Sisera, complaining at the cruel cold world before it was even completely out. A child worthy of its mother. One more shove, and the water creature was out on dry land.

"Okay? Is the baby okay?" Isabel gasped. Time had speeded up into a dim whirl, the universe collapsed inward, then out again.

Daniel hovered over her, the infant held in one hand. "The cord's still stuck inside."

The afterbirth had to come out. She made herself cough twice, like Ruth had done. She could not feel inside anymore, but something slid out past her leg. "You have to check...the placenta...that it's all there."

"I'll do my best. It's hard to tell—"

"Did you tie the cord? Was the knife sterile?"

"Yes, yes."

"Is the baby okay?" she insisted.

"She's fine, I think. Got all her arms and legs. I haven't counted the toes yet."

"Let me have her now."

Daniel set the infant on her bare chest. She was so small and floppy. Isabel guided the infant's mouth with her finger until it found the breast. The head with its tiny mouth actually sucked for a minute or so, then let go, eyes half open, almost a dreamy expression.

Isabel watched hard. The little face was wrinkled, the head battered and the nose pressed to one side. Still, she wanted to remember this sight as long as she lived.

A pattering sound filled the trees, the early-morning rainfall, right on schedule. "Help me up, please," said Isabel.

Daniel took the baby, though Isabel's eyes kept following her, and he put his arm under her shoulder to help her up. "Can you make it through the window?"

"Not yet. I need a shower anyway." The fine raindrops fell and splattered, coursing into rivulets down her skin, washing away hours of sweat and blood and fear.

For the first day, then the next, she stayed inside the cell, alternately dozing and eating. She ate hungrily, building up for the milk to come in. She kept Jael with her all the time, almost jealously, until she was too exhausted to stay awake. Jael sucked strongly, and she hoped the milk would come in soon. It came not all at once, she realized, but as a gradual thickening and whitening of the antibody-rich substance that had leaked out before.

The strength of her own feeling for the infant at times took her breath away. Despite the odors, the diapers that could not be cleaned thoroughly, the still-present ache of her torn insides knitting back together, none of it counted for anything the moment she could see this perfect new creature. Such tiny fingers with little fingernails like specks of mica, and such an exquisite little yawn when Jael stretched in her sleep. Even the scent of the scalp, with its perfect swirl of baby hair, was indescribable. Her skin was so delicate that the blood vessels shone through, coloring her limbs red; she would darken with time, as African babies did. It was impossible for

Isabel to have imagined beforehand how she would feel; it was as if she had never seen a baby before, although she had helped deliver several. She wondered whether Daniel would feel the same way. She guessed that he did by the way he held the child and watched her as if nothing else existed.

By the end of the week, the exhaustion and the impossibility of their condition returned, redoubled, to overwhelm her. She could walk but a short distance yet, for her insides still felt as if they were falling out. Jael's needs were continual, around the clock, with no escape from that hungry mouth. Yet it was at her most peaceful, when the infant slept soundlessly in her little bed of fleece, that Isabel felt most undone. She found herself thinking would it be kinder to strangle the child as she slept, now, rather than let her grow up in this appalling cage? It was impossible to say aloud all the wild contradictory impulses she felt, but she clung to Daniel, convinced that somehow she could get through it all, if only the three of them stayed together.

In the long run, though, the three of them together could not last. Isabel herself was still bleeding heavily, there were not enough rags to keep up with it. There might be something wrong, perhaps a bit of placenta still attached to the uterine lining, and she had to have it checked out by a doctor. As for Daniel, he looked pale as he had the year before; without his medicine, his days were numbered.

While the infant nursed, Isabel's thoughts quieted again. She found herself thinking again of the keepers and their Queen. If the Queen was their lord of life and death, then perhaps she would be a presence to appeal to. Surely if the keeper Queen felt anything for her offspring like that which Isabel felt, she must take pity on Isabel's situation. Perhaps the Queen did not know what was going on; how closely did she look after her "zoo"? The Queen might take a more sympathetic view than those eyeless, armless keepers.

"Daniel? Are you awake?" The three of them lay in a cozy heap on the floor of the cell. Jael was not too messy, she could wait a bit. Outside, the birds were just tuning up for their morning concert.

"Yes, Isabel."

"What if we petition the Queen herself to let us go?"

Daniel raised himself on one elbow. "How do we do this? How do we even find the Queen?"

"Ask the pylon. Somehow."

The pylon loomed ahead against the night sky, bathed in concentric circles of infrared. Isabel walked toward it slowly, carrying Jael asleep on her chest, her tiny head cupped in Isabel's hand as round as an egg. Daniel kept close to her protectively.

Slowly the concentric circles faded away. Traces of a domed ceiling appeared within the hexagonal pyramid. It was the geodesic dome of the Queen cell. As the joints between the dome's polygonal tiles came into focus, Isabel waited expectantly for the Queen.

But the Queen did not appear. Minutes ticked by and still the cell stood empty. Outside, the din of the tree frogs pressed to her ears, the bright infrared bats swooped after insects, the pungent scent of a passing mother skunk entered her lungs, while before her the pylon with its Queen cell stood empty of life.

"They should show us the Queen budding off keepers." Daniel sounded disappointed. "They must be displeased with us again."

Isabel frowned and her pulse quickened. Something was different about the pylon tonight; she could not put her finger on it, was it the pylon itself...or the platform on which it stood? "Daniel—that platform looks different. It's not the same surface as usual, it's a different hue and texture."

Daniel's angelbee floated closer to the airwall. "Perhaps so. What does that mean?"

"It means—" She swallowed and held the baby tighter, her heart pounding. "The pylon's domain must have changed connection, through the extra dimension. Instead of giving out onto that place in the corridor, it connects...somewhere else." To the Queen cell.

"Then it must be an invitation." He put his arm around her. "Let's go. Thee wanted to see the Queen."

They walked slowly forward, angelbees ahead to penetrate the airwall. As they stepped onto the platform within the pylon's domain, the familiar "lift" in gravity bounced in Isabel's feet. Around them now, in all directions, rose the jointed panels of the dome, mostly hexagons with occasional pentagons to generate curvature, enclosing a space of about the volume of her mother's house in Gwynwood. There were angelbees, a dozen or so, lurking above the pylon. Still, no sign of the Queen.

A thought struck her and she turned suddenly cold. "Daniel—what if they got the Queen? The Shades—that was their aim." She dug her fingers into Daniel's arm. "They could be here, ready to jump on us!"

"Easy, now. There's no sign of danger—"

"They could be here any minute. Anyway, something's got to be wrong. The Queen can't just be gone."

"Thee is right," he quietly agreed. "Something is amiss. Let's go."

XLI

ISABEL DID NOT return to the pylon again. Daniel ventured there in the daytime, where the "connection" of the airwall seemed to have reverted to its usual site in the maze of fog-filled corridors. Yet, while his angelbees might explore at will, there could be no escape from the surveillance of the keepers.

During the day Isabel kept Jael fed and watched her grow, feeling the immense tug of Jael's tiny hand clenching her finger. Between nursings Daniel would take the infant for an hour, staring into her eyes until she fell asleep. As Jael slept, with her eyes shut tight and her mouth drawn small between her rounded cheeks, her expression reminded Isabel of something she had seen before, but she could not recall where.

Isabel took to exploring the hypersphere again with her angelbee eyes, watching the drama of nature's many creatures. The possum, the blackbirds, the mother skunk, all spoke to her loneliness.

"Isabel!" A voice came, one morning, a familiar voice, but not Daniel's. "Where does thee come from, and where is thee going?"

"*Peace Hope?*" Hurriedly Isabel called back her angelbees. The airborne eyes returned to look upon herself, but no Peace Hope was to be seen.

Daniel got up quickly, his form luminously infrared, holding Jael. His eyes were wide with surprise, and he extended a hand to something Isabel's angelbees could not see. Then, without sound or warning, he and Jael simply vanished. Isabel's angelbees could see nothing left but a bit of unfocused blur in the foliage.

"*Daniel, where are you?*" She pulled off the scales and her eyes blinked furiously, blinded by the light until her pupils could readjust.

"Here I am." Daniel was watching her, puzzled, his arm around Peace Hope.

"We're here, silly." Peace Hope stood there on her

crutches, her long blond hair streaming over her shoulders. One blue eye was open, the other closed, capped by an eye-spot scale, the angelbee hovering close at her shoulder. "Oh, Isabel, I've missed thee for so long. What is this beautiful Looking-glass Land?"

Isabel ran to hug her, and Daniel and Jael, too; for just an instant, she had lost them forever. Her heart was still slowing down, and she could barely speak. "It's really you. I don't know what happened—I couldn't see you."

Peace Hope said, "My angelbee couldn't see thee, either, with thy scale on, nor the keepers. And the keepers can't see me, so far as I can tell."

Daniel shook his head. "I don't understand. What's going on?"

"My angelbee must be a variant strain," said Peace Hope. "The biology book said that sometimes, when conditions get bad, one partner of a symbiosis may revert to an independent form. That must have been what happened to this angelbee," she said, glancing over her shoulder, "the one whose scale Becca passed on to Isabel." The one that had followed Isabel day and night, until the time she had popped its daughter. "But the ones Isabel is using now must be the keepers' strain," Peace Hope added. "That is why thee couldn't see me."

"So yours is somehow independent?" Isabel asked.

"Independent of the keepers," Peace Hope explained. "It chose me as a partner. The two different strains must put out microwave interference, somehow, each to hide its own class of partners from the other. Maybe on the keepers' planet there are predators—"

"Or warring bands of keepers." Becca's first angelbee must have been the original parent of the mutant strain. No wonder the keepers had sought to trap her.

"Isabel—is that adorable baby thine? What is his name, or hers?"

"Her name is Jael," said Daniel, cradling her.

"But, Scatterbrain, Daniel disappeared, too, when he touched you. Does that mean we all can escape the keepers' notice, with you and your mutant angelbee?"

Peace Hope considered this. "I hadn't thought of that. Yes, that should do."

"*Then what are we waiting for?* Quick, let's get out—before they catch on."

So the three of them crept slowly down the path to the pylon, Isabel and Daniel taking care to keep a hand on Peace Hope's shoulder. Jael, thank goodness, was asleep, breathing noisily beneath Isabel's chin. In the distance occasional angelbees hung among the tree branches. Isabel could not tell whether they were watching or not. "Does everyone know about the scales now? Do they know how the angelbees work?"

"I told only Teacher Matthew," said Peace Hope. "After I saw Daniel in the Pylon, I told him. He helped me figure out what I was seeing."

"Teacher Matthew?" Matthew had always been so cautious about the angelbees.

Peace Hope added, "I can't imagine how you got used to two angelbees at once. It took me days to get my eye straight with one."

"We had little else to work on," observed Daniel. "No more college to study."

The thought of college brought a sharp pang to Isabel. Here she was, on the run from the keepers, a baby on her back, and further than ever from her dream of attending the Sydney Uni.

But nothing would stop her, she vowed, with a sudden renewal of vision. When she got home, none of it would stand in the way of her getting a real education, one way or another.

Ahead of them stood the pylon, its rainbow-colored surface blank to human vision. Now Isabel and Daniel would have to follow Peace Hope with her angelbee blindly through the corridors of fog.

Isabel had second thoughts. "Those Shades—Did you run into anybody?"

"What do you mean?" Peace Hope asked. "I don't think so."

"What will become of us once we get back?" Isabel wondered. "Won't the keepers catch up with us soon enough?"

"A good question." Peace Hope stopped and leaned on her crutches. The crown of her lucky Red Queen poked out of her shirt pocket. "I've got some more eyespot scales in the candle box, from offspring of this one. They should all be the right strain of angelbee. They might protect you."

"Why, soon there'll be enough for everyone in Gwynwood, then. What's more," Isabel realized with growing excitement, "our angelbees can walk us through the Wall! We'll be free!"

Peace Hope lifted her crutches, and her angelbee descended to penetrate the airwall. The three humans crossed through the pylon's domain and entered the darkness. For Isabel it was hard, even harder than she expected, to follow blindly with no clear sense of what lay ahead. She reached out now and then to touch Jael's cheek. Still, there was no sign of keepers nor of Shades. Perhaps Peace Hope's luck was holding out.

Then an angelbee loomed out of the fog, a second one. Isabel gripped her friend's shoulder hard and nearly fell over. "Look—they must have found us!" Her voice echoed down the corridor.

"No, I can *see* that one." Peace Hope's angelbee turned, its eyespot rotating. "That's one of ours. It must be Teacher Matthew watching, in case I lose my way."

At long last, a pool of yellowish brightness appeared out of the journey through night. It was sunlight, true sunlight, the first that Isabel had seen in nearly a year. As they emerged at the Pylon of Gwynwood, Matthew Crofts was there to meet them, his smile as radiant as the sun. Matthew hugged them all, laughing and shaking his head. "You made it," he exclaimed. "What a surprise this will be!"

"Surprise? You mean—"

"We decided not to tell," said Peace Hope. "So nobody else would be in danger if we failed."

Matthew's eyes were smiling despite the wrinkles grown around them. Another recruit to the Gwynwood Underground.

XLII

THE SITTING ROOM was full of visitors. The true sun shed its red evening rays across the old couch where Isabel sat between her mother and her father, who cradled Jael in the crook of his arm and made exaggerated faces at her. The baby wore proper clothes for the first time, a clown suit donated by Debbie Dreher, who sat with Carl and the children nearby. Marguerite clung to Isabel and kept stroking her hair, as if her daughter might disappear again at any moment. Daniel and the Scattergoods were there, and Peace Hope sat enthroned in the big armchair, with an extra lilt in her voice, clearly making the most of her role as rescuer. "The keepers can't come after them again," she explained, "because our own angelbees will hide them in time. We'll make sure of that. Anna is keeping watch on the Pylon, to give warning."

The townspeople absorbed this. Carl cleared his throat. "Suppose they put us all to sleep again?"

Isabel said, "We can get out this time. Our angelbees can lead us out through the Wall."

Her words produced an unexpected hesitancy among those gathered. Debbie sat back suddenly, clutching her chubby one-year-old, Patience, transformed from the infant Isabel remembered. Matthew gripped the arm of his chair until his knuckles turned white.

Only Deliverance smiled, her eyes wide. "Why that means we can all go and live outside now! Isn't it marvelous?" she asked her mother.

Vera bit her lip and looked away.

Isabel was perplexed. What had she said? Could they not see that freedom was at hand?

Liza spoke at last, her Quaker cap pinned neatly as always. "We all long to cross the Wall, when we are ready. The town will consider this immediately. But now, Isabel, can thee tell us, did thee learn any better what the creatures wanted of thee, and Daniel and Becca; why did they take you from us?"

"We're an endangered species," said Isabel. "The whole human race."

Daniel added, "The keepers wanted us to learn that compassion is the key to survival. That is what I think. The accident with the keeper, when Isabel took the cylinder; that was a test for us, I'm convinced."

"But that's a lesson we all know," said Liza.

"Of course," Daniel agreed. "John Dickinson taught us that."

Isabel disagreed. "Those Shades didn't learn a thing from John Dickinson. Nor from the keepers, either."

"But for the keepers," Liza persisted, "why was it so important? Why did they voyage across space to rescue Earth?"

Daniel opened his mouth to answer, but thought better of it. "The truth is, we can't say for sure."

"We never saw their Queen," said Isabel. "I thought they would let us see her, somehow, to ask...I'm not sure what. But instead they led us to an empty cell." As if she herself were the equivalent of a Queen, with her new baby.

A knock came at the door. Isabel's first thought, as always, was someone for the doctor. Keith got up and headed for the door.

It was Anna, bundled in her coat, her slick black hair slightly askew. Isabel stood up quickly and hurried to meet her.

"The Pylon," said Anna. "It's—it's on fire. I don't know how else to describe it. It's gone all orange, with leaping flames inside, like the time we lit the bonfire around, remember? Only this time, there's no fire of ours."

The flames burned on within the Pylon by night and by day. Still there was no sign of fog, nor of keepers coming to seek their two runaways. After two days, Isabel and Daniel got up the courage to return to the clearing and see for themselves. The sight made Isabel's hair stand on end. No angelbees were needed to recognize the outpouring of light and heat—in fact, any angelbee that came close would be driven away.

"They've sealed us out," she told Daniel. "They're afraid of our new strain of angelbees. They've sealed out the contagion."

Daniel stood in the grass, his trim beard blowing back in the brisk autumn breeze, a breath of air not felt by them all that time in the hypersphere. Jael was strapped in a sling across his chest, soon to waken for milk time. "Perhaps we've been banished for choosing human company over their garden." The angels with the flaming sword. Even Yahweh was always such a jealous God.

"But what about the Sydney shipments?" asked Isabel. "Will those be banished, too?"

"That is the price of freedom."

It turned out that the Sydney shipments had become increasingly erratic, in any case, over the year past. Marguerite was hoarding and stockpiling medicines. Supplies for building were scarce, delaying the plans of Sal and Jon who wanted to reopen an old storefront on the highway and set up a grocery store, of all things. Meanwhile, there were hopeful signs from the *Herald*, reports that here and there the Walls were lifting. Overall, it seemed that the keepers were losing their grip.

Had the Shades really got the Queen? If so, what would happen next? Would the keepers take revenge at last? Isabel could not shake off a sense of foreboding.

At the Scattergoods', boarders had taken up in their former rooms; Liza just could not get on without a full household. The boarders offered to leave, but of course Isabel declined, insisting on bringing Daniel back to her old room on the hospital floor. Her father had kept everything as it was before, even Peewee in the cage, now grown too obese to fit inside her exercise wheel. The only thing new was a nest of bluejays that had set up house in the old gutter beneath her dormer window.

Jael had a hard time adjusting at first to the new surroundings. She threw fits of crying, spreading her limbs and throwing her head back, refusing to be diapered. At other times, though, she was developing a curious quiet alertness, a deeply watchful interest in her world.

While Jael was napping, Isabel slipped away to tell Peace Hope all about the hypersphere, and to find out what all had really gone on in Gwynwood for the past ten months. Peace Hope gave Isabel three eyespot scales which she had collected from angelbee offspring, one each for Isabel and Daniel, and one for Keith who wanted to try it out. The angelbees floated dutifully around the Scattergood house, all descendants of Becca's original angelbee, the one whose defection must have so scared the keepers that they took her away.

"I wish I could have stayed to see more of your Lookingglass Land," said Peace Hope wistfully. "I've never drawn a hummingbird from life before."

"Well I'm just glad to be out, thank you," Isabel assured her. "At least I didn't return empty-handed," Isabel added, thinking of Jael. Her breasts were feeling full already. She peered curiously at the latest stamp Peace Hope was drawing, an abstract model of balls and sticks. "What's that supposed to be?"

"That's an organic molecule, 'buckminsterfullerene.' A new line of stamps I started, inspired by chemistry class."

"Chemistry class?" Isabel was envious.

"Chemistry with Teacher Matthew, classical Greek with Mother, and I'm teaching art class. En archēi ēn ho logos."

"Of all the rotten luck, to miss chemistry."

"You only missed a month. You can take my book home." Peace Hope let the pen drop from her mouth and reached with her gripper-hand to a pile of envelopes on her desk. "I have something to show thee. I have a pen pal in Sydney. He's an engineering student at the Uni. His name is Christopher, and he writes lovely letters."

Isabel opened an envelope and removed a letter with a photo of a rather attractive young man, tawny-haired with freckles, one leg missing, probably to cancer. She read the letter halfway through, then looked up. "Scatterbrain, he sounds worse than that Pirate!"

"Doesn't he, though. I plan to visit him when I attend the Uni, after the Walls fall."

Isabel grew serious again. "The Walls are as good as fallen, already. What's the matter with this town? Why aren't they eager to get out?"

"It's not so much the Wall itself," said Peace Hope. "It's what lies outside."

"The keepers?"

"No, silly. The skeletons."

Of course, *los huesos*, the old pile of bones surrounding the town, bleached by twenty summers of sun. "That's no problem. We can clear our way through those."

"Isabel, the elders—they *know* all those people. They watched them all die."

She thought this over. "Okay, but—that was two decades ago, before I was born." Two decades seemed a long time to Isabel.

"To them, it's still like yesterday. I know. I asked Matthew, one night after chemistry class. He told me all about it. He talked on till daybreak." Peace Hope paused. "It was after that that he joined the Underground."

"Well, let them all talk it out, then, once and for all." That had been Becca's last wish, too, Isabel remembered.

Isabel paid a call on Ruth, to share what she could of Becca's last days in the hypersphere. Jael nursed, more alert than usual, her angelic eyes fixed upward adoringly at her mother, while her mouth chomped on the breast, making snuffling noises. What an odd hybrid creature an infant was, half angel and half piglet.

Ruth's Benjamin plodded across the room, his arms spread wide to keep his balance, an empty beehive frame clenched tightly in one fist. When something caught his interest in the next room, he dropped the frame with a clatter, then fell down on all fours again and sprinted through the doorway, still an expert crawler. Isabel watched curiously, thinking how different he was from the little naked kitten she had helped deliver the year before. Another year, and Jael, too, would be on her feet tearing up the house.

"Becca asked after Benjamin, often," she told Ruth. "She wanted to know how he ate, and what he'd learned to do." Isabel wished she had remembered more to tell Becca. "She asked after the bees, too. She wanted to know if the new queen took."

Ruth nodded. Ruth held in her hand an eyespot scale

which Peace Hope had given her. She turned it over curiously, poking her finger through the pupil hole. "So, with this, Becca came to 'see.'"

"That's right," said Isabel. "She gave us all the gift of sight."

"Could the children learn, too, do you think? Would it be safe for them?"

"I don't see why not." Isabel had not considered this. Little Benjamin, and even Jael, would grow up taking angelbee eyesight for granted. It made her feel suddenly old, to realize that her children would be born into such freedom.

Ruth said, "Becca always liked to hear the bees. She claimed she could tell different ones apart by the sound of their humming."

She remembered something else to tell Ruth. "Becca led a seder for us. We had to eat special things, and ask questions."

"That's Becca." Ruth flashed a smile. "She always loved to lecture. Even when Aaron was alive, she used to lead the seder."

"She answered my question about Abraham and Isaac, too. She said the point was, you had to be willing to give up your own child for the sake of God's peace." Isabel shook her head, as she switched Jael to the other side. "I still don't understand how you can think that way, with people like those Shades running around. I'd never give up my child."

"Well, she and Aaron used to argue over that one. But you should agree with that; you're the Quaker."

"I don't know what I am anymore. If God gave bees stings to defend their brood, why shouldn't humans do the same?"

"Bees can learn to be tame. Look how they let us rob their honey. Aaron used to make a 'bee beard' by covering himself with bees, from his cheeks down across his chest."

"But the bees know we're there to help them keep up their hive. They'll sting, if you make a wrong move."

"Not all bees even have stings. Some members of the genus *Trigona* are not aggressive at all, yet their nests are never attacked, even by army ants. If bees can figure out a way, surely humans can, too."

Isabel sighed. "I suppose so. I guess that is what I was supposed to learn out there. I'm not sure I learned anything."

Ruth rested a hand on her arm. "Of course you did. You've taught us a great deal. You taught us to see through the darkness, and to walk through walls."

Isabel cast her eyes down. "That's true, only..."

"Yes?"

"We have yet to walk through the Wall."

"That is true."

Isabel plunged into it. "Peace Hope says we have to talk about...about Doomsday, first. Before we can cross the Wall. That was Becca's last wish: that you would tell us about Doomsday, and the Death Year."

Ruth took a deep breath. "The town has been considering this very thing. You're right, we need to tell the story of the Death Year, before those memories pass away. But this time, you will have to live through that telling."

XLIII

THEY GATHERED IN the Scattergoods' sitting room, just as on that afternoon two summers before, when the townspeople had come to face the mysterious burning of the night sky. That had been a Sunday in August, the day that Isabel had challenged the people in the Meetinghouse in the name of the Wall, the Wall whose birth she had not been born to see.

Today was a Saturday evening, the last of October, and the survivors of Doomsday were going to tell how the Wall was born. Isabel sat on one of Nahum's spare wooden chairs and whispered furtively with Daniel and Peace Hope, anxiously wishing the baby was back in her arms, though Carl had promised to get her to sleep upstairs. Deliverance was there, and Sal and John who clasped hands demurely, notebooks on their laps. They all were expected to listen and take notes as a sort of oral history. Peace Hope was flipping through her audio cassettes, making sure not to erase her precious Lucy tape by mistake.

As if by unspoken agreement, those who were to speak had gathered in the opposite corner of the sitting room, by the west window where the sun's dying rays tinted their faces red. A beautiful sunset, the kind that the Little Prince would have loved and Isabel thirsted for after her months in the hypersphere.

Marguerite was one of those seated to the west, the doctor's chin nodding briskly as she spoke to Teacher Matthew, while Vera Brown interjected an occasional "I quite agree," in an unnaturally high tone of voice. Liza and Nahum sat together in silence. They were the only couple who had survived the Death Year together. Ruth, who had been nine at the time, chose to speak tonight, but Anna, who had been only three, came to join Isabel. The Drehers, who had married some years afterward, were looking after the children upstairs. Having lost Charity to the cancer just two months before, they chose not to relive the Death Year at this time.

Andrés had contributed pots of mulled cider and refried beans to help those gathered keep on through what promised to be a long night. "A fine night they chose, All Hallows' Eve," he muttered gruffly to his daughter, hiding his nervousness. "It sets my teeth on edge. Could they not wait two days? All Souls' is the holy day of remembrance. What fate was mine, to fall among heathens."

"Sh," said Isabel. "Once we open the Wall, you can go to Sydney, or even back to Chile, and find a priest again."

"And how do I get there, pray tell: in a rowboat, perhaps? A town that teaches Greek, but no geography." Andrés sighed and shook his head. "What use? There's no more Pope, so perhaps anyone can be a priest. Your friend Keith's a good enough priest for me."

Isabel smiled and squeezed his hand. Keith had declined to take part, saying he had recalled enough about the Death Year in Sydney and preferred to mind the hospital that night. Actually, Isabel suspected, Keith had become addicted to angelbee vision and planned to spend his Saturday night practicing on the local possums and owls.

Marguerite drained a cup of cider, then stared ahead, her full lips turned to stone. For a while there was a shared silence.

"It was a good year." Vera's voice broke the silence. "The year before, I mean. The price of eggs was down, we bought a new Toyota. Jem and I." Jem had been her first husband; Isabel knew only Ted Brown, the father of Sal and Deliverance, who had died of melanoma, the earliest hospital patient in Isabel's childhood memory. "You would never have guessed that—well, like I said, it was a good year."

Isabel wrote in her notebook, self-consciously making her o's wide and round like moons. On Peace Hope's tape deck the red light flickered.

"A year of peace," Marguerite agreed. "It's fair to say that. There was arms control, there was peace in Managua, where I worked at the clinic. There was a new drug for AIDS. It wasn't a bad year, compared to some."

"'Peace, peace, when there is no peace.' The peace was only skin deep." Nahum's voice came sharp; his dark-suited figure was imposing, his hair tied back severely as usual. "Peace founded on lies is no peace."

A short silence again. Isabel imagined Nahum sitting just like that behind bars, when he refused to pay taxes for the bombs. Andrés stood behind Marguerite massaging her shoulders, looking pensively out the window, where a trace of red from the sunset remained.

Matthew rolled his eyes upward. "It's worth remembering that tonight, Halloween, is the forty-third anniversary of the Moscow Link conference, when American and Soviet scientists jointly presented in public the phenomenon which they called nuclear winter. The concept originated, curiously enough, from Sagan's earlier observations of the persistence of dust clouds on Mars. Sagan could not have known that Earth's eventual survivors would owe their existence to visitors from far beyond Mars."

Isabel opened her mouth to ask a question, then realized she had about a dozen questions to ask at once. Listening, first, would be better.

"I was at my parents' home that day," her mother said quickly, "recuperating from my hectic schedule in Managua. Dad was out of town, on an action with the Plowshares. Mom had a two-hour commute from the Philly law firm; I never could see how she stood it. It was a beautiful, clear day, a bit of a wind from the west."

"Northwest," amended Matthew. "I remember seeing the weathervane pointing on top of the—" He stopped and swallowed a couple of times, unable to say the word "house." His house, what remained of it, stood just outside the Wall. "I wasn't spending the night there, because at the time Janet and I were separated."

It took Isabel a moment to realize what he meant. The final separation of loved ones was more familiar to her.

"A few people caught sight of the flash from Philadelphia," said Vera. "Jem told me he saw it, out of the corner of his eye, through his office window at the bank. I just recall the sound, like a giant thunderclap."

Ruth said, "Becca caught the flash. She was climbing a tree in the orchard across from the middle school during lunch break. She admired the view; you could see for miles."

Marguerite nodded. "It was an airburst; it must have set fires for miles around the city. The power blackout's the thing I recall," she added. "You could see lightning bolts leaping out of empty sockets. Little did I know it was the last electricity I'd see for two years."

"There was news on the shortwave," Matthew added. "On emergency stations, and also the BBC. New York, L.A., Washington of course—the list of hits was staggering. I suppose the Soviets got the same, though little news got out."

Ruth added, "Becca's parents took her to the hospital, but it was already full of casualties flown in."

Silence again. Beside Isabel, Anna's eyes were narrowed and her lips were pressed tightly together.

Liza said quietly, "We watched the black clouds spread along around the horizon. I remember watching with Nahum, shaking our heads at the sky. That was our second year of marriage."

Just then Vera choked and began to sob uncontrollably. Ruth went to her side to speak with her in low tones. She helped her up and led her out into the next room for a while.

Marguerite spoke, in almost a clinical monotone. "We were just inside the fallout zone. I posted warnings to stay indoors. Most did, but some were caught outside when the rains came. Doses received ranged from one to three hundred rads. Jem got a medium dose. He hung on for another three months."

Nahum added, "The shortwave told us not to eat any grain from the fields. But the shops were empty, and the fields were full."

"We all got sick, to one degree or another," said Marguerite. "A lot of folks left town, heading south mostly. The highways were clogged, day and night. By the third day refugees from Philadelphia were streaming in. My mother never made it—she was downtown—but my father did, I don't know how. He collapsed soon after arriving. His skin was all dotted with purple spots, spot hemorrhages."

Vera and Ruth quietly returned to their seats.

"The sky darkened more, every day," said Matthew. "Everything seemed to be closing up—banks, schools, gas stations. A gang came through town, plundering houses; they torched a few for the heck of it, the Sewells' and the Radnors' up the street."

Isabel paused with her pencil. So that was what befell the abandoned black hulk of a house they passed every Sunday on the way to Worship.

Liza said, "People were hungry of course. We had six months' worth of grain and dried milk in storage; it's a family tradition. We offered what we could."

"The people cleaned your house out in no time," Marguerite reminded her. "People came from miles around, and you couldn't say no. They took more than food, too."

"Praise God for that," said Nahum. "How was I to sleep in the valley of death, with that pile of earthly goods in my house? I had no rest until the house was empty."

The plain wood furnishings had all been crafted since Doomsday.

Marguerite said, "About a week after Doomsday we awoke to discover the Wall."

"It was just like a waterglass set over the area," said Vera. "It was the queerest thing; even the shortwave had no explanation. We tried to dig out, of course. We dug holes twenty feet down, thirty feet..."

"At first, we were the ones trapped," said Matthew. "I remember Angie, my nine-year-old, crying because I couldn't come out to her. She stood there with her face buried in Janet's skirt. Our Irish setter whined and lapped at them, trying to comfort them. Then Janet went back to the house, where Robbie was in bed with fever."

"My sister Sarah tried to send food in," recalled Liza. "Nothing got through, not even a lima bean. Sarah opened a sack of flour and tossed it in our direction, but it all blew back in her face. I can see her now, her face and hair all white with flour..."

"The sky outside kept getting darker," Vera said, "yet it was odd how a sort of murky light persisted in the sky above our trapped town. The dome of the Wall kept the black clouds out."

"The darkness," said Ruth, "the smoke-filled clouds outside, like a vision out of Night. That is the one thing I remember well. My father told me those clouds came from

Philadelphia...I had just attended the wedding of my cousin
that spring, at a temple in Northeast Philly. All my cousins
and nieces and nephews were there, all the children. As I
looked up into that dark stillness, I kept imagining the faces
of those children, turning into wreaths of smoke."

The sun had quite set by now. Andrés was lighting candles, new ones brought by Debbie Dreher, and their scent of
beeswax filled the room.

Vera went on, in an unnaturally high voice. "After the second week, I noticed my brother Gabe and the kids were wearing snow parkas when they came to the Wall. You could feel
the chill coming in, like a giant icebox with the door open.
And it was mid-July..."

"That's when the crowds began to collect," said Marguerite. "Hundreds, eventually thousands perhaps, to the warmth
of the Wall. They blamed us; they cursed at us, even shot
bullets which ricocheted back. One hit a child outside; I tried
to explain to his mother how to dress the wound. The child
died of blood loss. My father also died around that time."

"The animals came, too," said Liza. "So many deer, raccoons, possums, like the animals gathered into Noah's ark.
But this ark had no door."

"The animals were our salvation, for food," said Matthew.
"Janet got out the shotgun and took a deer now and then. She
managed to chop enough firewood, too, God bless her. We'd
had a stock for the wood stove, but that was long plundered
by then."

"Yes, Gabe did the same," said Vera.

"The Pylon," Ruth remembered suddenly. "The Pylon had
appeared by then. My friend and I found it there, in the field
past the Trans' place."

"Yes," said Vera. "We had no idea what it was, but when
the angelbees started appearing, we put two and two together.
Gabe said it was an alien invasion after all, not a human war.
Everyone was saying it. We all felt a lot better, God knows
why."

"A refuge of lies," said Nahum. "Lies built the Wall in the
first place. We have yet to give up on lies, though the hail has
long swept the refuge away."

Matthew nodded. "The extraterrestrials must have been

watching Earth for years, ever since they first detected our radio signals. Why did they never make contact? A slow-moving race, they watched and waited to learn about us, but in the end were too late."

"Alice was convinced she could 'talk' with the Pylon, somehow," said Liza. "Everyone thought she was crazy, an old woman bundled up in the snow, gesturing to an alien artifact." Yet the Pylon had "talked" to her, and kept on for those many years.

There was a long silence. Matthew opened his mouth twice as if trying to say something. "Janet finally told me Robbie had died," he said at last, his voice nearly inaudible. "I'll always remember the look on her face, in that moment. She said she couldn't bury him properly because the ground was frozen solid. I told her she ought to be wearing gloves. She said Angie was wearing her gloves because someone had taken the girl's gloves for her own child." Matthew choked on his words. "It was a neighbor, I won't say who; let the dead rest."

"They weren't all like that," Ruth observed. "There was an elderly woman from our temple who kept on knitting scarves for people the whole time."

"The darkness outside was indescribable," said Marguerite. "For months, you couldn't tell night from day. Only we had light, inside, and that was dim at best. We tried to help, setting fires on our side of the Wall; but then, we got short on firewood, too. We went without food for two weeks—until the first shipment arrived, miraculously, at the airwall of the Pylon. The first of many."

"I remember the day Gabe packed the kids onto the horse and said they were heading south. South where? I told him. I never saw them again. I guess I was lucky..."

"Janet pitched a tent right next to the Wall, leaning into it you might say, one of a long, unbroken line of tents and other makeshift dwellings. Angie and the setter huddled there all day. Janet never left for long, lest someone push them out. She had gloves again by then, from a corpse most likely."

"So many lay there, it was hard to tell the dead from the living. That is, the dying. I could tell some had a breath of life left, since Sarah tried to nurse a few."

"Firewood was getting scarce, Janet said. I saw our house ripped apart for firewood, a little at a time. The deer got scarce, too. A man shot the setter for meat, while Janet was out foraging."

"I can't say for sure exactly when Sarah died. She wasn't moving for a while. I finally faced it when the snow fell, covering the bodies. Black snow. This sounds foolish now, but I remember thinking, in my grief, at least she should have had white for a shroud."

"I knew when Angie died, because Janet stopped trying to feed her water. I tried to say...something to Janet..."

"We started our own graveyard, just inside the Wall. Why was that? I suppose we wanted to show them, we were dying, too."

"Those left alive outside started on the human bodies because there was nothing else left to eat. Janet kept watch over Angie, at first. Until one day she didn't come back."

"The last ones died, was it...November? December? I had other things to worry about, with all the patients expecting treatment upstairs."

"One man froze to death with his eyes open. He stared in at us all winter."

"I didn't think of it much, what with Jem dying, and I myself couldn't keep my food down. I miscarried at six months, because of the radiation, Dr. Chase said. When spring came, and the earth outside the Wall glistened as it began to thaw, I had the strangest feeling that all those bodies would wake up and come alive again. I still have dreams about it, sometimes."

IT WAS NEARING midnight when Isabel stepped out on the porch for a breath of air. The night sky was overcast without wind, the bare branches of trees carrying just a few dry leaves left. Isabel looked out, unmoving, her fingers cramped, her throat swollen although she had spoken little that evening.

The storm door squeaked open as a woman came out to join her. It was Anna, who came and put her arm around Isabel, drawing her close. Then Isabel found herself weeping soundlessly. "I'm sorry," she said in a husky voice, "it's silly but I can't help thinking of all those poor deer. Why did they have to go first? It wasn't their fault; they never paid any taxes."

"It's always been that way," Anna said, her round face shining like a moon set in the smooth darkness of her hair.

"It isn't right. If we humans had to mess ourselves up, fine. But couldn't we leave the animals alone?"

"Every creature is part of creation. They can escape their fate no more than we."

"The Bible says God gave us dominion over animals. I can't imagine why."

"The Buddha teaches to that, I think. I remember one of the *Jatakas* that my grandmother used to tell. In this tale, the Buddha appeared in the incarnation of a noble prince. One day in a forest the prince came upon a starving tigress, so desperate she was ready to eat her own cubs. Instead, the prince lay down and let the tigress devour his flesh. This deed of compassion was so noble, it is said, that for many years afterward the forest shone with a golden light. That is how humans were meant to govern the beasts."

Isabel nodded, and her voice steadied. "That is the kind of God the sheep and ox would have hoped for in the manger. It's easy enough for a God to sacrifice Himself for humankind; but for a tigress? That's the God for me."

IN THE MORNING, Isabel drove her family to Worship, as she had for so many years, though now it was a tight squeeze to fit her parents and Daniel and Keith in the back seats. Jael in her clown suit watched the scenery wide-eyed from her perch between Daniel's arms. They traveled the old familiar route, past the decayed highway and the burned-down Sewell place, up Radnor Lane through the pine forest. Isabel clucked absently to Jezebel, too deep in thought to give the mare much guidance. Fortunately Jezebel knew her way well enough. As the Meetinghouse appeared, with the cross and the Star of David perched crookedly atop the tar-paper roof, it occurred to Isabel to wonder what symbols the Buddhists chose to mark their worship.

The mood of the worshipers was curiously mixed. Sal and Jon, and Deliverance, looked sunken in the eyes as if they had slept little the night before. Peace Hope, in her usual gray Quaker dress, actually wore a white ribbon in her hair. Deliverance whispered that this defiance of plain dress and parental authority had caused some commotion at the Scattergoods'. As the star of their escape from the hypersphere, Peace Hope had taken full advantage of her enhanced standing in the town, offering her collected angel-bee scales to anyone interested. Even Ruth had accepted one, so that she might learn to "see" the way Becca had—and to make her way through the Wall, if she dared. What the keepers would have to say about all this was anyone's guess.

Worship began as always with the intensity of silence. Then Debbie led the programmed service, reading from the Psalm One Hundred Twenty-six, "Those who sow in tears shall reap with songs of joy." Sal and Jon were teaching the Sunday School now; as Worship closed, the youngsters piled in, raucous as ever. The Pestlethwaite twins, their fingers fluttering like butterflies as they signed, had grown a good head taller since she had seen them last. Miracle called to his sister Faith, "Let's go out and climb the Wall!"

Liza rose from her seat, calling in her strong voice for any announcements.

Peace Hope got herself up to speak, holding her crutches firmly, her ribbon conspicuous in her hair. "We have heard, now, of how the Wall came to be. The time has come to declare the Wall open."

Isabel's blood raced, and she glanced about the room. Matthew said at last, "Peace Hope is right. The Wall is open to anyone with an angelbee."

Liza nodded. "We must consider this immediately. Will those who can, please stay afterward to discuss the future of the Wall."

As the worshipers got up for tea, the children raced as usual around the long benches.

Where was Jael? Isabel wondered suddenly. Daniel was talking with Peace Hope, and the baby was nowhere to be seen. As the newest infant in town, Jael had to get passed around to everyone. Isabel scanned the faces and teacups to locate her.

From behind, near the door, came a voice: "My baby!" Isabel turned. Of all people, Jael was in the hands of Grace Feltman. Grace held the baby's head up well enough as she swung her back and forth, saying to everyone who passed, "See, my baby!" Nonetheless, Isabel shook her head in annoyance. She should have known Daniel would let Grace have Jael sooner or later. She took a step toward the door to reclaim her child.

The door opened with sudden force, as if kicked in, banging with a thud against the log wall. As startled heads turned, five Shades walked in, cylinders pointed straight ahead of them into the room full of people.

Isabel froze at the sight, the blood draining from her face. From behind came gasps and a scream.

Before her, Grace opened her eyes and mouth wide at the sight of the shaggy strangers in mirrorshades. "Visitors!" She lurched forward toward the man in front, whom Isabel recognized as their leader, Dirk Brendan. "You haven't seen my baby yet!" With that she half fell onto Dirk, who let the cylinder fall to his side as he caught the baby.

Jael reacted by reflexively throwing her arms out straight, then let out a wail, transformed in an instant from a wide-eyed angel to an indignant bundle of arms and legs. Meanwhile, Grace ran off, calling, "Aunt Li-iza, there's more visitors to see my baby!"

For a wild moment Isabel thought: They're hungry, they're raiding for meat, like the dead beyond the Wall.

In an instant she was there in front of Dirk, to snatch her child from his arms. Still struggling in the man's inexperienced grasp, Jael's hand knocked the glasses from his face, revealing flat gray-blue eyes that matched his sandy hair. As Isabel's hands closed upon the infant, her eyes met those of Dirk for the first time. A new thought struck her, almost in wonder: This apparition before her was a man, after all. Somehow, before in the Hive, he had seemed to her more alien than the keepers.

"Welcome, friends," came Liza's voice from behind Isabel. "You have nothing to fear from us. We invite you to share our table tonight."

Any plans for the Wall were overtaken by the confusion of absorbing the five new transportees. For that was what the handful of Shades turned out to be, a dubious parting gift from the Hive, whose residents had at last tired of the waxworms in their comb.

"Congratulations," Megan told Isabel. "I'll bet you're relieved not to be preggo anymore."

"Thanks. What brings you here?" Isabel asked warily.

"The rovers smoked us out of our camp," Megan told her. "When we got out into the Hive, they barred the way back with fire—I never saw such a thing, from those space cockies. Then they knocked us to sleep, and here we are."

"What about their Queen?" Isabel asked her. "Did Bob ever reach the Queen's cell?"

"Bob never made it." The line of Megan's lips tightened; her expression behind her opaque glasses could not be guessed. "He got caught in the crossfire..." She looked away, then back suddenly. "Of course, we reached the Queen cell. But what do you think? It was empty."

Isabel's mouth fell open. "So you never...hurt the Queen."

"We never found her. Nobody's ever actually seen her, that I know of. It stands to reason, doesn't it. Why would they let us get anywhere near her? What bloody fools they made of us, all that time."

Isabel thought of the Queen image she had shaped, and the images she had seen, the pregnant skeleton, and the empty Queen cell. She stared ahead, unseeing.

Daniel caught her arm gently. "Is thee all right?"

"Yes," Isabel whispered. Before her, Megan was turning away, at the approach of Vera Brown. "Daniel . . . What if there never was a Queen? What if she died, long before the keepers got here?"

His fingers tensed. "How could that be?"

"Remember, the lifespan of a Hive is a thousand years. If a Queen dies without replacement, perhaps the keepers go on living, obeying their caring instincts, seeking something to care for in her place, if not another Queen then . . ."

"Us?"

"The human race, a species threatened with a fate like theirs."

"But surely they could find another Queen," Daniel said, "on their home planet."

"Perhaps not. Perhaps," she added, her voice breaking, "the keepers all ended as we did." Or worse, lost their planet altogether, as Dirk had claimed before.

Dirk, meanwhile, was standing a few feet off sipping tea with Liza, who appeared to be trying to convince him to put aside his keeper cylinder for a while. Dirk shook his head earnestly, his mane of hair sweeping back across his neck. "Ma'am, you've got it backward. In fact, the firearm is the poor woman's best friend. It's the great equalizer: you don't need strength to use it. If you lived where I grew up, you'd be glad to tote a handgun."

"Would thee care to walk a city street where every purse contained a handgun?"

"At least we wouldn't need police anymore. Not that city cops were ever good for much. The cities were the breeding grounds of statist oppression. The best thing the space cockies ever did was to get rid of cities."

A sound arose, outside the Meetinghouse, a faint rumbling sound. An earthquake, Isabel thought; but no, it was a steady sound, from above. Children near the door raced out to see.

It was an airplane. "A turboprop," Matthew exclaimed, craning his neck upward along with everyone else. The airplane traced a straight line east across the blue sky, until it faded into the horizon.

Somewhere, a Wall had fallen.

THE NEW TRANSPORTEES were taken into various homes for the night. Marguerite, who was the most experienced at handling new arrivals, took Dirk and another man to stay in the hospital rooms. Isabel at first feared Keith's reaction once he recalled the role of the Shades in the destruction of his home district in Sydney. But if he felt anything, he showed no outward sign, soon trotting off arm in arm with the Shades' leader, exchanging unintelligible chatter from Down Under. Isabel herself wondered how she would sleep at night, knowing those people were in the house.

If the Walls were falling, even the deadland would soon be open. Where would she go? That evening, she found herself digging through the attic, reclaiming her own roots in the outside world. The dusty scrapbook had a picture of her Grandfather Chase, in his second "career" after duty in Vietnam, demonstrating at the missile factory he had broken into. That was in a suburb of Philadelphia; she would have to ask her mother where. Grandfather's face was as dark as Marguerite's, and he wore wire-rim glasses that gave him a studious look. He was smiling tranquilly, his hand resting on the wall of a huge orange missile tube splotched with letters in his own blood. The letters spelled, "Auschwitz." Grandfather Chase had lived to see those letters come true.

The next pages had baby pictures of her mother. Marguerite's skin had been pale at birth, like Jael's, although it had darkened later; Jael would darken, too. Isabel turned another page, and there were more baby pictures, Marguerite's two dead brothers.

The last picture was from Marguerite's graduation from Kenyon, a real college out in Ohio. It gave her a start to see her mother's face so young, echoing her own fiercely proud expression, the flat black cap with the tassel hanging down, standing between the two gateposts that marked the old entrance to the college. Did those gateposts still stand?

As she stood up in the attic to ease her back, the fullness

of her breasts reminded her it was time for the day's last nursing. Downstairs, Daniel had bathed the infant by now and bundled her up for the chilly night.

After the nursing was done, she held up Jael for one last look before setting her in the crib, which had been hers originally though it had circulated throughout the town since. Jael held her gaze for what seemed an unusually long time. "She has your eyes," Isabel told Daniel. "Like lodestars."

"Really?" He sounded abashed, and his cheeks colored in the candlelight.

Isabel laid the infant down, adjusting her head with care. Jael's eyelids shut readily, and her face assumed that serene look of an infant ready to sleep. Suddenly it occurred to her where she had seen that look before, the eyelids down, the lips drawn small between the rounded cheeks. It was the gaze of the Buddha figure in her old history book, the face of eternal peace.

When Isabel turned around, she saw Daniel sitting on her bed, his head out of the light, his shoulders shaking slightly. She was astonished to realize that he was crying, crying without sound.

"Daniel?" She held him close but felt helpless to comfort him. She had never seen him cry before, and it seemed to be shaking him apart inside.

"It is too beautiful," he said. "One pool of light, in such a vast darkness."

"Surely there's more hope for us than that."

"I thought the keepers held the answer, once," he reminded her. "But I can't believe that any longer. The keepers ended as we did, only worse: they lost their whole planet, and there was no other 'keeper' to save them."

"Only dying keepers left without a future." Queenless living ghosts, trapped forever in the universe outside the Wall. "But there's one thing," Isabel remembered suddenly. "The angelbees: they survived. They will outlive the keepers because they chose us."

Out the window in the dark, three of the silvery symbionts hovered faithfully, two of them swelling at the side, ready soon to bud offspring.

Daniel smiled fleetingly, and for a moment his eyes lit up

like they used to. "The angelbees taught me one thing, that living creatures glow like stars. And the stars...Do you remember the old paradox: If stars fill the sky to infinity, then why is the night sky not infinitely bright? The answer is that most of the stars are too far off for their light to reach us yet, though they've shined for a billion years. So their light shines on in the darkness, though we do not see it yet." He reached out to Isabel at last, responding to her touch. "It's important, to have a way of seeing through a dark time. To keep waiting, for the light to come."

Isabel tried to sleep, but her dreams kept ending with the appearance of a desperate Shade from around the corner. At last she sat up in bed, the sharp chill of night air hitting her face. Beside her, Daniel lay with his head turned away, fast asleep. She got out of bed, intending to get a drink of water from the pitcher in the hall. On the way out she felt for Jael in the crib, the tiny rounded bundle whose chest rose and fell reassuringly.

There was a light on in the clinical lab down the hall. She frowned and walked across to investigate, hugging her arms against the chill.

Keith sat there, one eye peering into the microscope, the other eye covered by an angelbee scale which he was trying to learn how to use.

"Specimens, at this hour?" she asked.

"I couldn't sleep. Here, take a look at this. It's from Carl's fermentation vat."

Isabel squinted into the eyepiece and focused the slide. Bright globes of yeast appeared against the dark field, some of them budding off like angelbees. Microbes could be symbionts too, producing beer and cheese, even aiding human digestion.

"What's with you?" Keith asked.

"Those Shades still worry me." Isabel shuddered. "I can't help it. I saw what they did with the cylinders before."

"No fear. I got the rayguns away from them."

"You what?" Isabel eyed him suspiciously. "Come on, Keith. What've you been up to?"

"I traded for them."

"Traded for what?"

"A keg of Carl's finest. They'd had a couple of pots by then already, you see."

Isabel was still suspicious. "You slipped something else in, too, I know you."

"Too right. Remember, these are the same guys that blew up Paddo. No way I'm letting those bloody breeders pull their tricks here."

Isabel grinned and gave his shoulder a playful shove. "You can say that again. Though God only knows what kind of folks will be coming out here in those airplanes."

"You'll get used to it. The first plane that stops here is taking me home."

"Really, Keith?" She felt a pang of sorrow. "I thought this was your home."

"It is, mate," he said softly. "But I heard from my lover, the last shipment before the Pylon shut down."

"He's still alive then! That's wonderful; I'm so glad for you."

"You'll be coming out to Sydney, too, won't you?"

"To the Uni."

"I'll show you the town. We'll see *The Magic Flute* at the Whale."

"Thanks." Watching the scale on his eyelid, Isabel thought of something. "Keith—let's not wait for the town to decide. Let's go out right now with our angelbees, to the Wall, and walk through."

Keith considered this, then he laughed shortly. "Sure, let's have a go."

They walked through the cemetery, listening to the swooping cries of barn owls who glimmered out of the foliage. Other bright things rustled and scampered across the pine needles, mice and squirrels stocking up for winter, all shining brilliant infrared against the cold ground. In the sky amid the still stars hung a late crescent moon. The keepers' red satellite, their dying Hive, slowly crossed the sky through Orion's uplifted arm. Somewhere there was the little hypersphere, with the little sheep she had left behind. *Le mouton*, would the sheep eat the flower or not?

Beneath the Wall, the ground was bare and dark. Isabel showed Keith how to bring down the angelbee and melt one's way, slowly, through. At the other side they stumbled forward, to the edge of the piled bones, human and animal, equally dark and cold. *Freedom*...

Carefully Isabel stepped onto the bones and climbed, one foot after the other. The wall of piled skeletons was only a couple of feet high, not so high as it had looked from inside. A child could climb it. She sat on top, balancing precariously on an uncomfortable perch, and her angelbee eyes looked out upon the deadland.

The deadland was no longer dead. Throughout the growth of wild grasses, a hundred bright little things were scurrying in and out of holes. Mice, they must be, probably common field mice. Some time in the past year a couple must have slipped out of Gwynwood with the angelbees, or perhaps just one, a pregnant cousin of Peewee's, released into the deadland like a microbe inoculated into a sterile flask. Now, as her angelbee watched from above, here were their myriad descendants, bright sparks appearing and vanishing in the dark like the Perseid shower. A living Christmas tree.

Keith had climbed up beside her. "Beautiful, isn't it. It gives me the oddest feeling, as if those were all the souls of the dead creeping out to claim their land." He paused, then added, "How long d'you think we've got?"

"How long? Until what?"

"Until the next Doomsday."

Her scalp prickled as she gradually realized his meaning. "I don't know. The keepers tried to teach us, but what did they know?" And what had she learned? Peace Hope had said once, about learning to draw, "One has to start out bad, to get to be good."

On impulse she took from her pocket Keith's cigarette lighter that she had carried throughout her captivity, an ambiguous token of power. *Haroset*. She turned it over twice, then tossed it away. It fell into a hollow between two long bones.

"It's not that killing is always wrong," Isabel explained. "It's just that even the most intelligent creatures in the universe are too foolish to be entrusted with a sword, let alone a keeper's cylinder. We'd all be better off like Grace."

"Really?" said Keith. "Those Shades could have mowed us all down instead. What good would Grace have done then?"

"Maybe it's too bad we let the keepers save us. We should have sacrificed our whole species, for the sake of the animals."

"What would the existence of animals matter, without humans to care? Who else creates meaning in the universe?"

To that there was no simple answer. Isabel shivered as the cold air penetrated her jacket.

"Who knows?" Keith added. "Habits die hard, but I kicked one. Fair go; we may make it yet."

"One can do it," Isabel agreed, "but a whole species? Maybe." Maybe the light would come.